NIGHT RIDER

Shaun Clarke

Hodder & Stoughton

Copyright © 2001 Shaun Clarke

First published in Great Britain in 2001 by Hodder and Stoughton
A division of Hodder Headline

The right of Shaun Clarke to be identified as the Author of the Work has been
asserted by him in accordance with the Copyright, Designs and Patents Act 1988.

10 9 8 7 6 5 4 3 2 1

British Library Cataloguing in Publication Data

ISBN 0 340 750 26X

Typeset by Palimpsest Book Production Limited,
Polmont, Stirlingshire

Printed and bound in Great Britain by
Mackays of Chatham plc, Chatham, Kent

Hodder and Stoughton
A division of Hodder Headline
338 Euston Road
London NW1 3BH

For Peter & Silvie

Chapter One

Getting them into bed is easy, Steve thought drowsily, *but getting them out is more difficult.*

Surfacing from sleep, he felt the woman curled up against him and instantly recalled the previous evening: the pub crawl that had started in Robinson's in Great Victoria Street, moved on to the Crown Liquor Saloon a few doors down, then progressed to the Golden Mile and finally terminated, full circle, as it were, in the lounge bar of the Europa Hotel, located directly opposite the Crown. That was where this woman, this pleasingly plump, curvaceous peroxide blonde with sky-blue eyes and full lips (he couldn't recall her name, but her lips had fulfilled their promise) had let him buy her a couple of drinks while flirting ever more boldly with him until the bar closed. After that, as always, the night became something of a blur, a vague recollection of the bright lights of the city centre, the new Belfast with its glass-domed shopping malls and modernized, well-lit thoroughfares, the soulless splendours that peace had brought, as they were driven in a taxi to his place, kissing and groping each other even during the short ride. Then stumbling into his fancy flat in one of the new apartment blocks overlooking the Lagan River — black, stippled, reflecting moonlight — to undress each other frantically as they made their way to the bedroom, leaving a trail of dishevelled clothes behind them, and fell across the big double bed in a tangle of sweaty limbs ... Now, here they were, still in the same bed in morning's pearly-grey light, one asleep, the other barely awake, both naked, white-skinned and none too glamorous. The real world had reclaimed them.

Christ! Steve thought. *Whoever she is, I'd better get her out of here!*

The woman had turned her back to him and was curled up in a ball, having pressed her rump into his groin, letting him sleep with his hands cupping her breasts. Obviously still asleep, she was breathing deeply and evenly, clearly as comfortable as if she were in her own bed.

Checking his wristwatch, Steve saw that it was just after eight a.m. He hoped, silently prayed, that the woman had a home or a job to go to fairly soon and, more importantly, that she wasn't the hysterical kind. Tentatively, not wanting to be too abrupt, understanding that the woman, sobered up after a drunken evening, might be embarrassed or outraged to find herself in a strange man's bed, he placed his hand on her bare, fleshy shoulder and shook her gently.

'Hi,' he whispered. 'It's morning.'

She shifted slightly, moving away from him, then gave a soft snore and murmured something, talking in her sleep. Sighing, Steve shook her again.

'Hi,' he repeated, still not recalling her name and wondering, ruefully, how many people in this one city were waking up under the same circumstances: strangers who had shared drunken intimacies and then had to face each other stone-cold sober in the following morning's harsh, revealing light. Too many by far, he was sure. 'Are you awake? I think it's time to get up.'

This time the woman briefly stopped breathing, obviously opening her eyes, blinking, probably gazing about her at the unfamiliar bedroom, the different view outside (the many building sites at the far side of the river,) and gradually realizing that she wasn't at home. Steve knew that this was so when, staring at the back of her blonde head, he saw it move a little, then heard a soft, despairing moan.

'Ack, Jasus!' she whispered. 'Don't tell me I ...' Her voice trailed off disbelievingly. Then she rolled away from him until she was lying on her side and staring straight at him. Her blue eyes were bloodshot. 'Oh,' she said, sounding hoarse. 'It's you, is it? *Now* I remember! Had a good time, did we?'

'Pretty good,' Steve said.

'I remember you in the bar – I remember that much – but that's all I remember. Jesus!' she exclaimed again, her eyes widening in shock. 'What's the fuckin' time, like?'

Steve checked his wristwatch again. 'Five past eight,' he said.

Suddenly galvanized into action, throwing the sheets off her and rolling, stark naked, off the bed, the woman said, 'Christ, I've got to get out of here! Sure I've got to get home before I get kilt! God, why do I *drink* so much?'

'Why do any of us drink so much?' Steve responded sardonically as he rolled off the opposite side of the bed. 'So who's likely to kill you?'

'My fuckin' husband, that's who,' the woman said as she frantically picked her clothes up from the floor, following a trail that led to the bedroom door and the corridor outside.

'You're married?'

'Of *course* I'm married! Couldn't you tell by the age of me?'

'You told me you *weren't* married,' Steve reminded her as he wriggled into his trousers while she returned from the landing and headed urgently for the bathroom, her clothes tucked untidily under her right arm. 'You said you were widowed.'

'Sure I'm a dreadful wee fibber when I'm drunk. Ack, Jasus, he'll kill me! Don't distract me, mister,' she continued as she rushed into the bathroom. 'Don't say another word. Just let me get dressed, like. You might make me a cuppa tea while I'm in there getting dolled up.'

'Will do,' Steve said.

Grinning, he put on his shirt, socks and shoes. Then, though not yet washed himself, he entered the kitchen-diner to put on the kettle. As it was boiling, he patted his hair down as best he could with his hands while glancing down through the kitchen window at the River Lagan, which flowed all the way from Lough Neagh, down through the Lagan Valley, through the centre of Belfast, then into the Victoria Channel and the Irish Sea. Pleased to note that the sky was clear and it wasn't raining (Belfast was enjoying a hot August), he proceeded to make tea and toast for himself and the woman frantically dressing in the bathroom.

'Oh, Jasus!' he heard her saying in the bathroom, agitatedly talking to herself. 'How the fuck am I gonna explain this? That bastard'll kill me!'

Grinning, realizing that the woman was talking about her husband, Steve poured tea into the two cups, added milk and sugar to his own, then started buttering the toast that had just popped up from the toaster. He was having his first bite of that toast when the woman emerged from the bathroom, again looking attractive, more recognizably the woman he had picked up the previous evening, with the make-up emphasizing her sky-blue eyes and full lips and her clothes, only slightly wrinkled, showing off her good, if slightly plump, figure. She glanced at him as if not really seeing him, then pointed at the spare cup of tea.

'Is that mine?'

'Yep. How do you like it?'

'With milk and two sugars.'

Steve put the milk and sugar in, stirred it and handed the cup to her. 'Toast?'

'No, thanks,' the woman said, then hastily gulped down some of the tea. 'This is all I've time for. I've got to get back real quick, like. With luck, that man of mine, unemployed as he is, will still be in his bed. Jasus, never again!'

'A good evening, though,' Steve said.

The woman rolled her eyes while taking another gulp of tea. 'Oh, yeah,' she said. 'Great! I just don't want to repeat it. I swear to God, I'm never gonna drink again.'

'Until the next time.'

'That's it, mister, I'm off.' She took a final gulp of tea, then placed the cup back on the table and glanced wildly around her. 'Jasus, where's m'handbag?'

'Hanging on the coat-hanger by the front door.' Slipping off the high stool that he had been sitting on, Steve led the woman to the front of the flat, removed the handbag from the coat-hanger and handed it to her, then opened the door. 'Nice to have met you,' he said.

'Aye, right, me too,' the woman responded distractedly. Then she automatically kissed him on the cheek and hurried out into the corridor. Grinning again, Steve closed the door behind her, then turned back into the flat.

Located in one of the many new apartment blocks that were springing up all over the city, the flat was impersonally fashionable, with cream-painted walls, Scandinavian-styled furniture, black leather settees and chairs, pine-board floors covered with Afghan rugs and carpets, framed reproductions of modernist paintings, and an entertainment unit that included hi-fi, DVD-TV with video, and a storage cabinet for videotapes and CDs.

Opening the sliding doors of the living room, Steve stepped out onto the balcony to glance in both directions along the winding River Lagan. Almost directly opposite were the round, glass-domed Waterfront Hall and, towering above it, the high-rise Hilton Hotel and bt.com buildings. To his right were the Queen's and Queen Elizabeth bridges, both packed with commuter traffic, and, beyond them, the Lagan Weir. Directly below him was the Laganside Walkway where people were already out strolling and jogging in the morning's grey light. Belfast had changed dramatically in the past few years – and Steve was part of that change.

Stepping back inside the flat, he closed and locked the sliding doors, then went to the kitchen-diner to finish off his light breakfast. This done, he placed the dishes in the dish-washing machine, went back into the bedroom, stripped off and entered the bathroom to have his morning shower. Approximately thirty minutes later, clean, dry and clothed in an open-necked shirt, denim trousers and suede shoes, he sat down at the computer in his small study to check his e-mail, share prices and bank statements. His share prices had all gone up, his various bank accounts were healthy, and most of the e-mails were either personal or concerned trivial matters about the various properties owned by him – including the very building he was living in.

Aware that peace was finally coming and that the new millennium would bring a building boom to Belfast, Steve, in partnership with some friends, had quietly invested in property even while still serving covertly in the city with the British Special Air Services (SAS) regiment. Though born in Belfast, where he'd also spent his early childhood, he had moved with his family to Kentish Town, north London, when he was eight years old. He'd joined the British army shortly after leaving school, transferred to the SAS and returned to Belfast at the tail end of the Troubles, as a covert SAS operative working for the notorious and by then supposedly disbanded 14th Intelligence Group.

Though it had been clear, even then, that peace, albeit an uneasy one, was going to come eventually, there were still plenty of hardline dissenters on both sides of the divide. It was the job of the 14th Intelligence Group to monitor their activities and, if necessary, remove them from the scene, either by imprisoning them or by having them terminated. Steve had been one of those called in to do this and he had certainly enjoyed the task, putting more than one terrorist behind bars while putting out the lights of some others. He had done so, however, knowing that the Troubles would soon be over and that once that came about the role of the SAS in British military affairs would be greatly reduced and, possibly, would end altogether. Though he loved soldiering, he had no intention of remaining in a peacetime army. So, once his time was up, he had left the army altogether and returned to Belfast to join his partners in their property-investment business.

Initially, in the late 1990s while the Troubles were still going on, they had purchased bricked-up houses in hardline sectarian areas where prices were rock-bottom. They'd left them as they were until the Troubles ended, then they'd renovated them and sold them for huge profits in a booming property market. Later, with peace bringing a massive building boom to the shattered city, he and his partners had used their profits to purchase old buildings and riverside sites that came with building permission. The old buildings had also been renovated, turned into apartment blocks, and brand-new housing complexes had been raised on the riverside sites, thus making Steve and his two partners rich. Now Belfast was, in general, a wealthy city and Steve was one of its wealthiest inhabitants.

After spending an hour answering all his e-mails, he picked up the telephone and dialled a number.

'Yes?' a woman responded.

'Hi. It's me, Steve.'

'I always recognize your voice.'

'You should; we were married long enough.'

'We're *still* married,' Linda reminded him.

'That's true enough.'

Linda was English and lived with their two daughters, Carol and Becky, four and five years old respectively, in the family house in Redhill, Hereford. She and Steve had met in Hereford shortly after Steve had successfully completed his brutal SAS Selection Training and just before he began his even tougher Continuation Training. Linda, at that time a secretary for a local firm of solicitors, had been having an evening out with girlfriends in a Hereford pub when Steve turned up with some of his friends to celebrate getting into the SAS after three weeks of what had sometimes seemed like hell on Earth. When he and his friends struck up a conversation with the three girls at the next table, he was instantly attracted to the brunette with the big brown eyes (Linda) and boldly, or drunkenly, asked her out on a date the following weekend. To his surprise, she agreed and from that evening on they were a regular item. They were married thirteen months later, a few weeks after Steve had returned from his SAS Cross Training in Germany and Norway, thus successfully completing his twelve-month probationary period with the Regiment.

The marriage was a success while they were still living in Redhill, in a house near the SAS base, Stirling Lines, with Steve involved in no more than routine duties. But it failed when Steve was posted to Belfast and took the family with him, moving them into a house in Holywood, just outside the city. Left alone in Holywood for days on end, surrounded by strangers and with only the children for comfort, Linda became increasingly concerned about the kind of work that Steve was doing in Belfast. Though he had never told her just what his new duties were, she knew that they had to involve counter-terrorist actions, which meant it was dangerous not only to him but to her and the children as well. The strain of living with this awareness drove her first to drink, then to a wide variety of sedatives; combined, they adversely affected her personality, thus scaring the children and poisoning her relationship with Steve. Finally, when the Home Office's Special Services Division (SSD) insisted upon securing their house *and* their car against possible terrorist attacks and, even worse, when Linda herself was compelled to undergo training with a UCBT (Under-Car Booby Trap) detector, she decided that it was time to get out. Not wanting to divorce Steve, but not wanting to live with him either – certainly not in Northern Ireland, where a knock on the door could mean death – she moved back to Hereford with the children, leaving Steve in Belfast.

During their separation, Steve, a promiscuous man when he'd been single, took up with other women and Linda became involved with another man. When Steve foolishly confessed to his affairs, she confessed to her own. Any chance of a reconciliation between them was doomed from that moment on. Though Linda never let her lover move into her house, she kept seeing the other man and told Steve that the relationship was a serious one. Hearing this, Steve knew that he could never return to his former home and decided instead to invest in property in Belfast and to return there when he left the service. Now, here he was, four years after his discharge in 1999, living permanently in Belfast, still friendly with his wife and flying to London once a month to spend a weekend with his two girls. It was a decent arrangement.

'So why are you calling?' Linda asked him, sounding friendly, at ease. 'Any special reason?'

'No. I just called on impulse. I felt like a chat.'

Linda chuckled. 'That's nice.'

'So how are the girls?'

'You only saw them ten days ago and they haven't changed much since then. They're at school right now, but I'll tell them you called.'

'Good. I miss them.'

'So you should.'

Steve grinned. 'And how's Dan?'

Dan was Linda's boyfriend. Steve had never met him, but Linda had talked about him. Dan was one of the solicitors for whom Linda had formerly worked. He had married and lost his wife to cancer before they had children. He had always fancied Linda, but had never made advances to her until she returned from Northern Ireland and applied for her old job (just to give herself something to do, as she had later explained to Steve, though the money had helped as well). Dan gave her back her previous position, informed her of his wife's untimely death, invited her out for dinner, once, twice, a third time, then became her lover, though they continued to live their separate lives. According to Linda, he was a quiet and decent man who only came to the house in Redhill for short, avuncular visits, never stayed overnight, and was a good friend (and surrogate father, Steve often thought with suppressed bitterness) to Carol and Becky. It was, in Steve's view, despite his secret bitterness, another decent arrangement.

'Dan's fine,' Linda said. 'He still hasn't moved in here and I still don't intend moving into his place, so stop worrying, Steve.'

'I'm not worried.'

'You are.'

'You can't live like that forever. Sooner or later, he's going to want to—'

'Or I'm going to want to.'

'That's right.'

'But it's not going to happen, Steve. You and I are still married and we'll stay that way. The kids want their daddy and you're their daddy and that's how it will stay. So how's *your* love life?'

'It comes and goes,' Steve said.

'Nothing lasting?'

'Not so far, sweetheart.'

'You're too busy making money,' Linda said. 'It's a long way from your days as a mere trooper in the—'

'Don't say it, Linda.'

'Sorry. A mere slip of the tongue. I won't. So presumably, since this call is purely social, nothing's changed in your life since we last met, all of ten days ago.'

'No, nothing's changed.'

'You got rich on the Troubles, you know that?'

'Yes.' Steve sighed. 'I guess so.'

'All those buildings bombed or burnt out by the paramilitaries

on both sides. Now rebuilt and being sold for a fortune. You
certainly didn't lose out by it.'

'I didn't bomb a single building,' Steve said, 'and I didn't
burn any down. Don't blame me for the money being pumped
back into blasted Belfast.'

'I don't,' Linda said. 'And I won't. I'm sorry; I shouldn't
even have suggested it. I'm just being bitchy.'

'Want me back, do you?'

'No, Steve, I don't. I'm perfectly happy being involved with
a man who doesn't live a high-risk life.'

'I don't live that kind of life any more. Now I'm as safe
as he is.'

'With you, nothing's predictable,' Linda said. 'Who knows
what the next few minutes will bring? Don't tell me! I don't
want to know!'

'You're so melodramatic.'

'I'm so sensible,' Linda said. 'So what are you planning to
do today?'

'Have a quiet day.'

Linda chuckled. 'Yes, right!'

'I still love you.'

'Only because I'm not there.'

'I'll call you soon.'

'You do that.'

Steve placed his phone back in its cradle and sank back into
his chair, staring first at the computer screen, which showed him
only a glittering cosmos, a screen saver, then glancing out beyond
his balcony to the river and the new buildings being constructed
on its far bank. He and his partners owned those buildings –
as they owned this one and a lot more in Belfast – but none
of it added up to any more than (as Humphrey Bogart once
put it) 'a hill of beans'. He loved Linda and his two daughters,
he wanted them back, and to compensate for his loss he was
shafting any woman who came along.

Shit, yes, have a quiet day.

Then the doorbell rang.

'Who the fuck ...?' Steve murmured, checking his wrist-watch, wondering if he had forgotten an appointment. 'No,' he said, recollecting. 'No appointments ... The cleaning lady ... Ah, right!'

Leaving his study, he went to the front door and opened it.

It wasn't the cleaning lady.

It was an aged gentleman called Daniel Edmondson, flanked by two policemen, both armed with truncheons and handguns.

'Houlihan's getting out,' Edmondson said. 'You're under arrest.'

Chapter Two

They had kept Houlihan in a special cage in the solitary-confinement wing and even then the guards who came to release him were sweaty and shaking. Houlihan liked that. He liked the feeling that he had that kind of power over them even when he was in the cage.

'No need for trouble now, Houlihan,' one of them said, releasing him from the handcuffs and ankle-chains while the other two guards kept him covered with their L2A3 Sterling sub-machine guns. 'You're getting out, so there's no need for trouble. Let's just take it easy now.'

'Aye, let's do that,' Houlihan said with a wolfish grin, the shadow of his enormous apelike body falling over the worried guard. 'Just let me get the fuck outta here.'

He had been in prison for three years, most of that time spent in the cage, chained up like an animal, in darkness and silence, isolated from the other prisoners, because his brand of violence was so extreme that normal prison security was not deemed to be adequate for him. So they had kept him in handcuffs and chained his ankles, then thrown him into a specially secured cage in the deepest, most inaccessible part of the jail, where he could bellow and swear for all he was worth, with no one to hear him. Three years caged up like the wild beast they deemed him to be. And now the beast, supposedly in for life, was being set free.

'There,' the youngest of the three guards said, unsnapping the handcuffs. 'You're all set to go, Houlihan.'

'I should wring your fuckin' neck,' Houlihan said as he rubbed his chafed wrists, 'before walking out of here. Just for the hell of it. Just for the pleasure, like.'

The young guard stepped back immediately, plainly concerned that Houlihan might make good his threat.

'Lay a hand on me, Houlihan, and you're dead. Make any sudden move and these two will open fire.' The other two had raised the barrels of their sub-machine guns, preparing to fire. 'Let's just walk out quietly. Once you're outside, you can do what you like, but you're not outside yet. Start walking . . . but slowly.'

'Shittin' your pants, are ya?' Houlihan asked.

'Just start walking, Houlihan.'

'Anything to get away from the smell of you. Okay, kid, I'm walkin'.'

Making no sudden moves, Houlihan stepped away from the cage and made his way across the large, rectangular room of unpainted concrete walls that had been built just to house his special cage. The two men with the sub-machine guns spread out to walk behind him, keeping their weapons aimed at him the whole time. The youngest of the guards, the one who had released him, fell in behind the other two, still holding the bunch of keys in his right hand. When Houlihan reached the open solid steel door at the far side of the room, he stopped briefly, allowing one of the two armed guards to step around him and take up a position just in front of him, leading him out.

Houlihan followed him, conscious of the other sub-machine gun being aimed at his spine. The first guard led him through the doorway, along a narrow echoing unpainted corridor, up a flight of steps and then into a cavernous area that had cells built on different levels and linked by steel catwalks that ran around the walls.

This particular wing of the prison had been constructed only recently to house the growing number of former paramilitaries who had turned to crime when the peace had left them unemployed as terrorists. A lot of them had once worked for Houlihan and would do so again.

When Houlihan followed the first guard onto the catwalk that ran across the middle of the vast holding area, a lot of the other prisoners clapped their hands, whistled, cheered and repeatedly banged their tin mugs against the bars of their cells.

Pleased to be so recognized and respected, Houlihan clasped his two hands together and held them triumphantly above his head as he crossed the catwalk, only lowering them again when he stepped off the far end and followed the screw through another doorway guarded by two more armed men. This doorway led into a wide courtyard with high red-brick walls and watchtowers on all four corners. The watchtowers all had searchlights and each was manned by a machine-gun crew and at least one crack rifleman.

This particular courtyard was also new. A lot of the jail had been rebuilt and security tightened after a mass breakout organized the previous year by some of Houlihan's men that had involved the extensive use of explosives. Imprisoned in his cage in the basement, Houlihan himself had not been among those who'd escaped. But the explosions triggered off during the breakout had devastated a lot of the former buildings and this had led to extensive renovations, including this new, secured courtyard.

'Where are we going?' Houlihan asked as the man ahead led him across the courtyard, aware that prisoners being released were normally checked out in the building he had just left.

'The warden's office,' the guard replied without turning his head. 'He seems to think you're a special case, so he wants to check you out personally.'

Houlihan couldn't be sure if this was true or not. Suddenly wondering if he was actually being released or if this was a set-up in which he could be 'shot while trying to escape', he looked up at the watchtowers but saw that no one was aiming at him. Then he glanced back over his shoulder and saw that the second guard was still following him, though holding his weapon across his chest, clearly not preparing to fire, while the third and youngest guard was bringing up the rear, his pistol still holstered. Relieved that he was *not* being set up, Houlihan turned his head to the front again.

The guard up ahead led him into the building where the warden's office was. When the guard stopped at a closed door, Houlihan stopped as well. The guard knocked on the door and identified himself to the man inside. Then, upon being given permission, he opened the door and stepped into the office, positioning himself by the side of the door with his weapon held across his chest. Houlihan followed him in and stopped just in front of the warden's desk.

The warden, Frank Harrison, was a heavy-set man with a flushed, mottled face, pale blue eyes and thinning grey hair. He wore a grey suit and a tie that identified him as a former pupil of the 'Inst': another fat-bellied Prod. He waited until the other two guards had also entered the office before speaking to Houlihan.

'You're being released back into society,' Harrison said. 'I trust you're pleased with yourself.'

'Aye,' Houlihan replied, grinning. 'Sure it feels grand, right enough.'

Harrison was not amused. 'Grand for you,' he said, 'but not so grand for this community. I'm sure you know that the decision to give you this early release – obscenely early, if I may say so – was not one that met with my approval.'

'Aye, I know,' Houlihan replied, standing upright to make himself seem even larger than he was, almost bursting out of the suit that they had given him, practically leering as he gazed down on Harrison with eyes of pure stone. 'I'm sure you feel like throwin' up right this minute. But don't do it in my lap.'

'You're an animal,' Harrison said. 'I always thought so and still do. As far as I'm concerned, you're the scum of the Earth and should have served the life sentence you were given.'

'Sorry to have disappointed you, boss,' Houlihan said with heavy sarcasm, enjoying himself.

'If I still had the authority to make you pay for that remark, believe me, I'd go the whole limit.'

'Too bad,' Houlihan replied. 'In five or ten minutes I'll be walking out those gates and there isn't a damned thing you can do about it. But sure it's good of you to attend to me personally, instead of letting your uniformed minions do it, as they do for the common folk. You're making me feel real important, like.'

'Think you're smart, do you?'

'I'll outlive you, boss, believe me.'

'You don't have to call me "boss".'

'Just bein' respectful, like.'

'Just being fucking sarcastic is more like it, because you've been pulled out of here.'

Houlihan, still grinning, shrugged. 'It's the way of the world, like.'

The warden leaned across his desk, resting his flabby chin in his hands, his blue eyes as cold as an Antarctic sky.

'Don't get too cocky, Houlihan. Don't let this go to your head. You're walking out of here, all right – forty years before you're due. But the highly placed shits who got you out did so for their own reasons – God knows what they are – and the instant they don't need you any more, you'll lose their protection. Then, if you make a single mistake, you'll find yourself back in here and when that happens I'll make you pay for your sins, believe me.'

'Dream on,' Houlihan said.

Harrison flushed with rage, clenched his fists and took a deep breath. Then he reached down to his side and straightened up to place a large manila envelope on the desk in front of him. He shoved the envelope towards Houlihan.

'Your worldly possessions,' he said. 'Take them, sign for them and then go.'

'Can I check them first?'

Harrison shrugged. 'Of course.'

Deliberately winding the warden up, Houlihan made a great show of removing the items from the envelope one by one – wallet, ballpoint pen, comb, banknotes and coins – and meticulously checking each item against the printed list that had been made up when he arrived at the prison. As he ticked each item off, he placed it in one of his jacket pockets.

After counting his money with infuriating slowness, he said, 'Looks like it's all here. Sure it's grand to know that there are still some honest cops.'

Harrison flushed with rage again, but managed to control himself. 'Escort this piece of filth to the main gates,' he said to the three guards standing behind Houlihan, 'and throw it back out into the streets.' He then turned his cold, sky-blue gaze on Houlihan. 'You'll be back,' he said, 'and I'll be sitting right here, waiting for you.'

Houlihan grinned. 'Aye, right. Old and grey and toothless, no doubt. Now can I get the fuck out of here?'

'Yes,' Harrison said, tight-lipped.

When he nodded at the men standing behind Houlihan, the one with the pistol opened the office door to let Houlihan and the other two guards leave the office. They did so.

The two guards, marching one on either side of Houlihan, though slightly ahead of him, led him out of the administration building and across the courtyard, under that hot August sun and the eyes of the men in the four watchtowers. When they reached the main gates, the young guard with the pistol stepped in front of Houlihan to present the release form to the man inside the security booth whose far door was on the outside. This man checked the document, stamped it, handed it back to the young guard, then opened the door of the security booth to let Houlihan enter. Houlihan started to enter. Then, grinning, he turned back to the young guard.

'Still shittin' your pants, are you?' he asked.

'Just leave,' the young guard replied, 'and don't worry about me.'

'Glad to see the back of me, are you?' Houlihan asked.

'*Please*, Mr Houlihan!'

'Let me tell you something, kid. You're not bad as the Filth goes. I mean, you treated me with as much respect as you could muster when you had me in chains. But you're still the Filth, kid. You were one of my fuckin' screws. So in future, whenever you're off duty, when you're out there in the streets, when you're with your wife and children, with your Mum or your Dad, and I happen to come across you – I'll recognize you, believe me – take it as read that you're gonna be dead meat. You understand what I'm sayin'?'

The kid nodded.

'Good,' Houlihan said. 'At least you're intelligent. Enjoy your time while you have it. Now fuck you and those two friends behind you, standin' tall with their popguns. Fuck you all, and *adios*.'

Houlihan stepped into the security booth before any of the three guards could make a retort or, just as likely, angrily attack him. Once inside, he slammed the door behind him and stood there, that wolfish grin on his face, until the Filth on duty opened the door at the other side. This particular piece of Filth, who didn't know Houlihan from Adam and therefore was not frightened of him, simply nodded, indicating the real world, and said, 'Out you go, pal. You're a free man again.'

'I was *always* a free man,' Houlihan retorted. Then he brushed past the guard and stepped outside.

Sunlight washed over him. He blinked, rubbed his eyes and saw green fields, blue sky – and a crowd filling the road in front of the barrier lowered across the main gateway.

Instantly surrounded by friends and relatives, Houlihan was hugged, had his back slapped and shook a lot of hands while hearing a babble of greetings and congratulations on gaining his freedom. Closing his eyes briefly, then opening them again, he saw his wife Maeve and one of his daughters, Kathleen, both overweight like him, neither of them attractive, wearing forced grins. Doing their duty in public, though terrified of him in private, they both kissed him on the cheek and then stepped away to let some of his hard men press in upon him. They, too, were grinning while slapping his shoulder blades, squeezing his arms, shaking his hands, welcoming him back to the real world, hoping to be favoured by him in the days to come. Meanwhile, the men and women of the media were taking his photograph, shoving microphones into his face and hurling a barrage of questions at him.

Clearly, he was still big news on the outside.

'Mr Houlihan, what are your feelings on being released from a life sentence after serving only three years?'

'Would you be willing to confirm, Mr Houlihan, that the British Prime Minister was personally instrumental in—'

'Is it true that your premature release from prison was part of an appeasement deal with—'

'My client has nothing to say at this moment,' Houlihan's solicitor, Jack Parnell, said loudly, pushing his way through the jostling crowd to place his arm around Houlihan's broad shoulders and hurry him towards the silver-grey Daimler parked beside the Visitors' Centre bus, which was empty right now.

As the camera bulbs continued flashing, Parnell's assistant, Katherine Crowley, led Houlihan's flustered wife and daughter to the taxi that had brought them here and would take them back home.

Katherine Crowley looked like a movie star, the sexually deprived Houlihan thought, as he took in with a quick, hungry glance her long blonde hair, alabaster skin, pert tits, broad hips and impossibly long legs, all emphasized by a skintight black miniskirt, low-buttoned white blouse under a black-and-white striped casual jacket of impeccable cut and, of course, stiletto-heeled shoes. Certainly not a piece of everyday Belfast crumpet. That was something special there.

Seeing her, Houlihan sucked his breath in, then released it again. He felt a hardening in his groin.

Once at the Daimler, even as Houlihan was clambering awkwardly into the rear of the vehicle, Parnell said to the media pack, 'Right now, my client wishes only to be reunited with his family and friends and then to put this disgraceful miscarriage of justice — the one that had him wrongly imprisoned — behind him. We have no other comment.' He then slipped into the back seat of the car beside Houlihan, slammed the door shut and told the driver to take off.

The driver did so, moving smartly away from the barrier lowered across the main gate of the prison. He headed along the road that curved between green fields towards the Visitor's Centre, then onto the road that led to the A26, also known as the Maeve Road.

'Good one,' Houlihan said, taking a packet of cigarettes from his jacket pocket. 'That one about a disgraceful miscarriage of justice. Sure ya should get an Oscar.'

Parnell grinned. 'Recommend me.' Though he was going bald, with only small patches of wiry red hair still sprouting around the back of his head and above his large, pear-shaped ears, framing a chubby-cheeked, smooth-skinned, pink, bland face and deceptively innocent green eyes, he looked a lot younger than his thirty-five years and much softer than he actually was. He was impeccably dressed in a light grey suit with a smart shirt, tie and black patent-leather shoes. Parnell could charm the birds out of the trees and that worked well in court, particularly when he was defending his criminal clients, one of whom was Houlihan. 'Sure some of the worst actors in Hollywood get Oscars, so why *not* me?'

Houlihan pulled one of the cigarettes out of its packet,

studied it, sniffed it, then said, 'This is the packet they took off me when I went in three years ago, but sure it still seems fresh enough.'

'Fresh enough to kill you,' Parnell, a non-smoker, retorted. 'Another nail in your coffin.'

Houlihan placed the cigarette between his lips, lit it with a match from the box that had also been taken off him three years back and only returned ten minutes, ago, and inhaled. While exhaling through his hairy, twitching nostrils, he said, 'Sure if you don't go one way, you go another. So what's the odds, like? Might as well enjoy yourself while you're here. You don't know when or how you'll be struck down, so all the rest is bullshit. Thanks for bein' there to meet me and for keepin' those bloodhounds off my back.'

'Actually, I *called* those bloodhounds there,' Parnell said. 'That's why they were waiting at the main gate and not in the Visitors' Centre, where they'd normally be. I wanted them to be there, right outside the prison gates, when I gave my impassioned little speech about a miscarriage of justice. Hopefully that'll encourage the already troubled Police Service of Northern Ireland to give you a wide berth.'

'Good dodge,' Houlihan said. 'So what happens now, Jack?'

'I'm taking you straight home,' Parnell said. 'Maeve and Kathleen have arranged a homecoming party and you really can't miss it.'

'A party? Ack, fuck it!' Houlihan exclaimed in disgust, glancing out the window of the car to see cows and sheep grazing in the gently rolling bright green fields of Lisburn, beneath a blue sky streaked with clouds that were as white and fluffy as candy floss. 'What I want, after three years inside, is to get my cock sucked and my leg over — not a lot of hypocritical homecoming shite with my fat wife and dim daughter and a bunch of fuckin' neighbours and friends. Couldn't you get me out of that one?' he whined.

'Not really,' Parnell said, unperturbed. 'Given the contro-versial nature of your premature release, I think it's safe to say that the press and other media are going to be crawling all over you and that you should be seen, at least for the first few days, as a loving husband and father who has the respect and friendship of his neighbours.'

'My neighbours respect me, all right. Everyone knows *that*.'

'Your neighbours *fear* you,' Parnell corrected him. 'And if you want your cock sucked and your leg over, why *not* try Maeve for a change? At least until the media lose interest in you.'

'Jasus!' Houlihan exclaimed with a grin. 'The very thought of me and Maeve doin' it again! I mean, we gave it up years ago when I found better elsewhere. If I tried it now, the shock'd be liable to kill her, so I don't think I'll try it, thanks.'

Parnell sighed. 'Okay. Let's not give her a heart attack. Let's just put on a show of solidarity for the media – a nice wee home-coming party for family and friends – and then, I promise, we'll do something about the other thing.'

'I can't wait,' Houlihan said, already feeling lustful and starting to breathe heavily at the mere thought of sex. 'It's been three years and I've built up a right load. I need to unload today. At least, no later than this evenin' – *before* I go to bed with that fat bag, if you get my meanin'.'

'I get your meaning,' Parnell said, thinking of Houlihan's unfortunate wife and feeling a certain sympathy for her. He had been Houlihan's solicitor for years, defending his many foul deeds, and by now he knew the Big Man inside and out: knew his gross appetites, his insatiable nature, his coarse animal drives and dangerous, almost total lack of self-control. *Of course* Houlihan would need sex this evening. He would not be able to wait any longer, and would therefore do it blatantly, carelessly, in full view of the world, as it were, if he, Parnell, didn't arrange something more covert.

'Right,' he said as the car turned onto the A52, heading in the direction of Belfast. 'Put up with your homecoming party, meet your family and friends, then go out this evening for a couple of pints with your old buddies. Go to the Hibernian Bar in the Falls, shake hands with any old friends there, then say you're having a few private drinks upstairs with me and Frank Kavanagh and Pat Connolly. We'll all be up there with women pretending to be Kavanagh's and Connolly's girlfriends, though they're actually a pair of pretty talented whores. There's a bed in the wee room out back and you can have an hour or so in there with either one – or both – of those tarts. Either one, or both together, will do you proud. Will that be enough time?'

'*Five minutes* will probably be enough time, the way I'm feelin' right now. I'll probably explode like a cannon at the sight of 'em.'

'I'm sure they'll manage to revive you,' Parnell said, 'and let you start all over again – less excited, with luck. If not, count sheep and think of England.'

'Fuck England,' Houlihan retorted. 'I've had England up my arse for years. So what about Wild Bill?'

'Ready, willing and able,' Parnell said. 'In all fairness to him, he hasn't tried any fancy tricks since you went inside, though he's nominally been in charge of the gangs on both sides of the divide, including your lot. He's told me, however, that it's too much to handle and – as he can't be guaranteed the loyalty of your men, despite the help given to him by your trusted lieutenants Kavanagh and Connolly – he'd rather have you back than inside. Also, since he has enough problems with the Prod splinter groups, he needs your support to keep the various Catholic groups in check – so that's another good reason for cooperation rather than conflict. He wants to have a council meeting when things settle down.'

'What things?'

'The media frenzy. Your early release has stirred up the piranha fish and they're going to be swimming around you for the next couple of days. Once they've had their fill, they'll drift off somewhere else and find something new to write about. But until then it's best that you and Wild Bill stay well apart. How's about a meeting next weekend? Clandestine, of course.'

'Okay,' Houlihan said, gazing out of the vehicle as it passed through the small town of Dundrod. Though he had been inside for three years, he hardly registered what he was seeing, being distracted by thoughts of the party awaiting him in his modest, though recently renovated, house in one of the many side streets off the Falls Road. The improvements to his house – and to many others in the area – had been made with some of the vast amounts of EU money still being poured into the province to encourage the political peace. That 'peace', however, while ostensibly making the province seem more stable, had led to a great deal of unemployment among the former paramilitaries on both sides. So a lot of them, otherwise unemployable, had turned to organized crime, thus turning the Belfast of 2003 into a city resembling the Chicago of 1930. Houlihan had benefited greatly from that situation and hoped to do so even more in the future, particularly now that the British Government had released him and would be shit-scared of interfering too much with him.

Nevertheless, though feeling good with himself, he could have done without the homecoming party being organized for the benefit of family, neighbours and so-called friends. 'So-called' in the sense that few friends, as he had learned to his cost, could be trusted, at least not in his game. Still, he would play along with it through the afternoon, then quietly sneak away to partake of the pleasures arranged by his solicitor.

Parnell was the best investment he'd ever made. A good solicitor, meaning a bright, bent solicitor, was worth his weight in gold. Parnell shone like pure gold.

They said no more to each other until they reached Belfast and, eventually, the area known locally as 'the Falls'. Not surprisingly, the Falls Road had changed little in Houlihan's absence. It remained a lively thoroughfare of ramshackle shops, countless pubs, bookies, video-rental establishments, churches and social clubs. Narrow terraced streets ran off it. As usual, there were plenty of people about, none of them looking wealthy, the women entering and emerging from the shops, burdened down with shopping bags, the kids playing in the side streets, the men either hanging around the entrances to the pubs and bookies or at selected street corners.

This was Houlihan's domain. He controlled every inch of it and most of those in it. His criminal territory spread west to Ballymurphy and Turf Lodge, east to the west side of Royal Avenue and north to approximately Cupar Way where it spilled into the Shankill, one of the many Protestant enclaves controlled illegally by William 'Wild Bill' Moore. This was Houlihan's realm and he was back to reclaim it.

When the driver turned the Daimler along a street off the Falls Road, Houlihan saw the familiar rows of modest terraced houses without gardens, one of which was his inherited family home. Of course, he was now wealthy enough to move to a better area. But the front for his lucrative criminal activities was a frozen-food processing business on the Duncrue Industrial Estate, down near the shipyards, so remaining here in the Falls had been helpful to his frequently repeated claims that he was an honest working-class man and wished to remain so. However, staying in the Falls also had the covert advantage of placing him four-square in the centre of his criminal empire (for so he liked to think of his strictly limited reach) and of making him highly visible to the locals. Now he saw a lot of those locals – a few of whom genuinely respected him though most of them actually feared him – coming out of their homes to look on or wave their greetings as the taxi up ahead deposited Maeve and Kathleen on the pavement in front of their modest house.

Not so modest today, though, Houlihan thought when he saw that more reporters had mingled with the many relatives, friends, neighbours and gang members who were gathered around the door of his house to welcome him back. Some were there voluntarily, others because they had been ordered there by the very same hard men who were now mingling with them.

The Daimler pulled up to the kerb in front of the house just as the taxi left.

'Remember,' Parnell said to Houlihan, lightly patting the back of his thick, hairy wrist. 'Just smile and be humble and tell everyone how glad you are to be home.'

'What about those reporters?' Houlihan asked.

'I'll deal with them,' Parnell said. 'I'm coming into the house with you and I'll stay for about an hour. I'll talk to the reporters on the way in, telling them exactly what I told the others, so all you have to do is be civil to them, give them a smile and a wave. But don't let them inside. When they see that the party's continuing, they'll gradually drift away. I guarantee that they won't be there when you leave the house tonight.'

Houlihan nodded. 'Okay.'

Breathing heavily because of his enormous bulk, he clambered out of the car and was met by clapping, cheering and a veritable chorus of bawled or shrieked greetings. Instantly, the reporters moved in with their babble of overlapping questions.

Placing his arm around Houlihan's broad shoulders, Parnell pushed him gently through the crowd while repeating almost verbatim what he had said outside the prison. 'My client has nothing to say at this moment. Right now, he wishes only to be reunited with his family and friends and then to put this disgraceful miscarriage of justice – the one that had him wrongly imprisoned – behind him. We have no other comment.'

Surrounded by the welcoming crowd, Maeve and Kathleen smiled dutifully as Parnell's movie-star assistant, Katherine Crowley, pushed them into their own house and Houlihan, urged on by Parnell, followed them in, waving and smiling as he went. Parnell then closed the front door firmly, locking out the reporters.

The people inside the house, jammed in like sardines

all the way to the back door and, possibly, to the small, brick-walled backyard, suddenly erupted into whistling, cheering and applauding, noisily welcoming the conquering hero home.

Chapter Three

'For your own good, of course,' Daniel Edmondson said with a wicked grin as he stood in the corridor outside Steve's flat with the two police constables flanking him, both bearing arms and in full uniform. 'To protect you from the wrath of Houlihan. May I come in?'

'Can I refuse?'

'Not really, dear boy. There's a riot squad downstairs in a parked van and a sledgehammer comes with the normal kit. Let's do it the easy way.'

Sighing, shaking his head disbelievingly, Steve stepped aside to let Edmondson enter the flat. When the older man had brushed past him, Steve closed the front door, keeping the two cops outside.

'Wonderful!' he said sardonically as he followed Edmondson into the living room. 'What a sight for my posh neighbours to see! Two armed cops guarding my front door. Thanks a million, Edmondson.'

Debonair as always — albeit now visibly ageing — in his pinstripe suit with immaculately polished black shoes and his old school tie (Eton), Edmondson stood with his back to the window, outlined against the city skyline at the far side of the River Lagan, and shrugged forlornly while spreading his hands, palms out, in an elegant gesture of helplessness.

'How else could it be done?' he asked rhetorically. 'We're under instructions to place you under arrest for your own protection and this—' he nodded, indicating the policemen outside the closed front door '—is how it's normally done. Now it's just a matter of showing you the official documentation and then—'

'Don't bother,' Steve said when he saw Edmondson reaching into the inside pocket of his pinstripe jacket. 'I'm sure you've got everything you need. Bastards like you always have. But what the fuck are *you* doing here? Why not some local minor government official? And, more importantly, just what the fuck is all this about? Did I hear the name *Houlihan?*'

Edmondson nodded. 'That's correct.'

'You said he's getting out of prison?'

Edmondson nodded again. 'Today, as a matter of fact.'

'Jesus!' Steve exclaimed softly, automatically. 'That bastard was supposed to be in for life. How the hell did he get out? And what are *you* doing here? Why the fuck aren't you back in Whitehall, rotting slowly with all the other lice in the woodwork? What the hell are you doing here personally? Am I dreaming, or what?'

Edmondson sighed and turned slightly to the side, glancing over his shoulder at the view beyond the balcony: the Waterfront Hall, shaped like a giant hamburger; the high-rise, strictly linear Hilton Hotel and bt.com buildings, neither blindingly attractive; the gantries, cranes and scaffolding of the many contruction projects in the rapidly expanding city; the narrowing views of the gorse-covered mountains – all on the other side of the River Lagan.

'Nice view,' he said. 'Sweet location. You must be rolling in money.'

'I bet there's nothing I can tell you that you don't already know. So Houlihan's out and you've come here to arrest me for my own protection. Yeah, I'll bet! You've come here personally, all the way from London, just to make the kind of arrest that would normally be done by the local cops. What the fuck *is* this, Edmondson?'

'You've asked me so many questions,' Edmondson said, 'I can't possibly answer them all at once. May I sit down?'

'Yeah, sit where you like.'

Edmondson glanced about the room, then indicated with a nod of his silvery-grey head a soft armchair at one side of the glass-topped coffee table. Table and chair were in front of the fireplace in which there was an artificial coal fire, heated and illuminated by electricity, this being the modern age. 'What about that?'

'Fine,' Steve said, barely able to keep the disgust and disbelief out of his voice. He knew Edmondson. This particular urbane English gentleman was a leading member of MI5 and, more importantly, the agency's representative at COBR, pronounced 'Cobra'. Though originally COBR was an acronym for the Cabinet Office Briefing Room, it had somehow been adopted as the name for a top-level management team that met regularly in a basement room in the old Home Office in Whitehall to discuss matters that were deemed too serious and secret to be raised even with the Prime Minister. As COBR was involved with matters of both internal and external security, including terrorist threats to the nation, it was presided over by a highly placed anonymous civil servant known only as 'the Secretary'. Its members included representatives of the various intelligence agencies, the Senior Foreign Affairs Minister, the Commissioner for the Metropolitan Police, the Supreme Commander of the Combined Services, and the Commanding Officer of the Special Forces Group. This organization, based at the Duke of York's Barracks, Chelsea, included the Special Air Service (SAS), of which Steve had once been an enthusiastic member.

As the MI5 representative at COBR meetings, Edmondson had been the brain behind a lot of the most daring counter-terrorist operations undertaken by SAS forces in a period when the Regiment as a whole had had little to do because of the lack of major international conflicts like the Falklands and Gulf wars of the 1980s and 1990s respectively.

Steve had been one of those recommended to Edmondson by the CO of the Special Forces Group as suitable to take part in undercover operations in Belfast at the tail end of the Troubles. Working covertly with the supposedly defunct 14th Intelligence Group, or 14 Int, he had been tasked with terminating the activities of the Catholic and Protestant paramilitaries who were trying to disrupt the peace initiative with a series of bombings and assassinations. Having completed his tasks to Edmondson's satisfaction, Steve had been called back repeatedly to undertake other special missions dreamed up by Edmondson at COBR meetings. These included the tracking and capturing of paramilitaries who had, with the coming of peace, shifted from political terrorism to organized crime – men like Houlihan. Thus, having been involved with Edmondson quite a few times, Steve knew him to be clever, pragmatic, charming ... and utterly ruthless.

'Very cosy,' Edmondson now said, sinking gratefully into the soft armchair and glancing about him. His keen gaze fell on the glass ashtray on the glass-topped table just in front of his immaculately trousered knees. 'Ah,' he said, obviously pleased and reaching into the side pocket of his jacket. 'I see an ashtray! Can I take it that means I can ...?'

'Yes, you can smoke,' Steve said without moving from where he was standing, still wondering what the hell was going on here.

'Excellent,' Edmondson said, taking a cigarette from the packet he had pulled out of his pocket. After lighting it, he exhaled with a pleased smile, sighing as he did so. 'We smokers feel like lepers these days,' he said, 'so it's doubly nice to be able to light up in a flat with an ashtray. I don't suppose ...?'

'Jesus! Don't tell me you're going to ask me for a drink! You're asking for my last drop of gin before you arrest me for my own protection? Surely even you aren't that brass-necked!'

Edmondson smiled and shrugged. 'What can I say, old boy? The sun's blazing outside and I grow old and am in need of some liquid refreshment. Would you deprive a poor pensioner?'

Edmondson did, indeed, look old, Steve thought, with his silvery-grey hair thinning and his matinée-idol good looks webbed with fine lines. He had lost a lot of weight, which didn't suit him, but his gaze remained bright.

'Yeah, I heard you'd retired,' Steve said, going to a cupboard against the wall facing the patio to collect a bottle of gin and a bottle of tonic water. 'So how come you've turned up here with a couple of policemen? Are you actually working in Belfast these days? Is your retirement a cover for covert MI5 operations in this fair, this *peaceful* city of ours? Tell me, Edmondson, I'm dying to know. Why are you here and not mowing a lawn in Buckinghamshire with all the other retired civil servants, brigadiers, admirals and suchlike boring old farts?'

'You're being cruel to me,' Edmondson said without rancour while exhaling a couple of smoke rings and watching them disappear.

'Yeah, right,' Steve said as he poured the gin and tonic into a tumbler. 'And you don't even deserve it.'

'Well, do I?'

'You've got as much blood on your hands as any terrorist who ever operated in this city. You just wash your hands more often, that's all. You have that civilized veneer.'

'I merely serve my country,' Edmondson said, 'and there isn't always a clean way to do it.'

'That's your excuse,' Steve said. He went into the kitchen to take some ice cubes out of the fridge and let them slide out of his clenched fist to splash into the tumbler. Then he returned to the living room and gave the drink to Edmondson. 'Okay,' he said, 'you've got your little drink. So why did they pull you out of retirement and what are you doing here in Belfast?'

'I'm officially retired,' Edmondson explained, 'but I still work part-time for Whitehall, three afternoons a week, which is just enough to keep me from being bored and to let them retain the benefits of my vast experience.'

'I'll buy that,' Steve said. 'But what's so important that they'd send you personally to Belfast? And what's this about Houlihan being released? Where, when and how?'

'The recently renovated and expanded Maghaberry Prison near Lisburn. This afternoon. He walked out a free man.' Edmondson held his glass up in the air and then raised one eyebrow. 'Aren't you joining me, dear boy?'

'Final drink for the condemned man?'

'No, not quite that. Who knows what a civilized chat between us can eventually lead to? So go on, have that drink.'

'Gee, thanks,' Steve said. 'I'm given permission to drink in my own home. That's real decent of you.'

Edmondson merely smiled and sipped at his gin and tonic while Steve went back to the cabinet to pour himself a Bushmill's whiskey, neat. He took a sip, then walked back to take the soft chair facing Edmondson. 'So how the fuck *did* Houlihan get out? I thought the bastard was in for life.'

'So did I,' Edmondson said. 'We went to so much trouble to nab him and put him in there – but, lo and behold, he walked out a free man this afternoon. There's no justice, is there?'

'Not much that I've seen in my time. You'd know, of course, since it's you and your kind who make the rules. So who engineered that bastard's release and why did they do it?'

'Not I, that's for sure. Not I and not my kind. If I had my way – if *we* had our way – Mr Houlihan would still be inside. No, I'm afraid we can't take the blame for this one. In fact, his release was arranged as part of an appeasement deal with a terrorist splinter group that was threatening to bring down the peace through a mainland bombing campaign.'

'If the British government didn't do as they asked.'

'Quite. And what they asked, or demanded, was that we release Houlihan from Maghaberry Prison.'

'Which means that the demand was made by one of Houlihan's criminal gangs.'

'Exactly.'

'And he walked free today.'

'Yes.'

'Jesus!'

'Quite.'

'So who authorized his release, if not the COBR?'

Edmondson sighed. 'The Prime Minister. Alas, he did it without consulting us. When we learned what he was going to do, we advised him against it, reminding him that Houlihan, even during the Troubles, had been widely viewed as a brutal, sadistic gangster masquerading as a freedom fighter merely to build up his criminal empire. We also reminded him that Houlihan, a supposed Republican, had, before being incarcerated, linked up with the Protestant gang lord, William Moore – affectionately known as 'Wild Bill' because of *his* violent nature – and that, with Wild Bill's help and despite the political peace, he'd created a reign of terror in the streets of Belfast. Finally, we reminded him that Houlihan, when in prison, was classified by the prison psychologist as a full-blown violent psychopath. So, we reminded our handsome young PM of all this and also warned him of the consequences of letting Houlihan out of prison to link up again with Wild Bill Moore. Unfortunately, our words of wisdom fell on deaf ears.'

'Why?'

'Alas, being media conscious, our PM was more concerned with the consequences of a breakdown in the peace for which he has, rightly or wrongly but certainly cleverly, taken a lot of the credit. The mere possibility of a mainland bombing campaign by a splinter terrorist group in Northern Ireland was enough to make him compromise and order the release of Houlihan. We could do nothing about it.'

'Except come here to arrest me for my own protection.'

Edmondson smiled. 'Well, let's face it, Steve: you were the

one who put Houlihan in prison, the one who caught him in the act and had him arrested, thus sending him on his way to prison, and you're now a prominent citizen of this fair city, not easy to hide. Now that he's free, Houlihan is bound to come after you. And we can't let that happen.'

Steve remembered the business of Houlihan's capture well. Just over three years ago he, Steve, had been working undercover as an SAS operative with the re-formed 14th Intelligence Group, tasked with tracking the movements of former Catholic and Protestant paramilitaries who had turned to crime when the peace rendered them unemployable. The two leading figures in the burgeoning Belfast underworld were Michael 'Mad Mike' Houlihan, formerly of the Provisional IRA, and William 'Wild Bill' Moore, formerly of the UDA.

A few weeks before he was due to leave the service, Steve had learned from an informer, or tout, that Houlihan was going to launch a full-scale attack on a Securicor van being used to transfer money from the vaults of a leading bank in the centre of Belfast. According to the tout, Houlihan, being a 'hands on' gangster who relished personal danger, was going to lead the raid personally.

Wanting to catch Houlihan red-handed, Steve had arranged for a six-man SAS patrol, led by himself, to be positioned in an unmarked van parked directly across the road from the bank on the Friday chosen by Houlihan for the raid. As anticipated, just as the money was being transferred from the bank to the Securicor van, another unmarked van roared up to the building and screeched to an abrupt halt. Houlihan and four of his men, all wearing CT body armour and masks, jumped out with all guns blazing, cutting down the men guarding the Securicor van and also killing the driver.

Instantly, Steve and his SAS men poured out of their own van to fire upon Houlihan and his men, shooting most of them down. However, Houlihan and one of his gang members managed to clamber up into the driver's cabin of the Securicor van and started off along the street. The gang member was driving with Houlihan beside him.

Steve himself raced up to the side of the van and raked it with a hail of bullets from his MP5 sub-machine gun, smashing all the windows, killing the driver, and causing the van to careen across the road, bounce up onto the pavement and smash into a brick wall between two shops. When Houlihan clambered out of the wreckage, dazed but unharmed, Steve and his men nabbed him and kept him covered until the RUC Headquarters Mobile Support Unit (HMSU) arrived to take charge of the suspects.

The following day, when the incident was reported in full by the media, the SAS came under heavy criticism for behaving like 'a bunch of cowboys' in a public thoroughfare, endangering the lives of passers-by. But Houlihan got a life sentence for the murder of the Securior guards as well as for attempted robbery and that, at the time, made it worthwhile.

As Houlihan, with his life sentence hanging over him, was being escorted from the courtroom, he stared directly at Steve, who had been a prosecuting witness at his trial, and said, 'Some day I'll make you pay for this, you SAS shit.'

Given his nature, his love of violent retribution, there was little doubt that he would, now that he was free, try to make good that threat.

'I'd *like* to believe that you're concerned for my personal safety,' Steve said to Edmondson, 'but I'm afraid it just doesn't ring true. What's your real interest here?'

Edmondson took a deep breath, then released it in a melodramatic sigh. 'We know for a fact that Houlihan continued to run his criminal gangs from inside the prison, sending out instructions through his many visitors and, of course, by coded messages in ostensibly routine telephone conversations with his family and friends.'

'I'll buy that,' Steve said. 'No way that he couldn't do that. The paramilitaries on both sides were doing that out of Long

Kesh, the Crumlin Road jail and Maghaberry Prison throughout the Troubles. Being in prison didn't hamper them at all, so it certainly wouldn't have hampered Houlihan.'

'Exactly,' Edmondson said. 'So, naturally, he'll personally take back charge of his gang members once he's out—'

'Which he is.'

'Correct . . . And now that he's free there's little doubt that he'll link up again with Wild Bill Moore and that between them they'll rule the whole city – at least, the criminal side of it . . . We simply can't let that happen.'

'How can you prevent it?'

Edmondson sighed again, shrugging, as if pained by what he was contemplating. '*You* can prevent it,' he said. 'You can do so by chopping off the two heads to render the main body helpless. You can do it. I *know* you can.'

Now that he was seeing the true picture, Steve was bleakly amused. 'I thought you came here to arrest me,' he said. 'For my own protection, of course.'

'Of course,' Edmondson replied, with a small smile. 'Without our protection, your life would be in danger because Houlihan, beyond any shadow of doubt, is going to track you down and kill you for what you did to him – a life sentence, no less. He's hardly likely to love you for that, is he? And you *know* he has a taste for vengeance, most violently wrought.' By this stage, Edmondson was sounding positively Shakespearean. 'So the basic thesis, dear boy, is that either we arrest you for your own protection or—'

'I get to Houlihan before he gets to me.'

Edmondson smiled with admiration. 'How bright you are! You've hit the nail on the head again.'

'So you want me to go out there and somehow neutralize Houlihan—'

'*And* Wild Bill!' Edmondson added promptly.

'Jesus!' Steve was truly disgusted. 'And if I tell you that I don't want to do it – or that I *can't* do it because it simply isn't possible — you're going to arrest me, supposedly for my own protection.'

Edmondson shrugged and smiled, spreading his hands in the air as if begging for clemency. 'What else *can* we do, dear boy? If Houlihan, within mere days of getting out of prison, assassinates a man known to have been one of our 14th Intelligence Group operatives before he became a respectable local businessman, we'll have a propaganda disaster on our hands. And believe me when I say that if Houlihan kills you, he'll certainly try to enhance his criminal reputation by spreading the word about who you are — or, being dead, *were*.'

'You're so kind,' Steve said.

'We have to face the facts, my boy. And on top of all that, we can't let Houlihan link up with Wild Bill to form what would almost certainly be the largest criminal enterprise in Great Britain and, possibly, Europe. Such a gang could effectively take over the whole of Northern Ireland, cross into the Republic and eventually link up with similar gangs on the mainland and in Europe, including the Russian *Mafiya*, which is already moving into London. Indeed, according to our intelligence, Houlihan and Moore have already had serious discussions about that very possibility and are planning to have meetings with *Mafiya* representatives. The very thought chills the blood.'

'You're being melodramatic.'

'No, I'm not. COBR has enough evidence to be convinced that such a link-up is seriously being considered by both sides — the Irish gangs and the Russian *Mafiya*. And since we can't stop the Russians, who are beyond our control, our only choice is to concentrate on the Irish and put them out of action.'

'So what if I say, "Fuck it. Arrest me and lock me up in some safe house for my own protection"? You won't be able to keep me locked up for ever. I could just sit it out. That might be better than some suicide mission to neutralize Houlihan and his Prod chum.'

'I'm not so sure of that, Steve. A lot could happen while you're away.'

'What does that mean?'

'It's surprising how much trouble even the most honest businessman can get into once he takes a long absence from work. I mean, what happens if, while he's away, the Inland Revenue decides that his business needs a thorough investigation and sets about doing it in his absence? They simply bully his staff into giving them access and they go through his papers with a fine toothcomb.'

'They wouldn't find anything on me,' Steve said firmly, 'even with a fine toothcomb.'

Edmondson sighed again and shook his silvery-grey head from side to side, as if despairing at Steve's ignorance.

'I'm afraid, my boy, that, honest as you may think you've been in your business dealings, you *did* make your pile by purchasing properties in some dodgy areas, the hardliners' ghettoes. So God knows how many tangled threads of illegality ran through those buildings before you actually became involved. Those tangled threads could eventually strangle you, Steve, giving you legal grief and even putting you out of business altogether. Then, of course, there are your partners to consider . . .'

'What about my partners? They're a pair of perfectly honest businessmen.'

'Are they? I wouldn't count on that. Business honesty, my boy, is in the eye of the beholder and the Inland Revenue, never mind the courts of law, interpret it differently from you and I. How easy it is, once a company is under investigation, for a simple lunch or some other gift from one businessman to another – or, perhaps, to a politician – to be viewed by the prosecutors as a bribe; for an offshore account to be seen as tax evasion; for a simple mistake in accounting to be viewed as—'

'All right, all right,' Steve interjected. 'I think I get the picture.'

'Ah, good,' Edmondson said, stubbing his cigarette out in the ashtray while looking pleased with himself.

'You really *are* a shit,' Steve informed him.

'Sticks and stones, dear boy.'

'You fuckers would really set out to ruin me?'

Edmondson shrugged. 'No choice, really. The good of the country comes first. So why not do the noble thing whilst also saving yourself all that agony?'

'Why not, indeed?' Steve said. 'It would seem that my goose is cooked either way.'

'Exactly,' Edmondson said. 'So can I take it you'll accept this little assignment?'

'This suicide mission,' Steve corrected him.

'Well . . .' Edmondson shrugged again. 'Have it your way, dear boy. Just give me the word: "Yes" or "No".'

'Yes,' Steve said. 'So how do I go about it? Do you have any ideas?'

'Only that we, the British government, can't be seen to be involved, so it has to be a covert operation and one without back-up.'

'Thanks a million,' Steve said, unable to hide his disgust, understanding that he was being placed in the dead zone of total deniability and that no help would be forthcoming if he needed it. He would be an 'Invisible' with no friends in high places and no 'official' sanction for the mission. He would be out there on his own, with no redress if anything went wrong.

He didn't want to do it. He was convinced it was suicidal. On the other hand, if he refused, the very same government that would now deny any involvement with him would ensure that he was financially ruined — always assuming that the mad, bad Houlihan hadn't killed him first.

Nice one, Steve thought.

'Are there any restrictions on *how* I do it?' he asked. 'Can I use weapons or does it have to look like an accident? Can I call in some old friends?'

'There are no restrictions, only recommendations,' Edmondson said. 'We just want the job done. However, it would be helpful if, when you neutralize one of them, you make it seem that it was the work of the other. That way we can turn one gang against the other, set them at each others' throats, destroy their unity and thus weaken them enough to enable the RUC — sorry, the Police Service of Northern Ireland — to pick up the pieces. As for calling in friends . . . No, I'm afraid you can't do that. The more people there are involved, the greater the chance of being exposed. Also, we couldn't pay them. We can't risk having any kind of payment traced back to us. So I'm afraid you'll have to do it on your own. Absolutely alone. There's no other way.'

'Anything else?' Steve asked.

'Nothing that I can think of,' Edmondson said. Then he finished off his drink, placed the tumbler back on the glass-topped table and stood up laboriously, again showing his age. 'Have you any last questions?'

Steve got to his feet too. 'No,' he said.

Edmondson nodded. 'Good luck.'

Steve showed him out. They did not shake hands. When Edmondson had left, Steve went out onto his balcony and studied the city on the far side of the river: the old buildings and the new, those that he had purchased and renovated to make a small fortune. He could lose that fortune — and an awful lot more besides — if he didn't do what was being demanded of him. If he didn't do it, he could also lose his life — and he was too young for that.

Sighing, feeling trapped, yet also excited, he went inside to pour himself another drink and let his mind wander.

Steve had a lot to think about.

Chapter Four

Houlihan couldn't believe how many people had managed to squeeze into his modest home. The small living room was so packed that the people could hardly bend their elbows. The sea of heads extended into the narrow kitchen and all the way out into the backyard in a haze of August sunlight. A lot of drink had been downed already and many faces were flushed, the guests cracking jokes and bellowing with laughter, the conversation incessant and noisy. You could smell the drink and the air was blue with smoke. This was a party in full swing.

The applause and cheering soon gave way to shouted greetings and a lot of handshaking and backslapping.

'Welcome back, Mike!'

'It's grand to see you again, Mike!'

'Sure you're a sight for sore eyes, Mr Houlihan. Now things might liven up around here.'

'A great day, Mike. Brilliant!'

'Howya doin', boss? Good to see you again.'

'Sure you're lookin' great, Mr Houlihan!'

Recalling the advice given to him by Parnell, Houlihan made a great show of hugging his wife Maeve and kissing her on the cheek. Then he did the same to his daughter Kathleen, who was standing beside the gorgeous Katherine Crowley.

Though Houlihan's daughter and Parnell's assistant had similar names, there all resemblance between them ended. It had never failed to depress Houlihan that both his wife and his daughter had inherited his unwholesome bulk and that neither woman could even compensate for it with attractive faces. While Maeve now had enough years on her to be able to wear her lack of good looks with comparative ease, Kathleen, still only twenty-three, about the same age as Katherine Crowley, was as plain as a barn door and not helped by her low intelligence and lack of humour.

Kathleen's unprepossessing appearance was only made all the more apparent by the close proximity of Katherine Crowley who, in this crowd of mostly working-class people, stood out like a shining beacon at sea with her movie-star features, smooth alabaster skin, golden-blonde hair, slim figure and expensive, sexy clothes. Even Parnell, with his finely cut grey suit, immaculately pressed shirt, colourful tie and gleaming black patent-leather shoes, looked out of place in this smoky room filled with generally dowdy dressers.

In truth, it was the presence of the sophisticated Parnell and his lovely assistant that reminded Houlihan that he *himself* was working-class muck, despite his hidden wealth, influence in the local community and secret desire to be something more than he was. Thus, while desperately needing Parnell and lusting after Katherine Crowley, he also resented them.

'Would you like a wee drop of whisky, Mike?'

'Aye, I would.'

'Here ya are, then!'

Houlihan didn't even know who was talking to him. He only saw the hand thrusting a big glass of whisky at him, so he took it and had a hurried sip, then glanced about him, trying desperately not to ogle Katherine Crowley.

'A good turnout, eh?' Parnell said to him.

'Ackaye, it is that, right enough.'

'Sure you have lots of friends, Dad,' Kathleen said. 'We

just let them know you were bein' released and that's all it took.'

'Good girl,' Houlihan said without warmth.

Looking at his daughter, he could hardly avoid also looking at Katherine Crowley, who was standing right there beside her. Instantly, he felt dizzy with lust. It had been three years, after all, without the touch of a real woman, only the arseholes of the nancy boys herded into the prison showers, the cream puffs so slim that you could pretend they were women, closing your eyes when you entered them, ramming their buttocks, thrusting hard to draw blood, excited by their slobbering, their moaning and groaning, their piteous pleas for mercy, which fell on deaf ears, sliding your hands over their smooth skin, squeezing here, pressing there, pretending, *imagining* . . . But even with all that, it was never like the real thing and certainly hadn't been enough to stop him being tormented by lascivious thoughts of women – *real* tits and ass, *real* cunt, wet and warm – or by erotic dreams that made him awaken to the guilt of sperm-soaked sheets.

Now, of all the women gathered together in this small house, including his fat wife and drab daughter, the one he least wanted to be near was the one standing right there in front of him: so sexy compared to the others that he was ready to come in his pants. Silently praying that his lust didn't show in his face, he decided, for his own good, to move on.

'Think I'll circulate a bit,' he said, avoiding Katherine's green eyes and catching Maeve's nervous gaze instead. Maeve, who'd felt the back of his hand more than once and who knew of his violent criminal activities (though feigning ignorance of them), had spent most of her married life in fear of him. 'Say hello to some old friends,' he added by way of explanation.

'Lots of those here, luv,' Maeve said. These were the first words that she had spoken to him since he had entered the house. 'And they're all dyin' to talk to you.'

'That's what old friends are for,' he retorted.

Moving away from her and the seductive Katherine Crowley,

he made his way into the tightly packed crowd, almost choking in the smoke, but taking pleasure from the smell of whisky and beer, neither of which had been permitted in prison. As he made his way to the narrow kitchen, virtually inching forward, shaking hands and exchanging greetings en route, he was reminded by the sea of flushed faces around him that most of the men gathered here were former paramilitary hard men, many scarred from fist fights, knives, bullets or shrapnel, and that they were now the cream of his criminal gangs. He did not have just one gang; he had a wide variety of them. They were like the old paramilitary (or, as the Brits would have it, terrorist) splinter groups and he had simply united them under his single rule, using a fist of iron to keep them in line. They were, of course, all Catholics, all former PIRA men. His former enemy, now his associate, William 'Wild Bill' Moore, was in charge of a similar organization composed of the worst, most criminal elements of the old UDA and UDR.

A right bed of snakes, when you thought about it, and ironic that they were gathered together here, in this small living room filled with Virgin Marys, paintings of other saints and Maeve's beloved framed photo of the present Pope.

Religion and crime, Houlihan thought. *They make good bedmates.*

Reaching the kitchen, also packed with guests, noisy and dense with cigarette smoke, Houlihan polished off his glass of whisky. He was greeted by more of his hard men and their wives, then was offered, and accepted, another large glass of whisky. Sipping it, he was confronted with his two sons, John and Peter, twenty-four and twenty-five respectively, as well as Pamela, one of his other two daughters, twenty-two, auburn-haired, pleasant and, like Kathleen, not pretty. The three of them took turns at embracing him, though none of them seemed at ease while doing so; they all seemed faintly embarrassed.

'Welcome home, Dad,' John said.

'Aye, welcome back,' Peter added.

'Me, too,' Pam said inexplicably, as if lost for words, as she gave him a brief hug.

'Sure it's grand to see you all again,' Houlihan said, loud and clear for the benefit of those listening. 'Even better to see you here than in the visiting room of that bloody prison. Sure you're all lookin' great. How are the kids?'

All of them were married with children and living in various areas of Belfast. His remaining daughters, Linda and Hope, were also married with children, but living farther away, Linda in South Armagh, Hope in Derry, which was called 'Londonderry' by the Brits and Prods. Houlihan didn't give a fuck about their kids, his grandchildren, but a man had to keep up appearances.

'Ack, sure they're doin' grand,' John said.

'Mine, too,' Peter added.

'Wee Sean's fine,' Pam said, referring to her only child while still looking faintly embarrassed.

Of course, Houlihan *knew* that his own children were uneasy with him, that they were basically frightened of him, because he had let them see him hammering their mother and had hammered them as well when they displeased him. Linda and Hope hadn't been able to take it, so had married young men who lived well outside Belfast. But the others, perhaps lacking that initiative, had remained in the city, though they saw as little of him as decency permitted. Not that Houlihan gave a damn. He wasn't family-orientated. What he wanted was power and the freedom to do just what he wanted. Nothing else mattered to him.

'Great!' he now boomed, mindful of those watching. 'Grand! Sure I'll come around in the next couple of days and pay youse a visit. I'll bring the kids somethin'.'

'Aye, right,' John said with little enthusiasm.

'I'm sure they'll be glad to see you,' Peter added without conviction.

'Of course, wee Sean's too young to know you,' Pam said

disingenuously, 'what with him bein' born a few months after you went inside. But it'll be nice for you to see him at last. Sure he's a lively wee tyke.'

'Ackaye,' Houlihan said. 'Sure isn't it a terrible thing when a man doesn't even get the chance to see his own grandchild, bein' locked up in prison for no good reason? Well, I'll come see him soon, love, I promise, and I'll bring a wee present.'

'Aye, right,' Pam said. 'I—'

But Houlihan had already lost interest. ''Scuse me,' he interjected, 'but I've just seen someone I've got to talk to. Sure I'll see youse all later.'

He had, in fact, been surprised on glancing out into the sunny backyard to see two of the men he was supposed to meet that evening in the Hibernian pub in the Falls: his most trusted lieutenants, Frank Kavanagh and Pat Connolly, the former black-haired and as big as a gorilla, the latter red-haired and as lean as a prizefighter, both of them with bottles of Guinness in their fists.

Still greeting other friends and relatives as he inched his way through the packed, narrow kitchen, almost choking in the dense cigarette smoke, Houlihan eventually managed to make it out to the relatively fresh air of the brick-walled backyard. The rear door had been opened to allow some of the guests to spill out into the entry where, as he recalled, many a man had either received a good hiding or lost his life during the Troubles. In fact, the litter-strewn entries behind the terraced houses were still used by Houlihan's men for punishment beatings or kneecappings, particularly under cover of darkness. Few people within earshot would respond to the screams of the victims for fear that they might be punished themselves, so the entries had their uses.

'What the fuck are you two doing here?' Houlihan asked when he reached his two friends.

They both grinned at him.

'Sure we couldn't pass up the chance for a free drink,

boss,' Kavanagh responded, waving his bottle gently to and
fro in front of his face.

'Ackaye,' Connolly added. 'We heard there was a grand
wee party goin' and we couldn't resist it.'

'I thought you two were going to meet me and Parnell in
the Hibernian pub this evening.'

'We are,' Kavanagh said. 'Sure that's no problem at all.
It's all been fixed up, like, by Parnell and we're gonna be
there. But what's the harm in comin' here first and sayin' a
quick hello?'

'No harm at all, Frank. Sure it's real grand to see you
both. So how are things with the boyos?'

By 'the boyos' he meant the gangsters, all former PIRA
paramilitaries, who ruled his various territories in the Falls and
the other predominantly Catholic areas of Belfast.

'No problems,' Kavanagh said. 'Sure everything's runnin' as
smooth as butter. Everything's hunky-dory, like. The money's
been pourin' in from—'

'That's it, Frank,' Houlihan said testily. 'Discuss our
business with half of fuckin' Belfast listening in.' He nodded
to indicate the drunken celebrants on all sides in that small
bricked-in space – a kind of miniature prison yard, in fact, as
he suddenly realized. 'Why not use a fuckin' megaphone and
be done with it?'

'Jesus, boss, I . . .'

'We'll discuss it this evenin', right?'

'Right, boss. Ackaye, that's right, right enough.' Kavanagh,
who had terrified many a man in his time, was now almost
blubbering with fear. 'Aye, tonight, then. We'll discuss it
tonight.'

'Right,' Connolly added nervously. 'Tonight, boss.'

'And just make sure you're there,' Houlihan told him.

'Christ, yes, boss,' Connolly said. 'No way otherwise, like.
No question about it. Here,' he added in a panic while bending
down to pick a bottle off the ground by his foot. Straightening

up again, he held the bottle on high. 'Have another drink, boss.' He sloshed the whisky into Houlihan's glass as if it was water.

Houlihan hadn't had alcohol in three years – except the odd nip of poteen made illicitly in the jail – and now the whisky was going to his head, making him feel inwardly luminous and powerful ... almost omnipotent.

'Jasus,' he said, feeling more friendly towards his erring lieutenants. 'What I'd give to get away from this fuckin' family do, this so-called fuckin' reunion, this media circus, and go straight to the Hibernian early. Have a few jars on my own before the women show up to oil my balls and coax the lead out of my pencil.'

'Know what you mean, boss,' Connolly said, nodding affirmatively. 'Sure it musta bin hard in the jail. I mean, three years without ...' His voice trailed off uncertainly when he realized that he was about to say something that Houlihan might not want to hear: an implication of how his enforced celibacy in jail was dealt with. Though banging nancy boys was perfectly acceptable in prison, it wasn't something a real man wanted to be reminded of once he was out. 'What I meant, boss, was ...'

Luckily, he was saved from committing a gross error when Jack Parnell pushed his way out of the crowded kitchen, followed by Katherine Crowley. When they stopped in front of Houlihan, he once more found it hard to keep his eyes off the woman.

'Right,' Parnell said. 'We've put in our appearance, so we'll be off now. I'll see you this evening in the Hibernian.'

'What time?'

'About seven.'

'Fuck!' Houlihan exclaimed in exasperation, glancing about him at the people packed into the small backyard, still trying to force himself not to look at Katherine. 'Can't I go earlier than that? Have a few jars before you arrive? Just to get the hell out of here.'

'No,' Parnell said. 'You've got to stay here and be seen as a good husband and father. Most of the press have gone, but there are still a few reporters loitering outside, waiting to pounce the instant you step out the door. They'll probably give up soon, get bored and take off, but I still think it's best that you stay here for most of the afternoon, at least until most of the guests have left. Then you can take yourself off, ostensibly for a few jars with your mates down in the pub, just like you did in the good old days. I want it all to seem natural.'

Houlihan sighed in frustration, but accepted Parnell's words of wisdom. 'Aye, right. I suppose I'll just have to stick it out. See you this evening.'

'You will,' Parnell confirmed, nodding as he turned away to begin pushing his way through the guests crowded around the kitchen door.

Despite himself, Houlihan stared at the woman, his hungry gaze taking her in from tip to toe: the golden-blonde hair, the moisturized full lips, the steady rise and fall of her breasts in that tight blouse, the long legs emphasized by the tight skirt and stiletto-heeled shoes. He was consumed by the sight of her, hardening in his crotch, burning.

Quickly, desperately, he shifted his gaze, but not before Katherine had caught its drift, looking her up and down. She gave him a slight, knowing smile.

'Nice to have met you, Mr Houlihan,' she said.

Houlihan nodded. 'Same here.'

'We'll probably meet again, in our office, when you visit Mr Parnell.'

Houlihan was slightly, pleasantly surprised by that remark, wondering if it was some kind of come-on. At the same time, he was confused by her slight smile, which seemed, at least to him, to be an odd mixture of invitation and mockery. *I'm probably just imagining it.* Yet when it struck him that Parnell might be fucking her, he was filled with resentment.

'Ackaye, that's true enough,' he said. 'Sure I'm bound

to be comin' to your office, so we're certain to meet again, like.'

'Exactly.'

'Right.'

'Till then.'

'Aye, till then.'

When Katherine, with another fleeting smile, turned away from him and pushed her way back into the kitchen, following Parnell, Houlihan observed the metronomic swaying of her hips, the perfect cheeks of her arse in the tight dress, with a lust that seemed to thicken his blood and made him almost light-headed. When, eventually, she had disappeared into the crowd, Houlihan turned back to his friends and saw that they, too, had been watching her leave, Kavanagh licking his lips while Connolly puffed out his cheeks to release his breath in a sigh.

'Jasus!' Kavanagh exclaimed softly. 'Sure that was some looker. You think Parnell's been in there?'

'How the fuck would I know?' Houlihan retorted, almost snarling, despite his intention to hide his true feelings. 'And what fuckin' business is it of yours?'

Kavanagh, who could murder his fellow man without blinking, blushed like a guilty schoolboy. 'Jasus, boss, I was just—'

'Keep your fuckin' gob shut,' Houlihan said, 'if you've got nothing worth saying.'

'Sorry, boss. I—'

'So what's that bastard Steve Lawson been up to while I've been inside?'

'Steve Lawson?' Kavanagh asked, his brow wrinkling as he tried to recall the name.

'Aye, Steve Lawson. The SAS bastard who bought me that three years in prison and is now back in Civvy Street in Belfast. I want that fucker's head on a plate. So what's he been up to?'

Relieved that the subject had been changed, and suddenly

recalling the individual concerned, Kavanagh poured another drink for his boss and then told him all he knew about Steve Lawson. Houlihan listened intently, feeling more drunk with every passing minute, more powerful, more enraged, but taking everything in, filing it away for future reference ... for the day when he would have his revenge for what that bastard had done to him.

As far as Houlihan was concerned, Steve Lawson was doomed.

Chapter Five

Steve had arranged to meet his old RUC friend Joe Williamson in the bar of Cutter's Wharf at seven that evening. Though he rarely exercised in a gym these days, Steve compensated for this by walking the city as much as possible, rather than going by car or taking public transport. So he left his flat a good hour before the meeting was due to take place and began to walk all the way to Stranmillis where the bar was located.

The sun was starting to sink when, wearing an open-necked shirt under a windcheater jacket, powder-blue jeans and brown suede shoes, Steve left his building. The evening was still warm, however, with silvery light reflecting off the river and the plate-glass windows of the buildings beyond the opposite bank.

Though Steve could have followed the river most of the way to Stranmillis, which many were doing in this fine weather, he preferred to meander through the centre of the city, which was more to his urban taste, being busier and with more to look at and be distracted by.

Turning away from the river, he went along Ann Street, past the grim guard-box and high black-metal fences of the Musgrave Street police station, then into Castle Lane, taking note of how lively those pedestrianized thoroughfares had become once the threat of terrorist bombings had ceased, the British Army had disappeared and the police had deliberately kept a low profile. Indeed, even at this time in the evening, a lot of the relatively new brand-name stores were still open, the streets were packed with pedestrians, and people were sitting on benches under the chestnut trees or at restaurant tables placed outside, taking in the sun while eating and drinking continental style.

Observing them as well as the ambience in general, the carefree *bon vivant* atmosphere, Steve recalled how different it had been a decade ago when the Troubles were still raging and the terrorists on both sides were causing mayhem. At that time, this area, particularly in the evenings, had been grim and desolate, with bricked-up doorways, caged shop fronts, steel shutters pulled down over plate-glass windows, whole terraces bombed out and turned into waste ground, and armoured troop-carriers, known as 'pigs', patrolling the almost deserted streets. All of that had changed with the coming of peace and now the centre of the city, much of it redeveloped with imposing glass-and-steel shopping malls, was thriving with late-night spenders as well as packed pubs and restaurants. There wasn't a troop-carrier in sight and the atmosphere was deceptively festive.

Deceptive because Belfast, as Steve knew, remained a dangerous city.

He had always loved this city because it was more like a town, small and easily traversed, and also because it was surrounded by mountains that had once been visible in every direction. Now, however, as he reached the end of Castle Lane and glanced east, he saw only the high buildings of Donegall Place.

Beyond those buildings, as he well knew, was the grim, deadly sprawl of the Falls.

Somewhere out there, in the Falls, Houlihan was once more on the loose and looking for him.

Turning into Donegall Place, Steve walked southward along the packed pavement towards the City Hall, recalling the days when this road was protected by grim army checkpoints manned with heavily armed soldiers in DPM clothing, steel helmets and GPVs. The barricades had been removed a few years back and the street had returned to stake its claim as one of the busiest shopping precincts in the city.

Soaring to 173 feet above ground level, the central copper dome of the City Hall was still impressive but, like any copper exposed to the elements, had tarnished green, looking like a mouldy cheese even in the sunlight and casting its shadow on the surrounding lawns where people were still loitering, taking in the slowly fading sunlight.

Skirting the City Hall, Steve continued down Bedford Street and then into the Dublin Road where, glancing eastward along the side streets, he did indeed catch an occasional glimpse of the gorse-covered slopes of the mountains, though the main road itself was packed with bars and trendy restaurants, most of them doing good business. Here and in the so-called 'Golden Mile', which included the Dublin Road but stretched to the far side of Shaftesbury Square, all the way up to Queens University and the Botanic Gardens, he saw how swiftly the young people of Belfast, a notoriously prudish, largely Protestant city, had come into the modern age since the peace. The girls, formerly fattened on potatoes and fried foods, were now as slim as fashion models and wearing minimal clothing that exposed lots of leg, stomach and breast. The boys were sporting black leather jackets, tight blue jeans and a wide variety of male jewellery, including rings through the ears and nostrils.

The times had certainly changed.

Leaving the Golden Mile behind, he walked along the quieter Stranmillis Road, with its red-brick Victorian houses, lush gardens and private driveways, then turned into the tree-lined Lockview Road, which eventually led him back down to the River Lagan. Located between the river and the quiet, tree-lined road, the bar-and-restaurant complex of Cutter's Wharf looked vaguely like a modernized boathouse, with picnic tables and benches in the L-shaped beer garden overlooking the river.

Steve didn't have to enter the building. He saw his friend, Joe Williamson, seated at a table in the beer garden with the flowing river in the background, facing in the direction of Governors Bridge, out of earshot of the other drinkers and with two pints of Guinness already to hand.

Pleased that Joe still assumed he would be punctual, which he always was, Steve approached the table and said, 'Hi, stranger! Long time no see!'

Joe looked up and grinned when he saw Steve. 'Have you come?' he said, using that oddity of greeting peculiar to the Ulster Irish. 'Long time no see!'

When he reached out with his hand, Steve shook it, then took the chair facing him. Wearing a light grey suit with shirt and striped tie, Joe was in his late fifties, with a genial, healthily flushed plump face, thinning grey hair and an expanding midriff. He raised his glass of Guinness in the air and Steve did the same. They touched glasses and drank.

'So,' Steve said after he had taken his first sip of the drink and was wiping his wet lips with the back of his hand. 'What have you been up to, my friend, since leaving the force?'

Joe had been an officer in the RUC for most of his working life but had asked for early retirement when, in the year 2000, the organization was renamed the Police Service of Northern Ireland. Joe hadn't approved of that. Though one of the least sectarian policemen that Steve had ever known – and Steve had met many – Joe felt that the RUC, despite its weaknesses, had done a dirty job well, taking abuse from both sides throughout a confusing conflict, and that changing its name for political reasons was an insult to all the men who had fought and died in the line of duty. Certainly, he wasn't the only RUC officer to have resigned during those tense, controversial days.

'Oh . . .' Joe shrugged. 'Keeping myself busy. A little bit here, a little bit there. Gardening, fishing, golf out on the course at Belvoir Park, and even a bit of sailing with the Royal Northern Ireland Yacht Club out at Cultra.'

Steve gave a low whistle of appreciation. 'That's a rich man's sport in a rich man's area,' he said.

Joe smiled. 'Well, I'm not rich and I never will be, but I have friends in all the right places. Do you want to hear the rest of this?'

Steve nodded. 'Go on.'

'I also work part-time in an advisory capacity for a small number of organizations that need help with security — banks, industrial complexes, even army bases and police stations — so that gets me out of the house as well. Of course, none of it's as exciting as the work we both did in the old days, but you can't expect everything.'

'The work we did in the old days was something special. Those were the most exciting days of my life. It's never been the same since.'

'I heard you were making a fortune in property,' Joe said. 'Surely that must be exciting as well.'

'A different kind of excitement — and even that only initially. Once you've made your first pile, it's just a matter of repeating yourself. I know exactly what I'm doing from one day to the next and that makes for a pretty boring life. It wasn't like that in the old days. They were unpredictable times. You didn't know what was coming up from one day to the next and that made for a life of constant surprises.' Steve nodded for emphasis. 'Yeah, I have to admit that immoral as it may seem, despite our dirty tricks, I was thrilled to be doing that work and I have no regrets. Or, at least, if I have a single regret, it's that I can no longer do it. The normal life kills me.'

'It's interesting that you should use the word "immoral",' Joe said, 'because certainly a lot of the work was just that, though we certainly did it for what we thought were good reasons. The end, I suppose, justifying the means.'

Steve knew what he was talking about. The world they

were discussing was another world altogether, one without rules, beyond morality, both dangerous and endangering, so bizarre that it had given birth to a wholly new, esoteric language: green slime and spooks; touts and turncoats and dickers; MIOs and Milos and Fincos and COPS, as well as MI5, MI6, and the RUC CID. It was a uniquely amoral, infinitely murky world in which even friends were enemies because no one intelligence agency trusted another.

While MI6, the intelligence agency secretly run by the Foreign and Commonwealth Office, and MI5, the security service openly charged with counter-espionage, were forever trying to undermine each other by withholding information or blocking each other's plans, the RUC, which had an almost tribal secretiveness, was running its Special Branch agents with scant regard for the needs or requirements of British Army security. At the same time, the RUC Special Branch was running its own secret cross-border contacts with the Irish Republic's Gardai Special Branch, which effectively left the other organizations floundering in the dark.

Because of this complex web of mutually suspicious and secretive organizations, the few SAS intelligence men in the province, including Steve, occupying key positions with the supposedly defunct 14th Intelligence Group or at the British Army HQ in Lisburn, had often been exposed to internecine rivalries when trying to coordinate operations against the terrorists. What linked them together, however, the SAS and RUC included, was the fight against terrorism, using any means at their disposal, no matter how questionable, including the use of turncoats and touts and not stopping at blackmail or neutralization. (This last being a polite euphemism for assassination or, more bluntly, murder.) It was therefore a world in which morality had little credence and where people like Steve and Joe, both supposedly decent citizens, were compelled to work undercover while closing their eyes to their own misdemeanours. They both had dirt under their fingernails and blood on their hands; they could never wash that blood and dirt off, but they had learned to live with it.

'Well,' Steve said, 'I'm not sure if the end, when it came, actually justified the means, given the state this country's in at the moment.'

'What state?'

'Criminal activity on a grand scale. Belfast, without sectarianism, has become Gangster City.'

Joe smiled and nodded. 'That's true enough.' Then he shrugged forlornly. 'But where else could it go? What do you do when peace comes and you have two or three generations of men who've never held an honest job and know only the rule of the gun? The paramilitaries of both sides financed their activities with armed robbery, intimidation, protection rackets, other kinds of fraud and extortion, money laundering, video piracy and, despite their protestations to the contrary, the smuggling and selling of all kinds of drugs. Given that many of those paramilitaries never knew any other kind of life and were, of course, often expert with weapons and explosives, what else could they do to make a living, never mind maintain their status, but turn to organized crime? In that sense, Belfast's present position as Ireland's crime capital was virtually preordained.'

'Not good,' Steve said.

'No, not good at all. And from what I hear, getting worse all the time.'

'You know who's in charge, don't you?'

'Yes, Mad Mike Houlihan lords it over the Catholic ghettoes while his former enemy, now his friend, Wild Bill Moore, struts his stuff with the Protestant communities. Those two gentlemen – or, more accurately, animals – have brutally carved the city up between them.'

'You've heard about Houlihan's release from Maghaberry Prison?'

'Yes. It's a bloody disgrace. That bastard's been responsible for half the crime in this city, including murder. He's also been responsible for the deaths of more than one police officer. Now the British Prime Minister orders his release. That's politics for you.'

'It sure is,' Steve said.

Joe stared quizzically at him, then raised his eyebrows, grinning, and said, 'You're the one who caught Houlihan robbing a Securicor van, aren't you? The one responsible for his prison sentence?'

'Yeah, that's right,' Steve said.

'He's not going to like you for that.'

'No, he's not,' Steve agreed.

'Is that why we're having this meeting? Is it something to do with Houlihan's release?'

'Could be,' Steve said.

'You think he's going to come after you?' Joe asked.

'That as well, but it's something more than that.'

'Okay, what is it?'

Steve glanced left and right to ensure that no one had come within earshot. The sun was now well down and darkness was falling over the stippled river and the chestnut trees lining both banks. With the air turning cold, a lot of people were leaving the outside tables and going indoors. Now there was no one nearby, no one to overhear, so Steve turned back to Joe and told him about Sir Daniel Edmondson's visit and what he had said.

When Steve had finished, Joe looked steadily at him for what seemed like for ever. Then, eventually, he let his breath out in a sigh and said, 'So they're telling you to neutralize Houlihan before he does it to you.'

'Correct.'

'And they're also saying that if you decide to disregard their warning – decide, as it were, to either ignore or simply avoid Houlihan – they'll arrest you for your own protection. Then, while you're in their custody, they'll let the Inland Revenue swarm all over your business and find something to pin on you.'

'That sounds about right,' Steve said.

Joe rolled his eyes and gave a low whistle. 'Lord,' he said, 'they certainly know how to sink to the depths. And they have you nailed either way.'

'Crucified,' Steve corrected him.

Joe smiled. 'So I take it you're going after Houlihan and his Prod friend, Wild Bill—'

'Correct.'

'—And you've come to me for some kind of assistance.'

'Also correct.'

Joe coughed into his clenched fist, then raised his glass of Guinness to his lips, had a sip and placed the glass back on the table. The sun had nearly set and a chill breeze was blowing. Joe shivered, then cleared his throat again.

'You're starting to sound as taciturn as Clint Eastwood,' he said eventually. 'What is it you want? I'll try to help, but please bear in mind that I'm no longer in the RUC, let alone the so-called Police Service of Northern Ireland.'

'But you're still in contact with your old friends. You still keep your nose to the wind and know what's going on.'

'That's true enough,' Joe said. 'So how can I help?'

Steve raised his index finger in the air. 'One: I want your advice.' He then raised his middle finger as well. 'Two: I want you to help me find the weapon, or weapons, I'll need. Will you go that far with me?'

Joe nodded. 'Yes. So what do you need to know?'

'Given the recent changes in Northern Ireland – the ongoing peace, which will make it impossible for me to disguise my actions as acts of terrorism, as political assassinations – what do you think is the best way to neutralize them?'

'You have to do this alone?'

'Yes.'

'With no help from the security forces?'

'Correct. I can't accept help from the police or the army. I have to be an Invisible.'

'Ah, yes, an Invisible!' Joe sighed melodramatically. 'A poor creature forced to dwell in the zone of total deniability, with no outside help, no redress, no back-up if anything goes wrong, no proof that he was working under orders. The godforsaken Invisibles. An interesting corruption of the original word, don't you think?'

'I suppose so,' Steve said, though he was feeling nervous and impatient, wondering where this conversation was leading to, wanting help and no more than that. Certainly not academic flippancy from an old friend. 'Can we just——?'

'The so-called "Invisibles" of Stalinist Russia,' Joe said. 'That's where that particular distortion of the word originated. In Stalinist Russia, when the State decided, for any reason, not to execute you or send you to Siberia for whatever crime you'd supposedly committed, they would instead take all your papers from you, including your identification papers, strike you off all records, thus denying you all your rights, and virtually turn you into an invisible person without the means to survive. In other words, you became one of Stalin's "Invisibles" and that was your sorry or nightmarish lot for the rest of your life. So you, Steve, forced by the British government to do its bidding while at the same time being denied any hope of recognition, irrespective of how things go, well or badly, have been reduced to our modern equivalent of one of Stalin's Invisibles. In other words, once you embark on this task, you'll no longer exist. That's something to think about, isn't it?'

'Thanks a million,' Steve said.

Yet he knew that his friend was right, that he had been, or was about to be, turned into an 'invisible man' who would have to fend for himself, risk his life, without any outside help and with no safe harbour if things went wrong. He was being cast out at the same time as he was being used and it didn't feel good.

'Okay,' Joe said. 'You have to do it alone. That means you can't attempt a strike from a moving vehicle, which would require a driver, and you can't arrange a complicated ambush.'

'True enough,' Steve said. 'So I have to choose a killing zone that offers me good protection and allows me to make my escape with all possible speed. My idea was to find some place — probably a pub — where Houlihan and Wild Bill meet regularly and do the job as they emerge. I could make my sniper position a car parked at the opposite side of the street, but they're bound to be surrounded by bodyguards. Almost certainly, even if I succeeded in neutralizing them both, the bodyguards would shoot up my car before I could make my escape.'

'They would indeed,' Joe agreed.

'So what I need is a sniper position that the guards won't be able to locate until I'm well out of their reach.'

'Which means a loft in a row of terraced houses opposite the killing zone. You enter the loft from a house farther along the street, preferably near the end of it, then mouse-hole along to the loft directly opposite the killing zone. You take up a position there where you remain, perhaps for days, until Houlihan and Wild Bill have their meeting. When they emerge from the pub and enter the killing zone, you neutralize them, then immediately mouse-hole back along the whole terrace and make your escape out through the end house while the bodyguards are entering the house that the shots came from. You get out of the street without them even seeing you. Just like in the good old days.'

'You've got it,' Steve said. In the good old days, the days of the Troubles, 'mouse-holing' had been a standard system for assassinations by SAS snipers. The sniper entered the house of a tout (or 'turncoat' or 'Fred') located near the end of the terraced street while the street's inhabitants were distracted with a full-scale raid by the security forces. Once the sniper was inside the house, he entered the loft and made his way from one loft to the next — 'mouse-holing' — until he was in the loft facing the killing zone. He would live in that loft for days until the job was done, then make his way back to the end of the street, from one loft to another, and slip out of the tout's house unseen. It was a strategy that rarely failed. 'So have you got any ideas for a killing zone with a row of terraced houses facing it and including a house that I could enter by? I know it's a pretty tall order, but ...'

'Not so tall,' Joe said, smiling. 'A few years back, before Houlihan went into prison, we had him under constant surveillance. One of his regular watering holes was the Hibernian pub, located halfway along a street running off the Falls Road and directly opposite a row of terraced houses. We'd deliberately moved one of our Catholic touts, a bachelor, into a house located at the end of the street, only three doors away from the Falls Road, and one of his functions, apart from spying on his neighbours in general, was to let our surveillance teams enter his loft under cover of darkness and mouse-hole along to the loft facing the Hibernian. We used that house for years, until Houlihan went into prison, then we rewarded the tout by setting him up in Australia. That house is still in the charge of the RUC CID, but they haven't actually used it since Houlihan went into prison. In other words, it's empty right now and you can use it without asking anyone. I have a key and can get another one cut from it, so you can use that house when you need it.'

'Perfect,' Steve said. 'So how often did Houlihan and Wild Bill meet at that pub? Did they have a regular evening?'

'Alas, they only met there once or twice a month and they had no set evening – it could have been any night of the week. There was no way of knowing which one.'

'Which means I may have a lengthy stay in that loft.'

'Correct.'

'Can you fix me up with the necessary kit?'

'Yes.'

'What about a weapon?'

'What would you like?'

'Since I'll only be firing from the other side of the street, I won't need anything special. Any good sniper rifle will do, though it has to have a night-vision sight.'

'What about a Lee Enfield .303 sniper rifle? That particular weapon was so commonplace during the Troubles – used by both the British Army and the terrorists of both sides – that no one will be able to trace it when you leave it in the loft after the job. Which you'll have to do, of course, as you can hardly escape into the Falls Road carrying a rifle.'

'Right,' Steve said. 'But I also need a handgun for personal protection. Any chance of a good old Nine-Milly?'

He was referring to the SAS's beloved Browning 9mm High Power handgun, more affectionately known to SAS men as the '9-Milly'.

'No problem. There were a lot of those floating around during the Troubles and most ended up in the hands of the paramilitaries, now the gangster community. So, yes, you can have one.'

'How soon?'

'Can you give me two days?'

'Yes.'

'So where do I deliver the groceries?'

'Can they be delivered, properly wrapped and packed, to that empty house in the street off the Falls?'

'Yes. They'll be dropped off at midnight, from an unmarked van, the day after tomorrow.'

'Great. What about the address?'

Smiling, Joe withdrew a small notebook from the inside pocket of his grey jacket, scribbled the details on the top page, tore the page off and handed it to Steve.

'Memorize the address and then burn the page,' he said. 'Even my handwriting could get me into trouble.'

Steve read the details instantly, memorized them, then withdrew a lighter from his pocket and set fire to the paper. When it had burned down almost to his fingertips, he released it, let it fall to the grass around his feet, then ground it to blackened dust under the heel of his shoe.

'I didn't know you smoked,' Joe said.

'I don't,' Steve replied.

'So how come you're carrying a lighter?'

'A lot of the women I meet are smokers,' Steve explained, 'and they always like having their fags lit for them.'

'That's part of your seduction technique, is it?' Joe asked sardonically.

Steve grinned. 'You might say that.'

Joe smiled in return, then finished off his Guinness, pushed his chair back and stood up. 'I'd better not hang around too long,' he said. 'I don't wish to be seen in the wrong company. You can now go into the bar, purchase another pint and light the fag of any lady you fancy. By the time you finish, I'll be long gone and this meeting will never have taken place.'

'I hear you loud and clear,' Steve said.

'Good luck, old friend. I think you're going to need it.'

'I can't argue with that.'

Joe smiled and walked away. Steve watched him leave, waiting until his old friend had disappeared into Lockview Road. Then he left the table to go into the bar, order another pint and, he hoped, find a lady begging for cancer, thus needing a light. He was not disappointed.

Chapter Six

Walking down the Falls Road, heading for the Hibernian pub, Houlihan, filled with drink, felt powerful and back in command. This was his territory and he loved the feel of it, the knowledge that he owned it and most of those in it, the people who feared him, paid him protection money, sold his videos and drugs, used his fruit machines, his betting shops, his social clubs, and in general bent to his will, terrified of his gangs.

Belfast had changed dramatically in the past few years — great new shopping malls of steel and glass, traffic-free zones with fancy restaurants and cocktail bars, everything new and gleaming. But the Falls Road had remained virtually the same, a throwback to the past, still a working-class strip of old-fashioned stores, fish-and-chip shops, hamburger joints, bookies, pubs and video-rental emporiums. No great social advances had been made here and Houlihan liked it that way because it made it easier for him to control the inhabitants, exploit their relative poverty and lack of security, keep them under his iron fist, have them nod respectfully or fearfully, as they were doing right now, when he passed them. Houlihan needed that respect, that fear, like other men needed air.

As he turned off the main road, into the side street where the Hibernian pub was, he looked at the grim terraced houses and was reminded of his own small place farther up the Falls, the house where he had lived all his life, originally because he had been born and raised there, more recently because he wanted to be on his own turf. He needed to keep his finger on the pulse, as it were, during the week. Of course, he was able to live in the style to which he had become accustomed, a rich man's style, when he went to his secret retreat, his much grander house near Cultra, at the weekends. There, away from his missus — who didn't even knew about the Cultra place — he had his drunken orgies with various friends and whores. And there he would, if he got the slightest chance, fuck Jack Parnell's sexy assistant.

Indeed, the very thought of Katherine Crowley almost gave him a hard-on right there and then. It certainly made him excited at the thought of what was to come pretty soon: the first touch of a real woman in over three years in that upstairs room in the Hibernian pub. He could hardly wait.

The Hibernian was about halfway along the street, sandwiched between the terraced houses. When Houlihan entered it was already busy downstairs, most of the customers being men who had dropped in for a pint or two on their way home from work, some still wearing their coveralls, others with peaked caps on their heads, all hazed in a pall of cigarette smoke. As Houlihan made his way to the stairs, old friends called out greetings, shook his hand or slapped him on the shoulder-blades, congratulating him on getting out of the clink and welcoming him back to the real world. Pleased, Houlihan returned the greetings, traded a few jocular remarks, stopped smiling only long enough to cast icy glances at old enemies, then left the main bar to take the stairs up to the private room reserved by his bent lawyer.

Parnell, Kavanagh and Connolly were already in the room, sitting around a large, darkly varnished oval table with the hookers who had been hired to masquerade as the current girl-friends of Houlihan's two lieutenants. Kavanagh and Connolly were drinking from bottles of Guinness, Parnell had a large whisky in front of him, and the two hookers were sipping what looked like gin and tonics. They all glanced up when Houlihan entered.

'Ah, ha!' Parnell exclaimed. 'You made it! Survived the party, did you?'

'Just about,' Houlihan replied. 'Christ, what a piss-up! I thought the fuckin' guests would never leave, though they did eventually. Was I ever glad to get out of there!' He nodded at Kavanagh and Connolly, then at the hookers. 'Hi.'

'Hi,' said the first girl, a plump blonde. 'I'm Julie.'

'Hi,' said the second girl, a slim redhead. 'I'm Peggy.'

Houlihan responded with another nod of his head, then glanced about the room. It looked like a bedsit, with a bed-settee, sink, refrigerator, shelves containing cups, saucers and dinner plates, and built-in cupboards for, presumably, cutlery. The window overlooked the backyard of the building and there was a closed door to his left: the door to the bedroom.

'A real little home from home,' Houlihan said. 'I'd forgotten all about it. You forget a lot when you're inside. So what can I drink?'

'What's your poison?' Parnell responded laconically, pointing to the refrigerator. 'We've got just about everything in there or in the cupboard beside it.'

'I had enough whisky at that party to down an elephant, so I'll settle for a bottle of Guinness.'

His icy glance flicked from one hooker to the other.

'I'll get it,' Peggy said, instantly jumping to her feet and going to the refrigerator. She was wearing a skintight red dress that showed everything she had, particularly when she bent over to reach down into the fridge.

'Fuck!' Houlihan exclaimed, breathing deeply, hardening already.

'What's that?' Parnell said.

'Nothing.' Houlihan pulled up a chair and sat facing the

blonde, Julie, who was wearing a clinging white sweater and hip-hugging miniskirt. Houlihan needed the table to hide his growing erection. 'So how did you spend your afternoon?' he asked of Parnell, wondering if the lawyer had fucked his sexy assistant, either over his desk or in his or her bed. The very possibility pained him.

Parnell shrugged. 'At my desk,' he said. 'Working as usual on behalf of my many clients – your own good self included.'

'Well, I'm glad to hear *that*,' Houlihan said, moving his gaze to the redhead, Peggy, as she returned to the table and handed him an opened bottle of Guinness.

'Thanks,' he said, taking the bottle and looking her up and down as she went back around the table to sit beside Julie. Long legs, good arse, great tits. The very sight of her choked him up.

'So what about you two?' he asked, turning to Kavanagh and Connolly for some distraction from his lecherous thoughts.

'Just went to pick up the girls,' Kavanagh said, nodding to indicate the two hookers, 'and bring them back here. I mean, we got here real early – about an hour ago.'

'Fuck 'em, did you?' Houlihan asked bluntly, glancing back at the hookers.

'Christ, no, boss!' Connolly said, looking nervous. 'Didn't lay a hand on 'em. Kept them clean and fresh just for you, boss.'

Houlihan stared unblinkingly at the two hookers. 'Is that true?'

Both hookers nodded affirmatively.

'Yes,' Julie said.

'Absolutely,' Peggy added. 'They just picked us up and brought us straight here and gave us a drink. We've just been sitting here, waiting for you to arrive. So ...' She shrugged and smiled coquettishly. 'Here we are!'

Houlihan was not moved by the coquettish smile. 'Where did they pick you up from?'

'From where we live.'

'Where's that?'

'We share a flat up the Malone Road.'

'You fuck your clients there?'

The hookers glanced quizzically, nervously, at each other, then nodded in unison.

'Yeah,' Peggy said.

'Naturally,' Julie added.

'How do you find your clients?'

'Mostly by word of mouth,' Peggy said.

'You don't walk the streets?'

'Fuck, no,' Julie said, then puritanically covered her mouth with her hand. ''Scuse me!'

'The Malone Road's a pretty good address for a pair of whores. What kind of clients do you get?'

'Good quality,' Peggy said. 'Middle-class, mostly. Well-heeled businessmen and civil servants and politicians. *That* kind of man.'

'Men of means.'

'Aye, right,' Julie said.

'You ever get men of God?'

'What?' Julie responded, looking even more nervous.

'Priests. Protestant ministers. Men of the church.'

Julie nodded. 'Ackaye. Naturally.'

'They're only human, after all,' Peggy added helpfully.

'What kind of thing do they like?' Houlihan asked, getting harder, bigger, hotter, breathing heavily.

'What?' Julie asked.

'You heard me. You know what I mean. The men of God ... What do they want from you?'

The hookers glanced apprehensively at each other then returned their gazes to him.

Julie shrugged. 'Well ...' She shrugged again. 'You know ...'

'No, I don't know. You tell me, whore.'

'Tell you what?'

'Do they want their cocks sucked?'

Julie nodded. 'Yeah, some do.'

'Do they want to fuck you up the arse?'

Her expression anxious, Julie nodded. 'Yeah, some.'

'Like you're choirboys, right?'

Both hookers nodded. 'Right,' Peggy said.

'Do some like to be tied up? Do they like to be whipped or otherwise abused?'

The girls nodded again.

'Filth,' Houlihan said. 'Hypocrites and perverts. You two whores from the Malone Road fuck men of God and would appear to have no limits to how low you'll stoop. So tell me . . . Is there anything you two cunts *won't* do?'

The hookers glanced at each other again, then looked back at him, though without actually meeting his cold gaze.

'For you,' Julie said, 'anything.'

'Yes, anything,' Peggy added. 'We don't say "No" to much. Anything you desire, Mr Houlihan.'

'Good,' Houlihan said. 'Finish your drinks and wait for me in the bedroom. I'll be there in a couple of minutes. It's been a long time — *too* long — so be prepared for anything.'

Now both of the hookers looked truly frightened, though they both nodded agreement.

'Right,' Peggy said.

'Anything you say,' Julie added.

They hurriedly finished off their drinks and went into the bedroom, closing the door quietly behind them. Houlihan let his breath out in a pained sigh, feeling his hardness, the burning heat, his pulsating groin, the inexorable rise of his violence.

'Fuck!' he exclaimed again.

'You'd better get in there,' Parnell said, 'before you explode.'

Kavanagh and Connolly chuckled while nodding agreement.

When Houlihan stared at them, not smiling himself, they both stopped laughing.

'I want that bastard Steve Lawson,' Houlihan said.

'You want him, you've got him, boss,' Connolly said. 'We know where he lives, in one of his own apartment blocks down by the Lagan. You want him dead or alive?'

'Alive,' Houlihan said. 'I don't want him to get off lightly. A fuckin' bullet through the head would be too quick for him, so I want him brought in alive. I want that fucker to suffer.'

'When do you want him, boss?'

'As soon as you can pick the bastard up. Any time after today. Let's get it over and done with.'

'Right, boss,' Connolly said.

'We'll just go and knock on his door,' Kavanagh clarified, 'and shove a pistol into his face and invite him to walk out with us. I don't think he'll refuse, like.'

'Not with a pistol shoved into his gob, he won't,' Connolly added, grinning. 'Sure isn't it wonderful what the barrel of a gun can do for a man's common sense?'

'So where do we take him when we get him?' Kavanagh asked.

'To the holding room out in Duncrue,' Houlihan said, referring to a particular room at his frozen-food processing business on a relatively isolated part of the Duncrue Industrial Estate – a soundproofed room with sheet-metal walls that was used for interrogations, torture, kneecappings and even more severe punishments, all the way down the line to termination. 'Call me as soon as you've got him locked up there and I'll come on over. We'll have a lengthy session with him, then kill the cunt, dismember him, pack his pieces into a frozen-food container and drive it out of there as part of our normal deliveries. We can dump the container into the sea en route to one of our regular customers. So long, Steve Lawson.'

'Beautiful,' Kavanagh said.

'Perfect,' Connolly added.

'I didn't hear that,' Parnell said. 'As your lawyer, I have to say this. Right now, I'm deaf, dumb and blind. This conversation never took place. I want my statement down on the record.'

Houlihan smiled bleakly. 'You legal bastards have it made. You can cut the cake any way you like and always keep the best piece. I should be so lucky.'

'Say your thanks that I'm on your side,' Parnell responded. 'Now, why don't you go into that bedroom and buy yourself some relief, then we'll all go back down the stairs and walk out like respectable people, letting these two—' he nodded, indicating Kavanagh and Connolly '—show off their supposed girlfriends. As your lawyer, I strongly recommend it. Let me earn my fee, thanks.'

'Ackaye,' Houlihan said, pushing his chair back and standing up. 'That's the thing to do, all right. Don't let anyone come up the stairs while I'm in there.'

'We won't,' Kavanagh said.

Breathing heavily, hard and hot, aroused to fever pitch, Houlihan opened the door of the bedroom and stepped inside. The two hookers were sitting side by side on the edge of the bed, which took up most of the space in the room. There were no windows. The walls were painted a plain off-white. There was a sink with a couple of towels draped over the wooden bars beneath it. There was a wardrobe for clothing, sheets and blankets. Both hookers, Houlihan noted instantly, were still fully dressed.

'Why the fuck are you still dressed?' he asked.

The hookers glanced nervously at each other, then back to him.

'Some clients prefer it that way,' Peggy explained. 'They like to undress us themselves, like.'

'Fuck that,' Houlihan said. 'Get your kit off – everything – then come and undress me where I'm standing.'

The hookers did as they were told, though they did it with the artfulness of experienced strippers, slowly, seductively, taking their time about it, letting Houlihan get a good eyeful while he fingered himself and grew even bigger and harder, drowning in his own heat. When they were naked, both voluptuous, a sight for deprived eyes, especially after that three years with the nancy boys, they came to him and, between them, undressed him slowly, languorously, while licking and sucking his bare skin, his ear lobes, his eyelids, his neck, his hairy chest, one tonguing his throat, an ecstatic feeling, pure rapture, while the other dropped onto her knees to take his pulsating hardness into her mouth and work her wiles on him.

'Ah, fuck!' Houlihan managed to gasp when that tongue had slipped out of his throat and the other tongue and lips had moved away from down there and the two hookers were stretched out on the bed, him standing beside it, looking down upon them, running his hands over them, bending his knees to rub his cock along a stretch of smooth, burning thigh, breathing harshly, dissolving.

'One that way, one the other way,' he gasped. 'Head to toe, me between you. A meat sandwich. You understand?'

They both nodded assent. The redhead sat up and stretched out the other way, until her feet were at the blonde's head, her mouth at the blonde's feet. He crawled in between them, made a meal of the blonde cunt, licking and sucking it, smelling it, tasting it, while the redhead made a meal of him, ingesting him, devouring him, and only stopping when he felt that he was coming and didn't want to – not yet.

'No!' he gasped. 'Fuck! Straighten up. Roll onto your belly. Let's do the priest and the choirboy.'

He fucked the choirboy, the redhead, recalling the nancy boys in the prison showers, shocked to find it coming back to him, inflamed by the very thought, shamed by the excitement that the recollection gave him. So he bit her neck and withdrew, rolled over to grab the other one, the blonde, pushing her onto her back, spreading her legs with a rough hand to go in the proper way, thrusting hard, with a vengeance, letting her know what a man was made of, a *real* man, a *hard* man, while the other one, the redhead, slid across him, soft breasts flattening on his spine, tongue lapping up his sweat, fingering his buttocks as if she knew what he refused to admit to, letting him have both, the choirboy and the woman, the prisoner's release and the prisoner's daily dream, his anus tightening on the knuckle, skin and bone, the sharp, feminine nail, while he pushed into the one below him, the blonde, a real man at last penetrating a real woman, losing his mind in pure sensation, his head filled with visions of other women pinioned beneath him ... blondes and brunettes and redheads, all young and slim and long-legged and full-breasted ... just like Parnell's assistant ... *Ack, Jasus, yes*, with eyes closed he saw her clearly, sensed her presence, almost *felt* her, even *smelled* her ... Yes, right there beneath him, her legs wrapped around his hips, her hands pressed on his spine, the fingernails cutting him, her belly rising and falling, slap-slap against his belly, his gross and sagging flesh, the years he wished to deny, her cunt sucking him in, closing around him, making him melt, while that other magical member, the finger of the redhead, moved in and out rhythmically to tighten the ring of his anus, making his buttocks quiver, sending the spasms darting through him; and he started coming, coming — *Ah, Jesus! Oh, Christ!* — wave piling upon wave, a veritable earthquake at his centre, the very elements colliding — so physical, so *sensual*, so overwhelmingly intense, every single instant of three years of sexual deprivation at last finding release in an electrifying jolting — and then he came — *Ah, fuck!* — in a series of wild convulsions, an uncontrollable seizure, spasm piled upon spasm, and exploded like a shotgun, shooting his wad into her, crying out some incomprehensible protest, almost sobbing, hardly aware of who he was, where he was, what was beneath him, quivering like a bowstring, gasping for breath, eventually breathing, breathing evenly, breathing normally, and rolled off the thing beneath him, that soft, warm trap, the spider's web of seduction, to look up and see, instead of the ceiling, a wide grin beneath a pair of mad eyes and a shock of dishevelled brown hair.

'Sure what the fuck would you be up to?' a gravelly, booze-addled voice enquired.

Wild Bill had arrived.

Chapter Seven

Steve entered the tout's empty house at two a.m., when no one was out in the street to see him. Letting himself in with the key given to him by Joe Williamson two days after their meeting, he closed the door behind him. Then he took a small torch from the side pocket of his jacket, switched it on and examined the dark living room.

According to Williamson, the house had been empty for four years now, since 1999 when the tout had been flown out to Australia. Clearly it hadn't been touched since then: the living room was still fully furnished and included a sofa, chairs, a television and the mandatory Virgin Marys and other religious bric-a-brac, all intact though covered in a fine layer of dust. The bric-a-brac had probably belonged to the tout's mother, who had lived here all her life and had died two years before the tout was lifted out.

The curtains had been closed but Steve couldn't risk turning on the lights. He used the torch instead, moving the beam over the floor until he located the big canvas bag that had been delivered by Williamson sometime the previous day. He didn't bother to open it and check the contents because he had faith in Williamson and knew that he would have got Steve everything he required. Certainly, judging by the bag's length and weight, the Lee Enfield .303 sniper rifle had been included.

Trying to make as little noise as possible, Steve humped the heavy canvas bag onto his right shoulder. Then, still using the torch, he made his way up the stairs to the landing that connected the bedrooms. Looking directly above him, he saw the trapdoor in the ceiling, which was also the floor of the loft.

After placing the bag gently on the floor, which, helpfully, was carpeted, Steve entered one of the bedrooms and found a wooden chair, which he placed directly under the trapdoor. Now even more aware of the need for silence, he stood on the chair and very gently pushed the trapdoor upwards. It was not on hinges, merely fitting snugly into its wooden frame, so he slid it gently to the side, where it rested on one of the ceiling joists. With the trapdoor cleared, he hauled the canvas bag off the floor of the landing, stood again on the wooden chair and pushed the canvas bag up through the opening, being careful to lower it onto its side, resting across a couple of joists, without making a sound. Once the bag was in the loft, he pulled himself up through the trapdoor, flopping forward until his chest and belly were resting on the joists beside the canvas bag. Then he wriggled forward until he was entirely in the loft. He straightened up as much as possible, standing in the half-crouch position with his feet on the joists and his head just below the criss-crossing wooden beams of the ceiling.

The loft was pitch black. When Steve removed his torch from his pocket and let it shine into the darkness ahead, he saw that the space under the terrace's roofs ran the whole considerable length of the terrace, from one house to the next, eventually disappearing in an even deeper darkness beyond the range of the torch's beam.

Quietly replacing the trapdoor, Steve picked up the canvas bag and 'mouse-holed' along the under-roof space, using the torch to illuminate the area directly ahead, advancing at the half-crouch to avoid hitting his head against the overhead beams and stepping in his rubber-soled shoes from one joist to the next. Knowing that the house facing the Hibernian pub was the twenty-second along, he counted off each loft as he passed through it and eventually came to the one he wanted: the one used by RUC and SAS surveillance teams several years ago.

Moving into the cramped space of that particular loft area, directly above the bedrooms of the house below, Steve moved the beam of the torch over the front wall and was pleased to see the peephole that had been used by his predecessors. He checked it. A slate nail in the roof had been removed and replaced with a rubber band that allowed the slate to be raised and lowered, thus providing a spyhole for the naked eye, binoculars, cameras or thermal imagers. Raising the slate, Steve peered through the hole and saw the Hibernian pub directly opposite, its front door closed and all its lights out at this early hour. Satisfied that he was in the right place, he let the slate drop back down over the hole and turned around to face the loft space.

This would be his uncomfortable home for an indeterminate period – until Houlihan and Wild Bill next met in that pub across the road. That meeting could take place tomorrow ... or a month from now. There was no way of knowing.

Sighing, thinking of what he had let himself in for, Steve kneeled carefully, unzipped the canvas bag and slowly, cautiously, unpacked it, beginning with the Lee Enfield sniper rifle, which he laid carefully across the joists.

Under normal circumstances, he would have used a steel tripod to support the weapon when he fired it but here in the loft he couldn't do that. First, because the legs of such a tripod would not span the space between the joists; second, because the position of the raised slate, which was at eye level when he rested on one knee, demanded that the rifle be braced against the shoulder and supported on the lower edge of the viewing hole.

The next item to be removed from the canvas bag, therefore, was a holstered Browning 9mm High Power handgun. Steve strapped this around his waist, with the holster resting on his left hip, slightly to the rear, the butt of the gun facing forward to enable him to make a quick cross-draw if he had to defend himself. Removing the handgun from its holster, he inserted a thirteen-round magazine, checked that the safety catch was on, then holstered the weapon again.

The rest of the kit, which Steve took out piece by piece and spread around him on various joists, carefully avoiding the floor, consisted of high-calorie rations, including chocolate, tinned meat and biscuits, water for drinking and personal hygiene, toothpaste and soap, plastic plates, cups and eating utensils, some books for distraction, a sleeping bag, rolls of toilet paper, and plastic bags for the disposal of his faeces and urine. He would shit and piss into the bags, seal them to make them airtight, then place them on the floor in the adjoining loft. It wasn't nice, but it worked.

Last but not least, the canvas bag contained half a dozen tongue-and-groove pine boards, each one four inches wide and six feet long. These were slotted together to make a single piece of wood measuring two feet by six feet. Steve laid this across some joists, giving himself a solid base, then unrolled his sleeping bag upon it.

With everything placed within reach on the joists around him, he took off his shoes and put an extra pair of socks on over the ones he was already wearing. In this way, he could pad about the loft without making any noise and also keep his feet warm when the loft got cold – as, indeed, it was right now at this early hour of the morning. Finally, satisfied that everything was in order and knowing that he had no need to keep his eye on the pub until it opened the next day, Steve gazed around the dark, cold, cobwebbed loft, shook his head resignedly from side to side, then wriggled into his sleeping bag and was soon asleep.

Chapter Eight

'For fuck's sake,' Houlihan said. 'What kind of madman are ya? How the fuck could you do that do me? Sure I nearly had a heart attack when I saw ya lookin' down on me even as I was comin'!'

'Ack, I just wanted to see you in action, like,' Wild Bill replied, grinning crazily, his wild blue eyes gleaming, his pigtail bouncing off the back of his neck as he chortled dementedly. 'And there you were, indeed, sandwiched between those two whores, shuddering like you were havin' epilepsy. Sure you came like a storm drain!'

They were not in the Hibernian pub but in a social club in the Shankill where Wild Bill had insisted they go once Houlihan had put his clothes on and where, a few years back, before the present so-called 'peace', no Catholic would have been allowed through the front door. In this club, they could drink the night away without worrying about closing time. There *was* no closing time here.

'Big joke, was it?' Houlihan asked, truly annoyed but trying not to show it.

'Aye, right. Just a laugh, like.'

'That lawyer of mine, Parnell, promised faithfully to let no one come up the stairs, let alone enter the bedroom, and yet you walked in as if you owned the place. I'll kill that cunt when we meet next.'

'Don't blame him,' Wild Bill said, still grinning crazily, his wild gaze taking in the club and its customers, particularly the women, many of whom were wearing clothes that showed off all they had for the edification of beasts like him. 'Sure he did his best, believe me. Actually stood up and tried to block my way, sayin' I couldn't go in there. So I pulled out my black-market SAS Nine-Milly and placed the barrel between his schoolboy eyes and said, "Oh, yeah? Who's gonna stop me, pal?" He went green around the gills and sat down again, his knees obviously shakin', and let me walk by him, into the bedroom. So I saw your big fat arse quiverin', risin' and fallin' between one whore's legs while the other whore was givin' your rectum a fine-tuning with her elegant finger. Looked good to me, like.'

'Fuck off,' Houlihan said.

But, having calmed down a bit, he said it without malice. No point arguing with Wild Bill. The Prod was a madman when it came to fun and games but he was brilliant when it came to serious matters, such as crime and control. Without his crazy Protestant friend, Houlihan would have found it difficult to control the various criminal elements of the city, particularly the Orange elements, so working with him was better than going against him. This way, both of them benefited.

Not that they were real friends. They could never be that. They had been enemies during the Troubles, doing damage to each other, and neither of them would ever be able to forget what the other had done. So, what they really were was fair-weather colleagues, using each other when they needed to. But the day might come when they would have a disagreement and end up with serious aggro.

Indeed, Houlihan was already having secret discussions with Russian *Mafiya* representatives in London about the possibility of a link-up, a strengthening of bonds, as it were, that would enable the Russkies to gain a firm foothold in Ireland, including the Republic, with the aid of Houlihan's mob of Catholic gangsters, all former PIRA paramilitaries. At the same time, the intention was to sideline Wild Bill's Prods, all former UDA men, before eventually, if necessary, obliterating the fuckers altogether. So Houlihan, though at present getting along with Wild Bill, didn't kid himself that they were really friends. More like uneasy partners.

'It was just a wee bit of fun, Mike. No need for embarrassment, like. No call for resentment.'

'No sweat, Billy-boy.' No one ever called William Moore 'Wild Bill' to his face, not even Houlihan. 'I have to confess, I was pretty fuckin' amused to look up, while my balls were still contracting, and see your gob smilin' down at me. I think the shock made me come twice, so I've that to thank you for.'

Wild Bill chuckled. 'Aye, I bet you have, all right. So, Mike, here's to your freedom!'

They both raised their glasses on high, touched them together for luck, then swallowed good mouthfuls of the Guinness. While wiping his wet lips with the back of his hand, Houlihan glanced around the social club, this Shankill social club, this den of Orange thieves, and saw that it was just like the Catholic ones: a big barn of a place, minimal decoration, lots of tables, a couple of bars, a sad excuse for a restaurant, lots of one-armed bandits, a stage for comedians, strippers and tenth-rate dance bands; and, of course, a dance floor for those who still did that kind of thing in the age of rock music. This being a Protestant club, you could take it as read that Wild Bill was getting a cut of the action while gradually bleeding the poor fuckers dry. Houlihan did the same in the Falls, so he could hardly complain.

'So what's Maghaberry Prison like these days?' Wild Bill asked, having spent a few spells there himself. 'Still good country livin', is it? Green fields, like, an' the fresh air of Lisburn.'

Houlihan shrugged his broad shoulders. 'A few changes all right, if you're talkin' about architecture, but otherwise it's pretty much the same. Course, ever since that big breakout, they've tightened up security and built a couple of new top-security wings. They put me in one of those. In a special cage, can you believe? Treated me like I was some kind of animal, though they never managed to break me.'

'Why the special cage?'

''Cause I kept beating up on guards and once attacked the warden himself. Naturally they clubbed me to shite but they *still* didn't break me. So then they built me this special cage in the solitary wing and kept me in it in chains, like. Ankles and wrists – the whole works. Those chains rattled with each breath I took but I didn't stop breathing.'

'Much as I admire your guts,' Wild Bill said, 'fuck that for a joke!'

'Still, you'd know what it's like, Billy-boy, havin' been inside yourself.'

'Ackaye, sure I do, right enough,' Wild Bill said sympathetically, 'and it's a right fuckin' hole.' He glanced about the big room, which was a riot of conversation, of drunken laughter and rock-and-roll music, taking particular note of the arse and tit available, the long legs in tight dresses, the ones he'd like a piece of. Then he turned back, breathing heavily, to Houlihan. 'Still, he said, 'you musta come across a few old friends in there. The kind you could talk to, like.'

'Aye, I did – at least I did until they put me in that cage. Met a quare few of my own lads, like, who were doin' their mandatory and were keen to keep in with me for the day they got out. Nat'rally they all did as I demanded, so even when I was in the cage, when most contact had been denied me, I was able to run my business from the inside – a helpful guard here, one of my own boyos there, friends or family members who came to visit and carried my instructions back to the Falls. So no problem at all, like, when it came to keepin' the business runnin'. And then, of course, I had you to keep my boyos, as well as your own, in line, so that ensured that things ran smoothly on well-oiled tracks. I have to thank you for that, Billy-boy.'

'Ack, sure, thanks aren't required. I wasn't doin' it just for you. A man has to look after his own interests, like, so it was a case of looking after your side to give less aggravation to my own. I mean, the last thing I wanted was to have your men operatin' like loose cannons in your absence. I didn't want the Law breathin' all over me, drawn to me by wildcat crimes that I'd no control over, so takin' charge of the whole operation, both sides as it were, *with your permission*—'

'Ackaye, you had that right enough,' Houlihan interjected, pleased to hear Wild Bill being so obsequious. 'Sure I passed the word to all my various gangs through my lieutenants—'

'Kavanagh and Connolly.'

'Right ... And once they heard that I'd authorized it, there was no way they were gonna go against you. That's why you had no problems there, Billy-boy.'

'Right.' Wild Bill had another slug of his Guinness and then glanced about the busy club. The one-armed bandits were flashing and making metallic ringing sounds, and a pale-faced ponce in a white dinner jacket, black trousers and bow tie was doing a pitiful imitation of Frank Sinatra singing 'Fly Me To The Moon', accompanied by an equally pitiful band. The dance floor was in semi-darkness but criss-crossed by beams of coloured light that made those dancing look unreal, the men and women lining the bar were producing a racket of conversation, and the atmosphere was growing ever more dense with cigarette smoke.

'Jasus,' Wild Bill said to Houlihan without removing his gaze from the women on the dance floor, 'I wouldn't mind dragging one of them out of here and into the back of my car. Fuck her till her eyes popped. Preferably without her permission and with her husband looking on, being covered by a couple of my men, like. The poor fucks fall to pieces when you do that. That's why marauding armies have traditionally used rape as part of their arsenal. I read that somewhere.'

Houlihan doubted that Wild Bill had ever read anything in his life, though the comment at least reminded him that his Prod friend had certain traits that could easily get out of control. Wild Bill *did* rape women while their husbands, restrained by his men, were forced to look on. It was one of his many so-called 'punishments' and not even the worst. When it came to punishing those who had crossed him, Wild Bill was diabolically inventive. He was a wild man, all right.

'Hey, there's somethin' I meant to ask you,' Wild Bill said, abruptly looking grim.

'Oh?' Houlihan took a swallow of his Guinness, then wiped his lips with the back of his jacket sleeve. 'What's that, like?'

'There's been a rumour goin' around that the Russian *Mafiya*, already well placed in London and at war with the Chinese Triads, is plannin' to move in on Northern Ireland, establish themselves here, then move from here into the south.'

Houlihan felt a flush of guilt. But he covered it by raising his bushy eyebrows, looking amazed and saying, 'No! You're shittin' me!'

Wild Bill shook his head from side to side, looking grave. 'No, I'm not, pal. That's the rumour I picked up from a pretty reliable source. Course, they didn't have any details, no real facts to hand. But the general gist of it is that the Russians are keen to exploit the growth of crime in Belfast city and, of course, the Bandit Country of South Armagh, which they view as virtually lawless, then, with their foot in the door, move in on the south.'

'Jasus!' Houlihan exclaimed, again acting surprised. 'This sounds like bad news to me. Those Russian bastards are even more ruthless and organized than the Sicilian Mafia, so they're not the kind we'd want aggro from.'

'It's not aggro they'll want initially,' Wild Bill said. 'It's cooperation. They can hardly come in here looking for firefights, so they'll want to talk first and arrange some kind of accommodation.'

'What the fuck does that mean?' Houlihan asked, feigning ignorance.

'Cooperation,' Wild Bill said. 'They'll try to make us an offer we can't refuse in return for a small part of our action. Then, once they have their foot in the door, they'll ask for a bigger bite and, if we refuse, those foreign fuckers, being by then well established in the city, will turn against us and try takin' over the whole works.'

'Jasus!' Houlihan exclaimed again, as if he couldn't believe his ears, though in truth he was already having secret talks with the Russians as the start of his grand expansion plan. That plan would not, in the end, include Wild Bill, but that problem would be taken care of when the time came. In the meantime, until he, Houlihan, was well in with the Russians, whose own plans he felt he could restrict if necessary, he still needed the support of Wild Bill and his gangs. This was a real dicey number, like. 'Sounds to me,' he said, trying to sound thoughtful, 'that if this really is on the cards—'

'It is!' Wild Bill interjected excitedly.

'—Then the Russians are going to have to talk to someone – and so far they certainly haven't talked to *me*.'

'Nor to me,' Wild Bill said.

'Well, if they haven't talked to you and they haven't talked to me, maybe they haven't made any kind of approach yet and are still talking among themselves about it.'

'No,' Wild Bill said, 'I don't think that makes sense. If the word's already out about what those bastards are planning, they must have made an approach already.'

'An approach to someone in Belfast?'

Wild Bill shrugged. 'Maybe Belfast. Maybe someone in London, where they're already well entrenched.'

'Who the fuck could they talk to in London that could help them here?'

'I can't be specific. But we certainly have a few old friends working for us in London, acting as liaison men with bent coppers or English criminals, buying or transporting weapons, sending information back about anyone who could help us here – easily bribed ships' captains, crooked Customs officials, Republican sympathizers who still think our Catholic element is fightin' for Ireland's freedom – so any one of them, those friends of ours, could have been approached by the Russians about the possibility of placing a *Mafiya* presence right here in the province.'

'If that's the case, then why hasn't our Irish friend in London already told us about it? Why is it still at the rumour stage?'

'That's what has me nervous,' Wild Bill said. 'Most rumours are based on fact and that particular kind of rumour wouldn't have started if there wasn't some truth in it. So clearly the Russians *are* interested in getting into Belfast.'

'Right,' Houlihan said, distractedly fingering the sweaty collar of his shirt and wondering how he could change the subject of this potentially damaging conversation. 'So—'

'So, obviously the Russians have already approached *someone* – one of our so-called friends – and whoever he is, he's not letting us know about it.'

'Why would he do that?' Houlihan asked, deliberately glancing about the crowded, noisy club as if this conversation wasn't all that important and concerned him only a little.

'Because most of our so-called friends in London are former PIRA men, some once placed high up. Any one of them, if approached by the Russians about an intrusion into the province, might take it upon himself to deliberately not tell us and instead secretly work for the Russians, helping them to get in here in return for a position near the top of their fly-covered shit-pile. In other words, maybe he's going to help them get rid of you and me, then take our place in a criminal Belfast run by the Russian *Mafiya*. It's not too far-fetched.'

Houlihan reluctantly returned his gaze to his Protestant friend, deliberately trying to look unconcerned. 'You don't think it's far-fetched?'

'No, I don't. Why else would a London friend approached

by the Russians not tell us about something so important? It has to be for the fucker's own profit.'

Houlihan nodded, looking thoughtful, as if accepting this theory with reservations. 'Well, maybe you're right.'

'Even if I'm not,' Wild Bill said, 'we have to find out either way. So let's both use our separate resources to find out if the Russians have in fact spoken to someone and, if so, learn just who that turncoat fucker is. Then we bring him in and string him up by his feet in an isolated garage for a lengthy interrogation – all out, no limit – to find out who his Russian friends are and exactly what he's promised to do for them. That should do the trick, like.'

Houlihan was deeply relieved that Wild Bill had not guessed who the turncoat was, since that guilty party was, of course, himself. He was even more relieved that Wild Bill remained in ignorance about the details of the Russian *Mafiya* connection because part of his, Houlihan's, master plan was to encourage the Russians to neutralize Wild Bill and so obtain a partial foothold in his Protestant territory. Houlihan would then take over the other part, which would leave him in command of even more of criminal Belfast, including a large portion of the Protestant territories that he could not, at present, remotely hope to control on his own. He could, however, control it with the help of the Russians who would not be subject to the old sectarian hatreds still cherished by Wild Bill's gangs and who would therefore be admirably pragmatic in dealing with any Protestant dissidents. Houlihan was willing to make such a deal because he did not believe, as Wild Bill had suggested, that the Russian *Mafiya* could ever fully control crime in Northern Ireland, let alone in the south as well. He was also willing to do it because the Russians would, in return for Houlihan's modest cooperation, channel their drugs to the province, place him personally in charge of them, and, if he played his cards right, give him the required protection when eventually he expanded his criminal activities to territories in which the Russians already had a strong footing – most importantly, from his point of view, the whole of the British Isles. So Houlihan, while immensely relieved that Wild Bill seemed ignorant so far of his own part in the plot, tried to look as if he had other things on his mind while nodding in agreement.

'Aye, right,' he said. 'Sure we have to at least look into it. You use your resources and I'll use mine, and if either one of us tracks that turncoat down, we'll bag him and then inform the other so that we can interrogate him jointly.'

'Agreed,' Wild Bill said. He finished off his pint and looked at Houlihan's glass, which was empty. 'Another pint?'

'Ackaye, why not?'

This club had waitress service for those using the tables, so Wild Bill waved his hand and snapped his fingers, trying to gain some attention. When none of the waitresses even glanced in his direction, he pushed his chair back and started clambering to his feet, preparing to grab one of the bitches by the hair of her head and bawl his order into her face while spitting all over her. Luckily, one of the waitresses, a buxom blonde with legs to die for, about eighteen years old, saw him and hurried towards him, smiling nervously, knowing just who he was, enabling him to sink back into his seat and feel important again.

'Sorry, Mister Moore, but we're so busy, I'm practically run off my feet. Sure what can I do for you?'

Moore responded by grabbing hold of her saucy rump and giving it a squeeze while fingering the crack of her buttocks. 'You can give me a handful of this for a start,' he said, 'and then maybe suck on this later on,' he added, indicating his groin with an airy wave of his free hand.

The waitress looked shocked, then smiled painfully, frightened of offending him. 'Well, really, Mr Moore, I . . .'

'All right, all right,' Moore said impatiently. 'Just a fuckin' joke, love. Make it two more pints of Guinness for now and we'll let you off scot-free.'

'Aye, right, Mr Moore.'

Looking immensely relieved that Wild Bill hadn't wanted more (since she couldn't have refused him for fear of her life), the waitress hurried off to fetch the drinks. Wild Bill watched her go, his gaze focused on her swaying hips, the quivering of her ample buttocks in that revealingly tight miniskirt. Then he lit a cigarette, inhaled, felt his crotch, exhaled a stream of blue smoke and turned back to the expectant Houlihan.

'So what are your plans, Mike, now that you're a free man again? What's first on the agenda? Anything big that I can help with and profit by?'

'That'll come soon enough,' Houlihan informed him. 'After I've had a couple of days of fun, readjusting to freedom, so to speak, and also gone through my own affairs, both legitimate and illegal, with a fine-tooth comb, finding out what's been happening in my absence and setting what's wrong to rights. Once that's done – and it should take about a week – I'll get back to you with a few proposals. What about a meeting this time, this day, next week in the Hibernian? I've come here to your fucking Orange club, so you can come to my place next week. What say you, Billy-boy?'

'Sure that's great,' Wild Bill responded. 'The same time, the same day, next week, but in the Hibernian. I'll be there. You can count on it, Mike. So what other plans have you?'

'A private score to settle,' Houlihan said. 'After three years in prison, it's like gettin' the lead out of your pencil: you have to do it real quick, like. Get it over and done with.'

'So am I allowed to ask you what it is or is it top secret, like?'

'Nothing secret about it,' Houlihan said. 'In fact, my men'll expect it of me. A matter of honour, like. I'm going to pick up the fucker who put me in jail and then, once I've got him, put his lights out.'

'Oh, yeah?' Wild Bill asked. 'Who's that, then? Nat'rally I should know, but I can't remember.'

'That former SAS shite-hole, Steve Lawson.'

'Ah, yes, I do remember him,' Wild Bill said, nodding. 'That bastard worked undercover for 14 Int. He put a lot of our men in jail and even more in their graves. If anyone deserves to be put under, that fucker does.'

'He'll be six foot under before you can blink,' Houlihan promised. 'My boyos are goin' to pick him up tomorrow and bring him to me alive. I want that fucker to pay his dues before he's put under, so I need him in one piece. Then I'll dismember him and bury the pieces and close the book on him.'

'Fuckin' A,' Wild Bill said.

Houlihan, having changed the direction of the conversation, heaved a sigh of relief.

Chapter Nine

Life in the loft facing the Hibernian pub was extremely uncomfortable. By the end of his first day, Steve's body was already aching from the effort required to crouch and balance on the joists or from bending over much of the time to avoid striking his head against the cobwebbed beams. By the end of the second day he felt dirty, cramped and blocked up from constantly inhaling the dust. By the end of the third day, he felt grubby, exhausted, claustrophobic and helplessly tense from not having seen Houlihan and not knowing how long he would have to remain here until the target showed up.

The heat was another irritant. Since it was summer, the heat in the loft built up throughout the long days and became almost suffocating during the early hours of the morning, only cooling down briefly in the few hours before dawn. Despite this, Steve still needed to move about quietly to avoid alerting the people living in the house below, so he had to keep the extra layers of socks on and his feet, as a consequence, were often sweaty and unbearably itchy.

The main problems, however, were domestic. As he could not cook hot food, he was forced to subsist on dry, high-calorie rations, the biscuits, cheese, tinned meat, chocolate and sweets that had been supplied. Although he had a couple of vacuum flasks of hot tea and coffee, he had to limit himself strictly to one hot drink a day and, for the rest of the time, he drank tepid water from plastic water bottles. As there was nowhere to wash, he could only clean himself with moisturized cloths and clean his teeth, or, rather, freshen his mouth, with spearmint chewing gum. But there was worse: this loft was not separated from the others (at least, by nothing as solid as a wall, only angled, criss-crossing beams) so he had selected the loft space of the adjoining house as his toilet, using plastic bags that had to be stored carefully once sealed. Since he was absolutely alone, this caused him no embarrassment. But shitting and pissing into the plastic bags while balanced precariously over a couple of joists was awkward. The sealing of the bags could be a smelly, messy business too if not done with meticulous care.

Sleep did not come easily. At first Steve had thought it a good idea to use a sleeping bag laid out on the wooden boards, but he soon found that every move he made caused the boards to squeak. This also made him nervously aware that he could, when sleeping restlessly, roll off the boards and fall onto the floor between the joists. Such an incident would alert the people below to his presence, especially if his fall damaged their ceiling. So, after a second restless morning in the sleeping bag, he had resorted to the old SAS method of sleeping while sitting upright against a wall of the loft with a blanket wrapped around him. This did not make for a particularly deep sleep, but it was better than nothing.

The most unnerving part of the whole business, however, was the constant need for silence lest the people living below should become aware of his presence. What this meant, in effect, was that he had to move as little as humanly possible, only when strictly necessary, and even then with the utmost care. This in turn made it almost impossible for him to relax in any way, to simply recline, let alone to take any kind of exercise that would have eased the aching of his cramped limbs.

By the end of the fourth interminable day, he was convinced that this particular surveillance task was worse than any that he had ever done with the SAS. In the old days, when engaged in a loft surveillance, the hardships had always been shared by a four-man team which offered, at the very least, the comfort of whispered conversation. Equally comforting was the knowledge that the team, using Pace Communications Landmaster III hand-held transceivers operating in the VHF/UHF frequency range or through the UHG band on their portable radio, could have daily conversations with the 'green slime', the SAS intelligence officers based in the military command network at Lisburn. Here in this loft, all alone, with no means of communication, Steve could not have such helpful conversations.

Thinking back on those better days with the Regiment, Steve recalled how he and the other members of the loft surveillance teams had constantly monitored the target building with a wide range of high-tech equipment. This had included Thorn EMI hand-held multi-role thermal imagers, standard-issue 35mm Nikon F3HP heavy-duty cameras with Davin Optical Modulux image intensifiers attached for night shots and, even more entertainingly distracting, advanced Surveillance Technology Group (STG) laser surveillance systems that enabled them to listen in to, and record, the conversations of the people inside the house being watched. This had been done with the aid of tiny fibre-optic probe cameras clandestinely implanted in the target building before the start of the loft surveillance. The fibre-optic camera picked up the sounds inside the target building and beamed them back to the optical receiver of the STG laser surveillance system in the loft, where they were filtered, amplified and converted into clear, if sometimes fragmented, conversation. Trying to make sense out of those often mysterious dialogues (murmured references to 'single shot', 'both knees', 'six-pack', 'house call', 'post office' or 'bookies', suggesting a combination of PIRA punishments, doorstep assassinations and armed robberies) was a healthy distraction from the nerve-racking tedium and discomfort of interminable days in the loft.

Unfortunately, Steve did not have that kind of distraction now, being on his own with no high-tech equipment and only able to eyeball the pub opposite through the spyhole. This he had to do without respite for as long as the pub was open each day, which was a very long time. So apart from the strain on his eye, the one peering through the peephole, having to crouch at the peephole on one knee, with his other leg raised in front of him, foot planted firmly for balance on the joist, caused pains to stab through his legs and made his spine ache.

Ironically, the oppressiveness of his own enforced silence and relative lack of movement was eased somewhat by the noises that came up from the house below: the radio, the television, the flushing of the toilet, the opening and shutting of doors, drawers and cupboards, the bedroom conversations and even, on the fourth night, the moans and groans as the married couple made love. Overhearing the sounds of sex, however, not only made Steve feel voyeuristically guilty but also reminded him of his own sexual deprivation. It encouraged him, particularly in the evenings when the pub had closed and he could ignore the peephole, to drift into erotic reveries in which he recalled the various women he had known and the sexual acts that he had engaged in with them. Such recollections were agonizing, vivid enough to be almost real, and they covered the whole spectrum of his love life, from his teenage years through his marriage to Linda and right up to his last romantic encounter: that pick-up in Cutter's Wharf shortly after his conversation with the former RUC officer, Joe Williamson.

Steve had, of course, deliberately entered the indoor bar in the hope of finding at least one attractive single woman, since certainly it was the kind of bar that women on their own could feel comfortable in. In fact, when he entered the bar there were three or four single women present and one of them, he saw instantly, was attractive. She was smoking a cigarette while sitting on a high stool at the counter. Using his old strategy for picking up women, Steve had stood beside the woman to order another pint and, when she placed her next cigarette between her lips, had instantly taken out his cigarette lighter and offered her a light. The woman, smiling, had accepted the offer and that, as Steve had intended, had given them a good excuse to talk to each other.

She turned out to be a married woman. But she was separated from her husband and, these days, just out for a good time. They ended up in Steve's bed, in his apartment overlooking the River Lagan, and what they did together there was hot indeed. The memory tormented him in the claustrophobic heat of the loft in the early hours of the mornings.

By the fifth day, with the silence closing in about him like an invisible wall and the filth and lack of exercise making him feel like crap, Steve had grown more distracted. His mental state bordered on disorientation, and he even suspected that he was starting to hallucinate in various small ways, such as imagining that he could hear sounds of movement where there were none and that he could smell himself with unnaturally heightened senses, particularly when it came to his bodily functions. Eventually, he became convinced that he could smell his own urine, albeit faintly, but once he smelled it (or *thought* that he smelled it) he couldn't forget it and the odour became stronger.

Nevertheless, he kept watching the pub across the road, wearily raising the slate to peer through the peephole for hour after hour, silently praying that Houlihan, preferably with Wild Bill, would turn up for another meeting.

It was now the sixth day. Steve had been here all that time without a sign of Houlihan and he couldn't help recalling, with an odd, clammy horror, Joe Williamson's comment that the timing of Houlihan's and Wild Bill's meetings was unpredictable and that they could take place as rarely as once a month. The very thought of being here alone for another month was a torment and Steve, despite his past training with the toughest army regiment in the world, wasn't sure that he could actually stick it out.

At some point he began wondering just what he was doing here. True, he knew he was here because he had been blackmailed into it by Edmondson, who had threatened him with financial ruin. But it was equally true that he was here because he knew that if he didn't kill Houlihan and, he hoped, his partner in crime Wild Bill Moore, Houlihan would certainly try to kill him. He was therefore here, in a real sense, for reasons of self-preservation. However, he was also here because his past actions had inexorably led him here, because his violent nature had drawn him to joining the army and then transferring to its toughest regiment, the SAS. He was here, in truth, because he had thrown himself fully into undercover work in Belfast, drawn by the excitement, the danger ... and, yes, the violence.

Now, with time to think about it, Steve was forced to face the fact that he was a man who thrived on high risk, a man who got a real thrill from being in a firefight with an enemy – like the one outside the bank when Houlihan had been captured. In truth, then, he was not too much different from Houlihan or Wild Bill; and he was here, when it came down to it, because, despite the discomforts and tedium of the loft, he *wanted* to be here. He did so because making money through property deals had given him little satisfaction, because he not been content since leaving the SAS, and because he would not rest until he had resolved this little matter of Houlihan. If he managed to do so, he would certainly do it without guilt or shame, having killed many men in the past without batting an eyelid.

This was why he had originally joined the army, then the SAS, and why he was now in this hot, cobwebbed loft facing a killing zone. He was here to recapture that old thrill by neutralizing the enemy.

What other kind of man, he now wondered, would join a regiment like the SAS? Why else join such a regiment?

Facing up to the brutal reality of his own nature made Steve feel less exhausted and certainly heightened his perceptions, helping to shake off his fatigue. But he was still faced with the prospect of more days, maybe weeks, in the loft and the awareness of that possibility lay upon him like mental chains.

By the end of the sixth day Steve was growing neurotically obsessed with his personal hygiene, with those smells that were tormenting him. He found he was repeatedly cleaning himself with the moisturized cloths (whereas previously he had been only doing it once each day) and even more obsessively wiping his anus and around his penis and testicles, in ever more frantic bids to get rid of the smell of urine that seemed to be growing stronger every hour and now wafted about him like a malignant spirit.

By the seventh day, Steve had started to wonder if he was losing his mind. He even considered retreating from the loft to preserve his sanity. He decided, however, to at least complete the rest of the day and the evening. Therefore, exhausted though he was and sniffing incessantly, neurotically, tormented by the smell of urine, he raised the slate over the peephole just before the pub doors opened and settled down in that awkward, painful kneeling position to observe the entrance until the doors closed again that evening.

This time his tenacity paid off.

During the long, hot afternoon, he saw no one other than the day time regulars entering the pub. But just after seven that evening, when his right eye, at the peephole, had started to blink incessantly from the strain of watching (it was, he thought, like squinting through the sight of a rifle for hours on end), Houlihan loomed into view, bulging out of his grey suit, his slab-like face even more grim than usual, perhaps because of his prison haircut. He was accompanied by two of his minders, both of whom would be armed.

Houlihan entered the pub with his goons.

Suddenly exhilarated, Steve blinked rapidly but kept his eye to the peephole, praying that Wild Bill too would turn up. Fifteen minutes later, he was feeling frustrated, thinking that Wild Bill wasn't coming. But a few minutes later the Prod gangster also appeared, looking like some over-age hippie with his long hair and ponytail. Like Houlihan, he was accompanied by two minders and all three of them entered the pub.

Galvanized into action, almost forgetting the smell of urine, but still moving as quietly as possible, Steve picked up his rifle to check it. Though satisfied with its readiness, he did not release the safety catch, but simply leaned the weapon against the front wall of the loft, beside the spyhole. This enabled him to keep looking through the spyhole and still pick up the gun, already loaded, in an instant. With luck, Houlihan and Wild Bill would not emerge from the pub until just before, or even after, closing time, which meant that Steve, the moment he saw them, would have just enough time to pick up the rifle, slide the barrel through the slot and get off his killing shots. He would then simply drop the weapon and leave it where it fell as he mouse-holed urgently back along the loft to escape from the tout's house at the far end of the street. With luck, he should be able to do that before the vengeful minders could get into the house below him and make their way up into the loft where, as they would know once he fired, the shots had come from.

Steve kneeled there and waited, keeping his eye to the spyhole for long stretches at a time and only moving it away slightly, briefly, every so often to take the strain off it. Though the silence in the loft was total, the raised slate let noise from the street in through the gap: cars coming and going, front doors opening and closing, people talking as they passed by on the pavement below, the odd burst of laughter from men emerging well oiled from the pub. Time passed slowly, seemed to stretch out forever, and as the sun sank and fewer people were seen in the street, the silence in the loft grew pervasive and, even worse, the smell of urine returned to torment Steve's nostrils.

Trying not to think about it, convinced that he was imagining it, he concentrated on watching the pub entrance. But he found it more of a strain as the darkness gradually deepened and the lights beaming out of the windows stung his tired eyes.

Then he heard an odd sound.

Startled, he glanced about him at his own gloomy cob-webbed loft space but couldn't see anything. Breathing deeply, again thinking that he'd imagined it, the smell of urine now a stench, he turned back to the spyhole and continued his visual surveillance in another deathly silence.

Then he heard the odd sound again.

This time, when Steve looked about him, the noise continued, a soft scraping sound combined with a muffled tapping. It seemed to be coming from the adjoining loft space, the one being used as a depository for his sealed plastic bags of shit and piss.

Now seriously concerned, even more aware of the stench of urine, which now was unmistakably real, Steve picked up his torch and turned it on. Then, shining the light down on the loft floor, he stepped, still wearing only the double sets of socks on his feet, from one joist to the next until he had reached the angled criss-crossing beams that separated this loft space from the next. He shone the torch through the beams, aiming at where he thought the noise was coming from: perhaps it was being made by a mouse or a rat. But he saw only the pile of plastic bags filled with his own shit and piss. The smell of urine, he noticed, was much stronger here.

Though the soft scratching and muffled tapping continued, there was no sign of movement over there.

No mice.

No rats.

Reluctant to accept the awful possibility that was forcing itself upon him, Steve carefully made his way through the loft beams, stepping now with even more care on the joists, frightened of making the slightest sound, edging across to the pile of sealed plastic bags, a veritable heap of shit and piss illuminated in the yellowish light of his torch. The soft scratching and tapping continued and was clearly coming from just under the outer edge of the pile of bags.

Breathing deeply, aware that the stench of urine was stronger here, Steve aimed the torch and still saw no movement, only the light reflecting off the plastic bags. With his heart racing, he kneeled on the joist nearest the bags. Then, with his free hand, he picked up the nearest bag and looked under it.

The soft scratching and muffled tapping became louder. But still nothing moved.

Trying now to control his harsh breathing, Steve placed the first plastic bag in the middle of the pile and then picked up another.

The noise became louder and the stench of urine became stronger.

Aiming the torch at the floor where the second bag had rested, he still saw no sign of movement. He therefore placed the second bag in the middle of the pile, beside the first one, and picked up another.

Instantly, his fingers became wet – and he heard the sound of liquid dripping onto the floor.

Shining the torch beam downwards, Steve saw that the bag of urine he was holding had somehow opened slightly. It was leaking, probably had been for days. The contents had been dripping onto the floor and, almost certainly, gradually soaking their way through to the bedroom ceiling of the house below.

The person below had obviously seen the stain and was scratching and tapping at the ceiling to find out exactly what was leaking. He, or she, had made a small hole all the way through to the floor of the loft ... and the beam of Steve's torch was shining down through it.

Someone cried out below, a man, shouting a warning to someone else.

'Oh, fuck!' Steve exclaimed softly.

Realizing that the game was up because the people below now knew that someone was in their loft, Steve switched the torch off and made his way back to his own loft space, guided by the moonlight beaming in through the spy-hole. Just as he reached the hole, he heard the front door of the adjoining house opening. Then a woman frantically called out a warning. Glancing through the spy-hole, he saw the woman hurrying across the road to the pub, still calling out frantically while on the move.

'Get some of them boyos out here!' she shouted as she mounted the pavement on the far side of the road, preparing to rush into the pub. 'There's someone up in my loft!'

Just as the woman stepped up onto the pavement, some men came out of the pub, heard what she had to say and glanced up at the loft wall of her house. Fortunately for Steve, darkness had now fallen and the men could see little, though some were jabbing their fingers at the loft wall as they talked excitedly to one another.

Then one of them ran back into the pub.

Steve knew what was happening. This was a strongly Republican street, filled with hard men, many of whom would have been members of the PIRA and, as a consequence, under the command of Houlihan. As the Hibernian pub had, during the Troubles, been a meeting place for PIRA members, known by the locals to have been under surveillance, those people down there, including the woman, would have known about security forces surveillance teams operating out of the lofts of touts all over the Falls. Given this, they would assume, correctly, that the person up in that woman's loft (which was where they thought he was) was some kind of spy, perhaps working for the Northern Ireland Police Force, formerly the hated RUC.

Almost certainly, then, the man who had just run into the pub had done so in order to tell Houlihan what the woman had told him.

Steve had to get out.

Cursing again, he turned away from the spyhole, removed his second layer of socks, then put on his rubber-soled shoes and his windcheater jacket. After removing the Browning 9mm High Power handgun from his holster, holding it in his right hand, he peered through the hole again and saw that some of the men who had already come out of the pub were advancing across the street to check for a spy-hole in the loft wall of the woman's house. Instantly, Steve dropped the slate back over his spy-hole, hoping that the men wouldn't see it falling back into place. Then, unable to wait for Houlihan to emerge from the pub, he mouse-holed back along the loft of the terrace, using his torch to light his way, until he had reached the loft space of the tout's house. Once there, he turned the torch off, lowered it as quietly as possibly to the floor, then listened intently while holding his handgun up against his right cheek.

While Steve had been mouse-holing along the loft, he had heard bawling in the street below, indicating that some men were running along the street in the direction of the Falls – the same direction that he had been taking.

Almost certainly, then, the men had known, or had just been told, that this house had once been the home of a tout and had been used as the entrance for the security forces' covert surveillance teams. If this was so, they clearly intended either to break into the house or to cover the exit until Steve tried to make his escape.

Steve listened intently. Hearing nothing directly below, though he could hear shouting from the street, he kept his weapon in his right hand while slightly raising the trapdoor with his left. Leaning forward to peer around the raised edge of the trapdoor, he saw the chair on the dark landing directly below but heard no sound at all. Satisfied that no one was inside the house just yet, he raised the trapdoor all the way, laid it across the joists beside him, holstered his handgun, then sat on the edge of the trapdoor opening and, balancing himself on both hands, gripped the edge of the opening and lowered himself onto the chair.

He had just placed his feet on the chair when he heard what sounded like a sledgehammer pounding against the front door of the house.

Damn! he thought. *Those bastards are coming in!*

It was indeed a sledgehammer pounding on the front door because its hinges started shrieking in protest, that dreadful sound soon joined by the sounds of splintering wood and breaking concrete. Then (Steve assumed from what he heard) the door was smashed off its hinges and crashed noisily onto the hallway floor.

Men were bawling as they burst into the house and started up the stairs.

Instantly, Steve jumped off the chair and bounded along the short landing as the first of the men below reached the top stair. As the unarmed man foolishly rushed onto the landing, clearly preparing to use his fists, Steve stepped out and kicked him brutally in the groin. Then he kicked him again, this time in the stomach, sending him bowling backwards down the stairs, crashing into his comrades as he went.

Wanting to discourage them from coming back up, Steve spread his legs before bending them slightly and aiming his pistol in the classic two-handed firing position. His intention was to fire a shot over their heads, into the wall behind them. But then he saw one of the men leaping over his fallen comrade and raising a pistol to fire at the same time. Steve fired his weapon instinctively, aiming for the man's chest. The man made a grunting noise, dropping his gun as Steve's bullet punched him backwards into the hallway.

Even before he had fallen to the floor, some other men were bursting in through the open doorway, all of them holding handguns. Steve fired at the first one, heard him cry out, then spun away, opened a bedroom door and hurried inside, not knowing what he would find there. But he had no choice.

He was in luck.

It was a small room with a single bed, a wardrobe and a window overlooking the backyard.

Initially Steve considered pushing the wardrobe across the door to prevent, or at least slow down, the advance of the men into the bedroom. He realized, however, when he heard their footsteps on the stairs, that he didn't even have time for that, so he simply slid the thin brass bolt across the door. Then he kicked out the glass in the window, cleared most of the remaining sharp shards by smashing them out with the barrel of his handgun, rested his backside on the window ledge, swung his legs over and started lowering his feet to the roof of the coal shed below.

This time, the men on the landing didn't need the sledge-hammer. Since the brass bolt was so small and fragile, one of them simply kicked the door open and raised his pistol the instant he saw Steve, still precariously balanced on the window frame.

Steve fired first, aiming squarely at the man's chest. The man gasped, clearly taking his last breath, and started falling backwards. His fall was blocked, however, by the big man standing directly behind him.

That big man was Houlihan.

Houlihan's eyes widened in recognition when he saw Steve on the window ledge. Then he disappeared, stepping away from the doorway, letting the dead man fall backwards to the floor as Steve aimed at him with his handgun.

Steve dropped off the window ledge and fell mere inches until he landed on the roof of the coal shed. He backed across the roof, keeping his handgun aimed at the window, until he had reached the brick wall that overlooked the entry behind the backyard.

A hand holding a pistol emerged from the smashed window, taking aim at Steve.

The man about to fire was Houlihan.

Wild Bill was standing just behind him.

Steve jumped off the roof of the coal shed just as Houlihan fired at him.

The bullet ricocheted off the top of the wall, spraying Steve with pieces of smashed brick and pulverized concrete as he

landed on his feet in the entry and instantly ran towards the
Falls Road, which was only three houses away. He started to slip
his handgun back into its holster, wanting to hide it under his
windcheater before he ran into the Falls. But two men appeared
abruptly at the end of the entry, both holding wooden clubs in
their hands and getting ready to use them.

The men were only a few yards away from him, blocking
his entrance into the Falls Road.

Steve didn't stop. He covered that few yards in seconds and
drop-kicked one of the men before either of them could even
raise his club. While he was kicking the first man, who screamed
when his balls were crushed, Steve struck out at the second man
with the butt of his handgun, smashing it into the man's temple
and splitting it open. The first man fell, still screaming, holding
onto his balls, as the second staggered sideways, obviously dazed,
with blood gushing from his split temple. Steve pushed him aside
and kept running until he had turned into the Falls Road.

Heading away from the street where the tout's house was,
he hid his handgun under his jacket. He deliberately didn't
run now, but he certainly walked as fast as he possibly could
without being noticed. Even at this late hour, the Falls Road
was still busy and that, as far as Steve was concerned, was all
to the good, even if it didn't actually guarantee his safety.

Indeed it did not. When he glanced back over his shoulder,
he saw Houlihan, Wild Bill and a whole gang of their minders
coming out of the side street and hurrying along the pavement
towards him.

Steve did the only thing he could. After firing a couple of
shots at them, making them scatter and terrifying the ordinary
citizens, who dived for cover into the doorways of nearby shops,
he ran across the road, weaving through the late-night traffic,
and raced downhill in the direction of Divis Street. He had
only gone a few yards when he saw a man about to clamber
into a red Vauxhall Cavalier. Instantly, he slowed down, walked
up to the man, placed the muzzle of his handgun between the

man's eyes and said, 'Give me your fucking car keys and then get the hell out of here.'

With his eyes widening in fear, the man handed over his car keys and then hurried off along the pavement. Steve holstered his 9-Milly, clambered into the driver's seat, closed the door and turned on the ignition. He screeched away from the kerb and burned along the road, heading towards the centre of town, though with no fixed destination in mind, just wanting to get away from Houlihan and give himself time to think.

Houlihan could easily find out where he lived and, having recognized him, would certainly go there to find him. For this reason, Steve could not return home – at least, not until Houlihan and Wild Bill were both out of the way, preferably dead and buried deep. Until then, for Steve to return home would be suicidal.

He was now a man on the run and would have to go underground.

Disappear, he thought. *Quickly.*

Chapter Ten

Having crossed the road in pursuit of his quarry, Houlihan was furious when he saw him hijack a red Vauxhall Cavalier and burn off towards the centre of nocturnal Belfast.

'Fuck!' he exclaimed, clenching his fists with frustration, silhouetted in the pale light of a street lamp. 'The cunt's got away!'

'Aye, right,' Wild Bill, standing beside him, responded. 'No point in tryin' to follow him now. By the time we got into a car, he'd be long gone and lost to us.'

'Did you recognize him?' Houlihan asked as he turned towards Wild Bill and the four armed minders.

'No,' Wild Bill said, falling in beside Houlihan and walking back up the Falls Road with two of their minders up front, two more bringing up the rear. Houlihan liked having minders. Apart from offering the protection that he surely needed, they made him feel like someone important: a politician or a king. It was good for his ego, like. 'I only caught a quick glimpse of him when he was balanced on that backyard wall,' Wild Bill continued, 'but I couldn't see his face in the darkness.'

'It was Lawson,' Houlihan said. 'That fucker, Steve Lawson. That SAS bastard who ambushed me and my men during the bank raid that got me put inside. In other words, he was the bastard responsible for copping me a life sentence. And that was him up in that loft, spying on the Hibernian.'

'Why?'

'*What?*'

'I didn't recognize Lawson, but I know all about him. He *used* to be in the SAS – he even tried to shop me when I was in the UDA – but since leaving the army, mere months after you went into prison, he's been making a fortune in property development. That guy's big around here. He's a respectable citizen. He owns the building he lives in and a couple of the buildings opposite and a lot of other properties around town. He has a fucking Lamborghini and a Mercedes-Benz and a silver-tanked Yamaha 400 motorbike that's worth a fucking fortune in its own right. Why the fuck would a guy like that be spying on us? Who would he do it for?'

'For himself,' Houlihan said. 'To save his own fucking skin. I don't think he was in that loft just to spy on us; I think he was there to put out my lights before I put out his. He must have known that I'd try to pay him back for what he did to me, so he decided to get me first instead. He was in that loft to put a bullet in my brain as I walked out of the pub. Luckily, his piss dripped through that floor and gave him away before he could do anything positive. Lucky for me.'

They were heading back for the street they had just left, pushing their way through the drunkards staggering out of pubs and cafés that were closing up for the night. Late-night taxis and buses rolled up and down the Falls Road, grumbling and groaning and rattling, their lights glimmering in the lamplit gloom.

'If he was trying to nut you,' Wild Bill said, 'he'd have had to use a sniper rifle, aiming through a spy-hole.'

'So?'

'So did your men find one when they went up into that loft?'

'I don't know,' Houlihan said. 'I sent some guys to investigate, but I was already halfway down the street before they entered that woman's house. We'll find out what was up there once we get back.'

'Aye, right,' Wild Bill said, remembering. 'You were halfway down the street before I even had the wit to follow you. So how the fuck did you know that the entrance to the loft was in that house near the end of the street?'

'Jasus, man,' Houlihan said, 'sure I've known that since the old days of the Troubles. That was when the SAS, working for the fuckin' 14 Int, used to keep an almost permanent surveillance team in that loft facing the Hibernian where our PIRA active service units were known to meet practically every day. Sure it was the joke of the whole fuckin' street, man! I mean, the tout whose house they were usin' as an entrance to the lofts was workin' both sides of the fence, passin' mostly useless information to the Brits while tellin' us everything he was learnin' from them. Sure didn't we know all along that the SAS were usin' that loft for surveillance, includin' high-tech apparatus that picked up our conversations? And didn't we deliberately feed them the kind of bullshit information that sent them scatterin' in all directions while we quietly got on with our real business elsewhere? I don't mean the loft of that oul' bag who sounded the alarm tonight – she only thought Lawson was up there because his piss was drippin' through her ceiling. No, it's the loft *beside* her house, the one directly facin' the Hibernian, and you can bet that he was only usin' *her* loft as a toilet. We'll find out soon enough.'

After crossing the Falls Road, they entered the side street where the tout's house was, only three doors down. A couple of Houlihan's hard men were standing guard outside the tout's house. The front door, having been hammered off its hinges, was still lying on the floor of the small hallway in a pile of dust-covered rubble.

'Anyone in there?' Houlihan asked.

'Aye, boss,' one of the hard men replied. 'Kavanagh and Connolly. Sure they went in to check out the lofts directly facing the pub. They haven't come out yet.'

'Any sign of the cops?' Houlihan asked.

'Ackaye. Sure they came by in a patrol car, but they were guys on your payroll and when I said that you'd be back in a minute they said, "Fine" and rolled on. They only stopped long enough to remind us to put the door back up and have it fixed properly tomorrow, so that everything looks normal again. They didn't want any aggro from straight cops and said you'd follow their drift.'

'Sure I do, right enough,' Houlihan said, grinning, thinking of the two cops in the squad car and of the many others on his payroll. 'They won't be reportin' any break-in. They'll let sleepin' dogs lie. Okay, you two, keep your eyes peeled and make sure no passers-by, drunk or sober, stick their noses in here. We'll be back out in a minute.'

'Anything you say, boss.'

Houlihan turned to his and Wild Bill's minders, saying, 'You lot wait out here. You come in with me, Billy-boy.' Together, he and Wild Bill entered the house, stepping over the fallen door, peering into the dust-covered living room to see that no one was present, then making their way up the stairs. Houlihan, who went up first, was just stepping onto the landing when Kavanagh lowered himself through the open trapdoor, placed his feet on the chair below it, then jumped down onto the floor. Seeing Houlihan, he nodded and said, 'Hi, boss.' Then he looked up again as a Lee Enfield sniper rifle was lowered through the trapdoor by someone else, obviously Connolly. Kavanagh took the sniper rifle off Connolly and then, as Connolly started lowering himself through the trapdoor, he held the rifle up to show it to Houlihan and Wild Bill, who were now standing together on the landing.

'Here it is, boss,' Kavanagh said. 'A good old Lee Enfield .303 sniper rifle. A favoured weapon of the British army and the

SAS. We found it in the loft directly facing the Hibernian, along with a lot of kit, including a sleeping bag and various domestic items – real SAS stuff. He was using the loft next door, that oul' bag's loft, as a toilet and his piss was leaking out of a badly sealed plastic bag to drip through the floor. He was there to perform an assassination, boss – not just for surveillance – and judging by the size of that pile of toilet bags, I'd say he'd been up there a long time.'

'Just as I thought,' Houlihan said. 'That fucker, Steve Lawson, was hoping to top me before I topped him. I'm goin' to have his guts for garters, have his balls for my breakfast. But first, let's talk to the people living in the house directly under the loft. I want to know if they were in on this or just an innocent party, like.'

'I think they were an innocent party, boss. That's the house of Missus Emily Magowan whose husband, Bob, was one of our most loyal PIRA members, shot dead in an SAS ambush on the road to the airport in 1996. She's a devoted Republican who hates the Brits, so she wouldn't be a party to this shit.'

'Let's find out anyway,' Houlihan said. 'You two,' he added, pointing at Kavanagh and Connolly. 'Put that door back in place as best you can, turn out the lights, then join us in the upstairs room of the Hibernian, comin' in through the backyard. Bring the rifle with you. When you get there, before you come upstairs, use the downstairs phone to ring wee Jimmy McNally, the carpenter, and have him come round here first thing in the morning to put this door back in properly, making it look exactly like it did before we broke in. You got that?'

'Got it, boss.'

'Okay,' Houlihan said to Wild Bill. 'Let's go.'

Together they left the tout's house and made their way back along the street until they reached the area directly facing the Hibernian pub. The pub was officially closed, but a lot of the customers were still loitering about outside, mingling with neighbours who had come out of their homes, all excitedly discussing what had happened. Ignoring them, Houlihan led Wild Bill to the house directly facing the pub and found Mrs Magowan standing outside, arms folded upon her ample bosom, wearing a flowered plastic apron over her plain grey dress and with a bright green scarf wrapped like a turban around her head. Mrs Magowan was forty-nine years old but she looked a lot older, having been affected dramatically by the violent death of her husband and, a mere eighteen months later, by the death of her eighteen-year-old son, who had blown himself up while trying to plant a bomb near an RUC police station for that PIRA, of which he too had been a fervent member. Mrs Magowan had no other children and rarely smiled these days.

'Mrs Magowan,' Houlihan said abruptly by way of greeting, staring steadily at her.

'I'd nothin' to do with it, Mr Houlihan,' Mrs Magowan said immediately, looking him straight in the eye. 'Sure that man was as quiet as a mouse in my loft and I didn't even know he was there until Mrs Lavery burst out of her house, screamin' that piss was comin' through her ceiling. That's the first I knew about that man in my loft, believe me. I'd nothin' to do with him bein' there.'

'I'd be willin' to believe that, Mrs Magowan, if it wasn't for the fact that the man appears to have been in your loft for a pretty long time – too long for you not to have heard *something*.'

'Don't shite me, Mr Houlihan,' Mrs Magowan said. Having already lost her husband and her only son, she had nothing more to lose and so was not frightened of him. 'You know that durin' the Troubles a lot of them murderin' Brits, especially the SAS, the ones who killed my husband, used the lofts a lot and could stay in them for days on end without makin' a sound. They used to operate in teams of four, not just one like your man, and *still* they could stay up there for days without the poor souls right below them knowing a thing about it. So don't say that your man couldn't have been up there without me knowin' about it, 'cause he could and he was.'

'All right, Mrs Magowan, I'm willin' to buy that,' Houlihan said. 'But I just had to ask, as I'm sure you appreciate.'

In truth, he would have liked to give her a backhand blow for her impertinence — loosen her dentures, belt her back into her own home — but her late husband and son were widely viewed as PIRA heroes. He couldn't be seen laying into the widow in front of her neighbours, so he forced himself to smile at her.

'Right, Mrs Magowan,' he said. 'Sorry to have troubled you. That man won't be hiding out in your loft again — I promise you that — so relax and take yourself off to bed and have a good kip.'

'That's just what I was plannin'.'

'Aye, right,' Houlihan said, again wanting to strike her but instead simply staring coldly at her until she turned away and went back into her house, slamming the door behind her. Houlihan then turned around to stare at the men and women gathered outside the Hibernian, even though it was closed. They were there, he knew, to gawp and gossip about what had happened, but he didn't want them hanging about this close to midnight in case they attracted the attention of policemen not on his payroll. 'And you lot,' he said, loud and clear and threatening, 'take yourselves off to your homes. It's all over here and there's people tryin' to catch up on their sleep. Away with you right now.'

Any possibility that some man in the crowd, given Dutch courage by the drink, would put up an argument was dispelled when Wild Bill gazed left and right, his eyes gleaming with a mad light, and when the minders moved in around him and Houlihan to remind the crowd that they were faced with a lot of hard men. The crowd broke up quickly enough, its individual members heading off in different directions, some to enter their own houses in this very street, others making their way back to the Falls Road and then on to their homes in other areas.

As the crowd was dispersing, Houlihan glanced at the closed door of the pub. Then he nodded at Wild Bill and led him and the minders along the pavement to the end of the street, around the gable end of the terrace, then back along the entry, stinking of urine and littered with rubbish, including used contraceptives and empty beer bottles, until they had reached the backyard of the Hibernian. Houlihan had a key to this door and he let himself in, followed by Wild Bill and the minders. They then made their way through the backyard and into the building through its rear door and kitchen, emerging into the main bar, which was empty except for the owner and his wife, Jack and Rose MacNee, who were stacking the chairs up on the tables prior to cleaning up the night's mess. They both nodded at Houlihan.

'Still beaverin' away there, are you?' Houlihan asked.

Jack nodded wearily. 'Ackaye. Sure runnin' a fuckin' pub is no joke. It's a dusk to dawn job.'

'But think of the good you're doin' the local community. Soothin' troubled nerves and the like.'

'Not my own fuckin' nerves,' Jack replied, perhaps referring to the fact that he had to pay Houlihan protection money to prevent his men from smashing the place up. 'And not those of the missus. So what was all that goin' on outside to cause all that excitement?'

'Someone up in the loft of Mrs Magowan's house. Just like in the good old days of the Troubles. Obviously keepin' their eye on your pub. So what have you and Rose been up to, Jack, to warrant that kind of attention?'

Houlihan was winding them up and it had its effect. Jack stared at him with widening eyes while his wife, the fat bag, stacking chairs up on a table, virtually froze and gazed fearfully at him.

'Someone was up in the loft?' Jack asked as if he couldn't believe his ears.

'Aye, that's right,' Houlihan said.

'Why in God's name . . . ?' his wife began, clearly shocked, almost stuttering.

'You don't think . . . ?' Jack asked, though he was too rattled to finish his own sentence.

Houlihan grinned. 'Sure who did youse think it was? The security forces like in the old days, checking youse out because this place was always known as a PIRA meeting place? Did youse think that the security forces had come back to keep an eye on you 'cause I'd got out of prison and was known to still drink my jars here? Is that what you were thinkin'?'

'We just don't want any trouble . . .' Jack began, sounding nervous.

'The old days is dead and buried,' his fat bag of a wife added, 'and we don't want any trouble from the Law. We just want to run a decent business and—'

'Not let anyone know that Mad Mike Houlihan,' Houlihan said, 'is still using your filthy oul' pub as his regular meetin' place. Is that it?'

'She didn't say that, Mr Houlihan!' Jack jumped in desperately. 'Didn't mean that, at all. We just meant—'

'Ack, shut your gobs, the pair of ya, and turn out the lights in this place and go to your fuckin' beds and let us go about our business undisturbed by your blatherin'. We'll be upstairs and we don't want to be disturbed and we'll let ourselves out the back way when we're finished. Understood?'

'Ackaye!' Jack said, sounding throttled, vigorously nodding his head and sending a pleading glance to his fat missus. 'Right, Mr Houlihan. Youse just go upstairs and get about your business, like, and we'll finish down here soon enough.'

'Right.'

'Right, Mr Houlihan!'

Grinning at Wild Bill, who grinned back, Houlihan led him and their minders up the stairs to the private room with the refrigerator and other amenities. Before anyone could settle down, Houlihan ordered a couple of the minders, one of his and one of Wild Bill's, just to keep things fair and square, to stand guard at the bottom of the stairs and ensure that no one other than Kavanagh and Connolly entered the building and came upstairs. When the minders had left the room, Houlihan and Wild Bill sat facing each other across the table and were served drinks by some of the other minders. The minders not being gainfully employed as waiters were compelled to stand along the wall by the table, neither offered a drink nor allowed to take a seat, thus being reminded of their lowly position in an unjust world. When Houlihan and Wild Bill had their drinks in their fists, they raised their glasses to each other in a toast.

'To crime,' Houlihan said.

'Which never pays,' Wild Bill retorted.

'So say the priests,' Houlihan said. 'But we're not in church now. Here's to you, Wild Bill.'

They each had a good slug of their whisky. Then Houlihan, smacking his lips with pleasure, said, 'So who'd have thought that bastard would go that far?'

'Steve Lawson?'

'Who else? Sure the fucker pissed through that woman's floor and had a gun in the next loft. He went back to his old SAS ways just to give me a nut job.'

'Ackaye, he did that, right enough,' Wild Bill said. 'But how the fuck did he know about that loft and how did he get in there?'

'We know how he got in – through that tout's house.'

'But who told him about the tout's house and who gave him access?'

'Jasus!' Houlihan exclaimed. 'I never thought about that. A good question, Billy-boy. Who, indeed?'

'He might have used that loft before. A lot of SAS did. But that would have been a good few years ago, before he became a successful businessman and respectable citizen. How did he know that we'd be meeting in this very building and, more important, like, how did he know that the tout's house was still empty? And who gave him a key? Sure he had to have had some kind of help from someone in the know.'

'Someone in the security forces?' Houlihan suggested.

'Or someone who *was* in them,' Wild Bill said, 'but still had good connections when and where required. An old friend of his, like.'

'So who'd be an old friend to a former SAS man?'

'A member of the British army, an RUC officer, or a tout that he'd kept in touch with.' Wild Bill shrugged. 'It could have been anyone, really. But for sure someone helped him.'

'We should draw up a list of his old friends,' Houlihan said, 'and narrow it down to those who're still here in Belfast and still connected, even if only socially, with their friends of the old days.'

'I'd recommend that,' Wild Bill said.

At that moment, Kavanagh and Connolly came up the stairs and entered the room. Connolly was holding the Lee Enfield sniper rifle under his coat, wrapped up in newspapers. He unwrapped it and laid it on the table between Houlihan and Wild Bill.

'There it is, boss. That's an old security forces weapon. I wonder where he got it?'

'From an old security forces friend,' Houlihan said. 'Someone with connections in the army or police force. The same person who gave him access to that tout's house. That bastard Lawson was given assistance.'

'We'll check it out,' Connolly said. 'Meanwhile, we've fixed the door of that tout's house back in place temporarily – just jammed it into the doorframe so it looks reasonably normal in the darkness – and I've just spoken to Jimmy McNally on the phone and he's comin' round first thing in the morning to put it back in properly.'

'Good,' Houlihan said.

'Any chance of a drink, boss?'

Houlihan nodded towards the cupboard and fridge. 'Aye, help yourselves, lads.'

'I'm havin' a whisky,' Connolly said to Kavanagh. 'What about you?'

'The same,' Kavanagh said.

Houlihan checked his wristwatch as Connolly went to the cupboard beside the refrigerator to pour whiskies for himself and his friend. 'It's one o'clock in the morning,' Houlihan said, 'and here we all are, still sittin' and drinkin'.'

'It's the excitement,' Wild Bill said with a grin as he held his glass up. 'We're having too much fun, Mike.'

'Fun, my arse!' Houlihan said. 'It isn't fun to *me*. I've got a loose cannon tryin' to gun me down and he's gettin' good help from somewhere.'

'So we find him and put his lights out,' Wild Bill responded. 'I don't see any problem.'

'The problem might be finding him.'

'We know where he lives, Mike. There's nothing secret about it. He has a penthouse suite in his own apartment block down by the Lagan, near the Queen's Bridge, practically opposite the Waterfront Hall. We just place the building under some surveillance of our own and pick him up the next time he attempts to enter or leave.'

'I don't think it'll be that easy,' Houlihan said. 'I don't think he's that dumb. He knows that I saw him and recognized him, so he'll assume that I'm goin' to come after him and that I'm going to know, or find out, where he lives. For sure we have to place his building under surveillance, but it's unlikely that he's going to go back there until this thing is resolved.'

'Resolved?' Wild Bill asked.

'He's after me and now he knows I'm gonna be after him. It's him or me now. It's as simple as that. So he's not gonna go back to his flat and wait to be picked up. He's gonna go underground.'

'And then go for you again,' Wild Bill said. 'The first chance he gets.'

'Aye, that's right.'

Wild Bill gave a low whistle, which did not amuse Houlihan.

'Aye,' he repeated. 'It's him or me now and I'm gonna make sure it's not me. We're gonna find him and turn him into mincemeat and serve him up in a can with a label on it. Today's special offer.'

'The problem,' Kavanagh said, taking a seat at the table while holding his glass of whisky in one hand, 'is how to find him if he goes underground.'

'Aye, right,' Connolly added, taking the chair beside Kavanagh and also holding a glass of whisky in his hand. 'Steve Lawson's ex-SAS and he was one of their best, a killer operator, as elusive as a ghost, ruthless and as sharp as a whip, striking swiftly and then disappearing before you got near him. If he does go underground, he'll go down pretty deep and be hard to find. He'll be like an invisible man.'

'He's not that good,' Houlihan insisted. 'No one's *that* good.'

'He's fucking brilliant,' Kavanagh said.

'Maybe,' Wild Bill said, 'having failed to kill you the first time and knowing now that *you*'ll be coming after *him*, he'll just give up and stay underground, not resurfacing until he's pretty sure that he's been forgotten or when, for some reason or other, he thinks it's safe to emerge.'

'And when would that be?' Houlihan asked.

'When you're off the scene,' Connolly said. 'Either having left Belfast for good—'

'Not likely,' Houlihan interjected.

'—Or when you're back, God forbid, in Maghaberry prison.'

'Or in your grave,' Wild Bill said with an evil grin. 'Either dead from nat'ral causes or topped by a future enemy – the Russian *Mafiya*, for instance.'

They all grinned at that, but Houlihan was not amused. 'All fuckin' unlikely scenarios, but I get the general drift. He could stay underground for a long time – and all that time I wouldn't know if he'd simply given up or if he was working on another scheme for topping me. I'd have no peace, like. Even worse, I wouldn't be on the offensive; I'd be on the defensive.'

'That's true,' Kavanagh said.

'A bad situation,' Connolly added.

'So we have to draw him out of his hiding place,' Houlihan said. 'Do something that'll make him show himself, sooner rather than later. In other words, force him into a confrontation.'

'And how are you gonna do that?' Wild Bill asked.

'With a bombing campaign.'

Chapter Eleven

Steve didn't go back to his apartment, but he *did* return to the building itself, determined to pick up his silver-tanked Yamaha 400 motorbike before Houlihan's men had time to get there. Reasoning that Houlihan would brief his men before letting them do anything and that the apartment building was unlikely to be placed under surveillance until the next day, he dumped the hijacked Vauxhall Cavalier in the centre of town, in Royal Avenue, which was practically deserted at this early hour of the morning. Then he made his way on foot to the Lagan River, stippled and serene in the moonlight.

The walk from Canal Quay to the apartment block, across Queen's Bridge, only took a couple of minutes. But Steve didn't take a step without carefully checking to his left and straight ahead (the river was to his right) for suspiciously parked cars or strangers out walking. Seeing no one, but still deeming it wise not to enter by the front door, he made his way around to the rear of the building and entered the premises by punching his code number into the control panel at the side of the iron gate. Inside, behind the high fences, were marked spaces for outdoor parking, individual parking bays and ground-floor lock-up garages, the garages being located directly under the flats.

After walking past his silvery-grey Mercedes-Benz, which was parked in a marked bay, Steve punched in another code number on the panel beside the door to his lock-up garage. The door opened automatically, vertically, to reveal his red Lamborghini and his beloved silver-tanked Yamaha 400 motorbike.

Steve's love of powerful motorcycles had begun when he did part of his cross-training with the SAS Mobility Troop. Although he'd never had the opportunity to use a motorbike during his duties with the Regiment (no Gulf War for him – only the mean streets of Belfast), he had purchased the Yamaha 400 shortly after receiving his discharge and had used it for frequent cross-country journeys when he was bored or frustrated. Indeed, so addicted was he to the kind of adventures that he had experienced with the various 'troops' of the SAS Sabre Squadrons, particularly the Mobility Troop and the Mountain Troop, that he had found himself increasingly taking long journeys on the motorbike through rugged terrain such as the Mountains of Mourne, the Wicklow Mountains or Connemara, where he could camp out just as he had when serving with the Regiment. For this reason, he had fitted the Yamaha 400 with two lightweight saddlebags, one to each side of the rear wheel, both packed with his civilian equivalent of an SAS survival kit. He also had a rolled-up sleeping bag and water-proof ground sheet, or poncho, permanently tied across the rider seat and supported by the wire-framed top of the saddle-bags.

The Yamaha 400 was Steve's home away from home, enabling him to sleep rough, under the stars, instead of boring himself to death in the comfort of the kind of hotels he could now easily afford. Knowing that he had to go underground until such time as he could eliminate Houlihan lest Houlihan eliminate him, which he would now certainly try to do, and convinced that he could not hide safely anywhere in Belfast, which was now virtually ruled by and divided between Houlihan and Wild Bill Moore, Steve had determined to get out of the city as soon as possible. Initially, he had thought to rent a holiday home somewhere in Antrim, near Lough Neagh, which would have offered a combination of isolation and easy travel to and from Belfast. But so convinced was he that Houlihan and Wild Bill between them had eyes and ears everywhere that he had decided to go into a state of near-invisibility by creating a hide, or lying-up position, in some densely wooded area near the city. Then he'd travel in and out from there every day, using only his Yamaha motorbike. This would be a rough, uncomfortable and lonely way to exist for a lengthy period of time. But it could, given his present circumstances, be the only way to keep out of Houlihan's clutches and thus stay alive.

Still convinced that this was the correct course of action, Steve removed the canvas covering from the motorbike, rolled it up, then tied it to the sleeping bag and poncho already stretched across the rider seat. After checking the motorbike as carefully as he would have examined a potentially booby-trapped car in the days of the Troubles, but finding nothing amiss, he wheeled it out of the garage and across the parking lot, again passing his Mercedes, then punched in the code that opened the gate. When the gate opened, he wheeled the bike out onto the road. As the gate was closing automatically behind him, he checked that no one was in sight, then sat on the saddle of the motorbike, turned the throttle, letting the engine roar into life, and moved off slowly. He picked up speed only when he was turning out of Rotterdam Street to go back across the Queen's Bridge.

As Steve crossed the bridge, temporarily dazzled by the floodlit Waterside Hall, Hilton Hotel and bt.com building and whipped by a warm wind, he glanced about him, looking back over his shoulder. Seeing no sign of movement, hearing nothing, with not a human being in sight, he heaved a sigh of relief and then, giving the motorbike full throttle, he shot off along Ann Street, desolate, lamplit, and eventually made his way through the quiet city centre to the Antrim Road and the M2 motorway.

Steve loved his motorbike. Loved the heat of it, the vibration beneath him, the comforting roar of it, the feel of the wind whipping his face, the world passing by in a blur like a ribbon of dreams. Most of all he loved it at night, when that ribbon of dreams became a river of light that rose and fell, winding like a snake, flowing back on both sides of him as the city receded. It didn't last long, of course: the city soon fell behind him, leaving him with broad, alluvial fields that rose and fell under the summer stars of this unusually hot August, this uncommon season in Northern Ireland, and were bordered with deciduous trees and hawthorn hedges. He went all the way to Antrim, which was not a long way, about only thirty minutes or so, then turned off the motorway to wend his way deeper into the countryside, looking for a reasonably protected place where he could set up his hide.

What Steve wanted was a densely wooded area – not that common hereabouts where the trees stood in long lines that bordered the low hills and gently rolling fields. But eventually, about halfway between the eastern shore of Lough Neagh and the western side of Antrim City, he found a broad swathe of hilly farmland with a wooded area overlooking the only road in the immediate area that could support motorized transport. If anyone found out where he was, they would have to drive up that road and he would see them coming.

'Beautiful,' he said, talking to himself without embarrassment.

Climbing the steep hill with ease on his motorbike, Steve soon reached the wooded area. He had to wend his way around the trees, the beam of his headlight creating bizarre chiaroscuro shapes in the dense foliage, until he found a suitably protected spot, a small clearing surrounded by trees, with a hedgerow running east to west and a brook running past it, a few metres away. While the hedgerow would provide him with excellent protection in the unlikely event that some local wandered up this far, it also gave him a good line-of-sight view of the road below.

Realizing that this was as good a spot as he was likely to find,

Steve parked the motorbike under the overhanging branches of one of the trees. Then he set about creating what would be his primitive home for an indeterminate period.

First, he removed the saddle bags, rolled-up sleeping bag, waterproof poncho and sheet of plastic from the motorbike and spread them out on the grassy ground. He used the sheet of plastic to cover the motorbike completely, then scattered loose earth and local vegetation over it to make it blend in with the trees. Next, deciding to base his hide – his lying-up position – on the classic long-term observation post (OP) of the kind he had used when serving with the SAS, and also mindful of the fact that he could not erect a tent, which would be seen by the farmer who owned the surrounding fields, he put up a hessian screen, with the waterproof poncho and a camouflage net for overhead cover, supported on wooden stakes and looped over one end of the hedgerow and secured with iron pickets and rope. To further disguise the overhead cover, he sprinkled it with grass, gorse and vegetation from the hawthorn hedge.

Once this basic form of protection had been set up, Steve used a small spade and pickaxe to dig out a rectangular area, approximately eight by fifteen square feet, with one end running under the hedgerow. He then dug a shallow 'scrape' under his camouflaged covering and rolled his sleeping bag out upon it. At the bottom end of this scrape, he dug a smaller one to be used as what was known in the SAS as a 'kit well' for the storage of water bottles, high-calorie food (canned goods, chocolate, biscuits and tinned milk) as well as his toiletries and other minor luxuries, such as books, notebooks, pens and pencils, a torch and a pair of small but powerful military binoculars, all of which had been carefully packed in the saddlebags of his much-used motorbike. His cooked meals would be bought in restaurants or cafés, either locally or in Belfast. He could wash himself and his clothing in the brook that flowed just behind the hide.

Once Steve had completed the hide, he scattered the loose soil from the scrapes a good distance away. He then made a camouflaged entry/exit hole in the hessian hanging to the ground at the rear end of the hide. Last but most important, he shaped a camouflaged rectangular viewing hole in the hedgerow and hessian covering the side of the hide that overlooked the road below.

He could now settle in.

Checking his luminous wristwatch, he saw that it was four in the morning and realized that he was very tired indeed.

'Beddy-byes time,' he said softly.

Stripping off his outer garments, but leaving on his vest and underpants, Steve crawled into the sleeping bag and closed his eyes, not really expecting to sleep, just trying to work out what he should do next, now that he was at least temporarily safe.

He had failed to kill Houlihan and, even worse, had let Houlihan see him long enough to recognize him.

Houlihan, having recognized him, would be more determined than ever to kill him.

It was now a simple matter of life and death.

If he, Steve, did not want to spend the rest of his life hiding out, an invisible man, he would have to try once more to terminate Houlihan.

'Fucking great!' he whispered to himself.

Nevertheless, he would not have to do it immediately. Instead, he would stay in this hide for at least a couple of weeks, perhaps a month, long enough for Houlihan's men to have conducted a massive sweep of Belfast and the surrounding area, including Antrim. With luck, when they didn't find him, they'd decide that he had fled the country entirely.

If they didn't find him within the next month, almost certainly they would come to that conclusion and give up the search for him.

Once that happened (and it was possible that Joe Williamson, who had his nose to the ground, could tell him when it did), Steve could move out of this hide and into more civilized accommodation, most likely a holiday home near Lough Neagh. From there he could venture daily into Belfast to spy on Houlihan and his friends, build up a pattern of his movements, work out the place to strike at him ... and then make the strike.

'And do it properly this time,' he said aloud.

So Steve lay there in his hide, working out what he would do, contemplating the next few weeks in this hole in the ground, alone, without home comforts ... Gradually he became aware that the thought didn't depress him as it should have done, that in fact it excited him, took him back to the good old days, his days with the SAS, when suffering this kind of discomfort and risking his life, as he was doing now, had given him the kind of thrill that most men, living their ordinary lives, could only dream of and that he, despite his Civvy Street success and wealth, had sadly, frustratingly, lacked since leaving the Regiment.

Shocked and thrilled to realize just how much he had missed this release from daily tedium, this flirting with death and the seductive lure of danger, the knowledge that he might not be that different from Mad Mike Houlihan – or Wild Bill Moore, for that matter – yes, shocked and thrilled by this knowledge, he did not fall asleep until first light.

When, eventually, he *did* fall asleep, he slept soundly, with no fear or guilt to disturb his rest.

He awakened, in the sunlight of noon, feeling like a new man.

An invisible man.

Chapter Twelve

'Lawson only has a few choices,' Houlihan said. 'He knows that I recognized him and knew he was trying to kill me and that I'm not going to take that lying down. So either he leaves the country entirely and doesn't come back or he goes into hiding and only emerges when I'm safely out of the way – either dead or in prison again, as you all kindly pointed out.'

This copped nervous chuckles from some of those gathered together in a supposedly abandoned house in West Belfast, though the building was actually used as a store for weapons and explosives. Ever since peace and the partial arms decommissioning, with the British army gone from the city streets and the police diplomatically keeping a low profile, it had become even easier to smuggle weapons into the city than it had been at the height of the Troubles. Naturally, Houlihan and Wild Bill had exploited this situation and now they had more weapons and explosives than they could possibly use at any one time. This particular house had been bricked up during the Troubles and had remained that way because the developers, sharp fuckers like Steve Lawson, hadn't yet got round to this area to buy up the houses, renovate them and sell them off for a considerable profit.

Though the bricks remained where the front door and windows had originally been, Houlihan had arranged for the bricked-up rear entrance to be reopened and a proper door put back in. As the new door could not be seen from the entry, being hidden by the high walls of the backyard, no passers-by – usually drunkards after somewhere to piss or lovers having a quick stand-up fuck – would notice that the house was being used. Houlihan's men, when they wanted to collect weapons or explosives, simply entered via the backyard door and then the new rear door of the house.

Right now, even as the men stood there, gathered around Houlihan, every room in the house was filled with weapons and explosives: blocks of Semtex, Soviet-made RPG-7 grenade launchers and SAM-7 missile launchers, Russian DshK 12.7mm heavy machine guns, Romanian-made AKM rifles, AK-47 assault rifles, .357 Smith & Wesson revolvers, Brazilian Taurus automatic pistols, thousands of rounds of ammunition, a variety of car bombs, firebombs, detonators, timers and mercury tilt-switches.

'So what do you think he'll do?' Wild Bill asked.

'I don't think he'll leave the country for good because he has too much invested here.'

'He could run his business from England,' Kavanagh said.

'He could, but he'd have problems,' Houlihan insisted. 'Sure he couldn't make himself too invisible in England if he tried to run his business from there. To run a business where you're living, never mind from afar, like, means you have to be in constant contact with people – on the phone, using e-mail, out and about – and that would make it pretty fuckin' difficult to keep a low profile, let alone be an invisible man. So, no, I don't think he's gonna leave the country completely. I think he's gonna stay right here – if not in Belfast proper, then somewhere around it. He'll lie low for as long as he thinks necessary, but he'll do it somewhere in the province – which means he can keep his eye on us as well as on his business.'

'Not good,' Wild Bill said. 'So, as you said, we have to

draw him out of his lair and the way to do it is with a bombing campaign.'

'Right,' Houlihan said. 'Since he's gone underground, we attack him where it hurts – his business – and force him to come out to defend it. That cunt has made a fucking fortune by exploiting the building boom of recent years and now, quite apart from all the houses he's renovated and sold on, he owns a lot of property in Belfast, including two or three new apartment blocks built on what used to be the waste ground of areas razed during the Troubles. So we bomb a couple of those blocks, setting him back a good few bob – or, to be more precise, givin' him a fuckin' major financial headache – and then he'll almost certainly have to come out of hidin' to protect his interests by ensuring that we don't do him more damage.'

'Good one,' Connolly said.

'Aye, I think so. I mean, once he comes out of hidin', the only way he can prevent us from doin' him more damage is to try to do what he failed to do before – put out our lights, like. And to do that, he's gonna have to show himself – though this time we'll be well prepared for him.'

'What does that mean?' Wild Bill asked. 'You're invitin' that fucker to come back and try to kill you – or us. But who's to say he isn't going to succeed? I mean, he may come out of hiding in the sense that he'll go for you, but he's hardly gonna advertise his presence until he has you – or us – in his fuckin' sights. That guy's a fuckin' assassin, a trained SAS sniper, a former 14 Int covert operative and reportedly brilliant at it, so he's gonna know what he's doin' when it comes to trackin' our movements and pickin' the right time and place to slot us. Given that, how the fuck can we be "well prepared" when he finally decides to make his move?'

'Ack, sure nothin's guaranteed,' Houlihan said pragmatically, though he was actually excited by the thought of the deadly cat-and-mouse game that was about to begin. 'But we know that he's gunnin' for us – or will be, you can bet, once we've bombed some of his precious buildings – so we simply make life difficult for him by surroundin' ourselves with bodyguards, takin' more precautions, and keepin' our eyes peeled night and day.'

'That's some fuckin' gamble,' Wild Bill said, not impressed. 'We invite him into our web and just pray that we manage to catch him before he gets us in his gun sights. We gamble that if we make ourselves virtually impregnable, he'll make some kind of major mistake, exposing himself, before he actually gets within firing range. Is that what you're sayin', Mike?'

'Aye, it is,' Houlihan confirmed. 'It's a gamble worth takin'. If we protect ourselves as completely as we did durin' the Troubles – surroundin' ourselves with bodyguards, dickers planted on every street, constant surveillance on our homes and our pubs and where we work, reinforced cars and under-car booby-trap detectors to be used before and after every trip – we should be able to frustrate him so much that sooner or later he's gonna grow impatient and make a mistake. Then, since we'll be watchin' for him night and day, we can pounce on the fucker. I say it's worth the risk.'

Wild Bill sighed, glanced at Kavanagh and Connolly, then looked around the sitting room they were using. The fact that the light, a bare bulb, was on gave him no cause for concern since the room door was closed and the only window, which overlooked the backyard, was bricked up. He and the others were seated on hard wooden chairs around a battered, dust-covered oak table, though the room contained no other furniture. What it *did* contain, however, was a lot of weapons, stacked up against every wall, as well as boxes of ammunition and explosives – a regular arsenal big enough to blow up most of the street it was in if anything went off accidentally.

Sighing again, Wild Bill turned back to Houlihan.

'Okay,' he said, 'I'll buy that. So when do we start and how do we go about it?'

Everyone, including Houlihan, turned to look expectantly at the small, prematurely wizened man who was seated at one end of the table, doodling in a notebook with a pencil and rubber, doing line drawings that no one could see, constantly erasing them and starting over again. Obviously in his late fifties, he was as slim as a reed, nearly bald, but with tufts of red hair jutting out above big ears and watery, weak-looking green eyes. The left side of his face had been burned in a fire, leaving most of the skin shrivelled and purple, like an ancient, dyed leather. All in all, though he commanded attention, he was not a pretty sight.

'Well, Dan?' Houlihan asked.

The man was Dan Farrell and Houlihan revered him because he had been with the PIRA for most of his life, certainly ever since his teenage years, and had developed an almost legendary reputation for the number of British soldiers, RUC policemen and innocent citizens that he had managed to kill in his many bomb attacks. Farrell had made just about every kind of bomb, from simple under-car booby traps (UCBTs) to firebombs that had turned hotels and bars into infernos. His work had included 1,500-lb Semtex and fertilizer jobs that had caused hideous devastation not only in Belfast, but in the West End and the City of London. Twice imprisoned during the Troubles, he had twice managed somehow to make bombs in his cell, smuggle the dismantled parts bit by bit into the exercise yard, reassemble them within minutes and blow holes in the prison walls to make his escape. Released from his last stretch as part of the peace agreement, he had instantly gone to work for Houlihan's criminal gangs and soon proved himself to be invaluable. Now, as everyone stared expectantly at him, he sniffed and scratched his right nostril and blinked his watery green eyes.

'Well,' Farrell began, 'if I have this correct, we're initially talkin' about two relatively new apartment blocks, both overlookin' the River Lagan, one located on the Laganside Walkway, near Queen's Bridge and almost directly opposite the Waterfront Hall, the other farther south along the river, neat the Albert Bridge.'

'Aye, that's right,' Houlihan confirmed.

'And the idea is to cause considerable damage to both buildings, beginning with the first-mentioned.'

'The one on the far side of the river,' Houlihan clarified. 'The one near Queen's Bridge.'

'Exactly,' Farrell said, sniffing again and blinking his watery eyes.

'Can it be done?' Wild Bill asked impatiently.

'Can you shit?' Farrell replied with a small smile. 'Of *course* you can! And there isn't a building standing in this city that I couldn't blow down.'

'So how do you do this one?' Wild Bill asked.

Farrell shrugged. 'I simply bomb it.'

'Yeah, right,' Wild Bill said, exasperated. 'But what *kind* of bomb?'

Farrell pressed his lips together, went, 'Mmmmmmm,' then opened his lips again. 'Let me see ... For a building of the size we're talking about, I'd recommend the use of a 1,000-lb mixture of Semtex and fertilizer explosive contained in milk churns, surrounded by cans of petrol and activated by a button job – remote control to the layman.'

'How does the button job work?' Wild Bill asked.

'It sends a high-frequency signal to a modified radar detector, a receiver/decoder device, that's connected to a block of Semtex in one of the milk churns. The knock-on effect does the rest: one milk churn exploding after the other, all igniting the cans of petrol. Most of the ground floor of the building will be completely destroyed and the floors immediately above it – at least, say, floors one and two – could come down, leading to the collapse of the entire building. Meanwhile, the cans of petrol will ensure that the ground floor is turned into an inferno from which nothing or no one will escape.'

'Fucking beautiful!' Houlihan said admiringly.

'I'm not sure that I understood all of what you said,' Wild Bill admitted, 'but sure it sounded real great, like.'

'Sounds great, all right,' Kavanagh said. 'But you're talkin' about a thousand-pound mixture of Semtex and fertilizer explosive in a lot of milk churns. You're also talkin' about a lot of cans of petrol. Where do you put them?'

'What?' Farrell asked, his brow wrinkling in confusion.

Kavanagh, an experienced PIRA member himself, spread his hands in the air as if releasing two white doves of peace. 'That's an awful lot of materiel, Dan. All those milk churns surrounded by cans of petrol. Where do we put them? Along an outside wall of the building, or what?'

Farrell shook his head from side to side. 'No. They have to be inside the building for maximum effect. No point in creating a ball of fire if it's outside the building.'

'So how do we get them in there?' Connolly asked. 'We just ring the doorbell and ask the porter if we can bring the stuff into his lobby?'

'No need for sarcasm,' Farrell said testily. 'My job is to create the bomb, friends; your job is to get it in there. Naturally, for this kind of device, the lobby is useless, but buildings like that sometimes have basements and that's what we need here.'

'It doesn't have a basement,' Kavanagh said. 'But it does have individual lock-up garages directly under the flats.'

'Are you sure?' Houlihan asked.

'Aye, I'm certain,' Kavanagh said. 'We've had the building under surveillance for the past couple of days – ever since that bastard Lawson was discovered in that loft – and before we sent our men out there, we got our hands on the architect's drawings for the place. No question that those garages exist ... and Lawson has one of them. He's in the penthouse apartment with four flats between him and his garage, but if you manage to blow up that garage, the whole works would come tumbling down.'

'But how can we get into his garage?' Houlihan asked. 'I mean, he's not going to *lend* it to us, is he?'

'No, boss, he's not,' Connolly said. 'We can't get into *his* garage, but we *could* get into the one beside it.'

'Oh? How?'

'I've been the one supervising the surveillance of the building and I had our lads check it out front and rear. Forget the front – there's only the front door. At the rear of the building, however, entering by way of Rotterdam Street, there's a kind of courtyard that has a combination of private outdoor parking in marked spaces, open parking bays located between semi-detached blocks in the building, and ground-floor garages, located directly under the flats. The courtyard is fenced in and has a steel-barred gate operated automatically when you either punch in the code number manually or use a remote control from your car.'

'So we're fucked already,' Houlihan said impatiently.

'No, we're not,' Connolly said with an unusual show of confidence. 'Sure I think I've found a way in there, boss.' He turned to Dan Farrell. 'This bomb of yours – all those milk churns and blocks of Semtex and fertilizer explosive and petrol cans – how do you transport all that shit to the killing zone?'

'In a van,' Farrell said. 'Naturally. The van is part and parcel of the bomb. The shell of the bomb, you might say. You load up the van and park it at the killing zone and then detonate it by remote control.'

'So how soon can you have such a van – the bomb – ready to go?'

Farrell smiled with quiet pride. 'I always have one ready and waiting,' he said, 'and there's one all set to go even as we speak, parked in our own garage out near Mr Houlihan's factory on the Duncrue Industrial Estate. Just give me the word, like.'

'Which still doesn't tell us,' Wild Bill said impatiently, 'how we get it into that car park.'

'We drive in,' Connolly said, now smiling his own smile of quiet pride. 'As I said, we've had the building under surveillance, front and rear, and we've taken notes on all the comings and goings.'

'Everyone but Steve Lawson,' Wild Bill said with his lopsided, slightly crazy grin.

Connolly grinned back and nodded. 'Aye, everyone but Mr Steve Lawson. Anyway—'

'Right, go on,' Houlihan said impatiently.

'These are people with money,' Connolly said, 'and they enter and leave the building a lot, particularly in the evening, probably to wine and dine, the rich cunts.'

'Aye, they'd do that sure enough,' Houlihan said resentfully. 'They'd be fillin' their guts in some fancy restaurants on the Golden Mile or elsewhere.'

'Right,' Connolly said, growing visibly excited. 'And one of those cunts is a woman who owns the lock-up garage right next to Lawson's, which means it's virtually under his penthouse apartment – four floors up, as I recall. That rich bitch comes home just about every evening between eleven and midnight. Give or take thirty minutes or so on either side, she's as regular as clockwork.'

'Keep talkin',' Houlihan said.

'So,' Connolly continued, 'if you disguise our van, our mobile bomb, as something official – Northern Ireland Electric or something similar – and park it just after sunset near to that courtyard gate, you won't have to wait long before the rich bitch from that buildin' returns home from her evenin' out. We start the engine of the van the instant we see her car arriving. She uses her remote control to key in the code number and the gate to the courtyard opens. As she drives into the courtyard, we follow tight on her tail. When she gets out of her vehicle, we jump out of the van, take her car keys off her and make her give us the code that automatically opens her garage door. When the door opens, we tie the bitch up, gag her, place her in the back of the van, then drive the van into her garage. We lock the garage door, using the same code, then drive out of the courtyard in her car. We drive back across Queen's Bridge and transfer to the getaway car, which should be parked where we have a clear line of sight to Lawson's apartment – say, facing Chichester Street in Oxford Street. I activate the bomb from there, using my button job. When we see the building explode, we get the fuck out of there in the getaway car, driving straight back to the Falls. It's a piece of piss, really.'

Wild Bill gave a low whistle of appreciation and mockingly clapped his hands together. 'Pure genius,' he said.

'A real treat,' Dan Farrell added.

'Can we do the first one this evening?' Houlihan asked. 'Anything against that?'

He glanced first at Dan Farrell, who shook his head from side to side and said, 'No, I've nothing against that. I'm all set to go.'

'What about you lot?' Houlihan asked, glancing at each of the others in turn. 'Can you think of any reason we can't do this?'

'No,' Kavanagh said.

'No,' Connolly added. 'Let's pick it up and run with it.'

'You?' Houlihan asked of Wild Bill.

'No argument,' Wild Bill said. 'I'm all hot to trot.'

Houlihan sighed with relief. 'Grand,' he said. 'So what time do we have?'

He checked his wristwatch but Connolly beat him to it. 'It's now eight thirty-five in the evening,' he said, 'so it's still light outside. But if Dan here has to get to the Duncrue Industrial Estate to pick up the van, he won't get to Lawson's apartment block until just after sunset. So the timing is perfect.'

'Great,' Houlihan said.

'So who does what?' Wild Bill asked.

'You want to come along?' Houlihan responded.

'Of course!' Wild Bill exclaimed. 'You think I'm a fuckin' eejit? Sure I wouldn't miss this for the world. I want to see it all happenin'.'

'And I want to make sure,' Houlihan said, 'that the fuckin' van, the bomb, goes into that garage, so I'm goin' there.'

'Which means you come with me,' Dan Farrell said.

'Right,' Houlihan said. 'So we need a getaway car. Which

means that I go out to the industrial estate with Dan here while you three—' he nodded in turn at Wild Bill, Kavanagh and Connolly '—you three go together in the getaway car and park it in Oxford Street, as close to Chichester Street as you can get. When we've finished at Lawson's apartment block, we'll drive across Queen's Bridge and transfer from the woman's car to yours. Then, when Dan here has set off his bomb, you, Kavanagh, will haul us all out of there and take us back to the Falls.'

'Neat,' Wild Bill said.

'What about the button job?' Houlihan asked Dan Farrell. 'Where will that be located?'

'In my fist,' Farrell replied. 'This is the modern world, ain't it? These days I use a radar gun that sends a high-frequency signal to a modified radar detector connected to the bomb's detonator. *Voilà! Kaput!*'

'Sounds like science fiction,' Wild Bill said.

'It's actually not that new,' Farrell informed him. 'We've been using the same device and similar ones for an awful long time. Like when we bombed the Cloghogue checkpoint, Romeo One Five, in South Armagh in 1991. I think that was the first time.'

Wild Bill gave another low whistle of appreciation. 'Shit!' he said. 'Real Flash Gordon stuff!'

'So we're all agreed to do it this evening,' Houlihan said, his impatience rising.

'Aye,' Wild Bill said, 'I think we're all agreed.'

The others nodded assent.

'Right.' Houlihan checked his wristwatch again, then raised his eyes. 'Let's move it,' he said. 'You lot take the getaway car, the Seat Toledo, and park in Oxford Street, like I said, and wait for us there. I'll go with Dan here to the industrial estate and come back with him in the car bomb. We should be at the apartment block just after dark. You'll probably hear the bomb exploding, even from where you're parked, so when you see us turning into Oxford Street in that rich bitch's car, the driver—'

'That's me,' Kavanagh said.

'Right,' Houlihan responded. 'The instant you see us coming, you turn on your ignition and get ready to take us all out of there.'

'What kind of car has she got?' Kavanagh asked. 'I need to know what I'm looking for.'

Houlihan glanced at Connolly, who said, 'A sky-blue Rover 97.'

'Right,' Kavanagh said. 'When I hear the sound of the explosion, I start looking for a sky-blue Rover 97.'

'That's it,' Connolly said.

Houlihan glanced at each of his men in turn. 'Okay?' They all nodded in agreement. 'Right, then, let's go.'

Excited, he pushed his chair back and stood up as the rest did the same. They left the bricked-up house by the rear door, emerging into the filthy, stinking entry, bathed in the sinking sun's pale light. Dan Farrell's own car, a red Skoda Octavia, was parked in the street at the end of the entry, so he and Houlihan parted from the others there.

As Dan drove Houlihan out of Andersonstown and along the Falls Road, passing the Milltown Cemetery where most of the deceased IRA and PIRA heroes were buried, Houlihan glanced at the graveyard's entrance and came over all sentimental, recalling his glory days and all the good friends who had passed away, shot to shit or blown apart while performing their patriotic duty. As the cemetery fell behind him, Houlihan realized that he could no longer remember how he had become involved with the PIRA and didn't even know if idealism had ever been part of it. It was, of course, possible that at one point, when he was still a teenager with strongly Republican parents, he had seriously believed he was engaged in a fight for freedom. But certainly, at least as far back as his memory now went, his use of violence, intimidation and other forms of antisocial behaviour had long since shifted from the idealistically political to the purely criminal. Nevertheless, perhaps to salve his wounded conscience, he let that brief glimpse of the gates of the Milltown Cemetery wash him in a tide of nostalgia for the glory days that he and Dan Farrell, his demolition expert, had once shared together.

'Ack, Dan,' he said as he was driven past that other Catholic ghetto, Turf Lodge, and on towards the increasingly non-sectarian, highly commercialized city centre. 'Sure all that talk about your car bomb reminded me of the good old days when we all worked together for a common cause. When did I first hear about you, Dan? Was it . . . ?'

'1979,' Dan said. 'That Narrow Water business, as I recall.'

'Jasus, was that it? I thought that was a South Armagh thing. I didn't know . . .'

'I was involved in it,' Dan said. 'I had a hand in the bomb-making. Sure that had to be one of the greatest days in IRA history and I'm proud to say that, though I was just learnin' my trade, I played my part in it.'

'Jasus!' Houlihan exclaimed admiringly as the car turned into the Donegall Road, a strongly Protestant enclave, one of those now ruled by Wild Bill, located almost directly opposite the Whiterock Road, which divided Turf Lodge from that other Catholic ghetto, Ballymurphy. 'Sure I remember it now! But were you involved in one or two of the bombings?'

'Three,' Dan said proudly, then abruptly changed the subject. 'Do you mind if I take the Westlink? It's the quickest way to the M3.'

'Go any way you want,' Houlihan said. 'I mean, why should I mind?' He turned to Farrell. 'Sure aren't the days when a Catholic couldn't get into that estate, no matter how good his business, dead and gone? Now we're all united in places like that, glued together by that EU money. This city's changed, all right.'

'It sure has,' Farrell responded, nodding sagely.

Glancing out of the car's window, Houlihan recalled the days when this area contained one of the most hardline Loyalist communities in the city — an area where a Catholic wouldn't have dared to show his face. Now, of course, it was controlled by Wild Bill's criminal gangs who were admirably non-sectarian when it came to the business. Yes, the times had certainly changed. 'So you were involved in both, were you?' he asked, referring back to their previous conversation.

'Ackaye,' Dan said. 'Truly a day to remember. Eighteen fuckin' paratroopers killed by two bombs, including a 700-pounder just like the one we're goin' to use this evening, except the one we're usin' this evenin' is even bigger.'

'Ah, right!' Houlihan said appreciatively, recalling that great day at Narrow Water, Warrenpoint, in Northern Ireland, just across the border from Omeath and the Cooley Peninsula in the Irish Republic, when a 700-pound IRA bomb, packed inside milk churns and surrounded by petrol cans, blew up a Land Rover and two four-ton trucks, killing seven members of the Parachute Regiment's 2nd Battalion. A second bomb, 1,000 pounds of explosives, also contained in milk churns, then blew up the gatehouse opposite Narrow Water Castle, completely destroying the building and killing another eleven men, thus making a total of eighteen dead, including two senior officers. 'But what the fuck was the third?'

'Mountbatten,' Dan said proudly. 'Earl Mountbatten of Burma. The seventy-nine-year old uncle of Prince Philip and cousin to the Queen.'

'Ah, that shite,' Houlihan said. 'Supposedly a friend to the Irish, though what man with royal connections could be? Sure the oul' bastard got what he deserved. So you had a hand in that as well, did you, Danny-boy?'

'Ackaye,' Dan said proudly. 'Sure wasn't he havin' his regular holiday at Classiebawn Castle in County Sligo, down there in the Republic, like, amusin' himself by fishin' in the bay in his boat ... what's its name?'

'*Shadow V*,' Houlihan informed him.

'Aye, right! So we planted a fifty-pound bomb in the bottom of his boat and blew the fuckin' thing to pieces. Killed him and his grandson and his fifteen-year-old boatboy, not to mention the Dowager Lady Branbourne. Of course Mountbatten actually drowned – he wasn't killed by the bomb. His legs were blown off when he was blown into the water, so he couldn't swim and he drowned. After that, I suppose, I couldn't do any wrong and the PIRA welcomed me with open arms. That's what being young does for you.'

'You and me,' Houlihan said, still wallowing in nostalgia, 'are never gonna be that young again. Still, we had our good times, like.'

'Sure we did, right enough,' Dan said.

'That burned face came from one of your own bombs, did it?'

'We all make mistakes.'

They said no more until they had come off the Westlink, driven along the M3 motorway and were entering the sprawling Duncrue Industrial Estate, next to the great Harland & Wolff shipyard that was dominated by its soaring yellow cranes named Goliath and Samson. The sun was sinking fast now and the industrial estate was a dead zone, with most of the buildings locked up for the night and not a soul in sight. Dan drove straight past the large prefabricated building containing Houlihan's frozen-food processing business, took the road that ran alongside its eastern wall, and braked to a halt outside a garage just behind Houlihan's building.

'All out,' Dan said chirpily.

When they were both out of the Skoda Octavia, Dan locked it, then used another key to open the garage. It was a pretty large garage, holding a lot of vans and trucks, but Dan led Houlihan straight to a stolen van that had been repainted with the logo of Northern Ireland Electric. The van had held that false logo for years because they used it a lot.

'We sit at the back of Lawson's apartment block in this,' Dan said, 'and anyone passing by won't give us a second glance. Also, the residents of the building will think we're there for some kind of routine job. No problem at all, like. Okay, boss, let's go.'

They clambered into the cabin and Dan drove off immediately, leaving the industrial estate and taking the M3 motorway back to the city centre, which was busy and brightly illuminated by street lamps and neon lights. Glancing over his shoulder, Houlihan saw little through the small window in the rear wall of the cabin, though he was uncomfortably aware of the fact that he was sitting in a powerful car bomb.

Returning his gaze to the front, he said, 'Is all that shit of yours in the back?'

'Of course,' Dan said.

'No chance of it goin' off by accident?'

Dan chuckled. 'No.'

Houlihan heaved a sigh of relief and said no more until they'd completed the short journey across town, come off the motorway at the Bridge End Flyover, curved back into Rotterdam Street and arrived at the small, car-packed area at the rear of Steve Lawson's apartment block. Once there, Dan parked slightly along from the steel gate of the lamplit courtyard. Then he turned off the ignition and applied the handbrake.

'Now we wait,' he said. 'Do you mind if I smoke, boss?'

Houlihan instinctively glanced back over his shoulder into the rear of the van, which was packed with explosives. 'What about that lot? Won't it explode if you light up?'

Dan grinned, then reached into the glove compartment of the van and pulled out what looked like a small torch. 'Not without this, it won't,' he said. 'This is the button job: the radar gun I mentioned. Until I send a signal to the car bomb, using this, there isn't a chance in hell of the bomb exploding.' He clipped the button job to the belt of his trousers, pulled out his packet of cigarettes and held it up in front of his face. 'Okay?'

Houlihan nodded. 'Okay.' He checked his wristwatch. 'Jasus, I hope someone comes along soon.'

'You can count on it,' Dan said, rolling down his side window, then lighting his cigarette and thoughtfully blowing the smoke out of the cabin. 'Connolly said they're in and out of this place like fuckin' yo-yos, spending their *gelt*. The filthy rich, don't you know?'

Houlihan didn't reply. He was now feeling tense, but also undeniably excited, thrilled to be starting this deadly game with Steve Lawson. Houlihan still loved doing this, personally taking part in the action, and the thought of what was soon to come practically gave him a hard-on. On the other hand, he was impatient, which was one of his weaknesses, and he could barely contain himself as fifteen minutes became a half-hour, then the half-hour became forty-five minutes with no one arriving. However, just as he was about to say something to Farrell, a sky-blue Rover 97 approached the closed gate of the courtyard.

Instantly, Dan, who was on his third cigarette, straightened up, flicked the cigarette out through the open window, then turned on the ignition of the van. The engine coughed into life, then ticked over smoothly.

'That must be the car,' he said. 'That's the blonde bitch who goes out practically every evening. Brace yourself, boss. We're going in.'

The Rover 97 slowed down as it turned into the mews and approached the courtyard at the rear of Lawson's building. The light from its headlamps reflected off the steel railings when it stopped in front of the closed gate. From where he was sitting, Houlihan could see the woman roll down her window to aim her electronic control at the closed gate and press the relevant keys for the code number. The gate opened automatically and the woman, after withdrawing her hand, drove on into the courtyard, which was packed with other cars.

Instantly, Dan revved the engine of his van and shot

forward on squealing tyres, following the Rover into the courtyard before the woman had the chance to close the gate behind her. Houlihan withdrew a Browning 9mm High Power handgun from the holster hidden under his coat and prepared to jump out. When the Rover stopped inside the courtyard, the woman heard the van squealing to a halt behind her and glanced back over her shoulder with widening eyes. Confused, she did not attempt to close the main gate with her remote control, but simply drove on a little and then stopped again, assuming that the van driver wanted to get around her. She was right. Dan wrenched on the steering wheel, shot around the parked Rover, and then came to a squealing halt right in front of it.

Houlihan and the woman emerged from their respective vehicles at the same time, the latter wide-eyed and now clearly frightened, the former advancing upon her as he raised the pistol in his right hand, aiming straight at her.

'What ...?' the woman began, staring first at Houlihan, then turning her gaze towards the van as Farrell jumped out and opened the rear doors.

'Give me your fucking car keys!' Houlihan said as he advanced upon the woman.

'What ...?'

'*Your car keys!*' Houlihan repeated, deliberately sounding as threatening as possible. 'Give them to me, you dumb cunt!'

Gasping, putting her hand to her mouth, possibly to stifle an automatic scream, the woman reached in through the open door of her vehicle, removed the keys from the ignition, then handed them, her hand shaking, to Houlihan.

Houlihan snatched the keys from her, then pushed her roughly backwards with his free hand and said, 'Now keep your fucking mouth shut and tell me the code number for the door of that garage.'

'What?' the woman asked, her senses rapidly slipping away from her as the fear congealed in her.

'*The code number for the garage!*' Houlihan repeated, his tone resembling the hissing of an angry snake.

'Six, four, two, three,' the woman said breathlessly.

'Six, four, two, three,' Houlihan repeated, wanting to memorize the numbers. 'Okay, punch those numbers in and open the garage door.'

'The garage ... ?'

'*Shut your mouth and do what I tell you!*'

Gasping again, throwing her left hand over her mouth again, stifling a scream again, the woman turned away from him and pressed the relevant numbers on the control box at the side of the garage. The door opened by rising upwards and backwards, sliding on well-oiled hinges into the garage, level with the ceiling. Then the frightened woman faced Houlihan once more.

'Get into the back of that van,' Houlihan said, now aiming his handgun right between her eyes.

'What?' the woman asked, clearly too dazed to fully comprehend what was happening.

'*Get into the fucking van, you dumb bitch!*'

Visibly shaking with shock, the young woman went to the back of the van, stopping beside Dan Farrell. She looked into that cramped space filled with milk churns and a lot of wires, then automatically took a step backwards.

'*Get in the fuckin' van!*' Houlihan hissed dramatically at the woman, indicating the open doors of the vehicle with the barrel of his handgun.

She glanced at the open doors with widening eyes, then looked fearfully, pleadingly, at Houlihan.

'Oh, please, no!' she exclaimed. 'If it's money, I'll—'

'It's not money and you're not going to be harmed,' Houlihan lied. 'Now get into that van.'

The woman backed away from him, shaking her head frantically from side to side, whispering, 'Oh, please, no! I can't! I'm claustrophobic. I'll go mad if you put me in there. Please, don't make me—'

But Houlihan cut her short by walking up to her, grabbing her brutally by the nose, twisting it until she had to open her mouth just to breathe, then shoving the barrel of the handgun into her mouth, all the time pushing her backwards towards the open doors of the van.

'You want do die now?' he asked rhetorically as he continued forcing her towards the van with the barrel of the pistol still in her mouth. 'Is that what you want, you dumb cow?'

The woman, bent backwards, shook her head from side to side, indicating 'No' as best she could with the barrel of the handgun still in her mouth.

'Then get in that fucking van!'

Removing the barrel of the handgun from her mouth, Houlihan twisted her around until she was facing the open doors, then shoved her violently forward until she was forced to clamber, now sobbing uncontrollably, up into the van. Placing his handgun back in its holster, Houlihan followed her in, followed himself by Dan Farrell. Before the woman knew what was happening, Houlihan pressed his fat belly to her spine, slapped his hand over her mouth to prevent her from screaming, wrapped his other arm around her waist to prevent her from breaking free, and held her in his vicelike grip while Farrell grabbed a roll of masking tape and pulled out a good length of it. He nodded, indicating that Houlihan should remove the hand that was keeping the woman silent. The instant Houlihan did so, even as the woman was about to release an instinctive scream for help, Farrell slapped the end of the tape down over her mouth, then rapidly, expertly, brutally wound it around her head half a dozen times until her lips were completely sealed. When he had done this, the woman went limp, almost fainting.

Houlihan pushed her onto her knees, then jerked her arms behind her back to let Farrell tie one end of a length of rope around her wrists and run it down to her feet. He pulled the rope taut, making the woman bend backwards until her hands were near her feet. Then he wound the other end of the rope around her ankles, leaving her hog-tied.

Shaking as she sobbed, though her gagged mouth allowed no sound out, she was thrown carelessly to the floor, between the milk churns filled with explosives.

Houlihan and Farrell clambered back out of the van and slammed both doors shut.

'You still remember the door code?' Farrell asked.

'Ackaye,' Houlihan said. 'Six, four, two, three.'

'So let's do it,' Farrell said.

While Houlihan went to take up a position by the control panel for the door, Farrell clambered into the driver's cabin of the van and drove it into the empty garage. Turning off the ignition, he got out of the van and then left the garage to stand beside Houlihan. The big gang boss then pressed the relevant numbers on the control panel and the door of the garage hummed and closed, locking the van in, with the woman still trussed up in the rear.

'Let's go,' Houlihan said. 'Here,' he added, handing Farrell the unfortunate woman's car keys as they walked side by side to the Rover 97. 'You drive.'

While Farrell took the keys off him and slipped into the driver's seat, Houlihan took the seat beside him.

'Where to?' Farrell asked.

'Back across Queen's Bridge,' Houlihan said, 'then left into Oxford Street. Keep going until you see Kavanagh's Seat Toledo.'

'Gotcha,' Farrell replied.

He turned on the Rover's ignition, drove out of the courtyard through the still-open gates, went along Rotterdam Street and turned onto the Queen's Bridge. At the far end of the bridge, he turned left into Oxford Street, drove on a little and braked to a halt almost directly facing Chichester Street. Kavanagh's Seat Toledo was waiting there for them. Connolly was sitting beside Kavanagh in the front of the vehicle. Houlihan and Farrell slipped into the rear beside Wild Bill.

From that position, they all had a good line of sight obliquely across the river to Lawson's apartment block.

'Everything went okay?' Wild Bill asked.

'Ackaye,' Houlihan replied. 'Sure it went like a dream.'

'A *wet* dream,' Farrell added. 'You should have seen the driver of the car that let us in. I nearly creamed my pants.'

'Oh, yeah?' Wild Bill said. 'So where is she now?'

'Locked up in the van,' Houlihan replied. 'About to be turned into fried chicken.'

'Sweet Jesus!' Wild Bill retorted. 'What a fuckin' waste!'

'Such is life,' Farrell said.

They all glanced automatically across the broad moonlit river to the Laganside Walkway. There was no one on the Walkway, but the lights of Steve Lawson's apartment block were clearly visible, beaming out into the dark sky.

'A lot of those shits are still up,' Houlihan said, 'watching TV or having supper, maybe drinkin' champagne – whatever the fuckin' rich do in the evening.'

'Well, aren't they in for a surprise?' Wild Bill said, grinning crazily. 'They won't be sleeping tonight, *that*'s for fuckin' sure.'

'Except maybe eternity's endless sleep,' Houlihan said philosophically. 'Okay, Dan, set your bomb off.'

Farrell unclipped the radar gun from his belt, aimed it at the building across the road and turned it on. For a couple of seconds nothing seemed to be happening. But suddenly the lights in the lobby of Lawson's building blinked off. Then the ground-floor walls and windows exploded, sending lumps of mortar and showers of glass spewing out over the Laganside Pathway in billowing clouds of dust and black smoke.

From where the Seat Toledo was parked, visibility was no longer that good, particularly with the lights of that lobby across the river now extinguished, almost certainly by the massive explosion in the garage at ground level. But the lights along the river bank were enough to let Houlihan and the others see something of what was happening, which was massive devastation – and, of course, though they couldn't actually see this, the loss of many lives.

The noise seemed to come long after the actual explosion, though this might have been an illusion. What the gangsters heard was, first, a muffled explosion as the car bomb went off in the garage, then a bass rumbling as walls were blown out or collapsed and, no doubt, as the dreadful fireball boiled up through the collapsing building, incinerating the van and (as Houlihan had realized) the lovely young woman locked inside it. Then came the distant sound of many windows exploding at once, followed by more muffled explosions as gas pipes and electricity cables were destroyed, leading to more destruction and fire.

Eventually, flames could be seen licking out of the ground floor where parts of the wall had exploded or collapsed and most of the windows had been blown out. The flames rapidly grew brighter and bigger, like phosphorescent, torn, flapping sheets, until they were licking up the walls to reach the second and third floors.

A great pall of smoke covered everything, blotting out the moon and stars.

Then most of the apartment block collapsed.

Clearly, the massive explosion in the garage, combined with the fireball, had demolished the ground floor of the building, destroying its walls and windows and thus weakening its ceiling and the first floor. Now, with one explosion leading to another – exploding gas pipes and steam pipes and boilers – the whole first floor had broken apart, falling into the demolished lobby and causing the floors above it to collapse, one after the other, as the walls on all sides fell away and crashed to the ground, raising massive, boiling clouds of dust and dense black smoke, though which red and yellow flames continued flickering.

Eventually, after what seemed like an eternity, the apartment block had been reduced to a skeletal ruin, unreal-looking in a shroud of boiling smoke and swirling dust and surmounted by a gigantic, spectacular umbrella of showering crimson sparks.

'Jasus!' Wild Bill exclaimed. 'What a sight!'

'Now let battle commence,' Houlihan said without a flicker of emotion. 'Okay, lads, let's go home.'

Kavanagh turned the car's ignition on and drove them back to the Falls.

Chapter Thirteen

Steve could scarcely believe his ears when he heard on the morning news that the apartment block he lived in had been almost destroyed by a bomb.

According to the news report, which he listened to through the earpiece of his small VHF radio, over forty people had been killed and many more had been badly injured when the building collapsed. The type of bomb used had not yet been ascertained. It had been planted by an unknown person or persons.

Steve knew instantly that the 'unknown' person was Mad Mike Houlihan.

Deeply shocked, he continued to listen to the news bulletins throughout the rest of the day and gradually learned, as the bomb site was examined and the police released more information, that the devastation had been caused by a massive bomb made with a mixture of Semtex blocks and fertilizer explosive. It had been driven into the ground-level garage next to his own in a van, the mangled pieces of which had been found scattered widely around the epicentre of the blast. The charred remains of a young woman had been found virtually glued by fierce heat to various interior surfaces of the demolished van, indicating that she had been inside it when it blew up.

Pieces of scorched rope had been found on one of the woman's dismembered hands and on the ankle of a dismembered leg, indicating that she had been tied up in the van, almost certainly by the people who had committed the atrocity.

A sky-blue Rover 97 had been found abandoned in Oxford Street, almost directly opposite Chichester Street. A vehicle-records check identified the car as belonging to Steve's neighbour and friend, Janet Lorrimer. Since Ms Lorrimer's body had not been found in the wreckage of the building and she had not shown up at work nor at any of her friends' places since the explosion, it looked increasingly likely that the remains found in the wreckage of the van were hers. The fact that the garage where the car bomb had been parked had been hers gave added credence to this notion.

It was believed by the police that the people who had driven the car bomb into the unfortunate Janet Lorrimer's garage, after binding her hands and feet and locking her up in the lethal vehicle, had made their escape to Oxford Street in her car and transferred to a getaway car at that point.

Resting in his OP-style hide above the rolling countryside of Antrim, concealed by the hedgerow and the camouflaged covering, watching darkness descend in great swooping shadows over the hills and glens, Steve felt a growing mixture of revulsion and almost ungovernable rage. The very thought of all those tenants in his apartment block being killed and maimed, not to mention the dreadful fate of Janet Lorrimer, made him think of Houlihan with a burning hatred that was infinitely stronger and more passionate than anything he had ever experienced before.

During the Troubles, when he had been in the SAS and determined to bring Houlihan down, he had been pragmatic about it, treating it as a job pure and simple — the hunting of a mad dog. But now Houlihan had personalized matters in the most dreadful way, filling Steve with a rage and disgust that felt almost physical in their intensity.

Initially, Steve had planned to remain in his hide long enough to grow a beard, a moustache and long hair to help disguise his features before he ventured back into Belfast. But after two days of listening to further news reports about the incident, each giving more details and, even worse, the names of those killed — yes, as the actual identities of the dead were revealed, thus making them real to him, compelling him to recall them individually, their features now clear in his mind, he could contain himself no longer.

Steve left the hide one evening, under cover of darkness, to make his way back to Belfast on his Yamaha 400.

By now he had the beginnings of a beard and moustache, though he still had a long way to go before his features were properly obscured by facial hair. Nevertheless, he felt that he would be reasonably safe at night and, besides, he had no intention of going where there were people who had formerly known him and who might recognize him. He simply had to see, with his own eyes, the remains of the apartment block, because otherwise he would have difficulty in accepting that it had actually been destroyed. The news of its destruction would seem like a bad dream.

Approximately thirty minutes after leaving his hide in Antrim, Steve was back in Belfast and approaching the eastern side of the River Lagan where his apartment block was — or had been — located. After deliberately parking his motorcycle a good distance away, in Upper Church Street, he walked across Queen's Bridge, which normally offered an impressive view of his building.

Alas, where the apartment block had stood there was now only a huge pile of rubble rising above wooden fences that had clearly been erected recently. Plastered all over the fences were signs saying *Danger! Keep Out!*

The building was gone for good.

Badly shaken by what he had seen, but now accepting the loss of the building and all those lives as a harsh reality, Steve glanced further along the river at his other apartment block, the one near Albert Bridge, and saw the lights of its many flats beaming into the night and, lower down, over the stippled, moon-reflecting, inky-black water.

What if Houlihan decides to bomb that one as well? he wondered, feeling chilled to the bone.

Looking in the other direction, at the huge pile of rubble behind the high fences, he realized that Houlihan had not destroyed the building solely as an act of vengeance, but to draw him, Steve, out of hiding.

So what if he didn't come out of hiding?

Would Houlihan bomb more of his buildings? Perhaps that one near Albert Bridge?

Shaken by what he was thinking, Steve returned to Upper Church Street, clambered onto his Yamaha and rode back to Antrim. He did not go immediately to his forest hide, but instead went into Antrim town, where he would not be known, and had a meal in a restaurant — the first hot food he'd had since fleeing from Belfast. When the meal was finished, he had the girl behind the counter fill up his two thermos flasks with hot tea. Then, his hunger satisfied and with enough hot drinks for the next couple of days, he drove on to the hide, high in the hills over Lough Neagh. After covering the parked motorbike with the canvas sheet, he camouflaged the sheet once more with soil and vegetation, then crawled into the hide to listen to the news on his radio.

As had become customary during the past two evenings, there were more news flashes about the bombing. But this evening he was shocked to hear one of his business partners, David Kershaw, a co-owner of the bombed building as well as of the one directly facing it across the river, giving an interview in which he stated that he had no idea who was responsible for the atrocity, that he had received no communications about it, but that he was worried because one of his two partners, Steve Lawson, had not been seen since the evening of the bombing.

'Do you think your partner, this Steve Lawson, had anything to do with the bombing?' the interviewer asked.

'No, certainly not,' Kershaw replied.

'So why do you think he disappeared the night of the bombing?'

'I've no idea,' Kershaw replied. 'Certainly, he didn't mention that he was planning to go anywhere, so his disappearance is a complete mystery to me.'

'Do you think he's still in the country?'

'Again, I've no idea. As you already know, he certainly didn't turn up at his wife's house in England, which suggests that if he's still alive, he's most likely still in the province.'

'Do you think he *is* still alive?'

'I would rather not speculate.'

'So why do you think that his apartment block – of which you are a partner in ownership – was the one selected to be bombed?'

'I really haven't a clue.'

'Did Mr Lawson have any enemies?'

'We all have enemies. But I don't think that Steve had enemies who hated him so much they would blow up an apartment block just because it was co-owned by him.'

'Is it not true that both you and your partner, the missing Mr Lawson, formerly served with the SAS in Northern Ireland?'

'I'm not at liberty to discuss where I or Mr Lawson were posted when in the SAS.'

'But the records show that you and Mr Lawson both served with the SAS in Northern Ireland.'

'Despite what the records show, I'm not at liberty to give details of my own or my friend's activities when with the Regiment.'

'Assuming that you both served in Northern Ireland, you would have made a few enemies among the terrorists. Do you think that any of them could have blown up that apartment block as an act of vengeance against you or Mr Lawson – or both of you?'

'Even if we *had* made enemies among the former terrorists

of Belfast – and I'm certainly not saying that we did – I think it would be far-fetched to imagine that they would take their revenge in such an outrageous way. The only people who *didn't* suffer from the bombing of that apartment block were me and Mr Lawson.'

'But you'll suffer in the sense that it's going to cost you both a lot of money.'

'Not true. The building was insured.'

Exasperated by David's refusal to be cornered, the interviewer tried a new tack.

'Do you think that the atrocity was carried out by a terrorist splinter group, as part of a campaign to disrupt the ongoing peace?'

'I doubt it,' Kershaw said. 'Why would a terrorist group blow up a block of flats inhabited only by civilians?'

'Gangsters?'

'That's possible,' David said. 'But I can't think of a motive.'

'Do you have any reason to believe that Lawson was in any way connected to the criminal elements of this city?'

'Certainly not.'

'Maybe he was kidnapped for ransom.'

'That's possible, but so far we've received no calls from anyone asking for ransom money or for anything else. Besides, a kidnapping for ransom wouldn't necessitate the blowing up of a whole apartment block. So the blowing up of the building – *and* Steve's disappearance – remain mysteries to me.'

'Will you be letting the authorities know if he calls you or comes to see you?'

'That depends on what he tells me. Assuming he's done nothing wrong, he must have good reasons for disappearing. If he turns up, I'm sure he'll be more than happy to speak to the authorities himself.'

'Is it your considered opinion that he will eventually turn up?

'As his friend, I'm naturally hoping that nothing bad has befallen him and that he will indeed turn up eventually.'

'Thank you, Mr Kershaw.'

Feeling very odd indeed at hearing himself discussed in that way, Steve listened to the rest of the news in a trance, hearing little. Then he switched the radio off, removed his windcheater jacket, and wriggled into his sleeping bag, still wearing his shirt and trousers. He tried to sleep but failed. With his mind in turmoil, he couldn't stop thinking about what Houlihan had done and wondering what he could do in retaliation.

Clearly, Houlihan had bombed that building to force a confrontation and, if Steve failed to emerge from hiding soon, might bomb another ... then another ... until Steve simply couldn't ignore him any longer. It was equally clear that he, Steve, could not wait to see if Houlihan was going to bomb another building. He had to move against the murderous bastard with all speed, starting right now.

Wriggling half out of the sleeping bag in order to sit upright, he picked up his cellular phone, and rang David Kershaw. David had, like Steve, worked on some complex, dangerous operations for the 14th Intelligence Group before leaving the army altogether, going into business with Steve, and moving into a big house in Holywood with his wife and three kids.

'David Kershaw,' a sleepy voice said.

'David, this is Steve.'

'Who?'

'Steve. Your partner. The one you were discussing on the radio just now.'

'Good God!' Now David sounded very much awake. 'Where the hell are you?'

'I can't tell you that,' Steve said. 'I have to stay low for a while. I'm just calling to let you know that I'm still alive and that I have to remain in hiding for a while.'

'By the way, I gave that interview about four hours ago,'

David said. 'But it was pre-recorded and only broadcast just now.'

'Fine. Makes no difference to me.'

'So is your going into hiding anything to do with the bombing of the apartment block?'

'Yes, but not in the way some people might think. I had nothing to do with the bombing of our apartment block. Almost certainly it was blown up by Mad Mike Houlihan, though no one's likely to be able to pin it on him.'

'Why would he bomb our apartment block? An old grudge against you?'

Not wanting to tell even David about his failed attempt to assassinate Houlihan, Steve said, 'Yeah, an old grudge. He's after me because I put him in prison and I've gone temporarily into hiding until I can work out what to do about him.'

'Why not just inform the police?'

'Houlihan was supposed to serve a life sentence and the British government sprang him after a mere three years. So, given those circumstances, do you think telling the police would do any good?'

David was silent for quite some time. Then, eventually, he sighed and said, 'No, I suppose not. So what *are* you doing?'

'I'm hiding out because now the police *and* Houlihan will be looking for me. Can I speak in confidence here?'

'Of course,' David said.

'Houlihan won't rest until he finds me and kills me, so I'm going to have to kill him first.'

David gave a low whistle. 'Just like the old days,' he said.

'Yeah,' Steve retorted sardonically. 'Just like the old days.'

'You think he's going to bomb more of our buildings?'

'I think he's going to try.'

'If he does, apart from the lives that will be lost, we'll be financially ruined. We'll never be able to get insured again. No more insurance, no more business.'

'Exactly. So I've got to eliminate him and, in the meantime, while I'm trying to do that, you've got to take every measure possible to secure our buildings.'

'We could evacuate.'

'No. That would just cause panic and encourage the police to ask more questions about me and my disappearance. Besides, we couldn't evacuate *all* our buildings and the individual houses we own – that just wouldn't be feasible. On the other hand, if you quietly go about making the buildings as safe as they can be made with state-of-the-art high-tech security systems while I, at the same time, make it known to Houlihan that I'm still in the province and gunning for him, I think he'll give up on the bombings and concentrate on finding me instead.'

'I think you're right,' David said. 'So, okay, I'll do that.'

'And make the fact that you're doing it known to the media. I want Houlihan to know that you're taking those extra security measures.'

'To discourage him.'

'Right.'

'So what are you going to do?'

'Play tit-for-tat.'

'A range war.'

'Something like that.'

'How?'

'Ask no questions and you can't be incriminated.'

'I don't mind being incriminated,' David said. 'I'm bored shitless being an honest businessman. Christ, you can't believe how much I sometimes yearn to be back at work for the 14th Int, risking life and limb. The only time a man feels truly alive is when he's flirting with death. I miss that a lot. So is there any way I can help you?'

'Not yet,' Steve replied. 'At least, not until I know exactly what I'm going to do. I think that for now you'd be better off securing our properties, protecting our tenants and dealing with the insurance companies and police, who'll doubtless be breathing down your neck – particularly with me being missing.'

'No problem. I can deal with all that. But if you need any other kind of help, don't forget I'm here.'

'I won't,' Steve said.

'Can I take it you don't want me to tell anyone that I received this call from you?'

'On the contrary, I want Houlihan to know that I haven't fled the country, that I'm alive and well. So when you inform the press about the extra security measures you're taking, you can also tell them that you've heard from me, that I denied categorically having anything to do with the bombing, that I had personal, private reasons for disappearing, that eventually I'll be turning myself in to the authorities for questioning, and that I refused to tell you where I was, apart from saying that I'm still in Northern Ireland.'

'What about Linda and the kids?' David asked.

The question instantly filled Steve with guilt. It was typical of him, he realized, that he should decide to go underground without even informing his wife, who could in turn inform the kids, that he would be gone for some time. Typical that he hadn't told her where he was going, or that he was going to be perfectly safe (the standard SAS white lie). Now, reminded of her by his friend, he actually blushed with shame.

'Shit!' he exclaimed. 'I never thought to call her and I'd better not call her now. Almost certainly, given the bombing and my disappearance, her phone will already be bugged. Can you call her for me?'

'Of course.'

'Tell her I'm safe – and lie with conviction when you tell her that I'm not in any danger or in any kind of trouble with the Law.'

'I'll do that,' David said.

'So what about *your* fucking phone?' Steve asked, suddenly thinking that he might have made a bad mistake here. 'Do you think *you've* been bugged?'

'I certainly thought of the possibility, but I've already

checked all my lines and so far I'm okay. They may get around to me eventually, however, so you'd better not call again.'

'If I have to get in touch again, I'll do it by e-mail from some cybercafé. I'll use a different cybercafé every time, which should make me untraceable.'

'Excellent,' David said. 'But let's terminate this conversation, just in case. Anything else?'

'Not for now. But you make that announcement first thing in the morning and meanwhile, before then, I'll drop Houlihan a calling card to confirm that I haven't forgotten him.'

'I won't even ask what that calling card is.'

'It's something simple and eloquent.'

'I'll bet,' David said, chuckling.

'Take care of yourself, buddy.'

'*You* take care of yourself,' David retorted. 'And get on that e-mail when you need me.'

'I will.'

'Best of luck.'

'Thanks,' Steve said.

Realizing that he had made a mistake in coming back here, that he should have remained in Belfast to do what he was going to have to do now, Steve turned off the cellular phone, clipped it to the belt of his trousers, then wriggled the rest of the way out of the sleeping bag and reached down into the smaller shallow scrape, the kit well, to withdraw his holstered Browning 9mm High Power handgun and strap it around his waist.

What he really needed was a small fireball, a home-made job. But since he had no explosives with him and no way of getting any, certainly not tonight, the 9-Milly would have to suffice for this particular task.

Crawling out of the hide, Steve glanced around him and saw only the rolling hills and glens, a vast jigsaw of shadow and moonlight. A light breeze was blowing, whispering through the trees and hedgerows. There was no sign of traffic on the road below.

After checking that the hessian screen, waterproof poncho and camouflage netting were all in place, he put on his windcheater jacket, then removed the covering from his motorbike and wheeled the vehicle silently away from the hide. When he was a good distance from the hide, he started the motorbike, turned its single headlight on, then threw his leg over the saddle and headed down the narrow, winding dirt track that led to the main road. There was still no sign of traffic down there.

Reaching the main road that wound between the moonlit, alluvial fields, he headed for the M2 motorway that would take him into Belfast. Traffic built up noticeably when he got onto the motorway, though at this hour, just after midnight, it was fairly light and he was, of course, as anonymous as he wanted to be.

The open spaces to either side of the motorway soon gave way to the industrial zones outside the city, the tree-lined streets of Bellevue, the ink-black slopes of Cave Hill and, finally, the sprawling housing estates of north Belfast.

Coming off the motorway, Steve took the Westlink to Grosvenor Street and from there went on up to the Falls Road. Though it was relatively quiet compared to what it was like in daytime, there were still taxis, private cars and late-night buses about, with men, women and teenagers, many of them obviously drunk, wandering in both directions along the pavements.

Steve ignored them. Weaving expertly between the other vehicles, using the skills he had learned with the 22 SAS Mobility Troop, he made his way up the Falls Road until he came to the street where the tout's house and the Hibernian pub were both located.

He did not hesitate.

Turning along the lamplit road, he saw that a couple of Houlihan's hoodlums were guarding the tout's house while pretending to be just loitering there, both of them smoking cigarettes. He went straight past them, not casting even a sideways glance, and kept going until he was approaching the Hibernian. The pub was closed and the lights inside were off, but two more of Houlihan's armed thugs were standing guard at the front door.

As he raced towards them, keeping to the left-hand side of the road, well away from the pub, they watched him approach. But they made no move, probably assuming that he was just a typical motorbike freak on his way home.

Your mistake, Steve thought with grim satisfaction.

Removing his right hand from the handlebars, he withdrew his 9-Milly from its holster and cocked it even as, with his other hand, he manoeuvred the motorbike until he was racing alongside the kerb on the wrong side of the road – the side that the pub was on.

Realizing now that something was up, the two hoodlums tensed and started reaching under their jackets for their handguns. But by that time Steve was about to race past them. He fired one-handed, one bullet after the other, managing to hit both men, making them jerk convulsively. Then he peppered the front window of the pub as he passed it, causing the window to shatter violently and shower the two falling men with shards of glass.

He emptied the gun's magazine, thirteen rounds in all, making a shocking, reverberating din, just before he finished his ride-by of the pub. Then he shoved the gun back into its holster and returned his free hand to the handlebars to weave rapidly left and right, tilting the motorbike dangerously low in both directions, just in case anyone shot back at him. In the event, no one did.

Turning the corner at the end of the street, Steve did not look back. He knew that he had managed at least to wound the two bodyguards, that the window of the Hibernian pub had been smashed to smithereens and that the interior must have been badly damaged as well.

This was his calling card, his message to Houlihan, letting

him know that battle had commenced and would not end until one of them was dead.

Contented, Steve drove back to his forest hide and had a good night's sleep.

Chapter Fourteen

Houlihan was burning up with humiliation, but he wasn't about to show it. As he walked down the Falls Road towards his meeting with his solicitor, Jack Parnell, in Parnell's offices in Castle Street – located right there in the centre of town to impress the lawyer's clients and, of course, his competitors – Houlihan either nodded curtly (to inspire fear) or threw a big grin (to inspire confidence) to those he passed. Which was, of course, the only reason why he was actually walking instead of taking a taxi. The important thing was to remain in the public eye, to be seen and remembered, so this walk, as well as being good exercise for a big man, was also done to make his presence felt on what he believed was his home turf.

Nevertheless, behind the hearty bonhomie and the fearless superiority (depending upon whom he was staring at), Houlihan was seething with rage and shame over Steve Lawson's shooting up of the Hibernian pub the previous morning – not to mention the wounding of two of his bodyguards. Houlihan couldn't get over the fact that Lawson had simply ridden along the street on a motorbike and shot up the pub *and* two of his men while still on the move. Even worse was the knowledge that the men standing guard outside the pub, supposedly hard men, had been so taken by surprise that they hadn't even managed to get their own pistols out before being shot by the daring night rider. One of those men had received a bullet in his right thigh, the other a bullet in the left shoulder. Both of them, instead of being sent immediately for medical treatment, had been taken to a garage just around the corner and there beaten black and blue as a punishment for being so inept. They were now in the hospital, all right, but with more than mere bullet wounds.

So now Houlihan, though appearing to walk alone, actually had two of his armed thugs walking ahead of him, both watching the road like hawks. Two others brought up the rear, unobtrusive enough by Houlihan's standards but also with their eyes and ears peeled for potential trouble. Other bodyguards had been tasked with keeping his house covered around the clock, working in four-hour shifts, four men to each shift, two standing directly outside his house, the other two at the far side of the road. Yet more guards were on duty at both ends of the street, also working around the clock in shifts. There were now bodyguards watching even the gates of his frozen-food processing business out in the Duncrue Industrial Estate. Finally, the meeting place for Houlihan and his lieutenants had been changed from the Hibernian to another pub, on the Falls Road and surrounded by busy shops, with a constant stream of locals passing by every minute of the day and most evenings. So if that fucker, Steve Lawson, wanted to get at him, he'd have to work a lot harder the next time. Houlihan didn't intend to have a repeat of the previous evening's debacle.

As he walked along Divis Street, unrecognizable these days with all the rebuilding that had gone on (the notorious flats had been knocked down and half of the surrounding area levelled to make way for the Westlink), Houlihan glanced about him and tried to remember it as it had been.

Less than ten years ago this area had been a maze of narrow terraced streets that bled into the fanatically Loyalist Shankill Road. Between them, the Catholics and the Prods had turned those streets and litter-filled entries into the worst killing ground in the Western world. During the

Troubles, he, Houlihan, had contributed to the killing, being the head of a PIRA active-service unit tasked with abducting, interrogating and murdering Protestants. During those days, too, Steve Lawson had been an SAS sergeant acting as a so-called undercover agent for the British army's hated 14th Intelligence Group, or 14 Int, tasked with terminating people like Houlihan.

Lawson had been a 'so-called' undercover agent in the sense that PIRA knew of his existence but simply couldn't track him down to neutralize him. As Lawson was then known as one of the SAS's best men, both respected and feared by the members of PIRA, Houlihan had taken a perverse pride in being singled out by him for special treatment. That pride had, however, turned to venomous hatred when Lawson and some SAS pals had ambushed Houlihan during the bank robbery, capturing him and handing him over to the RUC.

Houlihan was reliving that bitter humiliation now, when he thought of the ease with which Lawson had shot up the Hibernian pub, almost a sacred PIRA drinking shrine, and wounded two of his men into the bargain.

He was, at least, momentarily distracted when he entered Parnell's plush Castle Street offices and found that sexy bitch Katherine Crowley waiting there for him, hand outstretched, a small smile on her full lips, green eyes glinting in that frame of blonde hair, breasts rising and falling invitingly right under his nose. *Shit!* She sure knew how to take his breath away.

'Mr Houlihan.'

Just that. By way of a greeting, like. Whispering it as if out of a crumpled pillow case, letting him hold her delicate fingers in his big paw, the sweet smell of her scent wafting erotically over him to give him an instant hard-on. Jasus, what he was suffering!

'Miss Crowley.' With a curt nod, revealing nothing.

'So nice to see you again, Mr Houlihan.'

'Aye, right.' Gruff, non-committal, neither here nor there.

'Is Parnell waiting back there for me?' Indicating the main office with a nod of his burly head.

Another melting smile. A nod. 'Yes, he is. Let me show you in.'

She turned away from him to lead him into Parnell's office. The long legs in stiletto heels. *Stiletto heels!* The starched white blouse tucked tightly into the waist of the black miniskirt, so tight it showed the cleft in her arse. Jasus! What a sight! A man could come just glancing at it. Best raise the wide-eyed gaze, like. She could be Parnell's girl.

'Ah! Mike!' Parnell rose from behind his desk, slick in his light grey suit, his expensive shirt and tie, sparse red hair neatly combed, a bright smile to match his deceptively artless schoolboy's face. He did not offer his hand but merely used it in a languid wave, indicating the chair facing the desk. 'Good to see you, Mike. Take a seat.'

Houlihan took a seat. Katherine Crowley took another chair beside the desk, facing Houlihan, crossing her legs, glistening in sheer stockings, to take his breath away again. The bitch was tormenting him.

Parnell sat down again, looking important behind his desk, and raised his fine eyebrows inquiringly over eyes the same colour as Miss Crowley's. 'Tea? Coffee? Something stronger?'

Houlihan checked his wristwatch. It was only eleven o'clock in the morning. 'Sure I'll have a wee whisky,' he said, then glanced sideways, expectantly, at Katherine Crowley. She smiled, uncrossed her long legs and walked to the drinks cabinet that Parnell kept prominently displayed under a large landscape painting that meant nothing to Houlihan. When Katherine bent forward to pour the drinks, he automatically started staring at her pert arse in that tight skirt. Then he caught himself ogling her and forced his gaze back to Parnell. Was that wee bastard fucking her?

'So,' Parnell said, 'how's it been going?'

'Terrific,' Houlihan replied sarcastically. 'The Hibernian

pub and two of my men were shot up by a night rider on a Yamaha motorbike with silver tanks. Sure I'm over the moon, like.'

Parnell grinned. 'I take it you know who this night rider is?'

'I've a good idea, like.'

'Steve Lawson?'

'Right.'

Parnell grinned again. 'Well, someone *did* blow up his apartment block – no names, no pack drill – and I dare say he feels a little resentful. What happened to the Hibernian was nothing compared to what was done to his apartment block, so you should count your blessings.'

'Aye, right.' Katherine brought Houlihan the glass of whisky, leaning down as if about to melt into him, letting him see the heavy fall of her breasts under the starched white blouse, letting him smell her, before straightening up again.

Was she coming on to him? Was he imagining it? Was it purely his male vanity at work here? He had to wonder as she resumed her position in the hard wooden chair and again crossed her long, elegant legs, the tight miniskirt riding high up her smooth thighs.

Realizing that he was staring again, Houlihan wrenched his gaze back to Parnell.

'So what did you want to see me about?' he asked his smarmy, bent lawyer.

'Have the police been to see you yet?' Parnell asked.

'Ackaye,' Houlihan said, annoyed by the very recollection of those uniformed members of the Police Service of Northern Ireland crowding into his small house to give him a grilling in front of his wife and daughter. 'Sure they came to ask me questions about my whereabouts on the night of the bombing of Lawson's flats.'

'They paid me a visit,' Parnell informed him, 'to ask me the same questions about you.'

Houlihan had a sip of his whisky. 'And you said?'

'I told them what I told *you* to say: that as far as I knew you were in bed with your beloved wife at the time of the incident and that she would be willing to confirm that. You did say the same?'

Houlihan nodded, 'Yes.'

'And did they ask for that confirmation from Maeve?'

Houlihan nodded again. 'Aye.'

'She confirmed?'

'Nat'rally. She does as she's told, like.'

'Good. If it ever gets to court, which I doubt, Maeve, being your wife, couldn't be called as a witness anyway. But it's a help that she confirmed verbally to the police. I mean, an alibi like that is pretty unbreakable.'

'How strongly do they suspect me?'

'Right now, you're their number one suspect,' Parnell said bluntly. 'They know that Lawson was the one to capture you, leading to that prison sentence, so they're pretty sure that you're the one with the most reason to have a grudge against him. I did, however, point out to them that even *you* weren't likely to commit such a major atrocity merely to get at an old enemy and that they should, perhaps, investigate the possibility that Lawson did it himself, perhaps for insurance purposes, or that some criminal elements other than my client — by "my client" I mean your own good self, of course, — might have had business reasons for the bombing. Given that you've got a firm alibi, I don't think they can afford to ignore such a line of inquiry and it should keep them distracted for some time.'

'As well as making them think of Steve Lawson as a possible culprit.'

'Exactly,' Parnell said, smiling with self-satisfaction.

'Sure you're worth your weight in gold,' Houlihan said, grinning and glancing at Katherine Crowley, then quickly returning his gaze to the front again. 'I can't begrudge you that, Jack.'

'Thank you,' Parnell said with a nod and an even broader smile. Then he too glanced at Katherine Crowley, who smiled back, and Houlihan just *knew*, with a keen stabbing of jealousy, that they were fucking each other.

'You think they'll find anything on Lawson if they look into his business matters?' Houlihan asked.

'It's possible,' Katherine Crowley said, giving Houlihan an excuse to turn his head and stare directly at her. 'Very few businesses can prosper without committing some minor infraction here or there; and once your business comes under legal scrutiny, the slightest irregularity can seem like the kernel of a major offence. If nothing else, then, just getting the police to investigate Lawson's business – trying to find a reason why he might have had his own building bombed or why criminal elements might have done it – could, even if it doesn't turn up anything seriously illegal, at least present him, or his partners, with countless minor headaches. So it was probably worth pushing the police in that direction for the nuisance value alone. Being investigated can certainly make a business suffer.'

'Good,' Houlihan said. 'That's what I want. To make his business suffer and give him another headache while he's trying to put me in my grave.' Katherine smiled at him, encouraging him to say something that might please her. 'You're a pretty bright lady to be only a secretary.'

'She's not my secretary,' Parnell explained. 'She's my legal assistant, fully trained in the law and with only one year to go before she becomes a fully-fledged lawyer herself.'

Houlihan glanced at him, then returned his unblinking gaze to Miss Crowley. 'So I was right: you're a pretty bright lady.'

'I have my virtues,' she said.

Very few, Houlihan thought as he studied her face, which was beautiful, self-contained, slightly enigmatic and slyly, erotically challenging. *This smart bitch has the morals of an alley cat and that's just what I need. Fuck Parnell. I'll have to go for it, sooner or later, with her permission or not.*

His balls ached when he thought of it.

Turning back to Parnell, he said, 'Your legal assistant's already as bent as you are; this has to be good news for me.'

Parnell smiled. 'Can't be bad. So can I now give you some sound advice?'

'What is it?'

'A question first . . . What other plans do you have for wreaking retribution on Steve Lawson?'

'As my lawyer, I don't think you want to hear it.'

'Quite right,' Parnell said urbanely. 'I don't even want to hear from your own lips who bombed Steve Lawson's apartment block. So can I just say, speaking as your lawyer, that a repeat of that bombing – which, of course, had nothing to do with you anyway – could undo all the good work that Katherine here—' he nodded dutifully to the assistant he was clearly fucking on a regular basis '—has done in deflecting police attention away from you and onto Mr Lawson instead. One more bombing of that magnitude, involving the killing and maiming of a great number of respectable middle-class citizens, will force the police into taking the most far-reaching measures to investigate everyone remotely under suspicion – which would, of course, include you. So far the police are, as it were, giving you the benefit of the doubt. But we have to accept that this is probably due to their awareness that you were released from prison on the direct authority of the British Prime Minister and they don't want any flak from that direction. However, if another of Lawson's buildings is bombed, they'll have no choice but to intensify their investigations and focus more intently on you. Do you understand what I'm saying, Mike?'

Houlihan nodded to indicate that he understood, though he wasn't well pleased.

'So what am I supposed to do? Let that shite come for me without retaliating in any way? Just let him take his pleasure any way he wants to? His building was blown up – I'd nothing to do with it, nat'rally – but he's obviously blamin' me and has already started to harass me for it. Two fuckin' men wounded and the Hibernian pub shot to pieces – and that's only the start of it. So how the fuck am I supposed to get at him if I can't attack his financial structure by—'

'Don't say it!' Parnell interjected. 'I don't want to hear it!'

Houlihan sighed with exasperation. 'Aye, right. No more buildings will be blown up – not that I blew up that first one, you understand – and I'll just have to sit back on my arse and let him crawl all over me.'

'Find him,' Parnell said. 'Do everything in your power to protect yourself while casting your net far and wide. Apart from any other consideration, a lengthy range war between you and him would only intensify the police focus on both of you, so the sooner this situation is resolved the better for all concerned. So spare no cost in locating this man and then deal with him rapidly. Let this be dead and buried.'

'*He* will be,' Houlihan said.

'I didn't hear that remark,' Parnell said. 'Now go out and find that man and keep me informed on a daily basis.'

'I will,' Houlihan said.

Parnell pushed his chair back to stand upright, so Houlihan and Katherine Crowley did the same. Parnell offered his hand.

'Until the next time,' Parnell said. Houlihan shook his hand. 'Katherine will show you out,' Parnell added.

'Of course,' Katherine said.

She gave him a smile, her green gaze steady and catlike, then led him out of the office, her rounded hips swaying like a metronome, pert buttocks emphasized by the skintight skirt. After they had passed through the next room, which was her office, they entered the reception room where an elderly grey-haired woman, presumably the real secretary, was seated behind a desk and clearly too busy to be interested in them. Katherine opened the front door of the office suite, then turned back to face Houlihan, holding out her hand.

'Until the next time,' she said, almost whispering, making it sound like pillow talk.

'Aye,' Houlihan said, 'until the next time.' He gripped her hand, not squeezing it, just feeling the weight of it, the fingers as light as a feather in his big mitt, making him wonder what they could do to him if . . . 'Maybe we can meet before then,' he added. 'Somewhere other than here.'

'I don't think so,' Katherine said.

Houlihan felt his cheeks burning from humiliation and an instant rush of rage, so he released her hand, dropping it like a hot brick, then nodded curtly and brushed past her to get out of the office. He heard the door closing behind him, the soft click cutting through him, a whip on his bare back, and his feeling of humiliation only heightened his rage as he took the elevator down to the lobby. There a uniformed attendant sat behind a long desk, with security cameras peering down above his head. Knowing who Houlihan was, he nodded respectfully and Houlihan, who appreciated it when due deference was shown, nodded back and offered the best smile he could muster, given that he was still quietly fuming over Katherine Crowley's quietly brutal rejection of his overture.

He would have that bitch some day.

Making his way awkwardly through the revolving doors, his great bulk crushed up between them, Houlihan emerged to the grey light of a dull noon and found his four armed bodyguards out there, two standing at each side of the door. Kavanagh and Connolly were sitting in a red Vauxhall Vectra SXi saloon car parked at the kerb a few yards down the street. Having walked into town and already been seen by his loyal subjects, the Falls Road locals, Houlihan didn't feel like walking all the way back and had arranged to be picked up by his lieutenants.

After glancing left and right, checking the dense, noisy

traffic and the many pedestrians pouring in both directions along the pavements, doing their shopping here, in Royal Avenue and in the streets running off both sides of Donegall Place, he instructed three of the four bodyguards to take a taxi back to the Falls Road and take up watch positions outside the pub he was planning to visit. He waited until the bodyguards had managed to get a taxi, thus ensuring that they would be in position outside the pub before he got there. Then he slipped into the rear of the Vauxhall with the fourth bodyguard.

'Good day, lads,' he said as the bodyguard, having slipped in beside him, slammed the door shut.

'Good day, boss,' Kavanagh said.

'Nice day,' Connolly added.

'A bit on the gloomy side,' Houlihan responded.

'Ackaye, it is that, right enough. But sure August is nearly over and winter's already on the way, like. We've had the hottest summer in a long time; now the dark days are comin'.'

Houlihan sighed. 'Aye, you're right there.'

Kavanagh was in the driver's seat with Connolly seated beside him. Both men were armed and would act as Houlihan's minders until they were all in the pub, protected by the bodyguards standing outside. After releasing the hand brake and turning on the ignition, Kavanagh drove the car away from the kerb.

'So how's it goin'?' Houlihan asked as Kavanagh headed along the road in the direction of Divis Street.

'Okay,' Connolly said. 'Nothin' to report, like. Nothin's happened one way or the other since we last met.'

'No sign of Lawson?'

'No sign of him and not a peep out of him. I mean, no taunting phone calls or the like. He's disappeared like a vapour.'

'You've men out lookin' for him?'

'Just as you asked, boss. We've cast the net far and wide. We've people keepin' their eyes and ears peeled all around

Belfast, including the outlying districts such as Bangor and Holywood.'

'What about Antrim?'

'You want us to check Antrim?'

'Why not? Sure he may not be in Belfast. Logic says that he'd have bolted from the city to avoid bein' recognized, either by us or by his own friends.'

'Aye, right,' Kavanagh said while driving along Divis Street on the short approach to the Falls Road. 'We took that into consideration. But we don't think, assuming he's out to get you, that he'll hide out much farther away than Bangor or Holywood.'

'That's not necessarily true. I mean, we're talkin' about a former SAS man who was known to be brilliant at covert operations that required him to be alone in OPs, sometimes for weeks on end. We're also talkin' about a man who did a lot of surveillance work outside the city, in Antrim and in South Armagh. So while I don't think he'd profit from goin' as far away as Armagh, I'm pretty sure he might find it real cosy, like, to find himself a nice wee hide just outside the city.'

'Like in Antrim,' Connolly said.

'Aye, right. In Antrim. Travelling into Belfast as much as he likes on that fancy motorbike that he used the night he shot up the Hibernian and those two useless arseholes we had guarding the place. On that motorbike, he could get from Antrim to Belfast in twenty minutes or half an hour, so hiding somewhere out there would make sense to me.'

'Not so easy to do a search of Antrim,' Kavanagh said while driving up the lower end of the Falls Road, which was as lively as always, though looking rather grim in the early afternoon's grey light. 'Antrim City, yes, but to cover the countryside would be difficult.'

'Difficult, but not impossible,' Houlihan insisted. 'Sure your scouts can ask around. Start with Antrim City, then move outwards in all directions, takin' in the villages and small towns, askin' if anyone has seen a stranger comin' and goin' – buyin' groceries and petrol and the like – and mentionin' that he has a motorbike: a Yamaha 400 with silver tanks. If you cast a net far and wide enough, you're bound to catch something in it. Sooner or later, someone's bound to come up with somethin' that will lead us to where that bastard's hidin'.'

'Okay, boss,' Connolly said. 'We'll do that. We'll start on it immediately.'

'Good,' Houlihan said.

He was trying to sound and look calm, but beneath the surface he was still simmering with rage over Katherine Crowley's humiliating rejection of him. With the rage came the barely suppressed violence, the frustration and the urge to vent it, so by the time the car was parked at the kerb outside the pub, he was in an absolutely foul mood.

The bodyguard beside him clambered out first and respectfully held the rear door open for him. Lucky for him that he did, because had he failed to do so, Houlihan would have vented his frustrations upon him.

Glancing at the pub, Houlihan saw that the bodyguards he'd sent on ahead were already in position. One lounged on each side of the door, both trying to look as unobtrusive as possible, as if they were just waiting for a friend to arrive. The other bodyguard had taken up a watch position on the far side of the street, from where he could see if any of the traffic (such as, say, a motorcyclist) was doing anything unusual and from where, also, he could give covering fire, if required, for the men on guard outside the pub. As Houlihan watched, he saw the bodyguard who'd come with him, Kavanagh and Connolly saunter across the street to join his traffic-watching colleague.

Satisfied, Houlihan was about to enter the pub with Kavanagh and Connolly when he saw a familiar face that froze him where he was standing.

It was the young guard from the jail – the one who had unlocked Houlihan's handcuffs and escorted him to the warden just before his release – now wearing civilian clothing and clearly out shopping with his wife and two children.

The wife was a pretty young thing, in her mid-twenties, with bubbly black hair and a sweet-natured face; the children were a boy and a girl, about seven and eight years old respectively. They were standing together, the mother holding the hand of the boy, the young guard holding the hand of his daughter, in front of a furniture shop only two doors up from the pub. The young prison guard was talking to his wife while pointing at the window.

Though the young prison guard had always treated Houlihan decently, he *was* a guard nonetheless, one of Houlihan's former screws, and Houlihan had to loathe him for it. Remembering the promise, or threat, that he had made to the young guard just before walking out of the prison, and also seeing an excellent opportunity for venting his frustrations and violent rage over Katherine Crowley's rejection of him, Houlihan remained where he was standing and waited until the guard and his family had turned away from the shop front and were coming towards him. Then he stepped in front of them, blocking their way.

When the young prison guard recognized Houlihan, he turned visibly pale.

'You wee shit,' Houlihan said, oblivious to the guard's sweet-faced wife and the two small children. 'I made a fuckin' promise to you, ya bastard, and now I'm goin' to keep it.'

'Please!' the young guard responded, glancing sideways at his wife, then down at his two children, before looking back at Houlihan with wide, pleading eyes. 'Don't be starting anything now. For God's sake, not in front of my wife and kids.'

'All the better,' Houlihan responded. 'Let them see the kind of weak piss you are.'

'At least let them walk on,' the young guard said. 'Don't force them to—'

But he didn't get to finish the sentence. Houlihan reached out to grab him by the shoulders, then brutally butted him in the face with his forehead, instantly breaking the cartilage in his nose.

The woman screamed when she saw the blood pouring down her husband's stricken face.

'For God's sake—' the young guard managed to say. But again he was cut short, this time when Houlihan kneed him in the groin, butted him in the face again, further mangling the broken nose, then flung him violently sideways into the wall.

'Ack, Jesus!' the young woman exclaimed, shocked and disbelieving, before grabbing the hand of her daughter as well and pulling both children a few yards away. 'Help!' she screamed as Houlihan started battering her husband with his big ham fists. 'Someone please help us!'

Instantly, Kavanagh walked up to her and shoved his face into hers, glaring at her, practically spitting as he talked. 'No one's going to help your husband here. No one's going to talk to the police about what they've seen here. You understand, you dumb cunt? Get the fuck out of here and don't talk to anyone about this or you and your kids will be getting the kind of visit you won't forget in a long time. Now get out of here and take your fucking kids if you don't want them shat on.' Then he bawled, 'GO!'

The children burst into tears.

Galvanized by fear, the woman threw one last despairing glance to where her husband was being beaten up, practically hammered back into the wall. Then she tightened her grip on the hands of her children and hurried off, sobbing uncontrollably, along the pavement.

'Take that, you fucking cunt!' Houlihan was gasping as he hammered his fists into the blood-smeared, grunting young bodyguard. 'And that, you cunt! And that!' Hammer, hammer against the wall as the pedestrians hurried by, most recognizing Houlihan and so pretending not to see, not wanting to be involved, not even when the young guard slid down to the pavement, spitting blood and vomiting, and Houlihan started to lay his boot into him, first kicking his shins to make him cry out with pain, then kicking him sideways until he was stretched out on the paving stones, when he kicked him repeatedly in the side, breaking some of his ribs. Then, carried away by his own violence, swept up in an almost homicidal excitement, Houlihan kicked the young guard on the side of the head and was about to stamp on him, wanting to crush his skull, when Kavanagh grabbed him by the shoulder and jerked him away.

'No, boss!' Kavanagh said. 'That's enough! For God's sake, don't kill him. Sure you've done enough, boss. Let's get inside that pub before some fucker tells the cops.'

Houlihan nearly took a swing at Kavanagh, enraged at his interference. But then he realized that his lieutenant was right, that a beating was one thing, a killing another, particularly when it came to witnesses. So he nodded agreement, then dropped to one knee beside his bloody and battered victim, who would never look handsome again, nose broken, teeth missing.

'You listen to me,' Houlihan said, grabbing the young guard by the shoulder and jerking him into a slumped sitting position. 'If the police come – though I doubt that anyone around here's going to call them – you tell them you don't know who attacked you. I know where you live – you're in the phone book, you dumb cunt – and if the police find out about this I'll assume that you told them, so I'll have my men pay a little visit to your wife and kids. That would be a day you'd never forget, so you'd better not bring it on yourself. Now crawl home as best you can – I'd recommend a taxi driver who doesn't mind bloodstains – and don't ever let me see your face again. You got that?'

The badly bruised and bloody young man nodded, unable to speak through his split, swollen lips.

'Good,' Houlihan said. He threw the young man to the side, letting him flop face down onto the pavement, then stood up to let Kavanagh and Connolly lead him into the pub.

He had vented his frustrations over Katherine Crowley and he felt a lot better.

Steve Lawson would be next.

Chapter Fifteen

When Steve walked into the bar of Cutter's Wharf the next time, he knew that with his beard, moustache and longer hair, he was barely recognizable. This was confirmed when his old RUC friend, Joe Williamson, seated at an indoors table because the weather had turned cold, heralding the approach of winter, certainly didn't know who Steve was until the ex-SAS man, having crossed the stone-flagged floor, stopped at his table.

'Aren't you speaking to your old friends these days?' Steve asked.

'Pardon? Who—' Joe looked up in surprise and wrinkled his forehead in perplexity. Then, eventually recognizing Steve, he broke out in a grin. 'Ah,' he said. 'Very good! You should win an Oscar.'

'You keep saying that,' Steve said, 'but you still haven't personally recommended me out there in Hollywood.' He glanced down at the table and saw that Joe, having arrived early as usual, had set him up with a pint of Guinness again. 'You're a good man, Joe.'

'Too good for you,' Joe said.

After placing his crash helmet on the table beside his pint of Guinness, Steve took the chair facing Joe. He glanced automatically at the ceiling, looking for the bare wooden beams that used to be there and finding only a magnolia-painted plain ceiling.

'What happened to my beloved wooden beams?' he asked.

'An arsonist,' Joe said. 'Someone set fire to the building and the beams were a godsend to the pyromaniac. When they had to be replaced, it was thought wise to have a plain plastered ceiling just in case the culprit, smelling new wood, decided to return for a replay.'

'Sectarian?' Steve asked.

'Unlikely. No side took credit for it and even the RUC were convinced that it was the work of a private individual, perhaps one with a grudge against the pub. But that's one of the problems with living in Belfast, isn't it? Every accident – every gas explosion or fire set off by, say, a faulty electrical cable – is initially viewed as the work of a terrorist gang. We haven't got over that fear yet.'

'No,' Steve said. 'I guess not.'

He glanced at the people seated about him (thankfully, not too many and most of them out of earshot), then returned his attention to his friend, lifting his glass.

'Cheers,' Joe said.

'Cheers.'

They tilted their pint glasses towards each other in a mock toast, took a swallow of their Guinness, then placed their glasses back on the table.

'You look like one of those nineteen-seventies hippies,' Joe said. 'Like one of those freaks from Haight-Ashbury.'

'What would you know about Haight-Ashbury?' Steve said. 'That was before even *my* time – and I'm younger than you.'

'I know it was in California,' Joe said. 'San Francisco, as I recall. And I know the hippies looked like you do now. Still, I wouldn't have recognized you, so you did the right thing. Someone would have to be pretty close to you and know you well to recognize you now. I take it that the new look is to help you get in and out of Belfast in general – and the Falls in particular – without being identified.'

'Right,' Steve said. 'I'm pretty damned sure that after last week's little incident—'

'The shoot-up at the Hibernian pub?'

'Correct.'

'I assumed that was you.'

'What a bright man you are. So after that minor event, I'm sure that Houlihan will have targeted me for a far-and-wide search, with some of his people even watching the roads into Belfast and others being given my description and asked if they've seen me. So the change in my appearance was vital.'

'What about your motorbike?' Joe asked. 'They're bound to be on the lookout for a Yamaha 400 with silver tanks – and a machine like that isn't likely to be forgotten by those who see it. Particularly out in somewhere like Antrim, where it would be a pretty rare kind of vehicle.'

'You really *are* a bright man,' Steve told him. 'Trust you to think of that – you and me.'

'So you've changed it already?'

'Yep. For a Suzuki GSXR 750 sports bike, painted stark black and with no silver tanks, thanks.'

'Fast?'

'A real monster. The speedometer goes up to four hundred kilometres an hour. It climbs hills as if they don't exist, so nothing in Antrim or Belfast is going to bother it.'

'More importantly, it's not what Houlihan's men will be looking for.'

'Exactly,' Steve said. 'Also, I change my route each time I venture into the city and I avoid a set routine to make life more difficult for his search teams.'

'Excellent,' Joe said. 'Your SAS training stands you in good stead.'

Steve glanced around the bar again, noting again that it wasn't all that crowded (though these were early hours yet) and that the majority of the clientele were young business types wearing expensive clothes and with cellular phones resting between them on the tables. Convinced, therefore, that none of them were working for Houlihan, he turned back to Joe. 'So what did you think of that shoot-up outside the Hibernian?'

'Very impressive,' Joe said. 'The Wild West in Belfast. If that night rider had had a horse instead of a motorbike, I'd have thought he was John Wayne.'

'Very funny,' Steve said. 'But that night rider, whoever he was—'

'And I don't want to know.'

'Of course not. That night rider at least did a decent job of causing Houlihan aggro. Would you not agree to that, at least?'

'Yes, I would,' Joe acknowledged. 'The choice of target was particularly apt. For years – indeed as far back as World War Two – the Hibernian was revered as an IRA, later PIRA, hang-out where some of the movement's most notorious operations were planned. That reputation lived on into the present peace, despite the fact that the paramilitaries still meeting there were involved in organized crime rather than in politics. So shooting the place up was certainly a very clever move, propaganda-wise, on the part of the mysterious night rider.'

'I'm pleased to hear you say that,' Steve said, grinning again. 'Not that I'd anything to do with it, you understand, but I can still admire that kind of operation. It reminded me of my days with the SAS Mobility Troop. It was the kind of thing I used to imagine doing, though I never got the chance.'

'Mmmm,' Joe said. 'I see.' He took another swallow of his Guinness, put the glass back on the table, lit a cigarette and spoke while exhaling a stream of smoke. 'So what did you want to see me for this time?'

In saying this, he was admitting that he knew that Steve was the night rider, but was still willing at least to consider what he had to say. In truth, he was going out on a limb for Steve, but if the branch shook too much he might have to back off.

'That shoot-up, which might have seemed daring,' Steve said, 'was actually an act of desperation, undertaken because I had no explosives and no weapon other than the one I used – the Nine-Milly, of course.'

'I'd already sussed that,' Joe said. 'So what is it you want? More weapons?'

'Yes.'

'And explosives?'

'Yes.'

'What I got you the last time was all I could get you – and God knows, it was little enough – but this is peacetime Belfast and weapons control is now much more stringent. A Nine-Milly is relatively easy – a lot of old friends still have theirs, which is where I got yours – from an old friend, I mean – but anything more ambitious than that would be extremely difficult, if not impossible, to obtain. I can't go to old police friends, I promise you, and the British Army is out of the question.'

'I don't need anything big. I can't carry that much in the saddlebags of my motorbike. In fact, it's mainly explosives I need, with perhaps a sub-machine gun that can be broken down into its component parts and placed in a saddle bag. Plus, of course, a good supply of ammunition.'

'That's still too much for me. I simply can't help you with that kind of stuff.'

'So where do I go? Who do I approach? If you can't help, just give me a name. Stay out of it and I'll do all the rest. I just need a jump-start.'

Joe sighed. 'I still can't help you. I can't even give you a name. The police and the army are both hamstrung now. Given the peace and the pressure to pacify all sides, including the former terrorists, they have problems in even arming themselves.

The security around weapons distribution is incredibly tight, believe me, and I haven't got a friend in the province who could help you to get some.'

'So I'm fucked.'

'I didn't say that. I simply said that I didn't have a friend who could personally help you.'

Steve thought about this, wondering what Joe was getting at. Then he had a sip of his Guinness, wiped his lips with the back of his hand, and said, 'Are you trying to tell me that weapons *are* available, but that I'm the only one who can get them?'

Joe smiled and nodded. 'Exactly.'

'So don't tease me. Where are they?'

'In the arms dumps kept secretly by the paramilitaries of both sides after the so-called decommissioning.'

'"So-called" because the paramilitaries on both sides treated the decommissioning as a joke. They only paid lip service to it to keep the politicians happy.'

'Very good,' Joe said.

'So where are the arms dumps?'

'I don't know where all of them are — no one does — but I know where *some* of them are. I know because the men who hid the weapons were the paramilitaries who were into organized crime — men like Houlihan.'

'So?'

'So most of the arms dumps controlled by men like Houlihan are right here in the city — in bricked-up houses or warehouses out in industrial estates — and I happen to know where at least one of Houlihan's arms dumps is located.'

'Jesus Christ!' Steve exclaimed.

Joe smiled, amused by Steve's look of amazement. 'Now, as you surely must know, Steve, any police or army dump is bound to be under tight security.'

'Right. You'd need an army to fight your way into them.'

'Quite. But since the political peace, no one has dared even to question the paramilitaries about any weapons not included in the decommissioning – it would be viewed as politically insensitive, if you get my meaning.'

'I do,' Steve said.

'Good. So the arms dumps of the paramilitaries, particularly in Belfast and its surrounds, are kept just like any other commercial product: with the kind of routine security that most straightforward commercial companies use. What I'm saying, in effect, is that none of the crime barons in this city – say, Houlihan and his Prod pal, Wild Bill Moore – have felt the need to place their arms dumps under any special kind of security because they know that in the present political climate, neither the police nor the army are going to risk being embarrassed by bothering them. The peace is all. The peace is sacred.'

'So I can mount a raid against one of Houlihan's arms dumps – the one you're going to direct me to – without facing anything like police or army security.'

'You've got it,' Joe said.

'No bodyguards?'

'No.'

'Burglar alarms?'

'Yes – but routine.'

'Can I silence them?'

'Yes ...' Joe reached into his pocket and pulled out a small rectangular metal case, which he slid across the table to Steve. 'This is something I picked up from an old friend who's working on advanced surveillance and security systems in the experimental laboratories of the British Army's Northern Ireland HQ in Lisburn. It's brand new. Open it.'

Steve opened the box and saw that it contained what looked like a black-plastic rechargeable battery with two small bulbs in the top. He was going to pick it out of the box to examine it when Joe, after glancing nervously about him, said, 'Don't take it out; you can examine it later.'

Instead of removing the device from its carrying case, Steve closed the lid, then returned his gaze to his friend, raising his eyebrows inquiringly.

'It's part of a range of brand new experimental devices to be used for everything from long-distance surveillance to the blocking of radar and other electronic signals.'

'Including those used in modern burglar alarms and video surveillance systems.'

'Correct.'

'Beautiful,' Steve said. 'I could kiss you. So how do I use it?'

'The instructions are childishly simple and they're tucked under the blocking device, though I suspect you won't even need them.'

'Probably not,' Steve said cockily.

'Basically, there's an on/off switch on one side of the blocking device. You simply switch it on and a red light will then start blinking. You peel the protective covering off the magnetized metal base, then attach the device to the metal box of the burglar-alarm system. When the red light goes off and a green light comes on instead, you can take it that the device is working, neutralizing the security system without actually causing it to go off.'

'Sounds like a piece of piss,' Steve said.

'A piece of cake,' Joe confirmed in his more polite way. 'So did you come here on your brand new Suzuki?'

'I sure did.'

'It's out in the parking lot?'

'Yep.'

'Then go for it. Do the job this evening. Because you can only do it once. When you do it, Houlihan will guess that you're responsible and he'll ensure that you can't do it a second time. Do it now, this evening, before Houlihan even considers that you might try it. Get the weapons and the explosives that you need, leave your calling card just to torment him, then disappear again until you're ready to actually go out and tackle him.'

'I will, believe me. So where's his arms dump located?'

Joe pulled out his wallet and withdrew a business card, which he handed to Steve. 'Keep it for your souvenirs,' he said.

The card was for a Mr Aidan Shanahan, director of the Milltown Computer Centre in the Kennedy Way Industrial Estate. 'That's the legitimate business,' Joe explained, 'and you will, indeed, find the main showroom filled with computers, printers, scanners, software and the like. However, the warehouse in the rear is where they store the arms and explosives.'

'Where's the Kennedy Industrial Estate?' Steve asked. 'The name's familiar, but I can't place it right now.'

'It's located midway between the M1 Motorway and the Falls Road, just south of the traditional IRA burial ground in the Milltown Cemetery.'

'Ah, yes,' Steve said. '*Now* I remember! That industrial estate used to be a shit-hole, but it's grown a lot over the past few years.'

'EU money,' Joe explained. 'It's transformed the face of Belfast and helped an awful lot of people.'

'Unfortunately, the wrong people too often.'

Joe sighed. 'That's true enough.'

'So what's the estate like in the evenings?'

'Perfect for your purposes. Dead as a doornail. Most of the businesses close up some time between five-thirty and seven, so if you go out there any time after darkness has fallen, you won't see too many people around.'

'Great,' Steve said, then checked his wristwatch. It was now just after eight in the evening. Glancing through one of the windows of the bar, he saw that the light had dimmed, casting the trees along the river bank into deep shadow. 'Well, I'd best be making tracks,' he said to Joe. 'I'm looking forward to doing this.'

Joe nodded his understanding, then polished off his pint of Guinness. 'I'll leave first,' he said. 'It'll be another half an hour or so before the sun goes down, so you're in no great hurry. You're just being impatient.'

'Yes, I guess so.'

'You really love this, don't you?'

'What?'

'The life-and-death game. The flirtation with danger. The excitement of the hunt before the kill. Yes, maybe even the kill itself ... I think you like all of it.'

'I'm not sure what you mean,' Steve replied, though he felt a little uncomfortable. 'Yes, I certainly like the danger, but so do mountain climbers. Yes, I like the excitement of the chase, but that's not so unusual – certainly not in the kind of men who're drawn to a regiment like the SAS. But enjoying the kill ... Is that what you're suggesting? No, I'm not so sure of that. I wouldn't say that I actually *enjoyed* it. That's not what I'm in this for.'

'You're in this to save your own life – it's either kill or be killed. But I still say that making the kill gives you a thrill.'

'You make me sound like a serial killer,' Steve said, attempting levity, though he still felt uncomfortable with the drift of the conversation. 'I don't think I'm that type. The kill is simply the end of the chase and generally unavoidable. For me, the excitement is in the chase. That's why I joined the SAS.'

'So what do men like you do when you can't get into a regiment like the SAS? Or when you've been in the Regiment, enjoyed it, then had to leave it. Become criminals, like a lot of former terrorists?'

'Well,' Steve admitted uneasily, 'a lot of SAS men have certainly done just that after leaving the Regiment.'

'Why?'

'A low boredom threshold. They simply can't stand living a normal life, the boredom of the familiar, the restrictions of acceptable social behaviour. So rather than go crazy with boredom, they turn to crime for excitement.'

'Are you that sort, Steve?'

Steve thought about it and didn't like what he was thinking. 'Yes,' he confessed, 'I might be that sort. Why? Would that make me despicable?'

'No, not despicable,' Joe said. 'Just interesting. It might mean that you're not all that different from the men you're pursuing.'

'Men like Houlihan and Wild Bill Moore?'

'That's right,' Joe said with a smile. 'The dividing line must be thin.'

'Fuck you, Joe. Get on home now.'

But Joe merely smiled even more broadly and pushed his chair back to stand upright. 'Ah, well,' he said, 'who knows? Ours not to reason why; ours to—'

'Do or die. Well, that's what I'll do, whether or not it's in my nature. Thanks for your help, Joe.'

'My pleasure,' Joe said. 'Take care of yourself. Travel with care.'

'I will,' Steve promised.

He sat on for twenty minutes after Joe had left the bar, finishing off his pint, thinking of what Joe had said, and realizing that it was too close to the bone for comfort. Determined to forget it, to get on with the job instead, he drank the last of his Guinness, placed his crash helmet on his head, then picked up the small metal carrying case and walked out of the bar, into the gathering darkness of the evening.

His Suzuki GSXR 750 sports bike had been parked in Lockview Road and when he reached it he opened one of the saddlebags, placed the small metal case into it, then zipped it up again before slinging his leg over the saddle. After starting the bike, which roared dramatically into life, he turned into the Stranmillis Road and made his way back to the centre of town by way of the university area, turning left at Shaftesbury Square to take the Donegall Road.

Passing the many terraced streets that ran off the main road, Steve recalled how, during the days of the Troubles, this whole area had been a hardline Loyalist enclave ruled by intimidation and violence, with many unfortunates tortured and murdered in the 'rumpus rooms' of the grim, windowless social clubs. As an undercover operative for 14th Int, he'd had to work those mean streets, in serious danger every minute of every day, so he had known just how vicious they were. Those days were long gone, of course, and the area was being modernized, but Steve still felt his stomach muscles contracting slightly as he drove past that familiar terrain.

At the end of the Donegall Road, Steve turned along the Falls Road, heading south. To his right, beyond a line of chestnut trees, the tombstones of the City Cemetery flowed upwards, one row after the other, in gentle, undulating waves of uncut grass, to the base of the looming Black Mountain. Also on his right, he saw the darkening playing fields and the bowling green of the sprawling Falls Park. Mere seconds later, he passed the entrance of the venerated Milltown Cemetery, where the hunger strikers and other IRA heroes were buried; and, almost directly facing it, almost insultingly positioned, was the military-styled RUC Andersonstown police station, protected by high walls topped with barbed wire.

Steve kept going until he reached the next roundabout.

After going straight through the roundabout, he turned left into the Blackstaff Road. This eventually led him into the Kennedy Way Industrial Estate.

Like most industrial estates, it was a formerly shabby, recently modernized, sprawling collection of warehouses, storerooms and showrooms, some built of red brick, others prefabricated, all linked by a web of linear roads and roundabouts, though thankfully illuminated with overhead lights that burned throughout the night, just like the street lamps. Following the route shown on the back of the business card given to him by Joe Williamson, Steve rode around until he came to a building that had a sign along its front identifying it as the Milltown Computer Centre. A relatively new building, it was built in red brick and had large plate-glass windows along the front, overlooking smooth, gently sloping, well-tended lawns. A large annexe wing thrust out of the rear of the building, running parallel to the narrow road that ran up its eastern side.

Stopping temporarily in front of the building, Steve saw the steel box of an alarm system protruding from the wall above the main doors. Assuming that there would be a similar set-up at the side or rear entrance of the same building, he gunned the engine of the Suzuki and headed up the narrow side road. About halfway along the side of the main building, the showroom, he saw a side entrance, with a door that looked just like the door of an average house, though the steel box of another burglar alarm could be dimly made out about fifteen feet above it, making it roughly twenty feet above the ground. Steve drove on past it until he could turn around the rear of the eastern wing, which he assumed was where the weapons and explosives were kept. There was no entrance there: only a solid brick wall. Seeing that he could not enter directly into the arms dump via the rear of the building, he went back to the side door, turned off the engine of the Suzuki, and wheeled it across the road to park it against the wall of the building there.

Hidden in the darkness, Steve opened one of the saddlebags and withdrew the blocking device. He also withdrew his old SAS abseiling rope, which he had kept when he left the Regiment and later used for the scaling of trees, just to keep his hand in, during his many motorbike trips into the Irish countryside. He then went back across the road, crossed the lawns at the side of the Milltown Computer Centre showroom and stopped by the side entrance.

The small metal container for the electronic blocking device had a belt clip at one end so Steve clipped it to his belt. Thus unencumbered, he was able to unravel the abseiling rope and hurl it expertly upwards, two or three times, as he had been trained to do with the Mountain Troop of 22 SAS, until it had snaked across the flat roof the building, with its four-pronged grappling hook digging into the channel of the black-painted metal guttering that ran along the top of the wall. He tugged on the rope three or four times, each time more sharply than the last, to ensure that the grappling hook had taken a firm hold and, just as importantly, to check that the guttering would actually take the strain, which it appeared to be doing.

Satisfied, he secured the clip at the free end of the rope to the ring on his belt, took a few steps away from the wall, then swung his legs upwards until his feet were planted against the bricks. When the rope went taut, the guttering above remained in place. After deliberately kicking himself away from the wall a couple of times and swinging back to plant his feet against it, he was satisfied that the guttering would hold his weight. So he began his slow ascent, scaling the wall instead of abseiling down it, which was what the rope was normally used for.

Moving slowly and carefully, aware that his weight might still tear the guttering away from its moorings, he made his way up until he was level with the metal box containing the burglar-alarm system, about fifteen feet above the side entrance. Once there, he rested by planting his feet against the wall and pushing himself out until his legs were stretched to their full length and the abseiling rope was absolutely taut. This allowed him to let go of the rope and use both hands to unclip the blocking device from his belt, remove the device itself from its metal case, then once more clip the case to his belt to prevent it from falling to the ground and making a noise. He then removed the protective covering from the magnetized base of the blocking device and attached the device to the metal box containing the burglar alarms and video surveillance systems.

He flicked the on/off switch and a red light came on, blinking rapidly for about ten seconds. When the red light blinked out and the green light came on, he knew that the device was operating and that the security systems had been neutralized without setting off the alarms. Satisfied, he lowered himself back to the ground, leaving the rope to dangle where it was, hidden by the darkness.

He was now ready to enter the building.

Luckily, because of the high-tech security systems, the owners of the building had not felt it necessary to have anything other than a normal lock on the side entrance – a variation of the Yale lock common to most households. Steve was therefore able to use his all-purpose police key, one with adjustable edges, to find the setting that would fit precisely into the lock and open it. After a few minutes of patient experimentation, trying one edge after another, he was able to open the door and slip into the building.

When his eyes adjusted to the gloom, which was dimly illuminated by the light of the street lamps beaming in through the plate-glass windows, he saw that he was indeed in an immense showroom filled with computer hardware and software. Glancing to his left, in the direction of the eastern wing, or rear annexe, he saw, in the otherwise solid brick wall, a door similar to the one he had just opened. On his way to that door, he picked up two of the store's large plastic shopping bags. Once at the door, he opened it, using the same all-purpose police key, and then let himself into the rear annexe.

It was packed with weapons and explosives.

Knowing just what he wanted, Steve moved quickly around the warehouse, filling one of the plastic shopping bags with small blocks of Semtex explosive, electric initiators, clockwork timers, blasting caps, bridge wire and half a dozen Haley & Weller incendiary and fragmentation grenades. From the vast array of weapons available, he could have chosen the most up-to-date; instead, he opted for a good old-fashioned

Mk2 9mm Sten gun, if only because it could be quickly broken down into three sections (barrel, magazine and butt) and hidden in one of his saddlebags. Having chosen it for this reason, he instantly separated the three parts and placed them in the second plastic shopping bag. He then filled the bag with as many thirty-two-round box magazines as it could safely hold and placed both bags near the door that led back into the showroom.

Now he wanted to leave his calling card.

Being surrounded by all that he needed, he quickly made a crude bomb out of a small block of Semtex plastic explosive, an electric initiator, a blasting cap with bridge wire and a clockwork timer not much bigger than a wristwatch. He placed this simple bomb beside a huge pile of Semtex blocks and set the timer for fifteen minutes from now.

This was his calling card.

Picking up the two plastic bags, he left the rear annexe, made his way back through the vast showroom and left the building by the side door, closing the door carefully behind him but leaving it unlocked. He then crossed the road to his motorbike, which was still parked in the pitch darkness by the side wall of the opposite building. Once there, he put the two shopping bags into his saddlebags, one in each, then started the motorbike and began the ride out of the industrial estate. He was just entering the Blackstaff Road when his bomb exploded.

The first explosion set off another, even louder blast (the huge pile of Semtex blocks going up) that was followed by another series of explosions, one piled on top of the other, each one setting off another one, until the noise of the detonations sounded apocalyptic.

Steve didn't stop. But he glanced back over his shoulder just long enough to see an immense, jagged fan of silvery-white light spreading across the centre of the industrial estate, directly over where the Milltown Computer Centre had been, with yellow flames licking through it like giant phosphorescent fingers and coils of smoke spiralling out in all directions to form a billowing black cloud.

Exultant, Steve looked to the front again, gunned the engine of his powerful Suzuki motorbike and roared into the Falls Road to begin the journey back to Antrim.

Chapter Sixteen

Seated at a table in a private room in the pub that he had chosen as his new HQ, facing Kavanagh and Connolly, both wreathed in clouds of cigarette smoke and drinking neat whiskies, Houlihan was almost blind with rage.

'For fuck's sake!' he exploded. 'This time the bastard found one of our arms dumps and blew the whole fuckin' place to Kingdom Come. The police forensic boyos are crawlin' all over the debris to learn about our weapons and explosives. So now the cops are questioning Aidan Shanahan about the shit he kept there and that means, Jesus Christ, that sooner or later, even if he doesn't crack, they're gonna find out that I have a share in the business – and *that* means I'll be fucked.'

'Ring Jack Parnell instantly,' Kavanagh said. 'Get him on your case without delay. I'm sure he'll give sound advice.'

'Parnell's already been on to me,' Houlihan said, 'sayin' that I'm to get over to his office right away for a talk. We know what he's gonna talk about, don't we? That fuckin' bombed warehouse and the legal repercussions. Jasus! What I don't need right now is Parnell's highfalutin' legal shite. What I want is a way to find that fucker Steve Lawson, who was clearly responsible, and put his lights out before he does any more damage. What I want is to find out how he *knew* that we were storing weapons and explosives in the back of the fucking computer showroom. I mean, who the fuck *told* him?'

'Could have been anyone,' Connolly said unhelpfully.

'Oh, fuckin' great, thanks, that's all I fuckin' need to hear, you dumb bastard. Let's go out with a fuckin' megaphone and hail the whole fuckin' city and say, "Hands up, who done it?" If you can think of anything brighter, I'm all ears, you fuckin' wee lunatic.'

'Sorry, boss,' Connolly said, turning pale because he had seen what Houlihan could do to people when they upset him to the point where he lost control. 'I only meant—'

'That we narrow it down,' Kavanagh said helpfully. 'Like, who would be in a position to know about where our weapons are hidden?'

'What does that mean?' Houlihan asked, mindful that Kavanagh was considerably brighter than Connolly.

'Policemen, former or still serving army personnel, former paramilitaries or even one of our own men.'

'That's a pretty broad spectrum,' Houlihan said. 'An awful lot to consider.'

'Well ...'

'The thing is to track down that fucker Lawson and haul him out of his lair. We've got to find him and put him six feet under before he does us any more damage.'

'Right,' Connolly said. 'Now we know for sure that he's out there, prowling around the city. At least, he hasn't left the country, like.'

'So why the fuck can't we find him?' Houlihan wanted to know. 'I mean, we've got spies out all over the place, asking questions about a silver-tanked Yamaha 400 motorbike – not common hereabouts, I can assure you – and so far no one's come up with a thing. What is this? The fuckin' silver-tanked monster is invisible, or what?'

'As a matter of fact, boss,' Kavanagh said, 'I was just goin' to talk to you about that.'

'You were, were you?'

'Yes, boss.'

'So what were you gonna tell me?'

'One of the people living locally and employed on that estate worked late that evenin'. He was walkin' home along the Blackstaff Road – the road that leads into the industrial estate – just as the bomb went off and he saw a helmeted man burning out of the place on a Suzuki motorbike. He said the man definitely glanced back over his shoulder when the bomb exploded, though he then took off in a hurry.'

'A Suzuki?'

'Yes, boss. That's the point I'm making. I think the guy who burned out of there just as the bomb went off could have been the guy who planted it and I think, since he was on a motorbike, that he had to've been Steve Lawson. The reason, then, that we haven't so far received a report of a man on a Yamaha 400 with a silver tank is that Lawson, the smart cunt, almost certainly changed it for a Suzuki shortly after fleeing from Belfast. So we've been looking for the wrong kind of motorbike.'

'Fuck!' Houlihan said.

'A black Suzuki,' Kavanagh said, clarifying the matter. 'The witness didn't know what kind, but he said that it was black and it was *big*. So that's what we have to start looking for.'

'Instantly,' Houlihan said. 'Like today. Put the word out as soon as we leave this pub.'

'Will do, boss.'

'So now we know he's driving a black Suzuki instead of a silver-tanked Yamaha and we also know that to find our arms dump he had to have had contact with some fucker who has inside information. As you said, a former cop, a soldier or one of our own. So how do we narrow it down without taking the next fuckin' decade to do it?'

'Why not narrow it down,' Connolly said tentatively, having already come close to enraging Houlihan and not wanting to do it twice, 'to the people that he'd have had contact with when working for the 14th Intelligence Group?'

'What?' Houlihan retorted in disgust. 'You mean half of fucking Loyalist Belfast?'

'No, boss,' Connolly insisted, removing a handkerchief from his pocket and wiping beads of sweat from his forehead. 'Most of the people that Lawson worked with all those years ago were with the British Army – SAS or the 14th Int – and they were sent back to the mainland after peace was declared, so only a few of his original contacts would still be here. That means former members of the old RUC or, perhaps, someone from the British Army's HQ out there in Lisburn.'

'Yes,' Kavanagh added. 'Some of those fuckers would certainly know the whereabouts of our city-based arms dumps. So far, they've only kept their traps shut because of the politics. They don't want to cause offence, like.'

'Aye, it's the same with the cops,' Houlihan said. 'Sure a lot of those fuckers know where we hide our weapons; they just can't speak out because of the peace, like.'

'Aye, right,' Kavanagh said. 'So, yeah, I'd go for a source in the British Army.'

'Or in the Police Service of Northern Ireland,' Connolly said.

'Or a former member of the old RUC,' Houlihan said. 'A lot of those fuckers would certainly squawk if they thought it would do us damage.'

'So we can narrow it down to someone who was in the army and had strong connections with the police or someone who was in the police and had a line back to the army.'

'Right,' Kavanagh said.

'That's it,' Houlihan said, starting to feel a bit more positive. 'A two-way street. Narrow it down to one of those fuckers – either in the army or in the old RUC – and we'll have a good chance of finding our man. Get onto it, lads.'

'Will do,' Connolly said, dabbing at his forehead with a

handkerchief to remove the last drops of sweat, letting his racing heart settle down. 'The minute I walk out of here, I'll get onto it.'

'You'd better,' Houlihan said threateningly, making Connolly instantly start sweating again. 'Anyway, lads,' he added, slapping the calloused palms of his big hands on the wooden table, making it visibly rock and audibly squeak, 'get your arses out there and start finding that fucker Lawson, as well as the bastard who led him to our warehouse. Meanwhile, like I said, I've received a call from Jack Parnell, who sounded agitated, so I'd best be off to see him now. Any questions, lads?'

'No, boss.'

'No, boss.'

'Right, see youse later. I'll leave first, just to be sure. No need to make a target of the three of us, right?' And Houlihan grinned crookedly, fearlessly, as he pushed his chair back, stood up and left the private room, which was, in this pub, on the ground floor. Walking straight through the busy, smoky bar and stepping outside, he found his bodyguards waiting, one on each side of the entrance. His Volvo V70 XC was parked by the kerb, with a third hood seated behind the steering wheel. Houlihan took the front seat beside the driver, his two minders slipped into the rear seats, and the car then moved smoothly out into the dense traffic of the Falls Road, heading downhill towards Divis Street.

As Castle Street, where Parnell's office was located, was an extension of Divis Street, they were there in a matter of minutes. After telling his minders to keep the door of Parnell's office covered, Houlihan took a deep breath, feeling unusually nervous, and walked into the building.

He entered via the grey-haired old bag's reception area and was disappointed not to find Katherine Crowley waiting for him. He was even more disappointed when the old bag, trying to get Ms Crowley on the intercom, failed to do so and had to call directly through to her boss, Jack Parnell, who told her to lead the visitor directly into his office. Entering that office, Houlihan was further discomfited to find the exquisite Ms Crowley seated on the chair beside her boss, long legs crossed, letting him have a good look but staring impassively at him, not the slightest trace of that enigmatic, catlike smile.

Fucking bitch, Houlihan thought bitterly.

'Hi,' he said, by way of greeting, unable to think of anything else, sensing bad vibes in the atmosphere. 'You wanted to see me, right?'

'Yes,' Parnell said. 'Please take a seat.'

Houlihan took a seat. No one offered him a drink. 'Yes?' he said.

'You must surely know why I called you here,' Parnell responded, using his public-schoolboy voice, the wee educated-in-England prick.

'I've a pretty good idea,' Houlihan said. 'It's about the bombing of the Milltown Computer Centre.'

'Of which you're a silent partner,' Parnell said curtly.

'Aye, right,' Houlihan said, slowly burning up over the growing awareness that he was being talked down to, like a schoolboy in the headmaster's office. *Here comes the cane, like.* 'So I'm to blame for the bombing, I suppose.'

'Never mind the blame,' Parnell said even more curtly, almost contemptuously, while Katherine Crowley looked on to witness Houlihan's humiliation all the more closely. 'What I'm concerned about here is what the police forensics team are finding in the rubble and the kind of questions that I've already been asked by their detective colleagues.'

'Such as?'

'Is it true that you, Michael Houlihan, are a silent partner in the business organization behind the Milltown Computer Centre? Is there any link between this bombing and the bombing of the apartment block owned by Steve Lawson, who was the one responsible for landing your client – you again – in prison and has, since the bombing of his apartment block, disappeared? *Those* kinds of questions!'

Houlihan glanced at Katherine Crowley and saw her stony expression. So he turned, his anger rapidly building, back to Parnell.

'So?'

'So the bombing of the Milltown Computer Centre has brought to the surface an arms dump that up to now may have been quietly ignored, or buried, by a politically sensitive police force. But now they're going to be forced to investigate it thoroughly and report what they find to higher authority. And since they're already seeing, or imagining, connections between the bombing of Steve Lawson's building and your well-known grudge against him and his subsequent disappearance, this bombing of a building that was used as a secret weapons arsenal and, as will eventually be revealed, is owned in part by you ... since all of this is gradually forming a blindingly obvious pattern, I, your unfortunate lawyer, will soon be placed in a delicate position.'

'That's what lawyers are paid for,' Houlihan said with a sneer. 'Particularly bent lawyers.'

'Mr Houlihan,' Katherine Crowley interjected, sounding as icily lofty as a glacier in the Antarctic, thus forcing him to turn and stare at her beautiful, slyly contemptuous, naughty face. 'May I just say here that your inability to deal with a loose cannon like Steve Lawson has placed all of us — you included — in an extremely precarious legal position. Damage limitation can, of course, be applied if the situation is contained fairly quickly, but if you don't do that soon—'

'Do what?'

'Contain the situation by removing Mr Lawson entirely from the scenario—'

'By killing him.'

'I repeat, by removing Mr Lawson entirely from the scenario, then I'm afraid we may have to reappraise our relationship and—'

'What relationship?' Houlihan interjected, now truly burning up with rage at what he perceived was this bitch's contempt for him, wanting to humiliate *her* as she was trying to humiliate him, make her beg him to stop.

'Our professional relationship. Our *legal* relationship.'

'Aye, right. Go on.'

'So if you can't prevent a repeat of this unfortunate incident by somehow . . .'

'Yes?'

'*Neutralizing* Mr Lawson, then we'll have to seriously consider releasing ourselves from our obligations and—'

'Release yourselves from your obligations? You mean drop me as a client?'

'Well . . .'

Houlihan wanted to shove his cock down Katherine Crowley's throat while crushing the back of her head with his ham fist, humiliate *her*, crush *her*, lay waste to her while getting satisfaction from her, pay her back for deceiving him, leading him on, only to bring him to this . . . Yes, he wanted to *ruin* her.

'Okay,' he said, deliberately keeping his voice steady, staying calm, playing the good old Irish boyo. 'Sure I've embarrassed my lawyers and caused a wee fuss, so let me make amends, like, by assuring you that I'll find Steve Lawson and turn him into so much vapour. As for the police tracing my silent partnership back to the Milltown Computer Centre, you can take it as read that Aidan Shanahan will say nothing to incriminate us and will, indeed, soon be as conspicuous by his absence as that fucker Lawson. So, all in all, you don't have too much to worry about.'

'So how are you going to get Lawson?' Parnell asked.

'We'll find him,' Houlihan said with confidence. 'We have reason to believe he's living somewhere just outside the city limits, probably in Antrim, and that he's using an exceptionally powerful black Suzuki motorbike to get to and from the city. Given the rarity of such a motorbike in Antrim, particularly rural Antrim where he's almost certainly bound to be hiding out — SAS-style, naturally, so he's in a fuckin' hide in the hills — I don't think it'll take too long to find someone who's seen the fucker comin' and goin'. Also, since he couldn't have found out where our arms dump was without the help of someone who straddles the police force and the British Army, I'm pretty sure we can whittle that down to the few old associates he has left in the province. It might take a bit of time, but we can do it.'

'We don't have "a bit of time",' Katherine Crowley said. 'It has to be *now*.'

Houlihan could have killed her.

'So I'll do it as quickly as humanly possible,' he said, now almost choking up with rage and the need to contain it. 'But with the best will in the world, I—'

'For God's sake,' Parnell exclaimed, sounding seriously exasperated, 'what's the great mystery? Very few people who Lawson worked with remain in Belfast and the few who do so are easy to check out. What are we talking about here, Mike? A strong connection between the old RUC, the 14th Intelligence Group and Steve Lawson, right?'

'Right.'

'For Christ's sake, Mike, we have all of your own PIRA intelligence reports to hand and the strongest link between the RUC and the British Army that Lawson had during his tenure with the 14th Intelligence Group was unquestionably RUC Chief Inspector Joe Williamson. He retired on so-called principle just before the RUC became the Police Service of Northern Ireland and has since, while ostensibly being an old-age pensioner, been known to have spent most of his spare time socializing with his old RUC and British Army buddies — the Lisburn HQ, no less. So if Steve Lawson's connection isn't Joe Williamson himself, you can bet your balls that it's someone *close* to him — someone he knows.'

'Well ...' Houlihan began. But he was cut short when Katherine Crowley rudely interrupted, saying, with what sounded to him to be a great deal of impatience, 'So for God's sake, do we have to spell it out? You pick up this Joe Williamson for a little talk and, at the same time, you get those imbeciles you use as your private army to find a stranger riding an all-black Suzuki motorbike. And when you find him, you ensure that he disappears. It's as simple as that.'

Houlihan now *really* wanted to kill her, to strangle the bitch. But he was determined not to let her see him upset.

'Imbeciles? You're calling my men imbeciles?'

'Oh, for Christ's sake,' she said, more impatiently than ever. 'Is that all you can think about? Your masculine *pride*? I mean, we're trying to explain to you the gravity of the situation and you're offended because I called your men *imbeciles*? All right, I'm sorry, forget I ever said it, but please focus on what has to be done here to prevent us, your lawyers from bailing out.'

Houlihan turned to Parnell. 'This bitch is speaking for you?'

Parnell sighed, but nodded. 'Yes, Mike, she is. What she says makes sense to me. You simply have to get out there and find Steve Lawson, perhaps through the man who's giving him his information. And you have to do it immediately.'

'It takes time to track these things down, to find out who's responsible.'

'May I suggest the obvious?' Katherine said with what was now clear, cold contempt, while looking down at the open file spread across her sheer-stockinged, fine-boned knees.

'What's that?' Houlihan asked, wanting to strangle her and fuck her simultaneously. Those knees ... the sheer stockings ... the whole works. The bitch was driving him crazy.

'We're not *guessing* about Williamson,' she emphasized. 'According to this old PIRA intelligence report, which in fact we received from you, though clearly you hadn't read it,

Lawson's best friend, during his time with the 14th Intelligence Group, was RUC officer Joe Williamson.'

'Aye, I remember him,' Houlihan said, burning up at this latest insult but deciding to ignore it. 'Like you said, he left the RUC in protest when it was renamed the Police Service of Northern Ireland. So he's not in the force any more.'

'He may no longer be in the force,' Katherine said frostily, 'but he's retained his connections to it, attends its annual reunion dinners, often goes to the homes of former RUC colleagues and, perhaps more importantly, frequently visits the British Army's Northern Ireland HQ in Lisburn, which for most of his kind would be out of bounds. In other words, he's still in regular contact with the kind of strongly connected people, both in the police force and in the army, who know what's going on just about everywhere in the province. So he's bound to know a lot more than most.'

'That doesn't mean he's the source of Lawson's intelligence,' Houlihan said, determined not to be put down, though what she was saying certainly made sense to him.

'I'm not saying that he's *definitely* the source of Lawson's intelligence. But certainly he has to be top of our list.'

'Why?'

Houlihan thought that he had her there, but she promptly slapped him down.

'He's your man,' she said firmly. 'It can't be anyone else. I mean, for God's sake,' she added, tapping her finger on the open folder spread across her exquisite knees, sounding exasperated, 'it's right here in your own damned intelligence report – which, of course, you were too fucking lazy to read—'

'Now just a—'

'Shut the fuck up,' she said, the accent still resolutely middle-class, the tone as sharp as a whip. 'It's obvious from this intelligence report – which, I repeat, you didn't bother to read – that Steve Lawson, despite leaving the army and, therefore, the SAS, has remained close friends with Joe Williamson, who was – also according to your own intelligence report – a covert operative for the 14th Intelligence Group, acting as a liaison man between the RUC, the British Army and the paramilitaries on both sides of the divide. So he was then – and remains now – an invaluable source of information about all things concerning the security forces *and* the paramilitary organizations. Williamson, therefore, is the obvious choice when it comes to identifying Lawson's source of information. So why not pick him up and ask him a few questions instead of sitting here wanking?'

That was the last straw for Houlihan. Despite the humiliating realization that the bitch was right, he was totally incapable of taking the even worse humiliation of that final comment (*wanking*, no less!) and was determined to make her eat her own words in a way that she would never forget, irrespective of how damaging it might be, in the long run, to himself.

Fuck the future. Let it take care of itself. He would run with the present and suffer the consequences if necessary. He would go all out, no limit.

'Okay,' he said, keeping his voice steady, 'I'll pick up Joe Williamson. Anything else?'

'Just try to keep your nose clean,' Parnell said, 'until we can sort out this mess.'

'I will,' Houlihan said.

Secretly enraged, but trying not to show it, he pushed his chair back, climbed to his feet and hurriedly left the office, not bothering to say goodbye to either of them. Checking his wristwatch, he saw that it was nearly 5.30 p.m., which meant that Katherine Crowley would soon be leaving the office and, he hoped, making her way to where she lived. As Houlihan knew, this was in her own apartment in the upper Malone Road. After clambering awkwardly into the Volvo, having problems doing so because of his massive bulk, he gave his driver, Neil Dempsey, the address of Katherine Crowley's apartment. Dempsey duly drove the car to the leafy side street off the upper Malone Road. Once there, Houlihan told him to park about twenty metres down from the renovated and converted house that was now an apartment building, at the opposite side of the road.

'Now we wait for the bitch,' he said.

Of course, he didn't know how long he would have to wait because she might not come directly home; nor could he be sure that she would come home alone and if she didn't, he would have to come back another day. (If, for instance, she was being fucked by Parnell, she might turn up with him in tow.) His rage, however, was so great that he could scarcely contain himself and he was willing to wait all evening, if necessary.

Sitting there, Houlihan could not shake from his thoughts the way that Katherine and Parnell had talked to him, talked *down* to him, with her especially, having already led him on only to haughtily reject his advances, putting the boot in with relentless sarcasm and clear contempt. Worst of all, he could neither forget nor forgive her use of the word 'wanking' (spoken as if to a fourteen-year-old boy caught in the act) and was determined to make her swallow her own words in no uncertain terms. Now, while still lusting for her, he also loathed her with all his might, burned with fury at the very thought of her, and thus wanted her all the more, his lust magnified by his violent rage.

Yes, he would make her swallow her own words while swallowing him and degrade her in ways that she would never forget. He would have her begging for mercy.

Houlihan's luck was in. Katherine Crowley came home about an hour later, arriving in a taxi. Houlihan waited until she had paid the driver and was walking up the garden path before he clambered out of the Volvo and crossed the road to follow her. He reached the front gate just as she was placing the key in the lock of the front door.

As Katherine pulled the door open, Houlihan increased his pace and hurried to reach her before she could close it behind her. Hearing his feet crunching on the gravel of the garden path, she glanced back over her shoulder and saw him. Her eyes widened in surprise and she froze where she was, holding the door half open, the surprise rapidly turning into confusion.

'What . . . ?' she began as Houlihan reached her. But he cut the question short by brutally slapping her across the face with the back of his hand to send her jerking violently to the side, falling against the door. Before Katherine could right herself, Houlihan had pushed her back into the hallway, stepped in and slammed the door shut behind him. He caught a glimpse of her wide eyes, the confusion that was clouding them before the glaze of fear came as he punched her in the stomach and she doubled up, gasping and choking, her blonde hair falling down around her face.

Katherine's flat had a living room to the left and a bedroom to the right, so Houlihan grabbed some of that dangling blonde hair and viciously tugged it, making Katherine spin in towards the bedroom, still gasping and choking. He placed his boot on her backside, that gorgeous arse in the tight black skirt, and kicked hard to send her stumbling into the bedroom, dropping her handbag. She fell onto her hands and knees, trying to catch her breath, gasping. He stepped forward to take hold of her shoulders and turn her towards him, making her raise her hands from the floor and balance herself on her knees. He slapped her face twice more, making her head jerk left and right, though not making her bleed, since he wanted to leave no scars. Then he grabbed her hair again and roughly pulled her head back until she was forced to look up at him.

Katherine's blue eyes were now bright with fear; her mouth was open and gasping.

'You snotty bitch,' Houlihan said. 'You fancy, high-toned whore. Fucking Parnell while looking down your snob's nose at me, even while you're comin' on like a cock-teaser to whip me into a lather. You want me to stop wanking? Then you'd better help me, bitch. I'll take it out and you can have a taste of it, then we'll get on with the real thing. No wanking, you cunt. You're gonna do the job for me. You'll do that and then we'll do a few more things that you won't forget for a long time. Now open your mouth and keep it open, you cunt, and let's get on with the lesson. After this, you'll be mine.'

The nightmare closed in upon her.

Chapter Seventeen

Thinking that he was safe using the black Suzuki sports bike because Houlihan's men would be looking for the silver-tanked Yamaha, Steve, who was still using his forest hide in County Antrim, made regular reconnaissance trips into Belfast, hoping to track the movements of Houlihan, albeit from a safe distance. He wanted to learn if his quarry had any regular habits or movements that would be helpful in an assassination attempt. Aware that Houlihan would have men watching the main roads into the city, he varied his route as much as possible and otherwise relied on his recently grown beard, moustache and long hair to stop him being recognized by anyone who might have known him before or had been given an identification photo of him.

Nevertheless, tracking Houlihan's movements wasn't easy as the gangster had, since the bombing of his arms dump, surrounded himself with armed minders who stuck to him like glue and even guarded the street where he lived. These minders worked twenty-four hours a day in four-hour shifts. Also, dickers – young men used to keep their eyes peeled for strangers or the police – were always in place at both ends of any street that Houlihan was doing business in. Last but by no means least, because of the shooting up of the Hibernian pub, Houlihan had moved to a different pub, O'Sullivan's, located right there on the main drag of the Falls Road, with countless people passing it daily as they went about their business. So attacking him there without putting innocent people at risk would be a dicey business.

Things were not much different with Houlihan's Protestant friend, Wild Bill Moore. Steve now knew that he would have to neutralize Wild Bill as well – for his own reasons, not simply because it was part of his original brief from Edmondson. It was clear to him that since the Hibernian incident and, even more, with the subsequent bombing of the arms dump in the Kennedy Way Industrial Estate, Wild Bill would have joined forces with Houlihan's men to throw a cordon around the city, hoping to box Steve in. Effectively doubling the numbers of searchers like that would also enable the mobsters to cast their net wider to take in the outlying districts, almost certainly including Antrim, just in case Steve wasn't in Belfast. For these reasons alone, it would be imperative to neutralize Wild Bill as well. But, like Houlihan, Wild Bill had surrounded himself with all the security trappings of a powerful gang baron and was rarely to be seen alone.

Wild Bill was, however, more often together with Houlihan these days then he'd been before. This was helpful to Steve since he was operating alone and so couldn't track both men at once. He therefore concentrated all his attention on Houlihan and prayed that a situation might arise where he could neutralize both men at the same time.

Since Steve was experienced enough to know that he needed at least four hours' sleep each night and since Houlihan and Wild Bill invariably met in the evenings, he began his surveillance by following Houlihan throughout the day and generally stuck with him until just before midnight. If Houlihan hadn't returned to his own home by that time, Steve took himself back to his forest hide in Antrim anyway, believing that sleep was more important than anything that Houlihan might be getting up to in the early hours of the morning.

In fact, Houlihan had fairly regular habits, which Steve was able to observe from a distance. Because of the dickers on watch in shifts around the clock, Steve could not even enter Houlihan's street to eyeball his house from a reasonable distance. However, he always ensured that he was in an inconspicuous position in the Falls Road and from there he could observe that Houlihan, who had stopped walking anywhere because of his justified fear of assassination, invariably emerged from the Falls Road end of his street at about ten in the morning (a late sleeper, obviously) to be driven in his Volvo saloon car to his frozen-food processing business out on the Duncrue Industrial Estate. Houlihan always sat up front, beside the driver, and there were always two minders in the rear of the car whose bodywork and windows were, Steve surmised, almost certainly bulletproof.

En route to the industrial estate, the Volvo would stop at various points along the Falls to enable Houlihan, again escorted by his two minders, to enter a variety of shops, pubs, bookies and social clubs where, Steve was convinced, he was personally collecting his protection money, which would have been stuffed into the black briefcase that he always carried at such times. This business would take him up to approximately lunchtime, which would be spent in some local pub or, if he was meeting a business associate, which he did frequently, in a restaurant in the centre of town.

Again, because of the minders and dickers, Steve could only observe those business meetings from afar, as he didn't dare enter the pub or restaurant concerned. Nevertheless, while Houlihan invariably entered these establishments alone, leaving his minders outside to keep the entrances covered, he often emerged in the company of the people with whom he'd had lunch. While it was clear from their clothing and mannerisms that some of them were local businessmen, others had the appearance and body language of foreigners, almost certainly, in Steve's judgement, Russians. So convinced of this was he that on a couple of occasions he temporarily ignored Houlihan and instead followed his Russian-looking guests after they had bid

Houlihan farewell. In each case, the strangers had returned to a hotel, either the Europa in Great Victoria Street or the Hilton, near the Waterfront Hall and overlooking the River Lagan – and the ruins of Steve's bombed-out apartment block. Satisfied that they were visitors to the city, Steve, swallowing his bitterness over his destroyed apartment block and murdered tenants, followed a particular group into the lobby of the Hilton Hotel and was able to confirm, when they asked for their room keys in guttural broken English, that they were indeed Russians.

Clearly, then, as Edmondson had said, Houlihan was negotiating some kind of criminal deal with the Russian *Mafiya*. Though he appeared to be doing it alone. In which case, despite what Edmondson had thought was going on, he wasn't including Wild Bill Moore in the negotiations.

Houlihan might be thinking of cutting Wild Bill out when the time is ready, Steve thought. *He might even be thinking of using the Russian* Mafiya *to get rid of the competition, meaning Wild Bill. I might be able to use this.*

Keeping at a safe distance, feeling relatively safe because of his beard, moustache and long hair, Steve continued to follow Houlihan on his daily rounds. He noted that while Houlihan's mornings were spent personally collecting protection money, invariably his afternoons found him touring the general area of the Falls and other Catholic enclaves to check on the activities of, and collect money from, his drug dealers. Specializing in crack and ecstasy, they were mostly juveniles, addicts themselves who were desperate for money to buy their own drugs.

During the Troubles the IRA had insisted that it was not involved with drugs, though in fact the organization had certainly collected a lot of its revenue from drug dealers, only punishing those who failed to pay up. Houlihan was not so hypocritical when it came to his own drugs business and it was clear that he recruited his dealers mainly from financially desperate addicts and was ruthless in collecting his revenue from them. He was a man known to enjoy a 'hands-on' approach to his criminal activities, including the personal administration of punishment beatings or even more horrific forms of torture. But he was careful enough, when it came to drugs, to remain sitting up front in his car while one of his minders dealt with the addict on the pavement, either by collecting the money from him or, if the addict could not or would not pay up, giving him a good hiding right there in the street, in front of the startled passers-by. The minder would then return to the car and the vehicle would move on to the next dealer.

Also, every afternoon, once the drugs revenue had been collected, Houlihan would visit one of the many social clubs in the Falls and remain there for an hour or so, almost certainly to have a game of darts or billiards, which he was known to enjoy. Emerging from the social club at around five p.m. he would usually go to a nearby pub where he would spend an hour or so drinking with friends and, perhaps, discussing business with some of his criminal associates. Certainly, the friends included his two criminal former IRA lieutenants, Frank Kavanagh and Pat Connolly.

Like a dutiful father, Houlihan sometimes visited his sons or daughters where they lived in or around the city and certainly, every evening without fail, he returned home for approximately two hours. During this time, Steve surmised, Houlihan would eat his cooked dinner, watch the news and sports on television, then change his clothing in preparation for the evening. Invariably, his evenings were spent in either a pub or a social club, with his minders on guard outside, and frequently now, though on no fixed evening, which made matters unpredictable from Steve's point of view, he would have a meeting with Wild Bill. Such meetings now took place in O'Sullivan's pub on the Falls Road and, during the meetings, there were always at least four minders standing outside: two for Houlihan and another two for Wild Bill.

While Steve was keen to neutralize Wild Bill as well and would have preferred to have completed both tasks at once, he did not think it feasible to do it while both men were emerging from a pub on the Falls Road. First, their minders always bunched too closely around them; second, there were too many innocent passers-by and he couldn't put them at risk. So a double assassination outside O'Sullivan's wasn't on the cards.

There were, however, other possibilities.

Two or three times a week Houlihan would visit a well-known brothel in the centre of town. He would also be seen leaving downtown pubs, clubs or restaurants with women a lot younger than himself, almost certainly whores, and going with them to their houses or apartments.

Steve thought that there might be a way in there.

Another possible assassination venue was Houlihan's big house overlooking an expansive beach just outside the wealthy enclave of Cultra, between Belfast and Bangor, where he spent most of his weekends without his wife. Steve had no way of knowing what Houlihan told his wife about his weekends in the house near Cultra (it was possible that she didn't even know about it), but he certainly saw enough to ascertain that Houlihan went there to have a good time. Most weekends, the gang boss arrived early on the Saturday morning and returned to Belfast late on Sunday evening. Sometimes, if the weather was good, he would take to the sea for an afternoon's fishing in a rented boat, though he did this rarely — certainly not regularly enough for Steve to plan a hit from another boat.

Houlihan did not play golf. He did, however, appear to entertain every Saturday night, with most of his visitors, including the women, staying until the following day. This suggested extended parties or, possibly, full-blown orgies, about which certain rumours had abounded before Houlihan had been thrown into Maghaberry Prison.

Steve briefly considered getting into the building during one of those Saturday nights, when everyone would surely be distracted with sex or sleeping off the drink. But he discarded the idea because of the high risk to the guests as well as the difficulty he might have in finding what bedroom Houlihan was using in a house full of other people.

He had to think of another way.

With the weekend over, Houlihan always returned to his home turf, the Falls, and resumed his normal routine. That routine changed, however, shortly after he had paid a visit to his bent lawyer, Jack Parnell, late one weekday afternoon. After leaving Parnell's office, a clearly agitated Houlihan, instead of going to one of his customary haunts, was driven to a leafy street off the upper Malone Road. Steve followed on his motorbike. Houlihan's Volvo stopped at the pavement in that leafy street and remained there for a considerable time. Eventually, to Steve's surprise, a woman he recognized from his surveillance of Houlihan's associates as Parnell's legal assistant, Katherine Crowley, emerged from a taxi and entered a house a short distance away from where Houlihan's car was parked on the opposite side of the road. Houlihan immediately left his car, crossed the street and followed the woman into the house. Parked much further down the street, Steve could see little other than Houlihan entering the garden. But he obviously went into the building as well and did not emerge until many hours later, when darkness had fallen. After clambering back into the Volvo, he was driven away.

Assuming that Houlihan, after his tryst with Katherine Crowley, would be going straight home to sleep lovelessly with his unattractive wife, Steve did not bother following him. Instead he parked his motorbike by the kerb and walked along the dark street until he reached the gate of the house that Houlihan had entered. Protected by darkness, seeing no one around, he walked up the garden path to confirm, from the nameplates fixed beside the front door of the red-brick building, that it was a substantial former family house converted into flats and that Katherine Crowley did, indeed, either own or rent one of the flats. So this was her place, not Houlihan's.

For the next couple of weeks, Houlihan frequently visited

Katherine Crowley at her flat, albeit irregularly, always shortly after she had returned from her working day in Jack Parnell's office. Katherine Crowley, who Steve had always thought had the cool self-containment of a well-educated and spoilt beauty, seemed to change after that first evening with Houlihan. When coming home on subsequent evenings for another tryst with him, she seemed badly shaken, even frightened, though there was certainly no perceptible change in her physical appearance.

Clearly, she and Houlihan were having sex together. But, judging by the tormented look on her face, she was not enjoying the experience.

While pondering the oddness of the relationship, wondering about the fear visible in Katherine Crowley's expression, Steve considered the possibility of getting into her apartment and waiting there for Houlihan to enter. He finally decided against it for a variety of reasons: because of the difficulty of entering without the minders parked across the street seeing him, because there was no access from the rear of the building, and because of the close proximity of the other apartments and the consequent difficulty of escaping unseen. More importantly, the irregularity of Houlihan's visits to Katherine Crowley made it impossible for Steve to know in advance on just what evening he would be there. So he axed the idea of using the woman's apartment for any hit.

One weekend, when Houlihan was due for his regular pilgrimage to the house near Cultra, instead of being driven straight there as usual from his home in the Falls, he was driven to Katherine Crowley's flat where he picked her up in the Volvo and took her with him. Steve followed them and then, from a safe distance, kept the big house under observation.

Clearly, Houlihan had decided to change his routine. Instead of the customary large crowd of visitors on Saturday evening, he received only two other couples. Both left, Steve noted, just before midnight, presumably after a normal dinner and without the usual extended party. Obviously, on this occasion Houlihan wanted to be alone throughout the night with Katherine Crowley.

This presented Steve with the possibility of getting into the Cultra house the following Saturday evening when the only people in it might be Houlihan and Katherine Crowley. True, there would be the problem of the minders and, almost certainly, the burglar alarm and surveillance systems, but these problems, he felt, could be overcome as long as the house was not packed with other guests.

He decided to try it.

With another week to wait out, Steve continued to tail Houlihan every day. The big gangster's routine remained pretty much the same, including the irregular evening visits to Ms Crowley's apartment in the upper Malone Road.

On the Tuesday of that week it was reported by the media that Aidan Shanahan, manager of the recently bombed Milltown Computer Centre, had gone missing from his home a week ago and had not been seen since by his wife or by anyone else. It was believed by the authorities that Shanahan had either deliberately gone missing because he was under investigation by the police over the arms dump kept secretly in the storerooms of his computer business or because he had been abducted, and possibly murdered, by gangsters to prevent him from talking to the police. The matter was still under investigation.

Learning about this, Steve decided to arrange a meeting with Joe Williamson to find out if he had any clues about what might have happened to Shanahan. Joe agreed and they arranged to meet at seven p.m. the next day in the bar of Cutter's Wharf.

Joe didn't show up.

The following day, Thursday, Joe's dead body was found floating in the River Lagan. On the Friday, after a forensic examination had been completed, a police spokesman announced that Joe Williamson had been tortured and then shot in the head in a gangland-style execution before being dumped in the river.

Shocked and enraged, Steve resolved to get into the house near Cultra and put an end to Houlihan, at least.

He would do it tomorrow.

Chapter Eighteen

Houlihan was feeling great when he rolled out of bed that Saturday morning, away from his unloved wife. He was looking forward to another weekend in his big house near Cultra, with Katherine Crowley's company as an added bonus.

While he showered and shaved, Houlihan mused on the fact that his wife, Maeve, still snoring contentedly in bed, doubtless glad to be rid of him, didn't even know that he had a house by the sea. She assumed that he went to Cultra purely for the fishing and always stayed with his old IRA friend, Len Quigley, who had a luxury bungalow down there and was indeed a fanatical fisher. As far as Maeve was concerned, they were still working class and were lucky to own this small and unprepossessing home in the Falls, where she had lived all her life and was, being neither greatly imaginative nor ambitious, perfectly content — apart from her misgivings about Houlihan. So Maeve assumed that her husband went fishing every weekend, staying with a bachelor friend, and since his absence actually gave her a bit of a break from him, she wasn't about to ask questions. Houlihan was safe.

After finishing his ablutions, he dressed, ignoring the sleeping Maeve, then went downstairs to have what was for him an unusually light breakfast of toast, marmalade and tea. Normally he would have had a full fry-up of bacon, egg, sausage, tomatoes, soda bread and potato farls, but he was used to being served and couldn't be bothered to cook it himself. He also wanted to get out of the house as soon as possible, so he just popped the bread in the toaster and had breakfast the easy way.

Mere minutes later, Houlihan was out the front door and clambering awkwardly into the Vauxhall Vectra SXi saloon that had been waiting for him for the past half-hour and was driven by one of his minders, Neil Dempsey, while two other minders, Kevin Magee and Sam Meaklin, sat in the rear. When they were all strapped in, Neil drove smoothly away from the kerb, turned along the Falls Road, then headed across town for the upper Malone Road. It wasn't yet eight in the morning and the whole town was desolate and grim in the pallid grey light.

Yet Houlihan was in a good mood. A couple of days back he had stopped Aidan Shanahan from talking to the police by simply picking him up as he was walking along the street where he lived and driving him out to the Duncrue Industrial Estate where he was taken into a back room and shot through the head. Once dead, Shanahan had been chopped up into pieces that, along with the bone and gristle, were passed through a meat grinder to be turned into mincemeat. This was then pounded into regulation shaped blocks and packed automatically with the other tinned food.

In other words, Aidan Shanahan had disappeared for good and no body would ever be found.

Houlihan hadn't wanted Shanahan's body to be found because he wanted to confuse the cops when they started wondering what had happened to him. He wanted them to have two main possibilities to puzzle over: on the one hand, that Shanahan had deliberately disappeared in order to avoid further questioning by them and, on the other, that Shanahan might have been abducted and killed by men who didn't want him to talk to the cops about the arms dump.

In the event, this had worked. Shanahan's disappearance remained a perplexing mystery to the police, though happily the authorities were already leaning towards the theory that he had simply fled and was probably hiding out somewhere in England. The more that line of reasoning was followed, the further away from the truth the cops would get — which was exactly what Houlihan wanted.

Though Houlihan and Shanahan had been friends, the gang boss felt little regret about the Milltown Computer Centre director's fate because Shanahan had turned out, in the end, to be such a coward. Now, looking back on the execution, Houlihan took an almost gleeful satisfaction in recollecting how, when they had picked Shanahan up, making him sit in the rear of the Volvo between the two homicidal minders, Kevin Magee and Sam Meaklin, he had instantly started sweating, repeating desperately that he'd said nothing to the cops so far and wasn't going to say anything in the future.

The very sight of him in that terrified state was enough to convince Houlihan that Shanahan would never be able to stand up under police interrogation. If he were allowed to live, he would surely crack and talk, giving away the names of those who knew about the arms dump — including Houlihan's.

Believing this, Houlihan had ignored Shanahan's increasingly incoherent, terrified babblings and ushered him into the big cold-storage room behind the frozen-food processing warehouses and workshops. There he had been made to kneel on the floor with his hands tied behind his back while a plastic sack was tightened over his head to minimize the flow of blood when the bullet entered his brain. The cowardly fucker had pissed himself. He had sobbed and then vomited and might have choked on his own spew — a strong likelihood inside the plastic bag — had not the bullet, fired at close range by Houlihan, put him out of his misery.

Yella-bellies like that, Houlihan now thought as he gazed out of the window of the car, *deserve all they get*. At least Williamson had died like a man, despite what he had suffered.

Indeed he had. Two days after executing Shanahan, Houlihan had picked up Joe Williamson.

Like Shanahan, Williamson had been picked up in the evening as he was walking home. He too was then driven to the frozen-food processing works out on the Duncrue Industrial Estate. There he had been taken into the same big cold-storage room where Shanahan had died. After being forced to strip naked in that freezing atmosphere, he had been hung by his ankles from an overhead bar that was normally used for the hanging, on hooks, of the cattle carcasses that were chopped up and pulverized into mincemeat that was then frozen and packed in tin cans. Dangling upside down, Williamson, not a young man, had been tortured in several appalling ways until he confessed that he had, indeed, had various meetings with Steve Lawson and had passed information to him about the movements of Houlihan and Wild Bill Moore.

Though Williamson had initially denied that he knew anything about Lawson's whereabouts, repeated torture finally got him to confess that if he didn't know exactly where Lawson was hiding, he knew that he was operating out of a forest hide somewhere between Antrim Town and the eastern shore of Lough Neagh.

By that time Williamson was half dead just from hanging upside down for so long in the freezing cold, never mind the torture. So Houlihan had him untied and lowered to the floor where, still naked, he was made to kneel to have the plastic sack tied over his head.

Williamson kneeled on the cold floor but managed to say through bloody, torn lips, 'If you're going to kill me, just do it. I don't need that bag tied over my head.'

'It's for the blood,' Houlihan explained thoughtfully. 'To catch the blood, like.'

'Just throw a towel over my head when I'm dead. You owe me that much, at least.'

'Aye, right,' Houlihan said, respecting the man's courage. Then he shot him.

Houlihan decided not to have Williamson turned into mincemeat because he wanted the body to be found as a message to Steve Lawson that he Houlihan, was now on his case. So Williamson's corpse was placed in the boot of a car and driven to a lonely stretch of the Lagan Meadows to be dumped in the river.

Joe Williamson died like a man, Houlihan thought as he glanced out at the deserted lawns of Queens University, the mowed grass glistening with morning dew. *You've got to credit him for it.*

All in all, then, Houlihan was feeling good as the car left the university area behind and entered Malone Road where some of the stores were just opening and housewives with scarves on their heads were already out for some early-morning shopping. The knowledge that Lawson was hiding out somewhere between Antrim Town and the eastern shore of Lough Neagh was sure to produce him much more quickly. Houlihan already had men driving around the small towns and hamlets of that area, asking people if they had seen a stranger on a powerful all-black Suzuki motorbike. He was certain that, with the search area already so greatly reduced, they would not be long in narrowing it down to within a few miles of Lawson's hiding place. Once they did that, Houlihan would have his men encircle the area and keep moving inwards, rather like pulling in a big fishing net until the fish was caught. He could hardly wait for that moment.

Realizing that the car was slowing down, about to make a right-hand turn into the leafy street where Katherine Crowley was living, Houlihan instinctively straightened up in his seat, feeling pleasurable anticipation.

His conquest of Katherine Crowley, or, rather, his *degradation* of her, his destruction of her spirit and snotty superiority, had been one of his more satisfying recent adventures. He had made her swallow her own words, all right, on her knees, swallowing *him*, then he had made her strip naked and stretch out on her belly while he pummelled her with his gross weight. Then he had made her raise herself onto her hands and knees, as slim as a virgin youth, one of the nancy boys in the prison, and he had done to her what he had done to them despite the blood and the pain. He had slapped her face when she cried out, punched her into submission, twisted her arms, crushed her hands in his own huge fists, jerked her this way and that by pulling brutally on her hair, that long, luscious, golden-blonde hair. But he'd done it all in such a way that she was left with no visible bruises or other marks that could indicate to the likes of Parnell just what she'd been through. All the real bruises were inside – the knot of fear, the broken spirit – and when she was spreadeagled beneath him, flattened by his great weight, the breath almost pressed out of her, her lungs gasping for air, he pushed into her, breaking down her resistance, as if he was trying to disembowel her with his cock, the cruel thrust of his hardness.

'You teased it often enough,' he reminded her, 'so don't complain now. Take it lyin' down, as they say, an' it won't seem so bad. Fuckin' whore! Fuckin' snooty bitch! You don't look so superior now and you won't in the future. Now open your legs wider and then bend them back and up and let's see just how much you can take ... Ah, fuck! Jesus Christ!'

The very recollection of it excited him even now, as the car was pulling in to the kerb in front of her house. He'd been humiliated in Parnell's office, by Parnell himself and also by her, so by fucking her, Parnell's secret woman, he was not only punishing her but also getting his revenge for what he saw as Parnell's insolent treachery. No one could talk to him the way that they had and hope to get away with it. Now he was paying them back.

When the car stopped by the kerb, Houlihan said to Kevin Magee, speaking over his shoulder, 'Okay, Kev, you go and get her. Then take this seat.'

Magee nodded without a word and slipped out of the rear seat of the car to walk up the garden path and fetch Katherine. Meanwhile, Houlihan manoeuvred his bulk out of the front seat and stood by the open rear door of the vehicle.

When Katherine came out, wearing an open-necked shirt, tight blue jeans, a short windcheater jacket and shoes with raised heels, sexy as sin despite her subdued appearance and escorted by the slab-faced, broad-shouldered Magee, she slipped into the rear seat beside the other minder, Sam Meaklin. Houlihan squeezed in beside her, letting Magee close the door behind him. Magee then took the front seat and Neil Dempsey drove off again, this time heading for the A2 and the road to the seashore town of Cultra where the wealthy – including Houlihan – had their holiday homes.

'So how are you?' Houlihan asked as the car glided out into the traffic of the Malone Road, which was bordered by playing fields and sports grounds, woods and parks. This was a middle-class area, so Houlihan loathed it.

'Fine,' Katherine replied, though she could scarcely keep her distaste for him out of her voice.

Houlihan didn't mind that because she was now his victim. In fact, her unstated but manifest loathing for him only made him lust for her all the more. He felt the heat coming out of her.

'Comfortable there, are you?' he asked with dry mockery.

'Not really,' she responded. 'I feel like a slice of raw ham crushed up in a sandwich.'

He was pleased to note that, though degraded and crushed, she had not lost her spirit altogether. The complete breaking of that spirit was a challenge that he could not resist.

Now, in full view of Sam Meaklin, pressing against her other side, he placed his paw on the middle of her thigh and gave it a squeeze. It was impossible for Sam Meaklin not to see this. Thus Katherine was further humiliated and Houlihan was even more amused.

'Sure you feel nice,' he said. 'Ham sandwich or not.'

Katherine didn't reply. Houlihan saw the flush in her cheeks, either rage or embarrassment, and he smiled, moving his hand up higher until his fingers were slipping down between her inner thighs, just below the crotch. Meaklin saw this as well.

'So warm and soft to the touch,' Houlihan said. 'Sure it does a man's heart good.' He squeezed more ostentatiously, looking past her, grinning at Meaklin, then added, 'And does other parts good as well, right, lads?'

'Aye, right,' Meaklin said with a tight grin.

'With you, boss,' Kevin Magee added, raising his head to get an eyeful in the rear-view mirror and also let Houlihan see his broad grin. 'We know just what you mean, like.'

Katherine closed her eyes. Her cheeks were flushed with humiliation. When Houlihan squeezed her crotch again, she tried to open her legs, to let herself breathe down there, but being hemmed in so tightly by the two big men, she could barely move an inch. She breathed in and out, deeply.

'Ack, well,' Houlihan said, deciding to give her a break, removing his hand from between her tight thighs and slapping her left knee lightly, with mock affection. 'Sure we'll get into all of that later, when we're in the big house. We'll have a good wee time there, right enough, and then sleep like two lovebirds while the boyos here keep us well protected. Sure that's the be-all and end-all. Life is there for the livin'.'

Houlihan was deepening Katherine's humiliation by impressing upon her that his minders knew what went on between him and her in that house and were wide awake, guarding the premises, while he and she were going about it. He was treating her like one of his whores in front of his men. The degradation was crude but effective, making her squirm. Also, he never failed to remind her that if she displeased him, if she failed to satisfy him, he would pass her on to his boyos to let them do with her what they pleased – and what pleased them, he was keen to assure her, was often extreme. He knew that she now lived in dread of the very thought of that. She could become the plaything of the minders, most of whom were mad brutes. She could become a ruined rag doll.

'So how's Parnell?' Houlihan asked as they left the city centre behind and picked up the Holywood Road. To the west, the gantries and cranes of the docks were silhouetted against a slate-grey sky, beyond the Belfast City Airport; east was the lush greenery of Sydenham with its playing fields and bowling greens. Houlihan, a city man born and bred, couldn't stand all that greenery.

'He's fine,' Katherine said.

'You haven't told him about us yet, have you?'

Katherine shook her head. 'No.'

'So how have you explained to the wee shite why he can't come round to your place most evenin's like he used to? Not to mention the weekends.'

'He never came around that much,' she said flatly, unemotionally, like one of the walking dead. 'Most times we went to his place. So I don't think he's even noticed that I haven't invited him round to my place recently.'

'But you're still fucking him?' The question was asked in a perfectly normal tone of voice, not subdued at all, to ensure that the other men in the car would hear it. This, too, was part of Katherine's ongoing humiliation and degradation. 'You haven't cut him dead, like?'

'No, I haven't cut him dead,' Katherine replied, actually sounding relieved to have been given a way out of stating categorically, in front of Houlihan's men, that she was fucking her boss.

'And you're still fucking him?' Houlihan repeated, deliberately forcing her to speak the words she had so desperately wanted to avoid.

Katherine took a deep breath and released it in a sigh. 'Yes, I'm still fucking him occasionally.'

'What's that mean?'

'Well . . .' She hesitated, clearly nervous. 'Obviously, the nights I'm not with you.'

'Good,' Houlihan said, glancing out of the car to see that they were now cruising along the A2, heading for Holywood. 'I don't want him to know about us yet. Not till I'm good and ready. Not till the time's right.'

Katherine didn't reply. She didn't dare ask any questions. She had no idea what fate had in store for her; and now that her fate was in Houlihan's hands she dreaded even thinking about it.

'So what about the weekends?' Houlihan asked. 'Last weekend and this. How did you explain not seeing him over the whole of the two weekends, like?'

Again, he was deliberately asking these questions in front of his minders in order to humiliate her more thoroughly. He saw them all grinning. Only Katherine was not amused.

'I simply told him that I was studying for my legal exams, which are coming up soon, and that I'd have to work over the next few weekends without interruption. I said I was staying in a girlfriend's holiday bungalow in Bangor to get away from unexpected visitors and the telephone.'

'Did he ask if *he* could phone you?'

'No. I made it clear that I didn't want any interruptions and I think he respected that. I mean, he's a lawyer himself and had to do the same exams, so obviously he knows how tough they are and wouldn't think that my request for privacy was unusual.'

'Great,' Houlihan said. He placed his hand back on her left thigh, beautifully outlined in the skintight jeans, to give it a squeeze, convinced that Meaklin was getting an erection each time he saw it. Houlihan had seen the way that his minders looked at Katherine – with helpless lust and resentment – so he knew that they were jealous of him and fantasized about her. Knowing this gave him deep satisfaction, a greater feeling of power. 'You said the right thing, girl,' he added. 'Now let's have us a good weekend.'

They spoke no more for the rest of the journey, simply sitting in a silence you could have cut with a knife until the car eventually stopped in the driveway of the big house by the beach near Cultra.

It was a recently built mock-Georgian manor, with pillars around the front door and balustraded balconies around the upstairs windows, set in lush gardens that overlooked the sea and sloped gently to a private path leading down to the beach. Houlihan had deliberately asked for the house to be built facing the road, not the sea, because he always liked to know exactly what was coming at him; it had been designed, however, in such a way that the main living room and bedrooms overlooked the spectacular beach and the sea. The property was well hidden by a variety of trees, tall hedgerows and high drystone walls, with electronically controlled steel gates and the usual high-tech burglar alarm-and-surveillance systems.

Actually, it wasn't that big: there was no swimming pool or tennis court like some of the other houses in the area had. But to Houlihan, who neither swam nor played tennis, it was a mansion suited to his new standing in life: a symbol of his power and secret wealth. He was the poor boy made good.

Another vehicle preceding Houlihan's, an unmarked van, had brought a good dozen minders to cover both sides of the house around the clock in four-hour shifts. Some of these men were already in position front and rear, as Kavanagh informed Houlihan when he met him at the front door of the main building.

'As usual,' Kavanagh said, 'we'll have two men right here at the front door and another man covering the gate to the path leading up from the beach at the rear of the house. We have plenty of men, so there won't be any problem in keeping you covered at all times of the night and day. The rest of the men, those not already on watch, are resting in the usual rooms in the guest wing. Everything's hunky-dory, like.'

'Where's Connolly?'

'He just went out back to take that new minder down to the beach and clue him in. He should be back any second.'

Indeed, Connolly appeared around the gable end of the house at that very moment, looking wind-blown but grinning cheerfully.

'Ack, you've come, boss!' he said to Houlihan while automatically glancing at Katherine, who was standing silently beside him, before quickly, guiltily, moving his gaze away again. 'How are ya?'

'No different from when we last met – yesterday,' Houlihan said acidly. 'So how are things out back?'

'No problems,' Connolly said. 'I've just placed a man in position down by the beach gate and the surveillance cameras are covering the rear lawns. You can relax, boss, believe me. Have yourself a good weekend.' He couldn't help glancing at the hapless Katherine again when he said that: a glance full of lust and resentment. A man just couldn't help himself. 'You're well protected here, boss.'

'I'd better be,' Houlihan said threateningly, since he knew that he could easily frighten Connolly, unlike the more hardened Kavanagh. 'Okay,' he said, looking at Katherine and nodding towards the front door. 'Let's get inside.'

With the gazes of all the men crawling over her like spiders, making her shiver visibly, Katherine walked ahead of Houlihan and entered the house. Houlihan followed her in and was followed, in turn, by Connolly, who was carrying his boss's overnight bag. When they had entered the hallway, which was big and richly furnished, like the rest of the house, Connolly glanced again at Katherine, then stared inquiringly at Houlihan.

'Where . . . ?'

'Upstairs, in the bedroom,' Houlihan said.

As Connolly started up the stairs, Houlihan nodded at the silent Katherine to follow his lieutenant, then he followed her. Once in the bedroom, decorated in the rich reds and purples of a Hollywood-movie brothel, Connolly placed the overnight bag on top of a chest of drawers. Then he hurriedly left the room, closing the door behind him.

When Houlihan turned the key in the lock, Katherine flinched visibly.

Houlihan could barely wait. He hadn't had sex for two days. His body seemed bathed in lambent heat and his breathing was heavy.

'Now the fun starts,' he said.

He saw the dread in her green eyes.

Chapter Nineteen

Steve saw the men coming from a good distance away. More precisely, he saw a car coming along the desolate road that ran through the countryside below his hide and knew that it had to be carrying Houlihan's men: it was a blood-red Vauxhall Astra with – as he could see through his powerful military binoculars – a number plate that matched one of the registration numbers that he had jotted down in his notebook during his past few weeks of surveillance. In fact, he had seen the same car outside the Hibernian pub before he shot up the place and, later, outside O'Sullivan's in the Falls Road. So he knew, even when the car was still in the distance, that Houlihan's men were finally closing in on him.

After weeks spent alone in his SAS-style hide, either sleeping like a log after a long day of surveillance in Belfast or watching the low hills and gently rolling fields of the farmlands spread out below him, Steve had started to feel dislocated, removed from the real world

In truth, he felt like hell. It had been a long time since he had been in the SAS, so living rough had been even tougher than he'd expected. For a start, he had been forced to accept that he was ageing, that he was no longer the golden young god of war, and that his relative lack of vigorous exercise (apart from climbing trees during his motorbike trips to the country) had left him vulnerable to the aches and pains of a normal man of his age. Added to that was the discomfort of not eating regularly (cold high-calorie rations while in the hide; the odd hot meal in a fast-food restaurant at unpredictable hours) and having to sleep in a sleeping bag under the overhead screen of combined hessian sheeting, waterproof poncho and camouflage netting. Together, these coverings certainly kept the rain off him, but they didn't prevent the crosswinds from battering him or shield him much from the deepening cold of the oncoming winter. In fact, Steve had to admit that his life in the hide was bloody awful.

Yet he was, perversely, enjoying it. He liked being reminded of better days, being removed from the commonplace, getting a thrill, unsavoury perhaps, from the dangerous nature of what he was doing, this daily gambling with life and death. Despite the discomforts of the hide, the loneliness, the cold and damp, he was becoming addicted to roughing it; felt rejuvenated by it, gradually coming to realize just how bored he had been since leaving the SAS and becoming a businessman, buying and selling property. His low boredom threshold had turned him into a soldier in the first place, had then made him transfer to the SAS, helped to break up his marriage, driven him restlessly from one affair into another, and finally made him a successful businessman. But he had never quite shaken it off and now understood, as he had not done before, just how much he needed danger and excitement in order to feel fulfilled. Perhaps, as the late, sadly lamented Joe Williamson had suggested, he was not much different from the men he was pursuing. If so, he had decided, he might as well take as much pleasure as he could get from what could well be the last real adventure of his life. He might as well throw himself wholeheartedly into it, going all out, no limit ... So when he saw that car, the blood-red Vauxhall Astra, coming along the road that wound below the forested hill, he felt no fear at all: only the sharp edge of an excitement that brought all his senses to a state of electric alertness.

The car was advancing out of the early evening, well before

the September sun had sunk, though with the light just beginning to fade. Steve watched it through the camouflaged rectangular viewing hole that he had shaped from the hedgerow and the hessian covering the side of the hide that overlooked the road. He could, of course, have been asleep when the car came and not seen it until it was too late. But, luckily for him, he happened to be awake – ironically, not least because he was actually preparing to leave the hide and ride his motorbike to Cultra to attempt the assassination of Houlihan.

There was only one car visible on the road. But Steve assumed that Houlihan's men had somehow found out that he was hiding in this general area, between Antrim City and Lough Neagh, and that more cars were covering other parts of the countryside, throwing around it a cordon of men who would be moving inward, in an encircling movement in the hope of gradually closing in on him. If this was the case, the men coming towards him in that Vauxhall Astra did not necessarily know for certain that he was here but were merely driving around and checking out any likely locations for a hide: sheltered areas on high ground, just like the place he had chosen. So those men down there, even if they didn't actually know for certain that he was here, would probably drive up the hill as far as they could go, then spread out to cover the forested area on foot. They would, very probably, find the hide.

And, indeed, even as Steve was thinking this, the red Vauxhall slowed down to inch along the road at the base of the hill. When the car came close to Steve's hide, he saw that a man had rolled the rear window down and was scanning the darkening landscape with binoculars.

If that guy's in the back, Steve thought, *there must be at least four of them in the car.*

Picking up his own pair of British Army binoculars, he studied the car in close-up and saw that it was indeed holding at least four men, possibly five: two in the front and two or three in the rear. As he lowered his binoculars, the car went into reverse, backed along the road and then turned along the lane that wound up the steep hill.

The car drove up the hill towards the small forested area on its summit.

Knowing that the lane tapered off into no more than a dirt track (all right for a motorbike, but certainly not for a car) just before it reached the edge of the wood and that it then wound around to the south side of the hill, directly behind the hide, Steve remained where he was, peering through the rectangular viewing hole in the hedgerow. He watched the car until it had advanced as far as it could go, about twenty yards below the summit.

When the car stopped, before the men clambered out, Steve picked up the three pieces of his Sten gun – barrel, magazine and steel butt – fitted them together, loaded the weapon with a thirty-two-round box magazine and clipped another two box magazines to his belt.

Turning back to the viewing hole, he saw that five men had clambered out of the parked car and were breaking up into two separate groups. Three men spread out in a line to follow the dirt track around the hill. The other two advanced straight up the hill towards the OP, though it was obvious that they still hadn't seen it.

All of them were wearing the same type of grey suit, black shoes, shirts and ties. Three of them had pistols in their hands; one man in each of the two groups had an L2A3 Sterling sub-machine gun.

They mean business, Steve thought.

Keeping his eye to the rectangular viewing hole, he didn't move until the three-man team had disappeared along the winding track, clearly wanting to find out where it led. Knowing that it looped back into the trees on the south side of the hill, leading to the rear of his hide, Steve decided that he would have to move quickly.

The two men directly below him were still advancing up

the hill, about five metres apart, moving in and out of shadow in the fading light, and were now only about fifteen metres from the hedgerow that was protecting the hide. Steve inched the Sten's barrel through the viewing hole. He aligned the rear sight and foresight on the chest of the man carrying the Sterling sub-machine gun, took a deep breath, held it, then squeezed the trigger to fire a short burst.

Struck violently by the 9mm bullets, the man jerked convulsively, dropped his sub-machine gun and was still falling backwards to the ground as Steve shifted the barrel of his weapon a few inches to the left and fired a second burst at the man with the pistol. Shocked to see the convulsions of his friend as he fell, the man glanced sideways, then looked to the front again just as Steve's second burst struck him in the chest. He too was knocked backwards, staggering like a drunkard even as his pistol slipped from his numbed fingers. Then he dropped to his knees, looked down at his own chest, which was all smashed and bloody, and lost consciousness as he fell face down into the grass.

Instantly, Steve withdrew the barrel of his Sten gun from the viewing hole, turned away and left the hide through the camouflaged entry/exit gap in the hessian hanging to the ground at the rear. Moving at the half-crouch, darting from the protection of one tree to another, holding the Sten across his chest, he advanced until he came to a point that gave him a good line of sight to where the path ran into the edge of the forest before tapering off altogether under the trees.

He took up a firing position behind a thick tree trunk, concealed in the semi-darkness beneath the overhanging branches.

By now the other three men were racing up the southern slope towards the noise of the shooting, with one of them still coming along the dirt track and the other two spread out, one on each side of him. The three of them were about five metres apart. The one on the dirt track, a big man with broad shoulders and a granite face, was carrying the second Sterling sub-machine gun.

Determined again to put the most dangerous weapon out of commission first, Steve aimed along his sights at the chest of the big man with the sub-machine gun. He took a deep breath, held it, then fired a short burst.

Killed instantly, the man dropped his sub-machine gun as he collapsed. One of the other men, glancing around in surprise, received Steve's second burst. Crying out in pain, he dropped his pistol, clutched at a shoulder torn to shreds by Steve's bullets, and fell to his knees as the last man standing crouched low and advanced toward Steve's position, firing his pistol while on the move.

Some of the bullets went whistling past Steve's head on their way into the forest behind him, but others ricocheted off the branches right above him to shower him with falling leaves, splintered wood and dust. Spitting the dust from his mouth, he fell to one knee, aimed at the man still advancing uphill, now a mere few metres away, and fired a sustained burst in a wide arc to ensure that he could not miss his target.

He did not. The man advancing at the half-crouch screamed and threw his hands up in the air, letting his pistol fall. Then he spun away, punched sideways by the hail of bullets, and crashed into the undergrowth. Steve jumped up and ran towards him.

Another shot rang out. Steve dropped to the ground. He was showered in leaves and dust from the overhanging branches as the bullet ricocheted off the tree and went hurtling off into the forest. Glancing down the hill, Steve saw that the man he had wounded earlier was still on his knees, his bloody left arm dangling uselessly from the mangled shoulder, though he had retrieved his pistol and was holding it in his right hand. While he blinked repeatedly, obviously dazed, and swayed, dizzy with shock and loss of blood, from side to side, he tried unsuccessfully to fire it again.

Steve rolled to the side, then rose to one knee, protected by a tree trunk, and fired a sustained burst at the wounded man. The impact of the bullets made the man shudder convulsively before he fell backwards, still holding his pistol, to disappear into the tall grass.

Bursting out from behind the tree trunk, Steve advanced down the hill, weaving left and right, crouching low, until he reached the last man he had shot. Finding the man dead, though still clutching his pistol in rigid fingers, he turned away and crossed to the man who had been carrying the sub-machine gun. He too was dead. Steve then crossed the path to examine the third man and was relieved to find that he, also, was dead.

Five dead in five minutes, Steve thought. *Not bad going at all, kid.*

Realizing that he now had a good new cache of armaments, he took their weapons and ammunition from each of the three dead men. Satisfied, he went back to the hide and dropped these guns into the kit well, beside his own stack of explosives and ammunition. Since he already had his Browning 9mm High Power handgun strapped to his waist, he left the Sten gun in the kit well too and then, holding his 9-Milly in his right hand, left the hide again, this time making his way down the northern slope to check that the other two men were dead.

They were.

Feeling pleased with himself, not remotely shocked by what he had done, Steve holstered his 9-Milly and took the weapons and spare ammunition from the two corpses. Then he went back to the hide, where he added his most recent spoils of war to the kit well.

Thirsty, he took a long drink of water from his canteen. Then he prepared to leave the hide for good and remove all traces of its existence. The five dead men would eventually be found, since their parked Vauxhall Astra was bound to draw attention to them when daylight came, but Steve thought it wise to remove all traces of the hide. An experienced policeman, noting that the hide looked like an SAS OP, would assume, correctly, that an SAS man – or former SAS man – was responsible for the killings. With all traces of the hide removed, however, the five dead bodies might be seen as the victims of internecine warfare between organized crime gangs. So Steve strapped the rolled-up hessian screen, camouflage net, poncho and sleeping bag across the rear of his motorbike and packed everything else, including the dead men's captured weapons and ammunition, into his saddlebags. Then he sprinkled soil and grass over where his shallow scrape had been, making it look almost normal and hoping that a good rainfall would do the rest of the job of restoration for him.

It took him an hour to do this. By the time he had finished, full darkness had fallen.

Holding his motorbike by the handlebars, Steve pushed it down the slope until he reached the parked Vauxhall Astra. After resting the motorbike on its tripod, he checked the glove compartment of the car but found nothing of interest. Checking the boot, however, produced something priceless: a Barrett Model 90 rifle, capable of firing a .50 calibre bullet at nearly three times the speed of sound and killing a man at a distance of nearly a mile. Also in the boot was a Leupold & Stevens Vari-X III telescopic sight, which could magnify a target ten times and had a built-in range estimator as well as a facility for making windage and elevation adjustments. Between them, the rifle and the telescopic sight made, for Steve, a dream weapon. Even better, the boot also contained a goodly quantity of .50-calibre ammunition. Steve was exultant.

After removing the rifle from the boot of the car and attaching the telescopic sight, he wrapped it in his rubber poncho and tied it, well concealed by the rolled-up sleeping bag and hessian screen, across the rear of the motorbike. The .50-calibre ammunition just about squeezed into one of the already stuffed saddlebags.

Happy, Steve climbed onto his motorbike, started it up, then drove down the winding lane to the road below. Once there, he made his way to the M2 under cover of darkness, going in the direction of Belfast. From there, he would pick up the A2 and go on to Houlihan's house in Cultra.

Beyond that, Steve did not care to think. He would play it by ear.

Chapter Twenty

Houlihan could hardly wait to get his hands on Katherine —
though he had other plans for her later on, plans to do with
her ultimate humiliation.

The instant they were in the bedroom of the big house near
Cultra, though it was still relatively early in the day, he made her
drop to her knees in front of him, fully clothed though sublimely
curvaceous in her figure-hugging blue jeans and tightly belted
blouse, to work on him with her lips, quickly arousing him.
That she didn't want to do it was clear from the expression
on her face, the barely suppressed revulsion etched there. But
she knew enough by now not to refuse him anything, so she
simply closed her eyes and did what he wanted.

'That's it,' Houlihan said, running his fingers through
Katherine's hair, squeezing her head until it hurt her, moving
her this way and that to obtain maximum satisfaction. 'That's
the way to do it, girl. Sure you must've done this occasionally
for Jack Parnell, so it's nothing new to you.'

She couldn't answer, of course. Her mouth and tongue
were too busy. She had to listen to his mockery, his insults
and put-downs, while being forced to be his back-alley whore,
fully dressed and on her knees, engaged in a loveless transaction
that satisfied only him. He knew this and was thrilled all the
more by it.

'That's some mouth you have,' he said, tugging her hair, kneading her scalp. 'Sure you used it enough times to insult me or at least talk down to me; now you're using it for somethin' more constructive while payin' your dues ... Ah, Jasus, yes! Ah, Christ, sure that's grand! Why the fuck are you wastin' your time with the likes of Jack Parnell when you could be makin' a fortune in a brothel, doin' what you do so well ...'

Houlihan liked the sound of his own voice, liked to talk his way through his humiliations of Katherine, giving instructions or warnings as required, letting her know who was boss. Sure it was grand to be in control, using fear as your whip. What could be more exciting?

'No, no, don't stop! I'll break your jaw if you stop. I don't give a damn if you're tired – I want this drawn out ... Move your head ... Yes, like that. Come on, girlie, use that tongue! Ack, Jasus, oh fuck, hold off now. If I come too quick I'll beat you black and blue. There, there, that's it, girlie. Let me go for the moment ... Ah, Jasus, just look at the state of me, you cunt. Sure I'm as hard and as big as fuckin' Nelson's fuckin' Column and you're goin' to know what it feels like to have it inside you. Now get on your feet and let me unzip your jeans. I want to do it myself.'

Katherine rose to her feet, standing mere inches from him, and Houlihan reached down to cup her crotch in one hand while unzipping her jeans with the other. He slid his hand down and in, pressing and rubbing, then tugged the unzipped jeans down around her hips and said, 'I want to do this with my clothes on, so lie tits down on that bed with your knees on the floor.'

'Please!' she whispered. 'Don't! Not that. I just—'

Houlihan slapped her face, making her head jerk to the side. 'That slap won't leave a mark,' he said, 'but my clenched fist will, so don't aggravate me. Now do as I say, you cunt.'

She was visibly trembling now, not sophisticated at all, not a stuck-up bitch with a tongue like a razor: more like a scared child.

'Did you hear me, you cunt?'

'Yes,' Katherine whispered as she turned towards the bed and lowered herself to her knees. She turned her head sideways to lay her cheek on the quilt, then spread her hands out on both sides while resting her breasts and shoulders on the end of the bed and raising her rear towards him. Her jeans were down around her hips, revealing the round cheeks of her arse in sexy panties of white silk. Houlihan gripped the panties in both hands and abruptly ripped them off, making her flinch with shock. He held himself in one hand, put it to her and then pushed into her, not even considering lubrication because her pain was his thrill.

'Fuckin' Nelson's Column,' he said. 'Sure it could split you in two ... That's it, groan and moan all you want. Sure it just makes me hotter ... Not so proud now, are ya? Not as grand as you were. Sure what would your boyfriend, my lawyer, Jack Parnell, think if he saw you right now? Would he be shocked? Ashamed? Would he throw up on his fancy carpet? Or do you do it doggie fashion for him when you're not actin' the lady? Take *that*!' he said, pushing hard. 'And *that*!' Pushing harder. 'Are you groanin'? Did I hear a groan there? Is that pleasure or pain, girl? Jesus Christ, what an arse you have! Here it comes. Grit your teeth, bitch. Ah, Jasus! Ah, Christ! God Almighty, God help me!'

The great shuddering mass of him, spasm piled upon spasm, collapsing upon her to squeeze the breath from her body, his hot breath in her tangled golden hair, his sweat staining her crumpled shirt.

'Ah, fuck! What a whore you are!'

Houlihan had to rest after that. Even Hercules had to rest. He rolled off Katherine and lay there beside her, looking up as she stared sideways, her cheek still on the quilt, her shirt soaked in his sweat, her jeans down around her hips, her arse bare, with those tell-tale flecks of blood and God knew what other damage. She was moaning and shuddering, her hands opening and closing, racked with pain but too frightened to move, no longer a snooty bitch. He gasped for air beside her, his member shrinking, all done in. But the lust in his mind would give him no peace and so he told her to sit up and strip off.

'Bollock-naked,' he emphasized.

Katherine quivered like a bowstring, sucked her breath in, let it out, then rolled over and managed to sit upright, her face a mask of despair.

'Right now?' she asked dully.

'You're not fuckin' deaf,' Houlihan said. He was still lying there on his back beside her, still fully dressed, though his pants were unzipped and his flaccid member flopped out through his flies like a dead fish. He caught the look of revulsion on her face and it made him come back to life. There was the hint of new hardness there.

'A cunt is a cunt is a cunt,' he said. 'And it's the cunt I want this time. Now get your fuckin' kit off.'

Katherine stood up to remove her clothes. She didn't look as exciting without them. Undressed, she was certainly alluring but not as *sexy* as she was in those high heels, though she could still do the trick. As she undressed, Houlihan fingered himself, still lying there looking up at the ceiling. A wanker, she had called him – so he rubbed himself and was soon ready again. He'd show the bitch what a wanker was.

'Great tits,' he said. 'But they'll be sagging five years from now. A great arse, but it'll spread in no time and you'll have to hide it in loose skirts. Those great legs – Jesus Christ, the way you teased me with those legs! – but they're already becomin' thick around the thighs and you're not even thirty-five. Not so hot, are you, when you're not in your miniskirt and high heels and silk stockings, the blouse unbuttoned practically to the navel, crossing and uncrossing your legs while you lean forward to show off the creamy udders – not so hot *now*, are you? And what's happened to the superior look? The head back as you stare down your nose, lips curved in disdain and those lips, these great cock-sucking lips, mouthing high-toned sarcasm. Did you think I'd take that, you bitch? Well, look where it's got you. Lie down on that bed, you snooty cunt, and spread your legs the way you do for Jack Parnell. Let me do it like Jack does. *Thaaat's* it. Here I come.'

Houlihan lowered himself between Katherine's raised knees, letting her smooth thighs enfold him, entered her – awkwardly, though convinced that it was smoothly, convinced of his own skill – and then laboured upon her, belly slapping on belly, hairy chest on naked breasts, pushing in with a vengeance, no love evident in the movement, pushing in and withdrawing and pushing in even harder, ignoring her dryness, his inability to arouse her, having sex, the beast with two backs, to express his hatred and reduce her to nothing.

'Take that, you cunt!' he gasped. 'And that! And take *that* for good measure ...' Taking pleasure from her pain. Her despair his delight. Certainly not making love, not even simply having sex, but engaging in a brutal rape, carried out as an act of vengeance until he couldn't hold back ... 'Ack, Jesus, I can't stop it, it's happening, I'm comin'. Ah fuck, here I come! Oh, you cunt, Jesus Christ, God Almighty, Mary, Mother of God, here I come, God, I'm comin'! Yes, you cunt, here it comes! Fuck, yes, I'm exploding ...' Shuddering and shaking, the rolls of fat quivering, his breathing like bellows, his sweat dropping upon her, as he rose and fell upon her, the spasms whipping through her, to pound her with his mass of bone and blubber before collapsing upon her ... 'Jesus Christ! Ah, God! Oh, sweet Jesus, that's *it*. God, I'm fucked. Now I'm *really* fucked ...' Lying upon her, gasping for breath, his weight crushing her, winding her, both slick with sweat and exhausted, lying there like the dead. Then eventually his words split the lengthy silence, offering nothing at all ... 'That was good. That's enough. Jesus Christ, what a start to the weekend. Sure a man could do worse, like.'

And so the weekend began.

*   *   *

They went for lunch. Houlihan took Katherine to a restaurant in a hotel in Bangor, sitting at a table overlooking the sea, high above the beach road where he could see his parked Volvo, the minders standing nearby, packing pistols under their coats but otherwise looking normal, smoking cigarettes and chatting to each other while eyeballing the people passing by, looking out for likely assassins. Houlihan, looking down upon them, smiled. Then he returned his gaze to Katherine who, dressed again, looked sophisticated and glamorous, if unnaturally pale and somewhat distracted, her gaze focused inward.

'They all want you,' Houlihan told her. 'All those bastards who look after me. They get hard-ons every time you appear, so they try not to stare at you. They're frightened, you see. They know I'm a jealous man. They know that I'd kill them if they even looked sideways the wrong way, so they try not to look, they try so hard, and that just makes them want you all the more. So what do you think of that?'

Katherine gazed steadily at him for a moment, wary of him, despising him, concealing her true thoughts, a woman not yet completely destroyed, the flame of her steely will still flickering dimly. 'It's really not worth thinking about,' she said. 'I'm yours, after all.'

'Are you?'

'Don't you think so?'

'Sure you're not mine by choice. You're mine because I've made you my slave and you're too scared to run away.'

'Where would I run to?'

'You could lose yourself in London, Paris, New York. All you'd have to do is jump on a plane and never come back.'

'You'd find me,' Katherine said.

'Aye, I would, sure enough.'

'Then you'd punish me,' Katherine said. 'Even worse than you're doing now.'

Houlihan had to smile at that. 'At least you're honest,' he

said. 'You're not pretendin' that what we do together gives you a thrill. You're not pretendin' I'm the world's greatest lover. You're just takin' it lyin' down.'

'What else can I do?' she asked. 'I'm being punished and I'm taking my punishment because I don't have a choice. If I tried to pretend it's something more than that, I don't think you'd believe me.'

'I wouldn't.'

Katherine shrugged. 'Okay, then.'

'You think I've punished you enough?'

'More than enough,' she said.

But Houlihan shook his head from side to side. 'No, not more than enough. It hasn't even begun yet. You humiliated me, you cunt, you sneered at me, you talked down to me, and that's something I can never forget, let alone forgive. I've got a lot more in store for you, lady, and after that, even worse. You can't begin to imagine it.'

He saw the fear in her eyes, then, though contempt was there as well. 'Keep talking,' she said, 'and you'll scare me so much that I might actually try to escape. London, Paris, New York – maybe farther than that. If I fly far enough, I might lose you. If I'm frightened enough, I might try it.'

'Sure wherever you went, I'd catch you,' he told her. 'And then, as you rightly said yourself, I'd be compelled to punish you – and when it gets down to that kind of punishment, you don't want to know.'

'Tell me,' she said.

Houlihan nodded towards the window, lowering his gaze to take in the armed minders standing near his parked car, a sullen, wind-blown sea behind them.

'See them?' he asked rhetorically. 'I hire them because they're animals. They're animals and all of them lust after you – and the kind of things that give them their sexual pleasure simply beggar description. If you ran away and I caught you, I'd hand you over to them. I'd say do what you want with her. I'd say

I'm finished with her, she's past history to me, and you can share her between you, do what you want with her, use her any way you want until she's all used up and then slit her pretty throat from ear to ear and dump her into the Lagan. I repeat: those men are animals. Having your throat slit would be an act of mercy. What wouldn't be merciful, not even remotely bearable, would be the things those animals would put you through as they passed you from hand to hand. You'd have your own room, of course. A spartan room with a bed and a toilet. You'd have a two-ring burner and an electric kettle, just to keep you alive. You just wouldn't have a doorkey. No way out of there at all. But those bastards, those animals, *they'*d all have a doorkey and they'd all come and go as they please and expect you to service them. How many of them I can't count − thirty or forty, you name it − and they'd have you in every way you can imagine, in every fucking orifice. Some get their kicks from inflicting pain. Others have even more bizarre tastes. They're pederasts and sadists, perverts and psychopaths. Sure what we're talkin' about here is the arsehole of existence and those maniacs, all thirty or forty of them, would have you as their sexual toy. Then, when you were all worn out and possibly half crazed, they'd complain about you to me and I'd tell one of them to slit your pretty throat and dump you in the river. Do you believe what I'm saying?'

'Yes.'

'Well, that's good. Don't forget it. Now let's get back to that grand house by the beach. I have a special guest coming this evenin' and he'll expect to be entertained.'

'With dinner?'

'No,' Houlihan said. 'With you. That's part of your punishment.'

Katherine flinched visibly at that. He saw the blood drain from her face. Her left hand, resting on the snow-white table cloth, opened and closed convulsively. Good, he was getting there.

'Let's go,' he said.

As Houlihan had an account with the hotel, he simply signed the bill and then led Katherine out to the Volvo parked at the other side of the road. The return journey seemed to take no time at all and soon they were back in the big house and up in his bedroom.

'I'm going to have a wee nap,' he said, 'and I think you should do the same, so get undressed and come to bed.'

Houlihan stripped naked in front of her, not expecting her to like it, knowing how gross he looked when naked, an enormous, hairy brute. But Katherine managed to keep her eyes off him as she, too, stripped and then slipped under the quilt to lie beside him. Satiated, both in his groin and in his gut, he closed his eyes and pretended to sleep, though in fact he was wide awake and just wanted to force her to lie there to torment her still more.

She pretended to sleep as well. It was her way of escaping from him. Her eyes were closed but he could tell from her breathing that she wasn't really asleep. She was lying there in fear, wondering desperately when this would end – and, no doubt, she was thinking about his minders and what the psychotic brutes would do to her if he passed her on to them.

Despite Houlihan's belief that he was satiated, when he thought of what the minders would do to her he had another erection.

'Hey, you,' he said, opening his eyes again and throwing the quilt off him to show what he had.

Katherine opened her eyes.

'See that?' he said, pointing.

She nodded. 'Yes.'

'Sure a man can't possibly get to sleep when he has one of those. Get rid of it for me.'

'I—'

'Get down on me, girlie. You understand? That's it ... Ah, Jasus!'

Later, seemingly satiated again, he led her into his posh

bathroom and made her join him under a hot shower. He made her soap him all over, rub the soap off with her body, lick him all over to arouse him again and give him a hand job while the shower was still running. Then he turned her to the wall and pushed it in from behind and came when he heard her pained groaning. Then he withdrew, feeling grand. He turned the water off and stepped out of the shower, then turned back to hand her a thick towel.

'Dry me,' he said.

It was great to have a slave. Sure it made a man feel powerful. He was thrilled by her expression of abject humiliation, though she hadn't sunk as low as she *could* go: she had that still to come.

'Now help me to get dressed for dinner,' he said. 'I'll show you the clothes I want and you'll put them on me and you'd better be fuckin' careful about it. You catch my cock when you zip up my trousers and I won't be amused. Here, these underpants first. Help me put 'em on, girlie.'

Houlihan raised one foot, then the other, getting into his underpants, looking down as she kneeled on the floor and tugged the underpants up his hairy tree-trunk legs and around his crotch, where his cock was already hardening again.

'Press your lips there,' he ordered.

Katherine pressed her lips to his crotch, now warm in the underpants.

'Now help me get into these trousers ... That's it, now you're gettin' it. Never thought you'd be a servant one day, did you? Not a fancy legal assistant like you, all set to do her exams and become a lawyer. Now here you are, dressin' a fine gentleman and pleased to be doin' it. Better than bein' worked over by thirty or forty of my minders, that's for fuckin' sure ... That's it. Grand. Now this shirt and tie, you dumb cunt. We want to look good for dinner, don't we? Then it's your turn.'

She finished dressing him, a silent servant, obedient. Then, when he was ready, he ordered her to get dressed and told her what to wear. A pair of fine silk panties covering less than a string bikini would. No bra. A shimmering, skintight black dress, cut low to show off the bosom, its hem well above the knee. Sheer black stockings and stiletto-heeled shoes that made her legs seem to go on for ever. When dressed, she looked practically naked, but even better than that. She looked like something to eat.

'You're some fuckin' legal assistant,' Houlihan said. 'Okay, let's go downstairs.'

They left the bedroom and descended the stairs, crossed the lobby and entered the living room. There was only one other guest, a man with a ponytail, gaunt Calvinist features and bright, slightly crazed green eyes. He was wearing scruffy blue jeans, high-heeled boots and a badly wrinkled open-necked shirt. He was sitting on the sofa, in front of a low coffee table, having a whisky and smoking a cigar.

When Houlihan walked in with Katherine, the man looked the girl up and down as if he was inspecting a piece of merchandise.

'Jesus!' he exclaimed, his voice harsh. 'What the fuck have we here, Mike?'

Houlihan glanced at Katherine, then grinned and turned back to his guest. 'You like it?'

The guest nodded vigorously in affirmation. 'Fuckin' right. That's some piece. I wouldn't mind a bite of it.'

'Maybe later,' Houlihan said. Then he turned to the mortified, even more nervous Katherine, waving a hand to indicate his scruffy guest. 'This is a friend of mine,' he explained. 'Name of Billy Moore. He's a wee Prod but we can't hold that against him. After all, he likes Catholic girls with long, sexy legs, which is just what you've got.'

'Yeah, right,' Wild Bill said. 'I always liked them long legs. Wraparound legs, I call 'em. You've got a nice set yourself, doll.'

'You should see the rest of them,' Houlihan said as he poured himself a whisky. 'Show him the rest of them, Kathy.'

'*What?*' Katherine sounded shocked and disbelieving.

'Show Billy-boy the rest of your legs. Tug your skirt up and give him a good gander. He's our guest, after all.'

'Fucking right,' Wild Bill said.

'I—'

'Tug your skirt up,' Houlihan repeated in a vicious tone of voice that brooked no argument. 'Up over your panties. Come on! Don't be bashful. Give my friend here an eyeful.'

Katherine closed her eyes, took a deep breath and let it out in a sigh that expressed her humiliation. Then she took hold of the hem of her dress and tugged it up as high as it would go, until it was tight around her hips, revealing her panties. Seeing what he could see, Wild Bill responded with a low whistle of appreciation.

'Good, eh?' Houlihan said.

'Real wraparound legs,' Wild Bill replied. 'So what's for fuckin' dessert?'

'She is,' Houlihan said.

Katherine trembled to hear that.

It was clear to Houlihan that the subsequent lengthy dinner was an agony to Katherine. But he and Wild Bill enjoyed themselves, trading stories about their various criminal activities, including their prostitution rings, the drugs trade, the protection rackets, the intimidation, the money laundering and, of course, the punishment beatings and killings. Full details were supplied and real names were named, which was deliberate on Houlihan's part, since he wanted Katherine to know that she was hearing too much for her own good and would almost certainly, some time in the future, be made to pay for it, most likely with her own life. For the most part, Katherine ate silently, head lowered, saying nothing unless spoken to, and even then only whispering her replies. Such interactions were few and far between ... and never remotely pleasant.

'So what do you think?' Houlihan asked her at one point.

'What about?' Katherine responded.

'Do whores get into it because of circumstances or are *all* women born to be whores?'

'I ...'

'What? I can't hear you!'

'I'd say circumstances.'

'You mean women don't like fucking for its own sake? They *just* do it for money?'

'I didn't mean that. What I meant was—'

'They're all whores.' This was Wild Bill's contribution. 'I say women are all natural whores and can't get enough of it.'

'What about you, Kathy?' Houlihan winked at Wild Bill. 'Do you like fucking for its own sake? And can you get enough of it?'

'Please, I—'

'I mean, what about Parnell? Does he give you enough? Does he do all the things that I've done to you or is he shy when it comes to the meat and bone of it? Would he be shocked by some of the things you've done with me? Would he believe it was you, like?'

'I ...'

'The things she does with me,' Houlihan said, now addressing Wild Bill with a wink and a grin, 'are done so fuckin' well that you've got to believe she's had a lot of practice.'

'I'd have to judge that for myself,' Wild Bill said. 'Don't deprive an old friend, like.'

'I won't. But why not have a three-ring circus to add some spice to it?'

'Me and her and who?'

'Me.' Houlihan spelled it out. 'You take one end and I take the other and we keep changin' positions. That should spice it up nicely.'

'Sure I'm game if you are.'

'Okay, Billy-boy, let's go upstairs.'

'*No!*' Katherine cried out.

It was a cry of dread and revulsion, of naked desperation,

bursting out of her instinctively and cleaving the very air as she pushed her chair back and turned away to rush out of the room. But Wild Bill was too fast for her, leaping out of his own chair to grab her, wrapping his arms around her waist to lift her off the floor while she kicked and struggled and sobbed hysterically.

'Let's get the bitch up those stairs,' Houlihan said, 'and pacify her just enough to make her amenable when we both get stuck into her.'

'I can hardly hold her,' Wild Bill said, his arms still wrapped around her as she struggled and kicked wildly at the air, sobbing wretchedly, choking. 'The bitch is wriggling so much.'

'Settle down, you cunt,' Houlihan said harshly. 'You hear me? *Be quiet!*'

He slapped Katherine's face, once, twice, a third time, then punched her viciously in the stomach, just below Wild Bill's clasped arms. She gasped and sagged, the wind all knocked out of her, as Wild Bill swung her around, away from the table, her feet still off the floor, and carried her out of the room and up the stairs to the bedroom.

Houlihan followed. When he entered the bedroom, Katherine was on her hands and knees, gasping for breath, looking down at the carpet, her long hair hanging around her face like a golden-blonde veil, hiding her tears. Wild Bill was taking his shirt off, grinning crookedly, his gaze crazed, and Houlihan, seeing Katherine's raised arse, her open mouth, was aroused all over again and started doing the same.

He was just about to rip his shirt off when something exploded outside, blowing the windows in, filling the room with flying glass and billowing dust.

He heard Katherine screaming.

Chapter Twenty-one

As Steve rode his motorbike along the A2, through a sleeping Holywood and on to the road that led to Cultra, he wondered how Houlihan's men had learned of his whereabouts. He assumed that they must have discovered that he had changed the Yamaha for a Suzuki when they tortured Joe Williamson before killing him. Presumably, then, Houlihan's men had scoured the Antrim countryside, asking about a stranger with an all-black Suzuki motorbike until, eventually, they did indeed find someone who had seen such a man coming and going from somewhere in that particular area. From there it would just have been a matter of throwing a circle of men around the area and gradually tightening the cordon until they discovered him. It was clear, therefore, that if he didn't manage to neutralize Houlihan and Wild Bill later this evening, he'd better change his Suzuki for something else or they would find him again.

Just like they found Joe, he thought. *Poor fucking Joe.*

The very thought of what they had done to Joe filled Steve with revulsion and rage while strengthening his determination to get rid of Houlihan and Wild Bill before they did any more damage. Indeed, it had taken the murder of his friend to remind him of just how deadly Houlihan could be and to cause him to wonder just how far his reach went. Certainly, if Houlihan could throw a cordon around whole areas of Antrim, he had more men at his disposal than Steve had assumed and could strike out at just about anyone, including Steve's friends in Belfast. More worrying was the knowledge that Houlihan, because of his former PIRA activities, had built up a lot of underworld connections on the mainland and could probably locate anyone he wanted to find. Given that it was now open warfare between him and Steve and that he had already picked up and murdered one of Steve's best friends right here in the province, there was nothing that said he wouldn't consider striking at someone even closer to Steve's heart ... perhaps even his wife and children in England.

This possibility became frighteningly real to Steve as he rode along the winding coast road to Cultra, high above the great sweep of Belfast Lough. As he glanced down at the inky-black water streaked occasionally with moonlight, at once cold and seductive, a suicide's dream, he recalled that during the Troubles he had been high on Houlihan's hit list because of his SAS work with 14 Int. That being so, there could be no doubt that Houlihan would have found some way to get a profile of him, including details of his private life. As Steve knew, once PIRA had raised a profile on someone, they kept it constantly updated. Houlihan, who had organized his criminal business along the lines of the terrorist gangs, would almost certainly have kept Steve's profile up to date. So he would have the address of Linda and the children even though they were separated from Steve and lived on the mainland.

If he thought that it would help to rein Steve in, Houlihan wouldn't hesitate to abduct Linda and the children. He would threaten to kill them if Steve didn't turn himself in. No question but that Houlihan would do that if it entered his head. He was that kind of man.

Shocked to find himself thinking of this possibility, suddenly feeling irresponsible and quietly praying that such a thought hadn't yet entered Houlihan's head, Steve rode the motorbike even faster to get to Cultra as soon as possible. Arriving there about ten minutes later, he kept going, heading north, until he reached the beach area where Houlihan's house was. Once there, he rode around the dark, hilly roads until he came to the one that had the name given to him by Joe Williamson. Not wanting his motorbike to be seen by Houlihan's surveillance cameras, he parked it at the end of the road and walked along until he was close to the house he was looking for.

This was a tree-lined road of big, detached houses surrounded by gardens, spaced well apart, and hidden behind a profusion of trees, hedgerows and high, almost tropical foliage. Most of the properties overlooked the sea and were raised well above it. Houlihan's house wasn't ostentatiously large, though it was generously proportioned and set well back from the road in lush gardens, with a high stone wall and steel gates. Unlike the other houses, it faced the road and backed onto the sea.

Deliberately walking past the house, but on the other side of the road, far enough away to avoid any security cameras, Steve glanced into the property and saw that there was, indeed, a security camera over the front door and that a couple of minders were sitting in chairs, one on each side of the entrance, both clearly alert. He also saw the grey metal container box of a burglar alarm, mounted over the front door as a warning to potential burglars. But since the alarm would not go off until he had actually broken in, the alarm bell would start ringing too late to bother him.

Steve kept walking, hoping to seem like a casual passer-by on his way home. Reaching the far end of the road, he crossed over and walked past the garden of the last house in the road, checking to see if there was a way in from the rear. In fact, the houses had been built on a bluff overlooking the sea and the only way into them from the back was along private pathways that zigzagged up from the beach to the rear gardens. The sea, Steve noticed, was rough and noisy, with waves breaking dramatically over the rock outcroppings. Since this was a stormy night, there wasn't a soul in sight.

Turning back past the fenced-in gardens of the end house, he crossed the road again, then turned along the road that ran parallel to the one Houlihan had his house in. After walking to the end of that road, he turned right and walked downhill until he was back at the end of Houlihan's road, where his motorbike was parked. He hopped onto the bike, revved the engine, made a U-turn and drove off to find the beach road. Finding it in a matter of minutes, he was soon on the shore.

Keeping his eyes peeled, Steve drove on the impacted sand until he was about half a mile from the rear of Houlihan's property. Stopping there, he clambered off the motorbike and propped it up on its steel legs. The wind was strong here, but not strong enough to blow the motorbike over. The sea rushed and roared.

Removing his binoculars from one of the saddlebags, he scanned Houlihan's property until he could see the stone pathway that snaked up his terraced rear garden to the flat lawns surrounding the house. Even at this time of night, the path was romantically illuminated with ornately hooded overhead lights. At the bottom of the pathway, where it led onto the beach, was a closed gate and, leaning against the outside of it, a minder wearing a sea-green anorak, which doubtless concealed some kind of handgun. He was facing the beach.

Scanning the other properties, where a few lights were beaming out into the night, showing that some of the residents were still awake, Steve saw that most of them had similar pathways down to the beach, though none of them had guards at their gates. For a moment, he considered simply making his way up the unguarded pathway of the nearest house and getting into Houlihan's property from there, unseen by the guard down on the beach. However, he quickly discarded this idea as being unworkable because, once he launched his assault on the house, the minder on the beach would hear the noise and come up the path to attack him from the rear. No, that minder had to be silently neutralized before the assault proper was launched.

Glancing up and down the dark, windswept beach, Steve saw that it was still empty. The luminous dial of his wristwatch showed that it was just before midnight. Given the weather, cold and blustery, with the sky above filled with rain clouds that obscured a pale moon and the few stars, it was unlikely that anyone would show up on the beach at this late hour. If by any chance they did, it would be unfortunate for him. But as the beach was so long and open, he would at least be able to hide his weapon, perhaps even ride off, before they came near him. So he decided to chance it.

First, Steve removed the hessian sheeting from the rear saddle and unrolled it to reveal the Barrett Model 90 rifle with the Leupold & Stevens Vari-X III telescopic sight already attached to it. He picked the weapon up and leaned it against the side of the motorbike. Next, after removing some of the .50-calibre ammunition from one of the saddlebags, he loaded the rifle and then kneeled beside the motorbike to support the weapon on the rear saddle and hard-topped saddlebags. He was approximately half a mile away from the rear gate of Houlihan's property: since the Barrett could kill a man at a range of up to a mile, he anticipated no problems with this particular task.

Squinting into the telescopic sight, Steve moved the rifle until the minder came into focus and was fixed in the sight's cross-hairs, bathed in the eerie green-yellow glow of the night-vision optics. The man was still leaning against the gate, still facing the beach, and Steve moved his weapon again until the cross-hairs met over the target's chest. He then used the magnifier to make the man appear in close-up, as well as the facility for windage and elevation adjustments, and, finally, once more checked the position of the cross-hairs over the minder's chest.

He cocked the weapon, held his breath and fired a single shot.

The noise it made was shocking, seeming even louder than it really was. But since Steve was firing from half a mile away, he knew that it wouldn't be heard inside Houlihan's thick-walled house.

The man jerked violently, then was slammed backwards against the gate, practically punched off his feet by that single .50 calibre bullet, his arms and hands flapping wildly. He remained there for a second, then he slid down the gate, his spine still pressed against it, until he was on his knees. He remained on his knees for another couple of seconds, then, either dead or losing consciousness, he keeled over to fall into the sand.

Steve continued looking through the telescopic sight for some time, checking the man in close-up with the aid of the sight's magnification. When, after half a minute, the man still hadn't moved, Steve accepted that he was almost certainly dead – or at least mortally wounded.

Satisfied, Steve removed the weapon from its support position on the motorbike, rolled it back up in the hessian sheeting, then strapped it back across the rear saddle. Glancing left and right along the beach, he saw that it was still empty, so he pushed the motorbike across to where the sand met the bluff and parked it under a high, grassy outcropping, where it was unlikely to be seen if someone passed by.

Protected by darkness, he removed a small canvas bag from one of the saddlebags and slung the strap over his right shoulder, letting the bag hang down by his hip. He then removed the holstered Browning 9mm High Power handgun from the other saddlebag and buckled the belt around his waist, positioning the holster on his left hip, the butt of the gun facing forward, allowing him to make a quick cross-draw with his right hand. Finally, he removed the three separate pieces of the Mk2 Sten gun from one of the saddlebags, fitted the parts together, inserted a thirty-two-round magazine, clipped another to his belt, then slung the weapon over his left shoulder.

Steve loped off along the beach, heading for Houlihan's property.

As he ran, the wind beat at his face and body, moaning

eerily around him. The sea rushed and roared, exploding dramatically against rocky outcroppings, throwing up curtains of silvery spray.

Steve moved at a measured pace and only slowed down when, nearly half a mile on, he was approaching the rear gate of Houlihan's property. Just before he reached it, he dropped back to a walking pace, glancing up at the house to see that some lights were still on, both upstairs and downstairs, indicating that at least a few of those inside were still awake.

Lowering his gaze, he saw the minder lying motionless on the sand in front of the gate.

Steve kneeled down to confirm that the man was indeed dead. He was. Satisfied, Steve stood up again, checked the gate and the stone pathway at the other side, and was relieved to note that there was no sign of a surveillance camera or other security system. Obviously, any resident wanting to secure their rear-entrance pathways would, like Houlihan, have to use a personal bodyguard and would only use their high-tech surveillance equipment on the property at the top of the path.

Relieved, Steve opened the gate and dragged the dead bodyguard inside to dump him at the side of the path by the bottom steps, where he would not been seen in the unlikely event that a late-night visitor to the beach passed by. After closing the gate behind him, he took his 9-Milly from its holster, held it in his right hand, then started up the steep, zigzagging pathway, moving lightly from one stone step to another, until he was about three-quarters of the way to the top. Once there, he stepped off the path and entered the cover of the trees, high plants and other foliage of the terraced gardens where he was less likely to be seen by any surveillance camera that might be fixed to the rear wall of the house. Moving roughly parallel to the pathway, he soon reached the rear edge of the flat lawns and, shielded by a low hedge, was able to look out in comparative safety.

The lawns ran upwards to the back wall of the house. Downstairs was dominated by what looked to be a spacious living room with French windows leading out into the gardens. The curtains had not been drawn across the French windows and the lights in the living room were still on, though no one appeared to be in there. On one side of the living room was what seemed to be a kitchen, judging by the plates and cups dangling from the hooks of the large Welsh dresser set against the wall facing the windows (clearly visible because there too the lights were still on). At the other side were the windows of another large room, possibly a drawing room or guest wing, though the lights there were not on.

On the floor above, a series of French windows, three in all, led out onto balustraded stone balconies – obviously the balconies of the bedrooms – and lights were shining only in the middle one. Steve judged from this that if there were people in the other bedrooms, they would either be asleep or having sex in the darkness, which would, at least, mean that they were mightily distracted. So the greatest danger would come from the middle room, where the lights were on, indicating that the people in there were almost certainly still awake.

He would therefore make that particular room his first port of call.

Scanning the second floor again, he saw a surveillance camera scanning repeatedly north to south, systematically covering the rear, west-facing gardens. The camera did not, however, move far enough in either direction to actually focus on the balustraded balconies, so if Steve could get as far as the rear wall of the house without being observed, he could do what he had to before attempting to scale the wall.

Helpfully, there was a large garden shed at the other side of the low hedge, then two greenhouses between that shed and the house. A steel extension ladder lay beside the garden shed and was long enough to reach the balconies in front of the first-floor French windows.

Calculating that he could avoid the camera by advancing from one building to another each time the camera turned away from him, Steve holstered his handgun, waited until the camera had turned north, then scrambled over the low hedge and made his way at the half-crouch to the large garden shed. He remained there, hidden by the shed's back wall, until the camera had scanned the whole garden and was turning north again. Then he picked up the extension ladder and advanced, still crouching and being careful to strike nothing with the ladder, until he had reached the first of the two greenhouses.

Just before the camera turned back towards him, he lowered the ladder to the ground and stretched out in the grass at the northern side of the greenhouse, assuming, correctly, that although the building was made of glass window-panes, the camera would not see him in that position, protected by two walls of the greenhouse. If it had, it would have stopped and focused upon him; instead it kept turning away from him until it was again aiming north.

Rising carefully to his feet while lifting the extension ladder, Steve advanced from one greenhouse to the next, though this time he stretched out on the ground at the southern side, again protected by two walls of glass window-panes from the camera that was turning in his direction. Once the camera had turned away from him and was facing directly north, he rose silently to his feet and quickly carried the extension ladder to the rear wall of the house, beside the window of the room he had assumed was the kitchen.

Confident that the roving camera could not see him in this position, which was practically directly under it and therefore out of its line of sight, Steve inched along the wall, away from the kitchen, until he was just short of the living room. After resting the ladder silently against the wall, mere inches away from the edge of the nearest French window, the top step almost level with the balustraded balcony of the bedroom above, he made his way back to the window of what he had assumed was the kitchen.

As the light was still on, he pressed himself to the wall

by the window frame, then leaned out a little to peer in. It was indeed the kitchen. Even better, there was no one in there.

Lowering himself to his knees, now unconcerned by the constantly turning surveillance camera, Steve took a home-made bomb from the canvas shoulder bag. Not a powerful bomb, it consisted of a small block of Semtex plastic explosive, an electric initiator, a blasting cap with bridge wire, a twenty-foot length of detonating cord and the kind of remote-control firing device that was known to the SAS as a 'button job'. He didn't need a powerful bomb because the explosion, though modest, would make a hell of a lot of noise and, more importantly, blow up the gas boiler on the other side of the wall and thus set fire to the building.

After glancing around him and listening intently to ascertain that no minders were patrolling the grounds, Steve taped the bomb to a black-painted vertical pipe that ran alongside the kitchen window, then made his way at the half-crouch back to where the ladder had been positioned, letting the detonating cord trail out behind him. The ladder was positioned about fifteen feet from the kitchen and the explosion wouldn't harm him from that distance.

He removed the Sten gun from his shoulder and held it in his right hand. He would need his left hand for the button job and, seconds later, the ladder.

Glancing upwards, Steve saw that the light in the bedroom almost directly above him was still on. Glancing left and right, he neither saw nor heard any sign of human movement. He remembered, however, that two armed minders were guarding the front door and would race around to the back of the building when they heard the explosion. His intention, therefore, was to leave the building via the front door.

Be audacious, he thought. *Well, here goes ...*

Taking a deep breath, then letting it out slowly to ease his tension, Steve pressed the button job.

The bomb exploded with a deafening roar. A sheet of jagged

light was followed by fingers of yellow flame, a billowing cloud of dust, then a mass of debris that flew out of the wrecked kitchen like a shower of bullets. The first explosion was followed almost instantaneously by a second one – the gas boiler exploding – and this time the flames were a veritable fountain of fire that spewed outwards in all directions.

Instantly, swiftly, Steve clambered up the ladder, using his left hand to hold on while gripping the Sten gun in his right. Within seconds he was on the top rung, flopping belly down on top of the balustrade to twist sideways, fling his legs over it and plant his feet on the floor of the balcony.

A woman screamed inside.

Looking in, he saw the woman stretched out face down on the floor, wearing a skimpy black dress that had been flung up over her back to reveal her white panties. Two men, Houlihan and Wild Bill, were standing over her, both looking startled, both unarmed.

The French windows were closed. Steve simply kicked them open. The glass broke noisily, shards falling to the floor as both doors swung back so hard that they crashed into the frames on either side.

The bell of the burglar alarm started ringing.

Steve lowered his Sten gun and fired on the move as he advanced into the room. But Houlihan and Wild Bill had already turned away and were disappearing through the door leading into the upstairs corridor. Steve fired another short burst and bullets ricocheted off the doorframe, tore wood splinters from the door, peppered the walls and filled the air with swirling dust as the woman on the floor covered the back of her head with her hands, then bravely turned her face sideways to see what was happening.

Steve recognized Katherine Crowley.

Not having time to attend to her, he simply snapped 'Stay down!', then stepped over her and made his way to the bedroom door. There were more explosions from downstairs, more gas pipes blowing up, and then he heard the sound of three or four men shouting over the general clamour. He left the room slowly, crouched low, moving the barrel of his Sten left to right, scanning the corridor as he emerged, half expecting to find someone running at him but seeing only Houlihan's broad back disappearing around the corner where the corridor met the top of the stairs.

The burglar alarm stopped ringing.

Tendrils of smoke were coming up the stairs.

Footsteps were also coming up the stairs.

Instantly, without hesitation, Steve raced along the corridor and started firing down the stairs even as he stepped out into the stairwell. His sustained burst, fired in a broad arc, smashed into the chest of the minder with a pistol advancing upwards and sent him bowling back down the stairs.

Another minder, coming up behind the first, pressed himself to the wall to let the body fall past him, but fired hopefully at Steve as he did so. The single shot ricocheted off the wall behind Steve as he fired another burst that made the man on the stairs crumple before tumbling down the stairs to land in a sprawling heap on the floor beside his dead comrade.

Still holding his weapon in the firing position, Steve descended the stairs into clouds of thickening smoke.

At that moment, he heard someone on the stairs above and behind him and whirled around to start firing.

It was Katherine Crowley.

'Shit!' Steve whispered. 'I almost killed you!'

'I'm sorry, but I smelt the smoke,' she said, 'so I thought I'd better get out. Who are you?'

'Never mind. Just stay close behind me, but don't get too close. I could be shot at.'

'I understand,' she said, sounding calm. 'Don't worry about me.'

'I won't,' Steve promised.

Frustrated because Katherine had cost him valuable time,

Steve turned away from her and hurried down the last few stairs, stopping at the bottom only long enough to see smoke pouring out of the ruined kitchen while flames curled around the wooden door frames, setting wallpaper and carpets on fire. Though he assumed that the two men he'd just shot were the ones who had been guarding the front door, he still moved across the spacious hallway with particular care, glancing left and right, checking the entrances to the other rooms, and keeping the barrel of his Sten gun pointed wherever his searching gaze went.

This was just as well since a whole bunch of men, some wearing pyjamas, others fully clothed, some holding handguns, came bursting from the clouds of smoke pouring out of the kitchen. Realizing that he was faced with the rest of Houlihan's minders, the men due to work in later shifts who had probably been sleeping in a guest wing near the kitchen when the bomb went off, Steve did not hesitate to let rip with the Sten gun, firing in a broad, deadly arc that cut most of them down, either dead or seriously wounded, in one fierce, sustained burst. They were bowled over like skittles, bellowing, waving their arms, their legs buckling. Steve only stopped firing when his weapon ran out of bullets.

Instantly, he replaced the empty thirty-two-round magazine with the full one clipped to his belt. Then he checked the men on the floor. Some were dead and others were only wounded. But none were a threat to him.

When he heard a car starting up outside, he rushed to the front door.

Despite his rising frustration, Steve didn't run straight through that door, dropping instead to one knee, pressing his back to the door frame, then leaning sideways to glance around it and see what was outside.

A Volvo V70 CX saloon car had just roared into life, its rear wheels churning up the gravel as it started out of the driveway.

Even as the car was moving off, Houlihan was clambering

awkwardly into the rear seat and Wild Bill, looking very wild indeed, was running beside him with a pistol in his hand.

When Steve jumped to his feet and ran out through the doorway, raising his Sten gun to the firing position, Wild Bill fired a stream of bullets at him, making him throw himself to the ground. He rolled over a few times, out of Wild Bill's line of sight, then propped himself up on his elbows, preparing to fire again.

He was too late.

Before he could bring his Sten gun into the proper firing position, Steve saw Wild Bill throwing himself into the rear seat of the Volvo and slamming the door shut behind him as the vehicle raced along the driveway, its wheels noisily churning up more gravel before it went into a sharp, screeching right-hand turn to burn off along the dark road, heading back towards Belfast.

'Fuck!' Steve said aloud.

He banged his forehead two or three times on the ground, letting the sharp gravel cut him, punishing himself. Then he pushed himself to his feet and turned back to the burning house.

Katherine Crowley was standing in the doorway.

Chapter Twenty-two

'That fuckin' night rider again,' Wild Bill said as he sat beside Houlihan and Connolly, all of them squeezed into the rear of the Volvo speeding back to Belfast. 'A real SAS-style operation. It had to be him.'

'It *was* him!' Houlihan retorted, almost screaming. 'Sure I saw the fucker as clear as day when he kicked those French windows open and stomped into the bedroom. It was that mad fucker, Steve Lawson, all right!'

Houlihan was livid. He wanted to kill someone. He could still hear the explosions, smell the smoke, see the flames, as his lovely house in Cultra was destroyed right before his eyes. He still couldn't believe it.

'He always *was* a mad fucker,' Houlihan added, barely able to contain himself, wanting to wring someone's neck – anyone's neck – just to ease his frustrations. 'A real Captain Nairac type. A chancer who didn't know any limits and thought he was a cat with nine lives. Well, this time we'll prove the fucker wrong. This time we'll get him.'

'How?' Wild Bill asked.

'I'll think of somethin', Billy-boy, don't you worry, and this time it's gonna be fuckin' terminal. He'll be food for the worms.'

Glancing out of the window, he saw that it was raining,

silvery sheets of rain falling across a shadowy Belfast Lough to make the inky-black water ripple. Thunder growled in the distance.

'He may be mad,' Kavanagh said, speaking over his shoulder from his seat up front beside the driver, Neil Dempsey. 'But he sure as hell made a mess of that house.'

'And took down a lot of our men,' Connolly added from Houlihan's right side. 'I mean, that fuck iced at least—'

'Jasus!' Houlihan exploded, nearly coming off his seat, his slab of a face turning purple with outrage. 'I don't believe my fuckin' ears! I've lost my house and about a dozen of my men and you pair of shites are *admiring* that bastard! I should—'

'Calm down, calm down,' Wild Bill said, patting Houlihan's left knee as if it was the head of a favoured dog. 'They weren't admiring him, Mike. Just expressin' an understandable disbelief over what the fuck did. Even *I*'m havin' trouble believing it. You must admit, that guy's some operator. Credit where it's due, Mike.'

'Jasus! God Almighty!' Houlihan couldn't control himself. 'I'm trapped in a car with Lawson's fuckin' fan club, forced to listen to them singin' his praises while my fuckin' house burns down. I could kill all you scumbags.'

'What's that?' Wild Bill asked sharply.

'Jasus, Wild Bill, hold off there. Nothin' personal, you understand, just a remark that popped out with the anger. No offence meant, like, pal. But Jasus Christ! God Almighty! He burned my house down and shot a dozen of my men and you and me are fuckin' lucky to be alive – so, you know, I'm a bit pissed off, like, and in no mood to hear how brilliant Lawson is. I wanna hear how we're gonna get the fucker and what we're gonna do to him.'

'A fucking blowtorch,' Kavanagh suggested.

'After a six-pack,' Connolly added, referring to the practice of shooting, at close range, an individual's ankles, elbows and kneecaps – a punishment recalled fondly by all those who served with PIRA during the Troubles. 'Then hang him by his collar to the railings of some park and wave the knife a couple of times in front of his fucking eyes – letting him know what's comin', like – before slowly, oh, so slowly, cutting his throat. *That* should see him off, boss.'

'Ackaye,' Houlihan said enthusiastically. 'Somethin' like that, sure enough. That would do my heart a fair bit of good – and it's only what he deserves.'

'That's the spirit,' Wild Bill said.

They were now racing along the Sydenham Bypass, with Belfast City Airport spread out on one side of them, the playing fields of Sydenham on the other, both swept by the driving rain. The wind roared and beat about the car like some malevolent spirit.

'So where am I going, boss?' Dempsey asked over his shoulder.

'The Sports Club,' Houlihan said without hesitation, since he had no intention of returning home at this late hour. He wished instead to talk this disaster through and work out how to put an end to it, once and for all. 'I think we should have a war council to devise a plan of action for tomorrow. Nip this thing in the bud, like.'

'Are you sure, boss?' Kavanagh asked, glancing at the luminous dial of his wristwatch. 'It's nearly one in the morning.'

'So?'

'So I think we'll all be half asleep,' Kavanagh said, 'by the time we get there.'

'Fuck sleep,' Houlihan said. 'You think I can sleep after that shit? Could *you* really sleep after that? Could *any* of us? I ask you!'

'I'm wide awake,' Wild Bill confessed.

'Me, too,' Connolly said. 'I keep reliving what happened back there and it has my heart pumpin'.'

'Fucking Kavanagh, here,' Wild Bill said, grinning admiringly, 'he's as cold and immovable as an Antarctic glacier. He could sleep through a fuckin' earthquake and waken up feelin' great. That's a gift from the gods, like.'

Kavanagh grinned his tight, mean grin. 'Yeah, right, it's my gift. For sure, I could sleep like a log right now.'

'Don't even think about it,' Houlihan said. 'We're going to the Sports Club.'

'Right,' Wild Bill said. 'We'll calm ourselves down or waken ourselves up – whatever the case may be – with a few drinks and some fags. I'm sure we'll all manage to stay awake and come up with something constructive.'

'Great,' Houlihan said.

The Sports Club was actually a billiards hall, a large rectangular red-brick building with no windows, standing in its own small piece of fenced-in, concreted over land on the Andersonstown Road, in a short stretch packed with shops, bookies, furniture stores and the like, obliquely facing Roger Casement Park, the Gaelic football stadium. Houlihan had purchased the land and built the Sports Club with an EU grant only a few years ago, back in the year 2000, on the grounds that it would be used as a youth club and, with luck, give disenfranchised young men a healthy outlet for their energies and an alternative to sniffing glue, taking drugs, hijacking cars, mugging passers-by and beating up old-age pensioners just for fun. In fact, most of the EU money had gone into Houlihan's own coffers and the Sports Club, built with cheap labour to minimal standards, had been turned into a billiards hall only used by private members, his own men, with unlicensed alcohol served under the counter. Houlihan had also used the building extensively for his so-called 'war council' meetings and, just as important, for lengthy interrogations, kangaroo courts and the administering of severe punishments. Because the building was made of solid brick and had no windows, the screams of those being punished could not be heard from outside.

As the Volvo was coming off the Westlink to turn along the

Grosvenor Road, Houlihan's cellular phone rang in his pocket. Startled, he glanced in turn at Wild Bill and Kavanagh, both of whom shrugged their shoulders.

'Better answer it,' Wild Bill said laconically. 'It could be one of the few survivors.'

Not amused, Houlihan glared at him. Then, taking a deep, martyr's breath, he withdrew the cellular phone from his pocket and switched it on.

'Aye?'

'Houlihan?'

'Aye. Is that——?'

'Kev',' Kevin Magee said, sounding hoarse. 'Where are you, boss?'

'Where are *you*?' Houlihan asked testily.

'Just comin' off the A2, heading for the centre of town. Me and Sam, like.'

'Sam Meaklin?' Houlihan asked, referring to another of his murderous minders.

'Aye, boss, that's right. We managed to escape from the house, but now we don't know what we're supposed to do. I mean, where are you, boss?'

'We're in the Grosvenor Road, headin' for the Sports Club.'

'You're goin' to the *Sports Club*?'

'Aye, that's right.'

'*Now*?'

'Aye, now. Are you fuckin' deaf or what?'

'Sorry, boss, I just meant ... I mean, it seems a bit late for——'

'We're havin' an urgent war council,' Houlihan said, 'so you'd better get your arse over here. You and Meaklin.'

'Right, boss. We're on our way. See you there in five or ten minutes.'

'Good,' Houlihan said curtly. He switched his phone off and placed it back in his jacket pocket, then glanced at Wild

Bill. 'You hear that?' he said. 'Those two fuckers *escaped* from my house.'

'Lucky them,' Wild Bill said.

'You miss the point,' Houlihan retorted. 'Those two fuckers *escaped*, leaving that bastard Lawson still alive.'

'So?'

'So those fuckers are supposed to be my minders and they didn't *mind* too much at all. My fuckin' house was bombed, it's probably still burnin', I have at least a dozen good men dead . . . and those fuckers *escaped*. I want a word with those two.'

'They're your boyos, not mine,' Wild Bill said, 'so you know what you want, Mike.'

'I do,' Houlihan said.

They arrived at the Sports Club a few minutes later. Dempsey parked the car in the single-car port that had been cleared in front of the building, just inside the fence of eight-foot-high black metal railings. The building itself, solid brick, devoid of windows, had all the attraction of a public toilet, though its appearance certainly didn't bother Houlihan as he led his men and Wild Bill through the front door. Once inside, they switched on the lights, revealing two billiard tables, racks of cues, scoreboards and, at the far end, well away from the billiard tables, an ordinary long pine table with eight matching chairs and a small, horseshoe-shaped bar made of varnished pine boards and displaying, on the shelves behind it, only soft drinks. This was for the benefit of visiting policemen and other nosy officials.

While Kavanagh and Connolly raided the storeroom for bottles of stout and whisky and Neil Dempsey found the required glasses and brought them to the long table, Houlihan and Wild Bill seated themselves at the table, one at each end of it, like generals about to have a war conference. When Kavanagh and Connolly returned to the table, drinks were poured and cigarettes were lit. However, just as they were settling in, before the talk could begin, the front doorbell rang and Neil Dempsey jumped up to go and open the door. He returned with Kevin Magee and Sam Meaklin in tow. The suits of both were rumpled and streaked with earth; both men looked tired.

'Hi, boss,' Magee said.

'So you've come,' Houlihan responded curtly.

'Ackaye,' Meaklin said.

'I'm lookin' forward to hearin' what you have to say. But rest your feet first and have a drink.'

'Thanks, boss. We sure need it.'

Houlihan watched them intently as they sat at the table and cracked open bottles of stout. Magee poured his into a glass; Meaklin drank straight from the bottle.

'So what happened out there after we left the burning house?' Houlihan asked. 'I mean, we'd assumed that everyone inside the building had either been shot by that bastard or killed by the explosions. How did you two survive?'

'Pure luck,' Meaklin said. 'We weren't on duty when the first bomb went off—'

'There was only one bomb,' Wild Bill interjected. 'The other explosions were all in the kitchen – the gas boiler and pipes exploding. That's probably what you heard.'

'Aye, that could be true,' Meaklin said. 'Anyway, we were sleepin' in the guest wing with the other off-duty minders when the bomb went off. The camp beds we were sleepin' on were positioned tight against the wall separatin' the guest wing from the kitchen. So when the bomb went off – and, as you say, the gas boiler exploded as well – the wall was blown to shit, the blast turned our beds over and both of us were buried in debris and knocked unconscious. I recovered first and then I managed to revive Kev here ...' He nodded, indicating Kevin Magee who stopped drinking from his glass of stout to nod silent agreement. 'But by that time the fight was all over and the house was on fire.'

'That fucking cunt!' Houlihan exploded, then managed to

get enough of a grip on himself to add gruffly: 'Okay. Go on.'

'Well, when we made our way out of the guest wing, through the ruins of the kitchen, which was on fire and filled with smoke, we found most of our mates dead in the lobby, obviously peppered by the bullets of an automatic or semi-automatic weapon.'

'Yeah, right,' Wild Bill said. 'A World War Two Sten gun. Cheap, nasty, crude ... and fucking effective.'

Meaklin nodded. 'Right.' Then he looked back at Houlihan and continued: 'So, knowing that we couldn't check out the rest of the house – I mean, the fire was spreading all over it, like, so we—'

'Fuck!' Houlihan exploded. 'It was *all* on fire?'

Meaklin nodded affirmatively. 'Gettin' that way, boss. We could hear the sirens of the fire brigade in the distance, but my bet is that they couldn't have done much to save the house; the fire was too far gone for that.'

'Jesus Christ, I'll murder that bastard,' Houlihan said. 'I swear to God he'll be mincemeat ...' He almost choked, but eventually cleared his throat by coughing into his fist. 'Okay, get on with it. I assume you didn't hang around until the fire brigade arrived.'

'No, boss, we didn't. We went out the front door, hoping to find our car okay, and saw Miss Crowley escaping along the driveway with—'

'Fuck!' Houlihan exclaimed. 'I'd forgotten all about that bitch. So she wasn't killed either?'

'No, boss. She was running along the driveway towards the main gates with a guy who had a beard and ponytail – he looked like one of those old hippie types – but he was carrying some kind of sub-machine gun—'

'A Sten gun,' Wild Bill confirmed.

'Right ... And when he saw us, he turned back to fire at us, long enough to keep us pinned down and let the woman

reach the gate and run into the road. When the man ran into
the road as well, obviously following the woman, we got into
our car, which was okay, and burned out of there, turning
in the same direction as the man and woman had gone. But
by the time we reached the road, they'd both disappeared, so
we got out of there real quick, wanting to avoid the police
who'd be coming with the fire brigade. We headed straight
for the A2.'

'You managed to avoid the police?' Houlihan asked.

'Ackaye, we did. They didn't even catch a glimpse of us.'

'Good,' Houlihan said.

He had wanted to wring the necks of these two bastards for
not fighting it out with Lawson. But it was clear that they hadn't
had the chance and had, in fact, done all they could under the
circumstances. Now it was only Lawson's neck that he wanted
to wring – slowly – with his big, bare hands. Satisfaction was
everything.

'Shit,' Houlihan said, glancing at Wild Bill. 'This is real
fuckin' serious. When the fire brigade's done their business,
the police are gonna move in and find a fuckin' pile of dead
bodies in the ruins. They'll want to know what was goin' on
out there and that could lead to trouble.'

'It's your fuckin house,' Wild Bill said. 'So they'll soon be
swarmin' all over you, askin' rude questions.'

'I can stop that,' Houlihan said. 'Though I own the house,
it isn't in my name. I bought it from a bent businessman who
took the money for it, signed a separate agreement stating that
it's mine, but left the deeds in his own name at my request.
If the police check it out, they'll find the deeds, but not my
secret agreement, so it's his name they'll find. It's him they'll
interrogate.'

'And he's bound to crack and tell them the truth,' Wild
Bill said. 'Which puts you right back in the shit.'

'Not if he disappears and is never seen again,' Houlihan said.
'The cops will assume that he's the owner of the house and tie

his disappearance to whatever led to that bomb explosion and a load of dead men riddled with bullets. As for me, I'll be home and dry. No question about it.'

'That'll work,' Wild Bill said. 'But if he's gonna disappear, he'd better be gone by dawn, before the police knock on his front door. So where does he live?'

'Right here in Belfast. In University Street. He goes to work every weekday mornin' at nine.'

'In his car?'

'No, by public transport. He has his office in Chichester Street, so he just takes the bus.'

'Don't wait until Monday. Pick him up in a few hours, before it's light,' Wild Bill said. 'Ring his doorbell and snatch the fucker when he comes down to answer it. Put his lights out and bury the body where it won't ever be found. *That* should leave you home and dry.'

'Right,' Houlihan said, feeling relieved.

'Which still leaves Katherine Crowley,' Wild Bill said. 'That bitch saw everything and has no reason to love us, so she'll most likely sing like a bird. Let's pick her up as well.'

'Aye,' Houlihan said with only a little regret, having wanted to draw out that bitch's punishment until it drove her insane. 'Dead on. So we'll do that. Take her and Brian Turner — the bent businessman — out to our food-processing plant and turn them both into mincemeat.'

'I'd recommend it,' Wild Bill said.

'Which gets us back to Steve Lawson,' Houlihan said. 'I won't rest until I've got him in my hands. But how the fuck do we do that? The cunt's become a night rider, in and out like a lightning bolt, under cover of darkness, and living rough somewhere in the countryside, an invisible man. We just can't find the bastard.'

'What about those men you have throwing a cordon around Antrim?' Wild Bill asked.

'Don't even mention them,' Kavanagh said. 'I'm already

worried about them. All but five of them phoned in last night, before we went out to Cultra, to say that they'd covered the whole area and still hadn't found him.'

'All but *five*?' Houlihan asked

Kavanagh sighed. 'Yes, boss. We had five men covering the area between the west of Antrim Town and the eastern shore of Lough Neagh and they didn't phone in. Not one of them. They were all in the same car and although we know they were in that area, we don't know exactly how far they got. All we know is that they should have phoned in and they didn't. Now we have another carload of men out looking for them and I've told them to call me any time, night or day, if they find something.'

'So what's your suspicion?' Wild Bill asked.

Kavanagh sighed again. 'My suspicion is that they came across Lawson's hide but he managed to neutralize them – all five of them – before they got him.'

'Jesus!' Wild Bill said. 'If that's true, what we're dealing with is a one-man army and it's gonna take an awful lot of beating.' He looked along the table, directly at Houlihan, with a wolfish grin. 'You'd better find him, Mike.'

Houlihan felt a little paranoid at that moment, wondering if Wild Bill's comment was a challenge, if his grin was actually a sneer. He felt that his credibility was being questioned and his authority undermined. It was all due to that bastard Steve Lawson. The night rider was winning.

'Put a call through to that search team in Antrim,' he said to Kavanagh. 'Ask them if they found that missing car or the men who were in it. Ask them if they've even a clue as to what happened to it.'

'I told them they could call me any time, night or day. So if they'd found something, they'd surely have—'

'Just call them,' Houlihan insisted. 'It's possible that even if they haven't found the missing men they might have picked up at least a clue to their whereabouts. I mean, what can we lose?'

Kavanagh shrugged, then withdrew his cellular phone from his jacket pocket and put the call through. He got an instant response.

'Hi,' he said. 'It's me. Kavanagh. You haven't called, so I assume you haven't found those missing men. But have you found anything at all, even the slightest clue?'

Kavanagh listened intently to what seemed like a lengthy reply, his brow furrowing, his eyes gradually widening in shock, nodding his head repeatedly as if communicating by telepathy with the man he had called. Eventually, looking bemused, he switched his phone off and turned his veiled gaze on Houlihan.

'They found those missing men,' he said. 'They called me a few hours ago to tell me, but got no reply.' He checked his wristwatch and looked up again. 'So they would have called just as that fucker Lawson was attacking the house.'

'Which was why you didn't reply,' Wild Bill said.

'Exactly,' Kavanagh responded. 'They called to say that they'd found the missing car, a red Vauxhall Astra, but there was no one in it. It was parked off the main road, on a tarmacked lane that wound most of the way up to the forested summit of a hill, somewhere in farmland about halfway between Antrim City and Lough Neagh.'

'Where we suspected Lawson was hiding out,' Houlihan said. 'His old SAS stamping ground.'

'Right,' Kavanagh said.

'So why didn't they call back?' Wild Bill asked.

'When they couldn't raise a response from me, they decided to try later and, in the meantime, to check out what had happened to the missing passengers of the parked car. As the car was parked at the top of that lane – and as the lane tapered off into a dirt track leading into the forested area – logic told them to check out the forest.'

'Which would have been ideal,' Houlihan said, 'for the kind of hide favoured by the SAS.'

'They thought of that,' Kavanagh said with a slight hint of pride. 'So they checked out the area around the forest, then the forest itself.'

'And?' Houlihan was filling up with dread and felt slightly unreal. In fact, he felt *extremely* unreal – it was making his heart race.

Kavanagh shrugged and sighed. He looked all worn out. 'They found our five men. All dead. All riddled with bullets. They found spent nine-millimetre cartridges on the forest floor.'

'The Sten gun,' Wild Bill said.

'Right,' Kavanagh responded. 'Two of the men were found lying on the north side of the hill, close to the forest's edge; the other three were found on the southern slope, also close to the forest. So clearly they either assumed, or knew, that Lawson's hide was in that small forested area and they were hoping to box him in, front and rear. But he must have seen them coming up the hill and got his shots in first.'

'Fuck!' Connolly said.

'Jesus Christ!' Wild Bill said.

'Did you find that fucker's hide?' Houlihan asked, trying now to combat his dread by keeping his mind on the facts.

Be pragmatic. Get the facts. Use the facts. Let the facts lead the way. Just find Lawson and bury him.

'More or less,' Kavanagh said. 'He'd done a fucking good job of removing most traces of it. But even in the darkness, by torchlight, they could see that some of the soil looked fresh, as if it had been dug up somewhere else and then sprinkled there. So, given the way that those dead bodies were distributed in that small forested area, they were pretty sure that the two groups of men were moving in on a hide on the summit of the hill. No question that Lawson was there – but he's moved on again.'

'To Cultra,' Wild Bill said sardonically.

Houlihan was not amused.

'Back to Belfast,' he said. 'He's somewhere in this fucking city. He's just burned my house down, killed a load of my men, run off with my fucking woman, and left me in a damaging position with the police. That fucker is now breathing down our necks and moving in for the kill, so ... *We've got to find him!*

'How?' Wild Bill asked.

Pulled back from the brink of hysteria by that single word, that burning question, Houlihan got a grip on himself and brought his teeming thoughts back into focus.

'There must be someone we can use to bring him in,' he said. 'Someone close to his heart.'

'His wife and kids,' Wild Bill said without hesitation. 'Sure that always works a treat.'

'Ackaye,' Houlihan said. 'Sure it would, right enough. But that bitch and her bastards are in England and we don't have the time for that. We need someone closer. We can keep his missus and his fuckin' spawn in mind if we get really desperate. But right now we need someone closer. We need immediate action.'

'His business partner,' Connolly said, looking nervous, always cautious, frightened of Houlihan's dreadful wrath if he said the wrong thing. 'He has two business partners, but the one that's most important to him is that bastard David Kershaw. He was in the SAS with Lawson during the Troubles and right now he runs the business in Lawson's absence. They're like brothers, those two. They go a long way back. So Kershaw might even know where Lawson is hiding and we might be able to torture those details out of him. If we fail, however, if it turns out that he really *doesn't* know where his friend is, we just hold on to him for as long as necessary and spread the word where it's most likely to help us – to journalists, policemen and those army bastards that Lawson would've known in the past. We spread the word that we're holding Kershaw and will top him if Lawson doesn't stop his activities and give himself up

to us. My bet is that he will. He'll trade for Kershaw's release
– himself for his friend, like. So we just pick up Kershaw,
then sit back and wait for Lawson to call us. Once he calls
us, he's ours.'

'Brilliant!' Wild Bill said admiringly.

Taken aback by Connolly's plan, not having expected it
from him – not from him, of all people! – Houlihan sat straight
in his chair and placed his big hands, fingers outspread, on the
table, looking grimly at each of his comrades in turn, including
Wild Bill.

'So let me get this straight,' he said, coming painfully to
the realization that he was no longer in control of his own life
and that even minions like Connolly were suggesting, correctly
too, what he should do. The very thought made him quiver.
'We pick up that businessman, Brian Turner, and put out his
lights to prevent him from talking to the police about my
house in Cultra.'

'Correct,' Kavanagh said.

'Then we pick up David Kershaw,' Houlihan continued,
'presumably when he's going to work, and interrogate him
regarding Lawson's whereabouts. Should he, even under torture,
fail to tell us where Lawson is – really not knowing, like – we
then use him to draw Lawson in.'

'Correct again,' Kavanagh said with what sounded, to
Houlihan's paranoid ear, like outright sarcasm.

I'm losing their respect, Houlihan thought, *and it's all because of
that bastard Steve Lawson. If I don't find him and deal with him quickly,
there'll be no respect left.*

'Okay,' he said, after a lengthy, agonizing silence. 'Let's
pick them both up.'

'*And* Katherine Crowley,' Wild Bill said, thus undermining
Houlihan's authority even more. 'She was seen leaving the
grounds of your burning house with a man who had a
sub-machine gun – a Sten gun – and that man, despite his
beard and ponytail, had to be Steve Lawson. So your loving

Katherine Crowley fled with him – with Lawson, no less. So now we have to ask *her* a few questions about him – where they went when they fled that house; maybe where he is now – before we turn her into mincemeat. So we have to pick her up, too.'

'Let's go,' Houlihan said.

Chapter Twenty-three

Katherine Crowley stood in the doorway of Houlihan's burning house, looking straight at Steve as he rose from the ground. In those drifting skeins of smoke, illuminated by yellow flames, in her black skintight dress and high-heeled shoes, she looked like a dream. She also looked like salvation.

Hearing a siren wailing in the distance — the approaching fire brigade — and aware that neighbours might soon be gathering, now that the gunfire had ceased, Steve walked up to the woman.

'You'd better get out of here, Miss Crowley,' he said. 'You won't be doing yourself any favours by sticking around when the police arrive with the fire brigade.'

'You're Steve Lawson, aren't you?'

'Yes.'

'The one they call the Night Rider.'

'I suppose so,' Steve said.

'They're desperate to find you, Mr Lawson.'

'It's mutual,' Steve said.

'All right, let's go.'

Steve turned away from the burning house and Katherine went with him, heading along the driveway for the main gate. Glancing back over his shoulder, Steve saw two men emerging from the burning building, both holding handguns.

When they saw him and Katherine, they raised the guns to fire at them.

'Run!' Steve snapped.

As Katherine started running, Steve raised his Sten gun and fired a sustained burst at the two armed men, moving the barrel from left to right in a broad arc. Both men were quick, however, obviously professional, throwing themselves in opposite directions as the bullets peppered the walls around the front door and ricocheted off the concrete columns on both sides of it. Steve kept firing in short bursts as he retreated along the driveway, keeping the men pinned down long enough for Katherine to make her escape. Then he too ran for the gate and made it into the road.

Katherine was waiting for him there. The siren was coming closer and some people farther along the road had come out of their homes to see what was going on. The flames from the blaze had formed a great fan of crimson light across the night sky.

'Let's get the hell out of here,' Steve said. 'I hope you can run fast.'

'I can run as fast as we have to,' she said, taking off her high-heeled shoes, leaving herself barefoot and holding the shoes by their straps. 'So which way do we go?'

'This way,' Steve said, gripping his Sten gun in one hand and her wrist in the other and starting to run along the lamplit road, heading for the beach, pulling her with him when she didn't run fast enough and not slowing down until they had turned the corner at the far end. Once around the corner, however, he slowed down to a walking pace and released her wrist.

'Where are we going?' she asked him, sounding breathless.

'To the beach. I've got a motorbike parked down there. I'll take you back to Belfast.'

'God!' Katherine exclaimed softly. 'What a nightmare! I don't know where to turn.'

'You'd better think about it,' Steve said, 'because you

could be in trouble. How the hell did you get involved with Houlihan?'

'I didn't volunteer,' she told him. 'He'd wanted me a long time – sure I knew that – and so he just reached the end of his tether and decided to take me. He burst into my flat and took me over and that was the end of it. You don't say "No" to Houlihan.'

'He threatened you?'

'God, yes! And there's nothing he wouldn't do. So when a brute like that makes demands backed up by threats, you can take the threats seriously.'

'Weren't you Jack Parnell's girl?'

'Not quite, but we had a relationship. Easy come, easy go. No real demands on either side. It worked fine for both of us. Two adults behaving as adults do.'

'Did he know about Houlihan?'

'No,' she said. 'I didn't dare tell him. Houlihan made it clear that if I told Jack what was happening and Jack took offence, he, Houlihan, would put Jack six feet under.'

'He'd do that to his own lawyer?'

'No question about it. The man's a psychopath, not renowned for his self-control. Jack had threatened to drop him as a client and Houlihan wasn't too happy with him. So, yes, if I'd told Jack what was happening, he really could have ended up dead.'

'And you?'

'I was terrified. I don't like to admit it, but I was. I'd always prided myself on my courage, but Houlihan scared me mindless. He kept reminding me of what he'd do to me if I tried to resist him. So I didn't resist him. I swallowed my last vestiges of pride. But all the time I was wondering what my future would be, when or how it would end. I only knew that it wouldn't be pleasant and that I had no way out. I've never felt so afraid before.'

They had reached the path that led to the beach and they went down it side by side as thunder boomed in the distance and rain began to fall. Glancing often at her, entranced by her very presence, the sheer unexpectedness of being with this scantily dressed beauty in the dead of the night, her body clearly defined in the skintight black dress, hardly more than a piece of silk held up by two strings, her golden-blonde hair whipped by the wind, Steve felt increasingly, uneasily unreal.

'So what'll you do now?' he asked as they reached the bottom of the path and started along the dark, windswept beach, keeping well away from the sea that was breaking in roaring waves over the rocks. 'I mean, where do I take you?'

'Where else can I go except home? What choice do I have?'

'Your parents' place?'

'My Dad's dead and my Mum lives in Bangor and I don't want her threatened.'

'Friends?'

'Wherever I go, Houlihan's bound to find me, so I don't want anyone else involved. No, just take me home, please. I assume you know where I live.'

'Yes,' Steve confessed.

'You've had us under surveillance, right?'

'Yes,' he admitted again.

'Jesus!' Katherine exclaimed softly, sounding almost good-humoured. 'There was me working my arse off to be a good lawyer and now I'm on the wrong side of the law. Life's full of surprises, right?'

'Right,' Steve confirmed. He saw the motorbike ahead, still hidden in the darkness of the overhanging, grassy bluff. 'That's it,' he said.

Under Katherine's watchful gaze, he disassembled the Sten gun and placed the separate pieces into one of the saddlebags. He then removed his shoulder bag, the one containing the explosives, and placed that too in a saddlebag. Finally, he unstrapped the holstered 9-Milly and hid it deep, under the camping equipment. Then he zipped up both of the saddlebags and picked his crash helmet off the rear seat. He held it out to Katherine.

'You'd better wear this,' he said.

'No, thanks,' she replied. 'You're the driver. *You* wear it.'

'I'd rather you did.'

'It'd make a mess of my beautiful blonde hair,' she said with a sly smile, 'so why don't you wear it?'

'Okay,' he said. 'If you insist.'

'I do.'

'I can't argue with a lady.'

'Thanks for the compliment. I didn't get too many of those from Houlihan.'

'I'll bet you didn't,' Steve said.

Still holding the crash helmet, not attempting to put it on, he stared thoughtfully at her. Katherine was beautiful and sexy, but that wasn't his interest here. In fact, just being with her in these bizarre circumstances, in the dead of the night, on this dark, wind-blown beach — *just being with a woman* — reminded him of his wife. She, just like Katherine, was now in danger of becoming one of Houlihan's victims. Not only Linda but the children too — all of them useful to Houlihan — and the very thought of that pig having them picked up filled Steve with dread and a growing sense of guilt.

Time's running out, he thought. *In fact, there's no time left at all. I have to bring this business to a conclusion, one way or the other, and I can't be too choosy about how I do it. I have to use what's to hand.*

He would have to use Katherine.

'No point in standing here talking,' he said. 'You're already soaked through. Let's make our way back.'

Steve kicked the motorbike's support upwards, letting it lock automatically into place, then turned the bike away from the bluff and sat on the saddle. Glancing at Katherine, he saw that the rain had thoroughly soaked her flimsy black dress so that it clung even more tightly to her curves. Her long blonde hair, though also soaked by the rain, was wind-blown and still looked sexy. 'Get on behind me,' he said. 'Put your arms around my waist. Pretend that I'm the man of your dreams and don't let me go.'

She smiled. 'Okay, boss.'

When she was seated behind him, her arms around him, fingers intertwined, he said, 'Are you okay? You won't freeze?'

'Just get me home quickly.'

'Here we go,' he said.

Starting the bike up, Steve moved off slowly, letting Katherine get used to it. Then he accelerated, roaring along the beach before taking the uphill road. Once back on level ground, he headed for the A2. But he glanced briefly back to the general area of Houlihan's house and saw clouds of smoke billowing upwards through a flickering, spark-filled, crimson glow, indicating that the house was still burning.

'Fucking great,' he said aloud.

The ride back to Belfast took less than half an hour, but not one minute of it passed without Steve being conscious of the woman seated behind him, clinging to him, her breasts flattened against his shoulder blades, her belly warming his spine. He felt sensual, sexual, aroused by her clinging limbs. But he couldn't shake the feelings of guilt and fear for his family.

Yes, he had to resolve this once and for all, regardless of any immorality of the means he might choose. He had to use whatever was to hand, he thought again, and that did indeed mean using Katherine. Thus, as he drove along the upper Malone Road in Belfast, approaching her street, he knew exactly what he had to say to her. And exactly what he had to do.

Reaching the end of her street, Steve stopped the motorbike and placed his feet on the road.

'Home sweet home,' he said.

Katherine removed her arms from his body and slipped off the pillion to stand on the pavement right beside him. Though the rain had stopped, she was still soaked and the flimsy dress still clung to her, showing every curve of her belly and bosom.

'Thanks for bringing me home,' Katherine said. 'Thanks for saving my life.'

'I brought you home,' Steve said, 'but I haven't necessarily saved your life. Your troubles aren't over yet. You saw everything that happened back there and that makes you a threat to Houlihan. He's going to come for you, Katherine.'

When he saw the fear clouding her eyes, he knew that he had captured her.

'Come for me?' she said, sounding confused.

'He's going to have to kill you. He can't let you talk. You know too much about him – about him and Wild Bill – and you're also a witness to what happened back there in Cultra, so he can't let you live.' Then he repeated, deliberately, fully aware of what he was saying: 'He's going to come for you, Katherine.'

She stared steadily, thoughtfully at him for what seemed like a long time. Then she eventually asked: 'When?'

'Very soon, I'm afraid. Tonight. Tomorrow morning or the next day. Quite likely when you're leaving to go to work. His thugs will pick you up in a car. After that, you'll just disappear.'

Steve saw the deepening of the fear in her eyes and it made him feel like a louse. But he still did what he had to do.

'So I'll get out,' Katherine said desperately. 'You can help me. I'll just go to my flat and pick up what I can't live without – my passport and so on – and pack a bag and come straight back. Then you can take me somewhere else.'

'Where?'

'Pardon?'

'Where can I take you where he won't find you? Short of flying to Australia, there's nowhere you can hide – and he might even track you down in Australia. So where can I take you?'

Now the fear, though still there in her eyes, was partly replaced by the dawning hard light of reality. She looked at him quizzically.

'What are you saying, Steve? Just what are you driving at?

I'm not a fool, so you can tell me what it is without pissing around. So what is it?'

'Wherever you go, they'll find you.'

'You've already said that, Steve.'

'So there's really no point in going anywhere.'

'You mean I should stay here? Just let them pick me up? Let them take me away to shut my mouth once and for all. In short, let them *kill* me. Is *that* what you're suggesting?'

'Let them pick you up,' Steve said. 'That's all I'm suggesting. I know it's a lot to ask, but even when I find those bastards, Katherine, I can't get close enough to them for long enough. I have to strike where they're relatively isolated and where they won't be expecting me. They'll take you where I need to go – some remote killing ground – and if I follow them, I can take them by surprise. Then, with luck, I can put out their lights before they do the same to you.'

'"With luck",' Katherine said softly. 'That's not a guarantee, Steve.'

'Nothing can guarantee your safety any more, so what can you lose?'

'My fucking life,' Katherine said.

Steve sighed. 'Whether or not you do as I say, sooner or later you'll end up in a killing ground. So let them pick you up and then, with me following them, at least there's a *chance* that I can save you.'

'That's a hell of a gamble,' Katherine said.

'No, it's not,' Steve insisted. 'It's not a gamble at all. If you don't do what I say, they'll pick you up and kill you anyway – there's no question about that – but if you do what I say you'll at least be giving yourself a chance to live. So at the risk of repeating myself: what can you lose?'

She gazed steadily at him, her face revealing nothing. Then she offered a thin, deadly smile and said, 'You're a shit.'

Steve didn't respond.

'You make sense, but you're still a shit,' Katherine said.

'You've seen your opportunity and you're taking it and all the rest is bullshit. You should have been a lawyer, Mr Lawson. You'd be great in a courtroom.'

'As great as a bent lawyer?' Steve responded. 'A lawyer like Parnell?'

'Fuck you,' Katherine hissed. 'Women don't have your choices. We live in a man's world and the men make all the rules and we have to keep the poor fuckers happy to get anything out of them. I work for Jack Parnell – and I sleep with Jack Parnell – because he's one of the best lawyers in this city – bent, maybe, but good – and I can't afford to let the opportunity pass. You understand, Mr Lawson? I'm going to be a lawyer if it kills me—'

'Which it might.'

'—And when I succeed, I'm going to make sure that bastards like Houlihan and Jack Parnell – and *you* – don't continue to use this city as your fucking playground. You're *all* bent, Mr Lawson. You and your fucking army and your police friends and your paramilitary pals – you're all as bent as a hairpin. That's a feminine simile, Mr Lawson, but it drives the point home. So, yes, I'll do as you ask, but I won't do it because I respect you. I'll do it because, as you rightly say, I don't have a choice. Now sit here and watch me being picked up and then do what you have to do, good or bad, right or wrong. I'm in God's hands now, aren't I?'

'I'm afraid so,' Steve said.

'That's life,' Katherine Crowley said.

She bent to put on her high-heeled shoes. Her legs were exquisite. In sheer black stockings, they turned Steve's head. She turned away from him and walked off along the street. The pavements were still wet, glistening under the street lamps. The earlier high wind had given way to a light breeze that made the trees shiver. Katherine Crowley looked beautiful. She also looked unreal. She was a gorgeous apparition, pale flesh draped in black silk, her golden-blonde hair falling to her shoulders.

Steve was enchanted. But his negative feelings persisted. As Katherine walked away from him, perhaps walking to her doom, he realized that what she had said about him was not far from the truth. He was using her, not to save her life – which he only *might* do – but to complete what he had started: the intended but frustratingly postponed elimination of Houlihan and his Prod pal, Wild Bill.

Even more than that, as Katherine had clearly recognized, he was using her with the cold-blooded, selfish pragmatism that had shaped his whole life and that had enabled him to give up his wife and children to live a life of pure freedom. Now, given what that freedom implied, he wasn't sure that he wanted it.

You're fucked – and you fucked yourself, Steve thought. *Now just finish the job. Don't even think about the future.*

For, indeed, as he certainly knew, there might be no future.

Katherine Crowley, that lovely apparition, was swallowed up by the darkness as she entered her apartment house. Steve stood there, leaning against a lamp-post, waiting for Houlihan's men to arrive and take her away.

He did not have to wait long.

Chapter Twenty-four

Houlihan sat up front in the Volvo beside the driver, Neil Dempsey, as the car moved at a steady pace through the early-morning darkness, heading for Katherine Crowley's street off the upper Malone Road. He wasn't feeling his usual confident self.

In truth, Houlihan was still suffering from the disturbing sensation that, for the first time in his life, he was not in control, that somehow matters were slipping out of his hands and that Steve Lawson, a loose cannon, a single individual, was somehow winning the game. At the same time he felt a contradictory excitement in the knowledge that things might soon come to a head, that conclusions were being reached, and that this conflict between him and Lawson might soon be resolved, one way or another.

Surprisingly, given the number of men Houlihan had working for him, as against Lawson's one-man band, he was still haunted by the uneasy possibility that Lawson might win. He couldn't imagine how (Lawson was just a lone operator, for God's sake!) but the poisonous thought was there in his head and could not be shaken loose.

For him, Steve Lawson had become something almost supernatural, an elusive apparition, a night rider who came and went like an angel of vengeance, leaving a trail of destruction behind him. Even worse: Lawson's recent exploits had turned him into an heroic figure to the denizens of Belfast's underworld, thus further undermining Houlihan's authority and eroding his confidence.

Now the time had come to put an end to Lawson, sooner rather than later. Maybe, with luck, even this morning, before the dawn broke.

Let me see the cunt's face, Houlihan thought as he glanced out through the windscreen at the lights of the Malone Road, the heavy clouds drifting across the few stars, a baleful moon coming and going. *Let me get my hands on him.*

Right now, of course, he was about to get his hands on Katherine Crowley, who would, if he had his way, not live long enough to see the dawn. She had seen too much already, heard too much, and she had also run away from the burning house with Steve Lawson. So she must have had some kind of talk with him and might even know where he was right now. He might even have taken her home. He might be in her flat at this very moment.

Houlihan licked his lips at the thought, though in truth that possibility seemed too good to be true. Nevertheless, he itched with the urge to interrogate that sexy bitch before putting her under for good. Though he also felt a twinge of regret that his lengthy humiliation of her, so enjoyable to him, would soon come to an end.

'We're nearly there,' he said to Wild Bill, who was sitting in the rear seat, smoking a cigarette – which Houlihan strongly disapproved of since it stank the car out. 'It's the street after this one.'

'Good,' Wild Bill said. 'I want to get this show on the road and then get back to my bed. Pity about the bitch, though. Real pity. She sure as fuck is some looker. You had a good piece there, Mike.'

'Aye, I did, right enough. But easy come, easy go, I say. There's plenty more where she came from.'

'A dime a dozen,' Wild Bill replied agreeably, 'no matter how good they look. Naked, they all look the same anyway. One cunt looks like another.'

'That's true enough, I reckon, when you get right down to it. One cunt *does* look like another!'

'Still, it'll be a shame to kiss her goodbye.'

'Aye, right, a real shame, like.'

Though Houlihan and Wild Bill were talking like old mates, the best of buddies, the Prod gang boss had, in fact, recently become yet another reason for Houlihan's discontent, his belief that things were slipping out of his control.

About a fortnight ago, Frank Kavanagh had told Houlihan that a couple of Wild Bill's hoodlums had been spotted in the lobby of the Hilton Hotel when Houlihan was having a meeting there with members of the Russian *Mafiya*. It was Kavanagh's belief that those men had not been there by accident, but were, in fact, tailing Houlihan on Wild Bill's instructions. If this was true, it meant that Wild Bill had found out about Houlihan's plans for making a deal with the Russians and, even worse, had learned that he, Wild Bill, had been excluded from the negotiations.

Houlihan had become convinced that this was so when, over the next few days, Wild Bill once again started making sarcastic remarks about a circulating rumour regarding a forthcoming *Mafiya* infiltration of Northern Ireland, reportedly being master-minded or, at least, supported by an unknown local criminal.

That unknown criminal was, of course, Houlihan.

Even now, as the car carried him towards Katherine Crowley's place, Houlihan was sweating at the thought of what Wild Bill might have learned through his covert surveillance. Houlihan knew that if Wild Bill had learnt of his negotiations with the Russians, he would turn against his present partner in crime.

Not that Houlihan was entirely to blame. Already, according to Houlihan's sources, Wild Bill was arranging a secret merger with the drug barons of Antrim in order to double his man-power. If that deal went off, Wild Bill would end up being bigger than Houlihan and would use his increased strength, his greater number of men, to wipe Houlihan off the map. Then, perhaps, he might even make his own deal with the Russians.

So now Houlihan was thinking that after neutralizing Steve Lawson, he would have to do the same to Wild Bill.

Clean the slate and start all over again. No Night Rider to contend with. No Wild Bill to be betrayed by. Just me and the fucking Russian Mafia. It's the only way forward.

'Let's hope the other lads aren't havin' any problems,' Wild Bill said, obviously referring to the other planned abductions. He sounded for all the world like Houlihan's best buddy, loyal and true.

'I don't think they'll have problems,' Houlihan replied. 'I mean, it's pretty routine, right?'

'Right,' Wild Bill said. 'If they're efficient, there shouldn't be any difficulty.'

'Are you suggestin' that my men aren't efficient?' Houlihan asked before he could stop himself, letting his suppressed bitterness show.

'No, no!' Wild Bill responded in a placating manner. 'Sure your men are the best in the business, Mike, and don't we all know it? I didn't mean the remark the way it sounded. It just sort of slipped out, like.'

'Aye, right,' Houlihan said.

It had been agreed that the abductions should be done in three separate cars. So while Houlihan and Wild Bill were picking up Katherine Crowley, two others cars had been dispatched to pick up the businessman, Brian Turner, and Lawson's partner, David Kershaw, with Kavanagh and Connolly dealing with Turner and Kevin Magee and Sam Meaklin dealing with Kershaw. Both teams had been ordered to take their captives straight to Houlihan's frozen-food processing factory out on the Duncrue Industrial Estate, where Houlihan and Wild Bill would also be taking Katherine Crowley. Many a man had been interrogated at length in that big, freezing warehouse, then shot through the head and either turned into mincemeat or dumped in the river. The same was going to happen to the three being picked up this morning, with the possible exception of David Kershaw who might be held as a pawn to bring Lawson to light. However, Turner and Kershaw would not be picked up until about nine in the morning, so Katherine Crowley would be the first to be dealt with out in that warehouse.

The Volvo turned into the street where Katherine lived and pulled up in front of the converted house where her flat was.

'You want me to come with you?' Wild Bill asked.

'Aye, you might as well. I think she'll come quietly, but you never know, so you could be useful if there's a bit of a struggle, like.'

'A fuckin' knuckle sandwich should silence her.'

'I'll hold her, you hit her.'

'Right,' Wild Bill said.

They clambered out of the car, then Houlihan leaned down to speak through the open door to Neil Dempsey. 'You get ready to take off in a hurry,' he said.

'I'll keep the engine tickin' over, boss.'

'Aye, you do that,' Houlihan said. Then he pushed the door almost closed and made his way up the path with Wild Bill by his side. This particular house had been converted into two rather grand flats, one upstairs, the other on the ground floor, and Katherine had the ground-floor one, which included a garden. Houlihan had forced Katherine to give him his own key and he used it now to let himself and Wild Bill into the hallway. The bedroom was on one side of the hallway, the living room on the other, and the light in the living room was still on. Houlihan walked in. He found Katherine Crowley sitting in a deep armchair, smoking a cigarette and staring steadily at him. She had changed her clothes and was now wearing blue jeans, an open-necked shirt and flat shoes, as if she was ready to travel. Houlihan, with Wild Bill behind him, walked up and stopped just in front of Katherine to look down at her.

'You must have known we'd be coming for you,' he said.

'Yes, I knew,' she replied, sounding almost unnaturally calm.

'So why didn't you run?'

'You said it yourself: there's nowhere I can hide. So there was no point in running.'

'Where's Lawson?'

'How should I know?'

'Don't fuck with me, you bitch. You were seen running away from my burning house together, so where did you go with him?'

'He just gave me protection as I was trying to leave the building. He ran me back here on his motorbike, then he took off.'

'Took off where?'

'I didn't ask and he didn't say. He just told me to look after myself, then he shot off on his bike.'

'He's not hiding out here, is he?'

'God, no! He warned me that you'd probably come here to get me and advised me to pack up and leave. He said he couldn't help me more than that. Then, as I said, he took off, not telling me where he was going. Why *should* he tell me?'

'I'll find out soon enough whether or not you're telling the truth. God help you if you're pissing me around.' Houlihan turned to Wild Bill. 'Check out the flat, Billy-boy, and just make sure that Lawson isn't hiding here.'

'Right,' Wild Bill said. He removed a handgun from the holster on his left hip, then left the room to check out the rest of the flat, prepared to blow Lawson's brains out if he found him. He was fearless that way.

Houlihan turned back to Katherine.

'We're taking you away,' he said. 'We have a few questions to ask you. We want to do it somewhere nice and quiet, somewhere your screams won't be heard. And, believe me, you *will* scream. Scream now, though, while we're leaving this flat, and you'll not live for long. Do you understand?'

'Yes.'

'Okay, girl. Now put that cigarette out, put your coat on and get ready to leave. You understand that as well?'

'Yes, I understand.' Katherine stubbed her cigarette out in the ashtray, then stood up and went into the hallway to fetch her jacket. Houlihan went after her and stood right behind her while she put on the jacket. Wild Bill came out of the kitchen at the end of the hallway and said, 'Everything's clean. There's no one else here.'

'Fair enough. Let's get of here.' Houlihan gave Katherine another warning look. 'And don't forget what I told you: no cries for help or you'll be dead in a second.'

'I'll be quiet,' Katherine said.

When they left the building, Houlihan closed the door quietly behind him, then locked it with his own key. With Houlihan on one side of her and Wild Bill on the other, Katherine was marched down the front path to the parked car.

'You get in the front,' Houlihan said to Wild Bill who grinned and said, 'Right.' Katherine slipped into the rear seat and Houlihan, too big and awkward as always, got in beside her and closed the door. 'Off you go,' he said to Neil Dempsey and the car moved off.

No one said a word as the car cruised through the darkness. The sprawling Duncrue Industrial Estate was not far away, only just out of town, off the M3 motorway, and because there was little traffic about they arrived there in no time. Houlihan had four buildings in all: two warehouses adjoining an enormous freezing unit, plus a combined administration and sales office. The sales office faced the main gate of the fenced-in complex and the words HOULIHAN'S: FROZEN-FOOD PROCESSORS were painted in three-foot-high letters above the plate-glass windows of the reception area. The giant cranes of the shipyards could be seen soaring skyward in the distance.

Dempsey did not drive up to the reception area. Instead, after passing between the electronically controlled gates of the high steel fence around the complex, he drove past the first building, turned around behind it, and stopped in front of the two immense warehouses adjoining the big freezing unit. The freezing unit was like a smaller warehouse packed inside a larger one, with sealed entry/exit doors leading from it into the two main warehouses. A lot of bright yellow electric-powered fork-lifts with heavy blades, used for lifting and transporting wooden pallets piled with goods, were parked in the lot outside the entrance to the warehouses; each of them had the word HOULIHAN painted on it in bright red.

The entrance to the nearest warehouse was surrounded by big piles of wooden pallets, which the fork-lift drivers used to transport the canned or boxed frozen food during the working day. The door to the warehouse was solid steel, about thirty feet wide, and when Dempsey aimed a hand-held remote-control unit at it, it opened by moving upwards and backwards until it was parallel with the concrete roof. A gently sloping steel ramp led into a huge basement and Dempsey immediately drove down into it.

The lights in the basement had come on automatically when the steel door opened.

The warehouse had separate floors, rather like a public car park, with the lower floor being the basement. The floors and walls were unpainted concrete. Access to the other floors was through the basement and then up steeply sloped concrete ramps. Dempsey, however, stopped in the middle of the basement, not far from an annexe room with no windows. Its walls were covered with metal sheeting.

He applied the handbrake and jumped out of the vehicle to run around it and open Wild Bill's door for him. When Wild Bill had got out, Dempsey opened the rear door to let Houlihan and Katherine Crowley out. Houlihan had his customary difficulty in getting his great bulk out through the car door; Katherine, being slim, slipped out with ease, though she shivered visibly when the biting cold hit her. She was trying to keep her lovely face composed, but fear was there in her unfocused gaze.

'This way,' Houlihan said to her.

As Katherine, still shivering, walked between Houlihan and Wild Bill to the room with no windows and ugly sheet-metal walls, she glanced about her and saw countless deep shelves stacked with huge packs of canned and boxed frozen food. Along the far wall – the wall separating this warehouse from the freezing unit – freezer suits with fur collars and big, padded gloves tied around them hung from steel hooks, looking like dead men on gallows. The word HOULIHAN was stamped in bright red across each of them.

At the door to the room with no windows and walls of sheet metal, Houlihan stepped aside to let Katherine enter. She did so. Houlihan followed her in, Wild Bill followed him and Neil Dempsey came in last, leaving the door open behind him. The room, which was as big as the average one-car garage, was lit with fluorescent tubes, which made everything look harsh. It contained only a pine table, approximately four feet by four, four wooden chairs, one at each side of the table, and a workbench upon which rested steel pliers, ice picks, a claw hammer, a bradawl and coils of rope. The pine table was badly stained.

Houlihan pointed to the wooden chair at the far side of the table, located directly under the harsh light of a twelve-inch fluorescent tube.

'Sit there,' he said.

Katherine did as she was told. Now she looked really nervous. Houlihan felt the old excitement, based on the thrill of domination, holding life and death in his hands, able to deal out a hell of pain or the ecstasy of relief, even if through death. He had heard many a scream in this place and each scream had strengthened him. The screams had come from his hands-on involvement and he was looking forward to that right now.

'How do you feel?' he asked.

'Frightened,' Katherine confessed.

'That's an honest enough answer,' Houlihan said, 'and sure I wouldn't have believed any other.' He turned away from her, went to the workbench and returned, holding the bradawl in his right fist. 'You know what this is?' he asked.

'Yes.'

'Tell me what it is, Katherine.'

'It's a tool used for boring holes in wood – before you put in a screw, say.'

'Aye, you're right. I might have known that you'd know. You're a bright woman and you have a practical streak, so you've probably used one yourself.'

'Yes, I have,' Katherine said.

'You've bored holes in wood with it?'

'Yes,' Katherine said.

'Have you ever tried to imagine what it would feel like to have someone bore a hole in your hand with this very same tool? And then to pin your hand to the table with it? Can you imagine the pain of it?'

Katherine closed her eyes. A shudder passed visibly through her. Tears came from her closed eyes and trickled down her cheeks. Then she opened her eyes again.

'Please don't,' she said. 'Sure there's nothing I can tell you. I'd never met Steve Lawson before. I only knew of him because of you. I didn't even know that I'd be in your Cultra house that evening, so I certainly didn't know that Lawson would turn up to bomb it. You and Wild Bill left me. You left me lying there on that floor. You both made your escape, forgetting me, and that man walked right over me. I could hear all the shooting. Smoke was pouring into the room. I knew the house was on fire, so I got up and made my way downstairs, where I saw Lawson shooting his way out. Naturally, I followed him. What else could I do?

We got outside and a couple of your men followed us out and started firing their guns at us. Lawson kept them at bay while I escaped into the road, then he joined me there. The rest you know about. He drove me home on his motorbike, he warned me to get out, saying that you'd come and get me, then he said he couldn't help me any more and he drove away on his motorbike. I swear to God, I don't know more than that.'

'No?'

'No. You can bore that bradawl through my hand, you can pull my fingernails out with pliers, you can break my fingers with that hammer, you can tie me down and do even worse to me, but I swear to God, I won't tell you any different, because there's truly nothing more that I can tell. Kill me if you want – I'm sure you will – but don't torture me because it won't do any good. I can't tell you what I don't know. I'll only tell you what I *think* you want to know if I think it will stop the pain. So don't do this. Please don't.'

Houlihan studied her for some time, impressed by her outpouring, but wondering just how much was the truth and how much a clever ploy. She was a lawyer, after all – or *almost* a lawyer – and it was the business of a lawyer to be able to act a role, ignoring the truth when it suited him or her. What the fuck was a lawyer, after all, except another professional liar in a court of law? Another person, man or woman, treating the law as something to be toyed with, as a game to be played. So Katherine Crowley, despite her marvellous performance, might not be speaking the truth. And in truth, there was only one way to find out: the way he had chosen.

Houlihan glanced at Wild Bill and received a broad grin as his colleague, or former colleague, moved his hand to and fro over his groin, mimicking a hand job, letting Houlihan know that he might not be averse to a little bit of pleasure with this bitch before they buried her for good. Her torture: his pleasure. Breathing deeply, still feeling slightly out of control, Houlihan stepped forward to lean over Katherine and look directly into her face, giving her his most malevolent stare.

'This is our Night of the Long Knives,' he said, referring to that notorious few hours in Hitler's Germany when the Nazis destroyed their own kind who had become their enemies. 'The night when blood flows freely and cries of pain go unheard. You understand, Katherine?'

'No.'

'You're not the only one being brought in here for interrogation and burial. A couple of others are being picked up, but not until the morning. A friend of mine, Brian Turner, the poor fool who owned that house, and David Kershaw, Steve Lawson's partner and best friend. They're both going to die. You're going to die with them. You're all going to die, but not before you sing like birds, and you'll do that because of what you suffer before you *beg* me to kill you. Be prepared, you wee bitch.'

Katherine closed her eyes again, wept silently, but did not say a word.

'They say an hour can be an eternity,' Houlihan continued. 'They say a minute, a fucking *second*, can be an eternity. So imagine what you're goin' to endure while you wait here for the others to turn up and go through their personal hells. I'm goin' to make you watch it, Katherine. I'll let you see what's been planned for you. You can watch us torture Brian Turner and put a bullet through his head – he'll be shot right in front of you: right here on this very floor – then you can watch what we do to Lawson's partner and best friend, that former SAS fuck, David Kershaw, before we kill him as well. You'll be forced to watch it, Katherine. You'll see it all from that very chair. The stains on that table are bloodstains and you'll see fresh ones this morning. Then and *only* then will it be your turn – and you'll know pain beyond reckoning. But for now ...' At this point he waved the glittering point of the bradawl in front of her eyes. 'For now we'll just give you a little taste, a wee preview, of what's in store for you tomorrow morning when we've done with the others.'

Wild Bill grabbed Katherine by her shoulders and Neil Dempsey grabbed her left wrist, holding it hard. Houlihan then pressed her right wrist to the table, the palm turned downwards, and raised the bradawl on high to plunge it into the back of her hand.

First one explosion, then another, then a third and a fourth, blasted through the silence outside the building.

They were being attacked from all sides.

Chapter Twenty-five

Or so it seemed. In fact, they were being attacked by one man, Steve, who felt that fate had dealt him a good hand, even though his resources were few and he had to bluff his way.

Steve felt that he was in luck when, waiting at the end of Katherine Crowley's street, he saw only one of Houlihan's cars pull up outside her house and only Houlihan and Wild Bill getting out of it. At the same time, he felt frustrated. He couldn't believe his eyes when he saw those two men, his prime targets, getting out of a car unescorted by bodyguards. But he could have killed himself for not being prepared.

He could, for instance, have tried to assassinate them outside Katherine's house, perhaps using the Barrett Model 90 sniper rifle. He consoled himself, however, with the thought that their brief walk from the car to the apartment building would have left little enough time for focusing the Barrett's telescopic night-vision sight, let alone getting off a decent shot. As for setting up the rifle and attempting to kill both men when they were leaving the house, they would certainly have been too close to Katherine to make the risk worthwhile. Finally, the noise of the Barrett being fired in this built-up area would have awakened half the neighbourhood and maybe hampered his chances of escape. So, although Steve felt frustrated at seeing both men alone and being unable to slot them there and then he felt justified in taking his other option, which was to follow them to wherever they took Katherine. This would be, he was absolutely convinced, an isolated killing ground.

Which turned out to be the case. When Houlihan and Wild Bill emerged from the house with Katherine between them (and, indeed, too closely hemmed in by them for Steve to have shot either man without risking Katherine's life), the Volvo that took them away ended up at Houlihan's frozen-food processing works on the Duncrue Industrial Estate, which was absolutely deserted at night. As for Houlihan's own buildings, they were enclosed by high metal fences and gates with the customary surveillance equipment, most of which was, in real terms, not much use when it came to fending off the average burglar, let alone an experienced former SAS man like Steve. Given his few resources — an antiquated Sten gun, his beloved Browning 9mm High Power handgun (the powerful Barrett Model 90 was relatively useless in a situation like this), a few grenades and, most valuable of all, his remaining few blocks of Semtex *plastique* — Steve decided that the best way to defeat Houlihan and his two buddies was to convince them that they were being attacked by a whole army.

Steve had seen Houlihan's Volvo entering the fenced-in grounds via the electronically controlled front gate. By moving around the corner of the fence on his motorbike, he had also seen them driving down into a spacious basement, the automatic door of which had remained open. The lights in the basement were on. Surrounding that doorway were piles of wooden pallets and bright yellow electric fork-lifts. Steve had no way of knowing what was down in the basement, but the presence of the pallets and fork-lifts made him think that it had to be a storeroom, or part of a warehouse, for cans and packets of frozen food. Exactly what part of the basement his targets were in, where they had taken Katherine Crowley, he also had no way of knowing, nor did he know if any other armed men were down there. So, clearly, whatever he did, he would have to do it quickly and he would, once inside the complex, have to be prepared for anything.

In other words, apart from working out how to get inside the complex, Steve could not plan anything. Once inside, he would have to play it by ear, which would mean taking a lot of chances.

Nevertheless, he would have to try it. Not only for his own satisfaction in finally putting an end to this filthy business, but also to save Katherine Crowley's life. He had asked her to gamble her life for him so he owed her this much, at least.

After parking his motorbike in a dark area between two of the overhead lights attached to the high fence, he removed his remaining blocks of Semtex from one of the saddlebags, four in all, as well as electric initiators, blasting caps and four wristwatch-sized clockwork detonators. Quickly and expertly, he made four crude bombs, each with its own detonator. He set the first detonator for fifteen minutes hence, then set the others to go off at thirty-second intervals, one after the other. The first bomb was left resting on the ground, against the bottom of the steel railings of the fence, about a hundred yards away from where his motorbike was parked. Then, moving at the half-crouch, he made his way around the whole perimeter of the complex, attaching a bomb to each of the other three sides of the extensive high fence.

Checking his wristwatch as he made his way back to his motorbike, Steve saw that he still had four minutes to go. Once back at his vehicle, he assembled and loaded the Sten gun, then slung it over his left shoulder. He also unbuttoned the leather holster for his Browning 9mm High Power handgun, ensuring that the weapon could be drawn rapidly, but he did not yet remove it from the holster. Finally, he clipped his remaining three thirty-two-round magazines for the Sten gun to his belt, as well as four Haley & Weller incendiary white-phosphorus hand grenades, which produced intensely bright, blinding flashes followed by useful dense smoke. In the good old days of the

SAS, they had been favoured for hostage-rescue operations. This situation, as Steve now saw it, was similar.

These, he suddenly realized, were the last of the weapons and ammunition that he had stolen from Houlihan's arms dump, so he had better put them to good use. He would not have another chance.

Checking his wristwatch again, he saw that he had less than a minute to go. With the Sten gun slung over his shoulder, he gripped the handlebars of the motorbike, slung his leg over the saddle and let the engine roar into life.

The first bomb exploded with an ear-shattering blast, blowing the steel railings of the high fence apart less than a hundred yards from Steve. Instantly, he headed for that spot on his motorbike. Thirty seconds later, the second bomb went off, blowing more railings apart in the eastern side of the perimeter fence. As Steve reached the first gap, where pieces of twisted, scorched metal were still smouldering, the third bomb went off directly behind the complex. Steve turned the bike in through the gap in the fence as the fourth bomb exploded. Roaring through the gap with the sound of the four explosions still reverberating in his ears, he headed straight for that wide-open entrance illuminated by fluorescent tubes. The bike bounced over the lip of the ramp and he was dazzled by almost painfully bright light.

As he went down the ramp, not knowing what he would find there, he took his right hand from the handlebar, reached across his chest to withdraw the 9-Milly from its holster, and expertly, thanks to his training with the SAS Mobility Troop, steered the motorbike with his left hand.

He soon found himself in a vast basement storeroom, obviously part of a larger warehouse, again lit with fluorescent tubes and stacked high on all sides with canned and packaged food.

His heart skipped a beat with pure panic and shock when he saw a bunch of men lined along the far wall ... Then he realized, with relief, that what he was actually seeing was a line of freezer suits with fur collars and with padded gloves dangling over the chest areas, just like folded hands. All were hanging from hooks on the wall.

As he reached the bottom of the ramp, which led into the vast, empty centre of the basement, he saw a couple of men – *real* men – emerging from a windowless room with sheet-metal walls thrusting out from the left-hand side of the basement.

One of those men was Wild Bill.

Steve didn't recognize the other, but he saw instantly that both men were carrying handguns – and preparing to fire at him.

Steve shot first, rapidly squeezing the trigger to fire about half a dozen bullets, making the two men hurl themselves to the cement floor as he turned the motorbike away from them, still using one hand, feeling the bike wobble dangerously. He shoved the handgun back into its holster as he came out of the turn and grabbed the other handlebar with his free hand. Then he roared back up the ramp, escaping from the basement, as shots cracked out behind him and bullets whistled past his head to ricochet off the concrete frame of the open door.

The motorbike carried him back out into the night where he came to a screeching, skidding halt.

The men in the basement were shouting at each other as Steve leaped off his motorbike and propped it up on its support leg before running back to the entrance, removing his Sten gun from his shoulder as he went. The wide door's mechanism hummed into life and the door started to descend. Realizing that the men below were hoping to lock him out, Steve dropped as low as possible, going under the descending door at the half-crouch, actually grazing it with the top of his head.

As the door slammed shut behind him, he saw one of the two men below running up towards him and preparing to fire on the move.

'Get him, Neil!' Wild Bill bawled.

The advancing man fired his handgun as Steve dropped onto his belly, then rolled across the ramp, letting the bullets whistle above him to ricochet noisily off the closed steel door. Still on his belly, Steve saw the man coming on, Wild Bill behind him, hugging the far wall and running past drums of petrol, holding what looked from this distance like a Heckler & Koch MP5 sub-machine gun.

Steve fired his Sten gun at the man – a short, wild burst, no time to aim properly – and the man screamed out as his left leg buckled and he fell onto the concrete ramp. Instantly, Steve swung the barrel of his weapon and fired a short burst at Wild Bill.

The bullets missed Wild Bill but hit the drums of petrol, which instantly exploded, creating a huge, roaring sheet of silvery-white flame. Wild Bill was thrown forward by the blast, bawling an incoherent curse as the back of his jacket caught fire. A bright yellow fork-lift was parked at the top of the ramp and he managed to throw himself behind it while beating frantically at his shoulder blades with his free hand, putting out the flames.

With Wild Bill temporarily, briefly, out of action, Steve turned back to face the man directly below him.

'I'm fuckin' hit!' the man was bawling to Wild Bill. 'The fucker shot up my leg. Ah, Jesus!'

At that moment Houlihan emerged from the room with sheet-metal walls. He had Katherine Crowley pinioned in front of him, one bulky arm locked across her throat, and was holding a pistol to her head with his free hand. He started backing towards the far wall of the warehouse, practically dragging the unresisting Katherine with him, staring over her shoulder.

'Get that cunt!' he bawled wildly.

The wounded man on the ramp was still holding his pistol and was not about to give up, even though his left leg was bent at a most peculiar angle, obviously smashed by one or two bullets. When he rolled onto his belly to fire his pistol again, Steve fired another short burst, moving the Sten's barrel from left to right, with only the man's head and shoulders to aim at. The head became an exploding pomegranate as the bullets smashed into it.

At that moment, Steve heard the fork-lift roaring into life.

Turning to the left, squinting against the brightness of the raging wall of flames that was now eating at the wooden shelves along the walls, his breathing ragged from the smoke that also made his eyes water, Steve saw that Wild Bill, having put out the flames of his burning jacket, had worked the accelerator levers of the fork-lift to send it careening across the concrete ramp without a driver. Will Bill was running behind it as it trundled noisily towards Steve, clearly about to run him over.

Steve rolled out of the way, down the ramp. As the fork-lift moved past, giving Wild Bill a clear line of sight at him, the Prod gang boss raised his MP5 and fired a short burst that shattered the concrete ramp surface and raced in a spitting, zigzagging line towards Steve, luckily passing just behind him.

Steve reached the bottom of the ramp as the driverless fork-lift crashed into the wall above him, coming to a shuddering, shrieking halt in billowing clouds of pulverized concrete before sliding sideways down the ramp, knocking over more drums of petrol as it went, until it came to another shuddering halt near Steve. It lurched to one side, sending drums rolling all over the concrete floor, before coming to a final stop, upright again as it bounced on its fat rubber wheels.

At that moment, Wild Bill came running down the ramp, firing a sustained burst from his MP5. But Steve had already rolled out of the way to take shelter behind the fork-lift. He jumped up to fire a short burst from his Sten and saw Wild Bill making a sharp right-angled turn to race to the nearest wall and take shelter behind a stack of wooden pallets. Steve fired at the pallets, then at the drums of petrol lying overturned nearby. The drums exploded with a deafening roar into sheets of flame and clouds of oily black smoke.

Wild Bill screamed in agony.

As a couple of bullets ricocheted off the fork-lift, obviously fired by Houlihan, Steve dropped down and moved around to the back of the machine. He glanced over his shoulder at where Wild Bill, still behind the stack of pallets, was now engulfed in the flames that had spread across from the exploded drums of petrol. They had ignited the wooden pallets and set Wild Bill's clothing on fire.

Wild Bill had let go of his MP5 and was screaming dementedly as he beat desperately at his own body and limbs, trying to put out the flames.

Instinctively, Steve jumped to his feet and ran across the ramp, removing his own jacket as he went. Wild Bill's shirt and trousers were burning. His hair was on fire. The skin of his face and hands was black and blistered and appeared to be melting in the flames. Steve threw his jacket over him, pressing it down to smother the flames. Wild Bill screamed even louder at the agony of it, though the flames at least went out. Steve slung his Sten over his shoulder, grabbed Wild Bill by the ankles and dragged him, still screaming, away from the blaze. He left him lying there, in the middle of the ramp, screaming and whimpering, to make his way back to the pallet jack and climb up onto the driver's seat.

'Help me, Houlihan!' Wild Bill managed to yell. 'Don't leave me here, Mike!'

'Go fuck yourself, Billy-boy. It's too late for you now. Sure, I can't do a fuckin' thing for you, so take it like a man, boyo.'

'Help me! Ack, Jasus, I'm in agony! *Don't leave me like this!*'

'Goodbye, Billy-boy. *Adios.* You're all on your own now.'

'Jasus, Houlihan! *No!*'

But Houlihan was still retreating across the vast warehouse, away from the advancing smoke of the blazing petrol, the burning shelves and pallets, still with one arm clamped across Katherine Crowley's throat, the barrel of his pistol at her temple.

'Put your fucking hands up,' Houlihan bawled at Steve, 'or I'll put a bullet through this bitch's head! Believe me, I'll do it.'

'Don't listen to him!' Katherine shouted at Steve. 'He'll just kill us both anyway!'

Shifting his big hand to slap it over her mouth, Houlihan bawled, 'Be warned, she'll get a bullet through her head! Give in and I just might let her go. If you don't, she'll have no chance. Do you want that on your conscience, you fuckin' patriotic, hypocritical shit? Do you want to make that decision?'

But Steve didn't give in. He gambled with Katherine's life instead. He twisted the accelerator levers of the fork-lift, making it whine and jolt into life. Then he shot across the floor to ram into an enormous stack of wooden pallets piled high with frozen foods, smashing the pallets apart, making the huge stack collapse so that pallets, cans and heavy cardboard packets rained down where Houlihan and Katherine were still retreating.

Instinctively, without thinking, Houlihan let Katherine go and ran away from the cascading containers, enabling Katherine to escape in the opposite direction, likewise away from that avalanche of foodstuffs.

Steve didn't see where she had gone; he had his own agenda now.

Houlihan backed towards the far wall of the warehouse. Steve, still driving the fork-lift, went after him. When Houlihan fired another shot at him, the bullet ricocheted off the steel frame of the driver's cabin, barely missing Steve, so he let go of the levers, jumped off and took up a firing position behind another high stack of pallets.

'*You*'d better give up, Houlihan!' he shouted. 'You've no men left here and you've only got a handgun. I've got a Sten gun and plenty of ammunition, including a couple of grenades – the good old flash-bangs. Give up or I'll blow the ears off you, then cut you to ribbons.'

A single shot rang out and the bullet, ricocheting just above

Steve's head, tore wood splinters from the front of the stack of pallets.

'Fuck you!' Houlihan bawled. 'Keep away from me, you bastard! You fuckin' lunatic, you don't know when to stop! Just get the fuck out of here before my men come and shoot you to pieces!'

With a combination of shock and excitement, Steve realized that he was hearing something he'd never expected: fear in Houlihan's voice. Houlihan, renowned as fearless, was losing his grip, perhaps imagining that his antagonist had friends all around the building (the four explosions that he had heard now multiplied in his memory) and that his number was finally up. Houlihan was contemplating his own mortality ... and the thought terrified him.

'You can't go any farther, Houlihan,' Steve called out to him. 'I can see you backed against that wall. If you don't throw down that pistol and put your hands up, I'll come at you with my grenades and this Sten gun. You won't have a prayer, then, Houlihan, so do the sensible thing.'

'Fuck you! Keep away!'

'Fuck *you*, Houlihan,' Steve retorted as he unclipped a grenade from his belt and released the pin. 'Try swallowing this.'

He threw the grenade, which flew as if in slow motion from behind the stack of wooden pallets, then fell out of sight. The resultant explosion was deafening, the force of the blast concussing and the accompanying flash of silvery-white light dazzling, temporarily blinding.

Steve jumped out from behind the stacked pallets as the light faded to be replaced by billowing black smoke that gave off the stench of cordite. He saw Houlihan, in desperation, pulling at a handle that opened a big door that led into the dangerously low temperatures of the freezer unit. There must have been an exit door in there because Houlihan, despite the freezing cold, backed into it while firing another shot at Steve. He then disappeared into the darkness or, at least, into the semi-gloom of that vast, frozen silence suited only to dead meat.

Steve started in after him and was instantly struck (it was like a physical blow) by what seemed like a solid wall of freezing cold. Backing out again, realizing that he couldn't stand the sub-zero temperature of the freezing unit for more than a few minutes without protective clothing, he removed the Sten gun from his shoulder, wriggled into one of the thickly padded, fur-collared freezer jackets that hung from hooks on the wall, then put on the thick gloves as well, even though he knew that he couldn't fire the Sten while wearing them. Considering this, not sure where the chase would end, he slung the sub-machine gun back over his shoulder and fumbled awkwardly until he had another grenade in his gloved hand. He would not be able to release the firing pin while wearing the gloves, but he calculated that he could remove the glove of his left hand just long enough to release the pin and throw the grenade with his gloved right hand. He might be able to do the same with the Sten gun – remove both gloves long enough to fire the weapon for a brief period – but, depending on how cold it was in there, he knew he couldn't rely on that.

Presumably, Houlihan, knowing where the exit was, was gambling that his vast bulk, all that muscle covered in fat, would protect him long enough for him to get through the freezer unit and out the other side without suffering too much. If not, he really *was* crazy.

Steve advanced into the freezer unit.

He felt the cold attacking his face as if stabbing it with ice picks and saw enormous blocks of frozen meat stacked high all around him. Even as he moved forward into that gloom, he felt the heat of the various fires in the warehouse behind him wafting in to raise the temperature of the freezer unit. As he made his way along the narrow corridors formed by stacked blocks of frozen food, he saw that the ice was already starting to melt – not much, but it was certainly melting, dripping, as the temperature rose marginally above freezing.

If Houlihan didn't stay too long in here, he might even survive.

Suddenly, a shot rang out and a bullet ricocheted off a block of frozen food nearby, showering Steve with chunks of flying ice.

Throwing himself to the floor, he wriggled a few feet backwards. He heard another shot ring out and was again showered with cascading shards of ice. He moved back to the edge of a solid wall of frozen food at the junction of four narrow corridors and circled around, following the L-shape of the corridor, making his way forward to where he thought the shot had come from.

Steve heard harsh breathing, then the tread of heavy footsteps and the ringing of metal against ice as Houlihan hurried off in the opposite direction. He was obviously banging into blocks of frozen food as he went and accidentally striking the ice in the narrow corridors with his broad shoulders and wildly waving handgun.

Steve stepped around a corner and saw Houlihan's shadowy form, like a great bear in retreat. He swiftly removed the glove from his left hand, released the pin of the grenade and threw the device before dropping to the ice-covered floor.

The explosion temporarily deafened him, hammering at him like a giant fist. When his ears recovered, he heard a high-pitched wailing, an almost feminine cry of pain, followed by a hoarse curse. Then footsteps – boots pounding on smooth, slippery ice – were coming towards him.

Glancing up, Steve saw Houlihan emerging from the gloom, looking even bigger than he really was in that narrow corridor of ice. One arm, obviously damaged, was oddly angled, dripping blood and hanging loose by his side. But his weapon was raised in his other hand and his face, which was covered with ice crystals, looked like a demented mask.

'You fuck!' he bawled. 'SAS cunt!'

Steve started to get to his feet. But he slipped on the icy floor, his feet shooting out from under him, making him fall, twisting to one side as he did, just as Houlihan fired his pistol. The bullet struck Steve as he fell, tearing through his right shoulder and left thigh, which were slashed by a searing pain even as he landed on the ice-covered floor. Houlihan took aim again. But then he too started slipping and reached out with his good hand to support himself, thus briefly losing his aim. And he was weakening, losing blood from his damaged arm. His balance going, he let himself fall slowly to his knees, where he fought to get his breath back. Steve took advantage of that, kicking his feet to wriggle backwards, and managed to get around the corner formed by more stacked blocks of frozen food, out of Houlihan's sight.

Steve had already been in here too long. Even though he was protected by the freezer suit and thick gloves, the temperature was still rising slowly, the cold was still intense.

Worse, with his left thigh wounded he couldn't stand upright and with his right shoulder damaged his shooting hand was useless, with or without the thick gloves. Houlihan, he knew, would come after him once he got his breath back.

Steve had no grenades left. His only chance was to get back to the warehouse, despite the spreading fires, and try to close the door of the freezing unit, locking Houlihan in.

When Steve heard the sound of Houlihan's footsteps, his harsh, animal breathing, he started wriggling frantically back the way he had come, through those narrow corridors of ice, towards the light that was beaming in from the warehouse, towards the heat that could help him.

Unfortunately, Houlihan had exactly the same idea and was advancing remorselessly behind Steve, catching up rapidly, until his breathing sounded like the panting of a giant bellows.

Steve continued wriggling forward, still down on his belly, ignoring the pain in his left leg and right arm. But just before he reached the doorway that led to the warehouse, to the light and the heat, Houlihan came up behind him and brutally stepped on the back of his ankle, preventing him from moving while sending a dreadful pain jolting up through his leg. Then Houlihan stepped over him, turned back in his direction, reached down and grabbed him by the shoulders to roll him roughly onto his back.

Steve looked up to see Houlihan staring down at him, ice crystals glistening on his lips, nose and eyelids, his gaze unnaturally bright and malevolent. He was framed by the light from the warehouse and by those distant, flickering flames.

'You cunt,' Houlihan said, spreading his legs and taking aim with his handgun. 'You piece of former SAS shit. Thought you'd beat me, did you? Well, look into the muzzle of this gun and count off your last seconds. It all ends for you right now.'

Feeling a fierce onrushing of almost supernatural dread, Steve closed his eyes and waited to die.

A single shot rang out, but Steve didn't feel a thing. When he realized that he hadn't been shot, he opened his eyes again and saw Houlihan slumping to the side, briefly holding himself upright by pressing his left hand against a wall of frozen food, then letting his handgun fall from numbed fingers as he slid down the wall of ice to the floor. He remained there for a moment, staring at his own chest, at the bloodstain spreading across it. Then he blinked a few times, as if trying to focus his eyes, and said, 'Billy-boy! What the fuck, Billy-boy? I thought we were—'

Steve kicked out again, pushing himself backwards. Houlihan fell forward, face down on the icy floor, both hands outspread.

He had been shot in the back.

Glancing beyond Houlihan's lifeless body, Steve, to his amazement, saw Wild Bill, horribly burned, black and blistered, his lips and eyes swollen, bone gleaming here and there where flesh had melted off it, sitting defiantly upright against one side of the doorway that led back into the burning warehouse. He was holding the MP5 across his outspread legs and had obviously switched to semi-automatic fire before shooting Houlihan with that single shot. He was a nightmarish figure.

The heat from the burning warehouse wafted over Steve and made the few ice crystals that had formed on his face melt. He felt the water trickling down his face and into his mouth.

'That fuck,' Wild Bill said, nodding to indicate Houlihan. Each word that passed his blistered lips obviously took a mighty effort. 'He left me there to die, the treacherous shit, and he knew exactly what he was doin'. He wanted it all for himself. He was wheelin' and dealin' behind my back, suckin' up to the fuckin' Russians, hopin' to cut me out completely, so he wanted to see me dead and buried and that's why he left me there. Well . . . the Fenian bastard's just received his due reward . . . Aren't *you* the lucky one?'

'Am I?' Steve asked.

Wild Bill gave a crooked, nightmarish smile. 'Not really,' he said.

Steve took a deep breath, placed his good arm on the icy floor, bent his elbow and pushed himself to an upright seated position. He studied his wounded thigh, the blood-soaked leg of his trousers, the torn flesh, then he sighed and slithered across the icy floor until he could rest his spine against the high wall of packs of frozen food. The ice covering the frozen food was melting fast now, he noticed, from the heat wafting in from the fires burning in the warehouse. Losing blood from his wounded arm and leg, he felt weaker each minute.

'You're dying,' he said to Wild Bill. 'You haven't a prayer. Nobody can survive that kind of burning and you're no exception. Why bother killing me, Wild Bill, when you're dying yourself?'

Wild Bill stopped grinning. 'Don't call me "Wild Bill",' he said. 'I hate that fucking name and you know it, so don't say it again.'

'Okay,' Steve said. 'Sorry.'

'I'm gonna kill you, you fuck, because I've wanted to for a long time. Because you made my life a misery when you were in the SAS and then you did it all over again as a civilian. I'm going to kill you, you fuck. Of course I know I'm gonna die but at least by killing you I'll die happy. You understand, dumb-fuck?'

Steve took a deep breath. 'I guess so.'

Wild Bill smiled again, then he lifted the MP5 off his burnt legs and aimed it at Steve.

'Here's lookin' at you,' he said, doing a fair imitation of Humphrey Bogart.

'Drop that gun,' Katherine Crowley said.

She had come out of the warehouse to stand just behind Wild Bill, backlit by the fire burning across the entrance and eating gradually at the shelves of stacked food. She had a pistol in her hand and was aiming it directly at Wild Bill as she moved around him until she was almost facing him but slightly to one side. Steve noticed that her hand was shaking slightly and that made him smile despite the pain he was in. She wasn't that tough, after all, though she sure had a lot of guts.

'This is the gun of your dead friend,' she said. 'The one lying back on that ramp and about to be cremated in that fire. It's loaded and I know how to use it, so don't think I won't. You're a fucking murderer and a rapist, a defiler of women, and you and that bastard Houlihan turned my life into hell on earth. So for that I'd willingly send *you* to hell. You'd better believe it.'

Wild Bill turned towards her, grinning at her with the utmost contempt. 'You'd shoot me down?' he said. 'You'd kill me in cold blood?'

'If you don't drop that weapon in five seconds, yes, I'll shoot you down like the animal you are. I'll kill you in cold blood.'

Wild Bill kept smiling, though his gaze remained contemptuous. 'You won't do it,' he said. 'You're a budding lawyer, not a gangster or soldier, and you're also a woman. Look! Your hand's shakin' like a leaf in a storm. You can't do it. You won't. Now get off my case, lady.'

He turned back to focus his stare on Steve and aim the MP5 at him.

When Katherine saw his finger tensing on the trigger, she fired her handgun.

One shot.

Into his chest.

Wild Bill jerked as if struck by a bolt of lightning before his eyes went out of focus and he fell sideways to the floor, letting the MP5 slip from his grasp and slide off his legs.

Katherine stared at her smoking handgun in amazement, perhaps in slight shock. Then she looked down at Steve.

'That man was an animal,' she said. 'Him and Houlihan – both animals . . . This is natural justice.'

'You'd better believe that,' Steve replied. 'It might help you to sleep in the future when all of this comes back to you. Now give me that handgun.'

She gave him the weapon. Fumbling because of his wounded shoulder, he emptied the magazine and placed the bullets in a trouser pocket. Then he applied the safety catch and wiped the weapon's butt and trigger before tucking it down behind his belt, thus ensuring that it would not be found by the police with her fingerprints on it. He glanced past Wild Bill's body, past Katherine, to where the fire was spreading across the warehouse, filling it up with heat and smoke.

'Is there any way out of there?' he asked her. 'Did you see any exit apart from that front door covered in flames?'

'Yes, I did. There's a side door that leads out into the showrooms. I made my escape that way, then changed my mind and came back here to see if I could help you.'

'Which you did.'

She smiled and nodded. 'Which I did.'

'Given my wounded leg – and no way, believe me, can I stand on my own – do you think you can help me stand upright and then walk me out of here before the fire brigade and police arrive to ask awkward questions?'

'Oh, I think I can manage that.'

'Then let's do it,' Steve said.

The beautiful Katherine Crowley placed her arm under his shoulder, helped him to his feet, then half walked, half carried him out of the burning warehouse, through the dark showrooms and out into the gloomy early morning.

They disappeared like mist when it clears.

Chapter Twenty-six

Steve had shaved off his beard and moustache and had had his long hair cut by the time he met Katherine Crowley in the relative anonymity of a wine bar in the West End of London. It was therefore no surprise that when she entered the wine bar, looking like a million dollars in a black skirt and jacket of deceptive simplicity, cut with understated elegance, with an open-necked white blouse and high-heeled shoes, her blonde hair still hanging loose, her green gaze still piercing, she didn't at first recognize him.

He had to leave the bar and step out in front of her to say, with a smile, 'I'm Steve Lawson, Katherine. How nice to see you again.'

She stared at him for a moment, not saying a word, then shook her head from side to side in disbelief. 'Well, well,' she said. 'Time moves on and people change. Don't complain because I didn't recognize you. Obviously I never saw the *real* you.'

'No,' he said. 'You didn't.' He checked his wristwatch, then looked up again. 'I don't know what your schedule is, Katherine, but would you care to have lunch?'

'I really don't have the time. We only get an hour's break at this convention, which is why I usually have lunch there. It took ten minutes to walk here and it'll take another ten to get back. That gives us exactly forty minutes. So a sandwich and a glass of white wine would be fine.'

'Let's take a table,' Steve said.

They sat at the nearest table, ordered sandwiches and wine, and made small talk until the wine arrived: the weather, the legal convention that Katherine was attending, what she thought of London and so on. As they talked, Steve kept glancing surreptitiously at her, taken aback at how sheerly beautiful she was, much more so than he had recalled. It was somehow nice to be thinking of her that way without actually thinking about trying to bed her. He was now back, albeit secretly, with his wife and children and he wanted nothing to threaten that relationship. He had returned to safe harbours.

'God,' he said when the sandwiches arrived and they were both nibbling at them, 'it seems such a long time! Certainly a lot longer than it's really been.'

'Given how little we knew each other,' she retorted, 'nearly a year *is* a long time. Given what we went through together in that very brief time, the time that followed seems even longer.'

Steve sighed. 'I guess so.'

He and Katherine hadn't seen each other since she had helped him escape from Houlihan's burning warehouse. While the fire spread and the fire brigade was approaching, Katherine had helped Steve walk the short distance into a nearby park, bound his wounds roughly with pieces of cloth torn from her shirt, then left him there, protected by darkness, while she caught a taxi (wearing her jacket over her torn shirt) back to her own place. (She had refused to try and ride his powerful motorbike; he couldn't take a taxi himself because of his highly visible gunshot wounds.) Then she'd picked up her own car and driven back to the park to collect him. After she had helped him to get into her car, weak and bloody as he was, he had given her the address of a house out in Lisburn and told her to take him directly there.

Once parked outside that house, in a moonlit, leafy street,

he had told her to go straight home, where she would now be perfectly safe, and make an immediate, anonymous phone call to the Special Branch of the Police Service of Northern Ireland, telling them about the planned abductions of Brian Turner and David Kershaw from their homes which were scheduled for that morning. Katherine had promised to do so, but when she asked whose house they were parked outside, Steve had refused to tell her. Instead, he had told her simply to help him up to the front door, wait until the man inside had answered, then hand him over to that man, take her leave immediately and forget that she had ever been there.

The man who came to the door was silver-haired and kind-faced and did not seem surprised to see the wounded Steve. He simply placed his own arm under Steve's shoulder, thanked Katherine for bringing him, then helped Steve into the house while closing the door, gently but firmly, in Katherine's face.

She had not seen Steve from that day to this. She had heard from him for the first time since then when, a few days ago, he had phoned to say that he had seen her name included in the guest list on the Website of the organization that was holding a legal convention in London. He had then asked if he could meet her. Just for old time's sake, he had added. Just for the hell of it. Just to trade a few interesting recollections.

'I'm game if you are,' she had said.

Now here she was, sitting in front of him, as beautiful as ever, sipping a glass of dry white wine, nibbling delicately at her sandwich, and studying his face with a slight, slightly mocking smile on her own.

'I often *wondered* what you would look like without the beard and moustache and long hair. Now, at last, I know.'

'Don't tell me,' Steve replied, grinning.

'Not bad at all. Much nicer than I would have thought. I'd imagined that, being a former soldier, you might have looked like one of Houlihan's thugs. But at least you're not *that* bad.'

'That's a backhanded compliment,' Steve said.

'Oh, I'm sure you can live with it. Anyway, the last time I saw you, you were being helped, limping and bloody, into the house of that silver-haired unnamed gentleman. And here you are, almost a year later, walking without a limp and looking healthy. Am I now allowed to ask who that gentleman was?'

'I won't tell you his name, though you could find out who he is by simply going there and knocking on his front door. Which I hope you won't do.'

'I promise not to. Cross my heart, hope to die.'

'Nothing too mysterious about him. Though now formally retired, he's a civilian surgeon who worked full-time for a legitimate hospital and part-time for the British Army's Northern Ireland HQ out in Lisburn, quite close to his home. He's a very dear old friend and he has a small surgery out at the back of his house, normally used for minor operations on his regular patients – boils, haemorrhoids, ingrown toenails, all that shit. So he patched me up there, let me stay in his cottage annexe for a couple of months until the wounds had healed enough not to require visible bandages, then packed me off anonymously over here, where I've been living, as it were undercover, politely ignored by a cooperative police force who insist that they don't know my whereabouts.'

'You must have friends in high places.'

'Ask no questions and I'll tell you no lies,' Steve said, thinking of Daniel Edmondson, MI5 and the good members of COBR in Whitehall. He didn't quite think of them as friends, but they had certainly helped him once Houlihan and Wild Bill Moore were out of the way. It was a devil's pact. 'I sold my part of the business to my good friend David Kershaw, happy just to be alive, then came here to England to disappear quietly with the help of friends who are, as you so neatly put it, in high places. So, here I am!'

'You saved my life,' Katherine said.

'I had no choice,' Steve confessed.

'Nevertheless, you *did* save my life and that's not something to take lightly. I was frightened at that time, *really* frightened. But I *did* make those phone calls to the police.'

'Yes, I know,' Steve said.

'You know what happened because of them?'

'Yes. My good friend David Kershaw, when I met him months later, certainly told me what happened to *him*. On receiving that anonymous phone call, a police anti-terrorist unit cordoned off David's street and picked up Houlihan's lieutenants, Frank Kavanagh and Pat Connolly, where they were parked just down the road from his house. Both of them are now serving life sentences.'

Katherine nodded. 'The same thing happened at the home of that businessman, Brian Turner. The police cordoned off the area and picked up two of Houlihan's murderous minders, Kevin Magee and Sam Meaklin, both of whom are also now in for life sentences. As for Turner, he was certainly lucky in that he didn't lose his life. But when it became known that he actually owned Houlihan's house, he was investigated by Special Branch and his criminal connections naturally came to light. So he, too, ended up in prison, though only for five years. Still, that's better than being dead, I suppose.'

'Much better,' Steve said. 'So what's been happening with you? Still with Parnell? Still sweating it out to become a lawyer?'

'"No" to both questions. With regard to the first, Parnell and I always had a kind of on-and-off relationship, easy come, easy go. But when he heard about me and Houlihan, instead of being sympathetic he sort of cooled on me and frankly, given his past advocacy of Houlihan, I simply didn't want to know any more either. Nor did I wish to help any more with his legal representation of half the worst criminals in Belfast. Luckily for me, I took my exams that year and passed with flying colours to become a real live-wire lawyer, so I was able to leave Parnell's company and strike out on my own. My business isn't very big yet, but it's getting bigger all the time and I'm certainly not defending any criminals. So that's where I stand right now.'

'Any man in your life?'

'Why do men always ask that?'

'I don't know. It just sort of popped out.'

'You fancied me, didn't you?' Katherine shrugged forlornly. 'Most men do. Luckily, most men are also frightened of me. Intelligent women aren't popular with little boys and most men are just little boys at heart. No, there's no man in my life at the moment, though I let a few pop into my flat now and then. Does that shock you, Steve?'

He grinned. 'No, it doesn't.'

'So what about you? You're living undercover, ho, ho, with the help of the British government or the Met or MI5 – I don't even want to know – but do you have a little woman on the side? I mean, how do you spend your nights?'

'Why do women always ask that?' Steve riposted.

'To get back at men,' Katherine said without hesitation. 'So, come on, let me hear your dirty secrets!'

'Why do you want to hear them?'

'Because Parnell knew all about you – through Houlihan, of course – and he said you were known as a womanizer, as well as being a man who loved danger. Your dangerous days are probably over, Steve Lawson, so what about your women? You being a *womanizer* and all.'

Steve shrugged, still grinning. He could have liked this woman a lot. 'I'm getting back with my wife,' he said. 'I think the time has come for it. I'll soon be able to surface again and live a normal life, with the cooperation of my old friends—'

'The ones we can't discuss.'

'Exactly. The ones we can't discuss.'

'Okay, go on.'

'But I've sold my share of the business in Belfast and once my unnameable friends tell me that I can resurface, I hope with their protection, I'll join my wife and kids in Redhill, Hereford, out near the SAS base, Stirling Lines, and then think of something else that I can do that doesn't involve guns. I've spent too long pursuing the wrong kind of excitement while harming decent people along the way. Now I think the time's come to pay the piper and that's just what I hope to do.'

'I hope you manage it,' Katherine said. She checked her wristwatch, raised her eyebrows, then finished off her single glass of dry white wine and pushed her chair back. 'I'm late already,' she said, 'by two minutes. I'm going to have to run now. You stay and finish your drink.'

'No,' Steve said, 'I can leave it. I'll walk you out of here and then let you hurry back. No propositions outside.'

'Thank God for that,' Katherine said.

They left together, stepping out of the relative peace and semi-gloom of the wine bar into the clamour and brightness of Leicester Square on a late summer's day. Standing there, in that big square filled with tourists, they faced each other and shook hands.

'Nice to see you again,' Katherine said.

'Yes, nice,' Steve responded.

'Maybe some other time, some other place.'

'That's a lovely, unlikely possibility.'

'What a line!' Katherine exclaimed softly. 'Enough to melt the hardest heart!' Then she smiled and turned away from him to lose herself in the crowd.

Steve watched her leave, appreciating her fine form, the sensual swaying of her hips, yet glad to know that they would not meet again and that temptation had been laid to rest, once and for all. He watched her until she was swallowed up by the crowd. Then he turned in the other direction to walk, feeling free at last, to the nearest Underground station.

The motorcyclist appeared suddenly, turning in from Charing Cross Road, making the pedestrians scatter wildly. But Steve saw him as if the whole business was happening in slow motion . . . in an absolute, unreal, eternal silence. The biker was not a Night Rider — he was riding in broad daylight — but in a movement that seemed to take for ever he aimed a handgun at Steve.

A single shot destroyed the silence in Steve's stunned mind. It sounded like a universe exploding and was followed by other shots.

Steve didn't hear those. He was gone before then. He felt the pain of betrayal, the grief of total loss. Then he plunged into a night without end, thinking, *No, you can't do this!*

Beyond that, there was nothing.

'Target down,' someone said into a cellular phone thirty minutes later.

'Very good,' Daniel Edmondson replied. 'Thank you. And goodbye.'

Silence reigned for a long time after that. At least until the next time.

There was always a next time.